❧ The Lady ❧

THE
LADY

Anne McCaffrey

Ballantine Books • New York

LIBRARY OF CONGRESS CATALOGING-IN-PUBLICATION DATA

McCaffrey, Anne.
The lady.
I. Title.

PS3563.A255L3   1987   813'.54   86-92092
ISBN 0-345-33675-5

Manufactured in the United States of America
Designed by Ann Gold
First Edition: November 1987
10 9 8 7 6 5 4 3 2 1

This book is dedicated to the memory
of a promising amateur jockey

ROBERT RICHARD EVANS
(October 24, 1964–August 18, 1986)
of Kilpedder, County Wicklow, Ireland

killed by the driver of a stolen car

sadly missed by all who knew and loved him—and me.

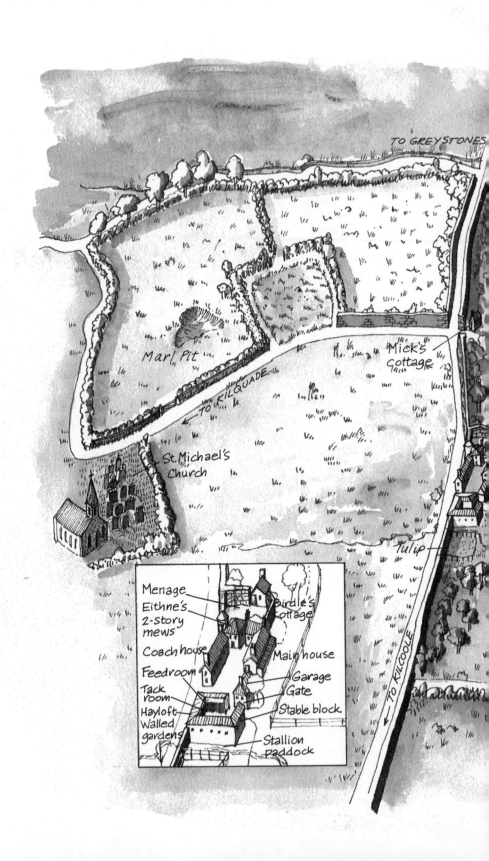

TO GREYSTONES

Marl Pit

TO KILQUADE

Mick's cottage

St. Michael's Church

Tulip

TO KILCOOLE

Menage
Eithne's 2-story mews
Coach house
Feedroom
Tack room
Hayloft
Walled gardens

Birdie's cottage

Main house

Garage
Gate

Stable block

Stallion paddock

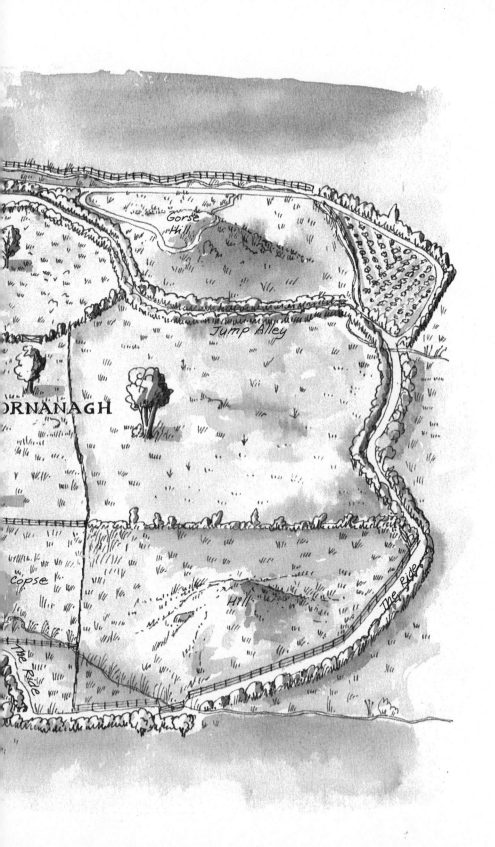

❧ *Acknowledgments* ❧

With no touch of sentimentality, this book would not have been written without my acquaintanceship with many Irish horses and ponies. They were the inspiration for the book—they and those who have dedicated much of their lives and energies to the horse, the noblest, bravest, proudest, most courageous, and certainly the most perverse and infuriating animal that humans ever domesticated.

Granted, I would not have written such a book without the sly persuasion of the glib-tongued Toby Roxburgh and, later, the shrewd insights of Pamela Dean Strickler, to both of whom I now tender gratitude and thanks. And I do very much appreciate the patience and tolerance of my agents, Virginia Kidd and Diana Tyler, for steadfastly encouraging me in this project, so far from my usual themes.

Thanks also to Catherine Ann Callaghan, who wore her eyes out on the microfiche records of ten years of Irish history, and to Jennifer Hatton Kiersey, who asked strange (to her) questions of many officials at the Royal Dublin Society and Bord na gCapall.

For their time in answering my odd questions, I am also very grateful to many notable Irish and English equestrians: Jan Regan, Jock Ferrie, Colonel Billy Ringrose, Dermot Forde, Michael Keogh, Ada Mathieson, Bernard Byrne, Joseph Tobin, Claire Devlin (who jockeyed the Dragonhold flat racehorses), the late Robert Richard Evans (who rode Dragonhold's two National Hunt horses) Georgeanne Johnson, Bobbie Evans, John Boyne, Pat Cleary, Joan, Helen, and Aidan Keogh, Helen Mangan, Aisling Smith, Greg Keating, Louise Cooper, Leslie Parker, and Simon Beirne.

• ACKNOWLEDGMENTS •

The unexpected djinns of all this were Hilda Whitten, who sold me my beloved gray gelding, Mister Ed, the first horse I ever owned, and Jane Kennedy Bloomer of Brennanstown Riding School, where old Horseface was boarded and where I served my stable management "apprenticeship."

However, without Derval Diamond, BHSII, and William Micklem, FBHS, this book would have been equally impossible. I can never adequately thank them for both inadvertent help and active corrections. Watching these two "bring on" horses developed a richer understanding and appreciation in me of this wondrously infuriating, stimulating, exacting, personally rewarding, and deeply subtle profession. For they, as riders and trainers, have the deep empathy for horse that provides the basis for much of my story.

—Dragonhold

Glossary

aids   hand, seat, leg, stick, and spur are considered "aids": a horse "between the aids" or "on the bit" is one ready to respond to any or all of the above-mentioned aids

alanna   Irish endearment—"little girl"

bascule   the natural curve of a horse's body over a jump

brushing boots   strap-on guard pads to prevent horse brushing his own fetlocks

chuffed   puffed up with pride

Dáil   Irish House of Paliament

ESB   Electricity Supply Board, usually abbreviated

exhaust   muffler on a car

farrup (v)   phonetic rendering of a horse noise

forehand   the front end of a horse, including legs—a horse "on his fore" is generally heavy on the hands and unbalanced

Gardá, Gardái   police—Gardá Siochanna

girth   band that runs under horse's belly to hold saddle on

hames   a mess

jumper   in most cases, a sweater

loo   UK euphemism for toilet

menage an outdoor ring, an arena for lunging or schooling horses

mucking out cleaning manure and wet straw bedding out of a stable

nick swipe or steal

nixer moonlighting—off-hours job or one not reported to employer

on the bit see entry for "aids"

over-reach bells rubber "bells" slipped over hooves to prevent hind hooves from clipping front hooves in wide, high, long jumps

oxer a wide spread fence frequently used in show jumping

quartering grooming a horse in four sections—generally in winter, by turning up one quarter of the horse rug at a time; otherwise a lick and a promise of a grooming

skipped out removing only recent droppings or wet straw/ shavings

stable rubber cloth used to "rub" horses down as final part of grooming

stone UK weight measurement—one stone equals fourteen pounds

swede traditional root vegetable, like rutabaga

sweet dessert

T.D. Teachta Dáil pronounced "chok-tah doil": Speaker in the House, meaning Speaker in the Dáil, the Irish Parliament, usually abbreviated to T.D.

• Glossary •

Táoiseach Prime minister—Irish

wellingtons rubber boots—"wellies"

whinge whining—Irish idiom

The Lady

❧ *1* ❧

*F*ollow the coast road to Greystones, turn right at Black-
lion, and watch out for the traffic haring up from the
town—some of the drivers buy their licenses at the post office.
Stay on that upper road past the Orchard Pub and continue
straight through the crossroads at Killincarrig. The right-hand
road leads to Delgany, and the left turns back down to the sea.
At Pretty Bush turn right and up the hill—mind the children
who play in the road—and continue on past Kilquade's cemetery. There's a grand view from there of the sea and the convent and the mountains, not yet greening with spring but with
twisted pines marching on the hill crests, outlined against the
bright sky. Just past the cemetery, on the left, is the beginning
of Cornanagh, property of the Carradyne family, landowners
since the first Carradyne did service for the Crown in the eigh-
teenth century.

Cornanagh means "hill of the beast" in the Irish, though many
wonder that the Carradynes, Anglo-Irish and for generations
loyal to the Crown, have retained the name. Except that the
Carradynes insist that the "beast" is a horse and they have
always been notable horsemen and women and breed some
of the finest hunters and hurdlers in the country. In that they
have become more Irish than English and, even during the
lean years and bad harvests of the previous century, made
profit from the production of colts and fillies.

If you drive into Cornanagh through the main gate and past
the old gatekeeper's lodge, the way is lined by massive syca-

mores and beeches, which legend has it were planted by the first Carradyne. The house, enlarged from an original farm manor of the late 1600s, faces east to the sea, with a gracious prospect of the undulating main fields and pastures of the estate. Past the house on the right are the extensive stables and then the huge walled garden, established in the mid-eighteenth century to amuse and delight the ladies of Cornanagh, sheltered from wind and storm, watered by the little stream that flows down from the hills and into the sea at Kilcoole. Old fig trees cling to its walls; pear, apple, and cherry trees flourish; and raspberry, gooseberry, and quince bear blossom and fruit in their time.

But to find the heart of Cornanagh, continue on the Kilcoole road past the formal entrance, past the high wall that girds the menage—the outdoor exercising ring—and to the strap-iron gates set between the old coach house and the stable block. Turn into the courtyard, past cow byrnes and right into the yard, its cobbled surface neatly swept on this February evening.

Lights, set high on the stable walls, illuminated the quadrangle. The horses all had their heads over their open upper doors, ears pricked, intent on the side that contained the foaling box.

A man of short stature, bundled with scarf, thick jumpers, and an ancient duffle coat against the chill, sharp wind, made his way across the courtyard to the stable block, absently whistling an old tune. He tugged his flat cap to secure it as the wind suddenly smacked against him and shrugged his broad shoulders into the warmth of his old jacket. The horses nickered softly at his passing and Tory, the black and white Wicklow collie, twitched his ears at the familiar step. The man stopped whistling and walked as quietly on the cobbles as he could in heavy leather work boots. He paused at the entrance to the stable, listening. Just then he heard a chorus of whickers from the animals inside, echoed by the horses in the quadrangle: a welcome if ever he'd heard one. Abandoning his cautious approach, he slid the door open and rushed to the center stall of the five in the barn.

Delight brightened Mick Lenahan's blunt, homely features into a smile as he saw the newcomer on the stable's straw.

"Ya do it every time, Frolic girl!" His voice was warm with approval for the big chestnut mare who hovered protectively over her newborn lying in the deep straw of the foaling box. "Ah, it's a grand big foal! The captain'll be that proud of you. Even if we never can catch you at it!"

He wheeled and, at a clumsy half trot, half canter, ran across both yards to the back door of the house. He entered with no ceremony, save to pull the cap from his graying, thinning hair, and pushed open the double doors into the dining room, where he knew the family was assembled at this hour. His noisy entry made everyone turn toward him: Isabel Carradyne with a frown, Captain Michael Carradyne rising from his seat at the head of the table, his expression expectant.

"She's done it again, Captain. A fine strong foal."

Michael Carradyne paused only to brush his napkin across his black mustache and bow courteously to his wife.

"Filly or colt?" he asked.

"Didn't wait to see, Captain dear."

"Oh, Mummy, may I go see, too?" said Catriona, the youngest of the current generation.

"Come on, Trina," her father said, ignoring whatever decision his wife might have made, and the three left the dining room, grabbing the first outerwear to hand from the crowded rack just inside the back door.

They ran across the courtyard. Michael Carradyne, ignoring the twinge of pain from a left leg once torn by shrapnel, followed awkwardly after his nimble daughter. Catriona outdistanced both her father and Mick and reached the stable block first. With fingers made cold by even that brief exposure to the February chill, she fumbled with the door latching. Once inside, she quietly approached the foaling box, blue eyes wide, her mouth breaking into a beautiful smile as she saw the dark foal on the straw. It was now sitting in the deep bedding, its long forelegs straight out in front of it, the back ones jutting outward to the left. Frolic whickered softly, secure in her trust of the humans.

"That's a fine foal, Frolic," Michael Carradyne said, coming to stand behind his daughter, his hands on her thin shoulders. The mare whickered once more, as if accepting his praise. Then she bent to nuzzle the newborn, licking the short strong neck.

As the three watched, the foal gave a massive lurch and, to their surprise, managed to stand erect on unsure legs that then buckled behind and made the little creature sit down. It gave a squeaky nicker of irritation and lurched up on all fours again, flicking the little brush of a tail.

"A colt, Captain," said Mick, "and as fine and independent a fellow as the Tulip has ever sired. He'll be dark, too, like his da, when that foal coat grows out. Another black Tulip."

Michael Carradyne, his blue eyes dark and shining, nodded in slow agreement. Then he glanced down at his young daughter. Her expression was enthralled, her mouth slightly open.

"Oh, Daddy, he's magnificent. The best of this year's lot. Oh, Frolic, you've done it again!"

At not quiet thirteen Catriona was just tall enough to see into the foaling box without assistance. She was a thin, slightly built child, who appeared considerably more delicate than she was, an illusion helped by a porcelain-fair skin framed by hair as black as her father's. Her eyes were the brilliant Carradyne blue, and the tilt of her curved eyebrows was all Carradyne as well. She had more grace about her than most preadolescents, probably the result of her riding, which had developed muscle control and an economy of movement.

Now the colt, plainly determined to succeed, managed first one forward step, then a second, though the hindquarters wobbled precariously. His dam encouraged him and presented her side. Two more steps and the colt was imperiously butting his dam's teats; latching on to the source of nourishment at the first try, he sucked lustily, tail flicking.

"A strong foal indeed if he's on his pins and nursing in the first half hour. Or could it be longer than that, Mick?"

"No, Captain, he'd only just been born when I got here. I'd wager anything she was only waiting for me to go for me tea to drop the foal." Mick shook his head at the mare's vagaries, but there was pride of her, too. "And isn't it just like a female!"

"A warm bran mash for her, Mick, with an egg thrown in," Michael Carradyne prescribed.

Mick grunted without rancor. He knew what to do but it was part of their relationship that the captain gave the order. Mick had come to Cornanagh as a scrawny, undersized twelve-year-old stable boy just after Michael's birth in 1918. Michael's father, Colonel Tyler Carradyne, had had as good an eye for a man as a horse and had quickly seen in young Mick Lenahan the raw material from which a first-rate groom, and a lightweight rider, could be made.

Mick didn't ride as much now as he had: the ground got harder every year, or so he said, and there were plenty to ride in his stead at Cornanagh. He was more use on the ground, having a shrewd eye for the slightest touch of unlevelness in a horse's stride. Since old Tyler had died, he had become the stallion man, for the Tulip trusted him as much as he did the Captain.

In a way, all of Tulip's foals were Mick's, for he was always present at their conception and at their birth as well, if they were bred from the Cornanagh mares.

"Not a bother on the colt, Captain dear, not a bother. He's more the spit of his sire than any we've bred."

As the colt was rump end toward them, Michael Carradyne laughed. "We'll see, we'll see. I'd say he'd weigh in at about nine and a half stone."

"He would that!"

Not one of Frolic's admirers wanted to leave the renewing sight of the newborn greedily eating. For those who love horses there is endless delight in the contemplation of a horse, moving, grazing, running, jumping. And a new foal in the barn was a pact with his past and a promise to his future for Michael Carradyne. For nearly two hundred years, Carradynes had been breeding horses in this very barn. This was Frolic's tenth colt, but Michael couldn't estimate how many foals had taken their first unsteady steps in this oversized box. He was conscious, though, of a sense of continuity with all the Cornanagh horsemen and -women.

Some foals arrived in less than perfect condition, despite all the care Cornanagh lavished on their gravid mares. On others there was an indefinable aura of promise. The strong look and uncompromising attitude of this fellow augured well: his conformation couldn't be faulted, and by the length of the leg on him, he'd make over sixteen hands of height. A well-shaped little head, slightly dishy, a good shoulder on his little frame, and a deep chest. Newborn hooves are silly, soft affairs, but his were hardening quickly as he strutted about, his longish ears wigwagging, his dark stump of tail twitching with impatience. He was Tulip's son indeed.

Reluctantly, Michael Carradyne tightened his hands on his daughter's shoulders. "Enough now, Trina. You've schoolwork to do. . . ."

"And the washing up." Catriona grimaced. She did not resist as her father guided her from the stable with an arm about her shoulders, but she kept her eyes on the mare and foal as long as she could.

"We'll have no worries about them now, Mick. You sleep in your own bed tonight."

"Didn't do me a mite of good for all my watching, did it?" Mick grumbled, glancing back at the mare. It was his practice to bed down in a nearby stall when mares were due to foal, just in case there was trouble. "You'll be telling Mr. Garden?"

Michael Carradyne grinned broadly at the little man. Mick, of course, would have heard that Jack Garden had bet that Frolic would produce a filly this year. Her unbroken record of colts must lapse, or so Jack Garden had insisted, and he had put his money where his mouth was.

Out in the windy cold the three parted, Mick turning left to the feed room to prepare Frolic's mash, Catriona hanging on to her father's hand on their way back to the house.

"Now, promise, Trina," her father said. "Don't irritate your mother by running out to see the foal every half hour."

"I know better than that, Daddy," she said solemnly. Then she added, "Besides, I've got hours of prep to do tonight. And it's not as if he were a puny foal, like Lady Madeline's always seem to be. We don't have to worry about him, do we?"

"No, we don't!"

Just as they were shedding their jackets, the dining room door opened. Philip and Owen came out, closing the door quickly behind them but bringing a puff of warmer air into the cold hallway.

"Filly or colt, sir?" Philip asked.

"Colt."

"The biggest, strongest colt ever," Catriona elaborated, her eyes shining so brilliantly that Philip smiled for his small sister's enthusiasm. "Why, he was up in two tries and nursing first go."

"Easily nine and a half stone," Michael Carradyne added with pride.

"Then Garden owes you a fiver, sir?" Owen asked his uncle.

"Now how did you know that?"

"Doesn't everyone in North Wicklow County?" Philip said, teasing. "What is this, her ninth or tenth colt?"

"Tenth," Catriona replied.

"Cheeky miss. Your chores!" said her father, and she obediently pushed open the kitchen door. "I think, gentlemen"— he put an arm about the shoulders of his son and nephew— "this calls for a glass of port." He steered them down the wide hall to the library door.

Catriona hurried through the kitchen, to the lounge behind it, and through the open door that led to the dining room, where her mother, her auntie Eithne, and Bridie were beginning to clear the table now that the men had left.

"What was it, Catriona?" her auntie Eithne asked.

"Oh, the loveliest colt," she answered as she cast a nervous glance at her mother's thin-lipped expression. Hoping to avert a scolding, she peered into the pudding dish. "Is there any left for me?"

Bridie nodded, but Isabel Carradyne said, "Not that you deserve any for that precipitous departure from the dining table, young lady."

"Come now, Isabel, it's not as if Trina is in the habit of leaping up from the table," Auntie Eithne began, falling into her customary role of family arbiter. "And her father gave her permission."

"Proper courtesy demands the permission of the hostess."

Eithne gave a bit of a sigh. Isabel Marshall Carradyne had once been a very pretty girl, and remnants of that beauty were still apparent in her fine features, but years of frustration and disappointment had etched lines from a thin, high-bridged nose to a now tight mouth.

Catriona looked wistfully at the pudding dish. It was lemon

sponge with her favorite custard sauce. She debated the wisdom of apologizing or waiting on Auntie Eithne's persuasion.

"Not enough of it really to keep, missus," Bridie said with a covert wink at Catriona, who never knew when the capricious cook would side with her.

"Oh, very well, then," Isabel capitulated. "See you don't keep Bridie waiting for you to clear. And mind, Catriona Mary, that you don't gulp it down. Sometimes your manners are no better than a tinker's."

Eithne Carradyne followed her sister-in-law into the lounge and smiled encouragingly at her niece before she closed the door.

Later that evening, as Catriona was slipping into her room, she heard the Tulip's strident call and peeked out her window into the courtyard. The lights were on, and she could see her father walking toward the old coach house, directly opposite the back of the house, where the stallion was stabled. She smiled to herself. Daddy was going to report to the Tulip, just as her grandfather had always done before crippling arthritis had tied him to his bed. First thing in the morning and last thing at night, the man of the house checked Cornanagh's stallion.

∿ 2 ∿

"**A**re you scribbling again, Catriona?" her mother asked, coming into her room with an armful of neatly folded clean clothes, which she deposited on the bed. She did not wait for an answer but came over to Catriona's desk by the window and twitched the notebook toward her.

"No, ma'am," Catriona said meekly.

"And what is all this about?" Isabel Carradyne picked up the book and read the lines already inscribed. *My first conscious memory was a horse race. My grandfather took me to it. It was really a point-to-point race which the Bray Harriers hold every year in February or March. I remember clearly that it was very cold that day but not rainy.* What on earth are you doing, Catriona Mary?"

"Miss Prendergast wants an essay of five hundred words about our first memories."

"Well, I should think you could find something more significant to write about than horses. Your brother Jack's ordination, for instance."

"But that wasn't my first memory, Mummie. I was five by then—and I remember my brother and all very well indeed," she added to divert her mother.

Isabel gave one of her sniffs but appeared mollified. "It was a wonder you didn't come home with pneumonia from the horse race that day." Isabel had started across the room and now turned, frowning. "How on earth could you remember that? You couldn't have been more than three."

"It was February, so I was nearly four."

"Don't be cheeky with me, miss."

"I'm not, Mummie, but I would have been four in April, wouldn't I?"

"You are altogether too bold, young lady."

"I'm sorry."

"And those clothes are to be put away neatly before you leave this room." Isabel Carradyne shut the door with more firmness than required.

"And Grandfather had a winner that day, too. The Tulip gelding." Catriona added once she heard her mother going down the stairs. She kept her voice low, though the only other occupant of the room was Clyde Cat, basking on the deep windowsill in what was left of the afternoon sun. "Grandfather treated everyone at the Willow Grove! And the gelding was sold on to an English buyer."

But Catriona didn't remember those last details on her own: she remembered because her mother was fond of mentioning Tyler Carradyne's falls from grace and temperance. And the essay was supposed to be from her own memories, not hearsay.

Her memory was especially vivid, comprising bright, but not warm, sunlight, and the sea sparkling beyond. She was up high—high enough above the ground to be on a level with the brush fence over which horses were pouring. She was not at all frightened by the fact that the horses seemed to be heading straight for her. She knew she was safe. She could also remember that her hands had been clumsy with cold despite her mittens (which she mustn't lose because they were new) and that her cheeks had burned in the freezing wind of her vantage point.

Noise was part of the memory, too: cheering, shouting, and the pounding of horses' hooves on hard ground. Despite the movement about her, the memory was static, a moment of time frozen forever at the instant the horses cleared the brush, with the sun, the sea, the cold, the noise, all imprinted in that moment of suspension.

When Catriona bent her head back to her notebook, she gasped, for her pencil had been moving of its own accord in the top margin, sketching the brush of the fence, the surge of straining horse heads and forelegs as they attacked the obstacle. She fumbled for the rubber in her pencil box to erase the errant sketch. Who was it had said a picture was worth a thousand words? If only Miss Prendergast weren't so mean about sketches, she'd already have doubled her English preparation.

Once the page was clean again, Catriona searched her mind for the exact words to describe that scene. Miss Prendergast was forever saying that one should use words precisely as well as grammatically. Determined to improve the vocabulary of her students, Miss Prendergast required each girl to learn twenty new words a month and be able to use them appropriately in sentences.

Just then movement in the courtyard below caught Catriona's eye: Mick was leading Frolic in, her dark brown colt foal, almost a month old now, skittering about in an excess of good spirits. Catriona half rose, not wishing to miss a moment. She laughed as she saw the little fellow pretend he didn't see his dam being led to the left into the yard. He trotted about the court, pausing to nibble a tuft of grass by the car shed. Then he shied, nearly upsetting himself, and ran on spokey long legs to catch up with Mick and his dam.

If Mick was bringing the mares and foals in, it was nearly time for evening stables. She closed her pad and stuffed it in her school bag. Wrenching off her uniform, she hauled on jeans and a heavy sweater. She was almost out the door when she saw the pile of clean laundry and, with a groan, hid it under the coverlet and then dumped her school bag on top of the lump. Padding downstairs in her stockinged feet, she located her wellingtons in the welter of boots by the door.

"Don't you leave this house, Catriona Mary Virginia," cried Bridie, opening the door from the kitchen, "without your hat and your scarf." Dinner odors, wafted out into the hall, spoke of a good meal and a spicy pudding for the sweet. Catriona obediently crammed the knitted cap on her head, wound the scarf about her neck, and shoved her feet into the clammy wellies.

That aromatic promise was obliterated as she left the house, which was only slightly less chill than the outside. But spring was in the crisp air out here, redolent with the smells of moist earth, rotting manure, and the acridity of newly spread fertilizer. Her mother and her auntie Eithne might fastidiously pinch their nostrils against the "farm smell" as they made for the garage, but Catriona took a deep breath of the combined scents that meant Cornanagh to her and exhaled with pleasure. She skipped as she made her way across the court to the main stable block.

This was the best time of day for the stables: when the horses were covered with their rugs for the night and eager for their dinners. The lights were on, and she could see the occupants of each stable as she went to the feed room in the corner. Mick and her brothers always complained that it was the most awkward position in the yard, for if you'd the hunters to feed in the courtyard, you'd a miserable walk of it on bitter or rainy nights as you struggled across the cobbles with the feed pots. When the horses had been kept only in the one yard, it had been convenient, but then Grandfather Tyler had turned the old cattle and pig byrnes into horse stables and the carriage house into luxurious quarters for the stallion and the hunter geldings.

As Catriona went into Blister's stable to pick out her pony's feet and rug him up, she could hear the rumble of male voices in the feed room next door. She was relieved by the easy conversational tone. The day had been cold but clear, so all the hunters would have been exercised and the young horses schooled. That meant her father would be in a good mood.

She ran her hands down Blister's near foreleg, feeling along the cannon bone for the bucked shin that had kept them from hunting the past three weeks. The swelling and heat were long gone. Even the scabby bits where the leg had been blistered were healing. If her father really was in a good mood tonight, she'd ask him if she and Blister could go on Saturday's hunt. It was at Willow Grove and would probably go up to Calary, which would mean more ditch and river than fly fences. And she'd promise to pull up if she felt any unevenness in Blister's going. He was a Connemara, and, as Catriona had heard her grandfather say often, "the perfect example of his breed: a genuine animal, go until he drops, never let you down."

Blister had very good stable manners, not like Sean Doherty's bay show pony in the next box. Blister knew which hoof to lift and he'd the most courteous habit of tilting the hind ones for you. She found his water bucket was full: Artie must have done it. Then she struggled to get the heavy old burlap rug spread over Blister's white shoulders. They'd had to clip him out this winter because the sturdy old pony had coated so thickly that it took him forever to dry once he'd sweated up.

"Getting on, Blister is," Mick had said as he worked the clippers through the heavy fur down the pony's neck. He paused for a moment, eyes on nothing as he did some mental calculations. "Your granddad bought that pony to teach your oldest brother to ride, so he's at least 30 years old." He clipped a few more moments, then switched off to give the head a chance to cool, running one hand affectionately down Blister's heavy neck. "All six of you kids learned to ride on him. 'Bout time you were promoted to something better."

"You mean it, Mick?" Catriona felt a surge of anticipation.

"Now, don't take me up wrong, Cat." Mick's cautionary tone brought her down to earth again. "You know your da's opinion of ponies." He jerked his head significantly in the general direction of Sean Doherty's fractious mount.

"But I ride the Prince much better than Sean does. . . ."

Mick leaned down to whisper his next words, putting his finger before his lips. "You and me knows that, Cat, but it don't do to say it in front of anybody else."

"But doesn't my father . . ."

"Yes, he does, all right enough, and you're why that flipping eejit manages to get the pony round a course. You've got more feel for an animal in your little toe than that spoiled fancy pants does in his whole body, but . . ."

"His father owns Ballymore Prince, and I don't." Catriona tried to suppress her sense of injustice, but she knew, as Mick did, that there was nothing to be done about it. She comforted herself with the knowledge that at least she had the chance to ride Ballymore Prince, and that it was her schooling that made the pony perform as well as he did . . . up until the moment the Prince realized that Sean, not Catriona, was on his back.

Generally Sean managed to get out of the ring without being shed. Catriona didn't like him in spite of the fact that she did feel sorry for him. He was scared of the Prince, but he was unable to stand up to his parents and tell them outright that he didn't want to ride. The Dohertys were what Isabel Carradyne called jumped-up tinkers, building providers who had made their fortune in the housing boom after the Second World War. They lived in a large and magnificently overfurnished house in Foxrock, and their children were given all the advantages, which naturally, as Isabel had said acidly, included the Pony Club and an expensive and otherwise useless show pony for the one son, to bring glory to his parents with his prowess in the show ring.

"What you need, Catie girl," Mick said, turning the clippers onto Blister's withers, "is enough length of leg to straddle the three-year-olds."

Catriona's eyes widened at such a marvelous future.

"You've more balance, a deeper seat, and better hands than even Philip has, if the captain would only look to see."

"He sees me on the Prince."

"He sees the bloody pony, not who's riding it," Mick said with considerable heat. "Put your mind to growing long legs, Catie girl, and we'll drop the odd word in the Captain's ear. I don't see many more seasons out of this old fella, so I don't."

For a moment, Catriona had been torn by conflicting thoughts: the sheer joy of being astride, say, Wicket, whom she would ride to such a standard that her father would have to compliment her, and the agonizing knowledge that Blister would go to the knackers once she outgrew him. For she knew her father's verdict for nonproductive animals. The pony was far too old to be sold on.

She remembered that scene now as she tied the baling string on the front of Blister's rug. It was old and so patched one didn't know if any of the original burlap remained. The top of the rug, over the withers, had a sheepskin patch that was nearly bald from years of rubbing, and the sides were stiff with urine and manure, but it kept the pony warm enough. Blister nuzzled her, snuffling into her hands, and then gave her a push with his mottled pink-and-gray nose, urging her to collect his feed. Laughing, she pulled his forelock. He lifted his head against her pull, as if resenting the liberty, then whuffled again, softly, as she went to get his bucket.

"Hooves picked out? Water bucket full? Rug on right?" Her father shot the habitual questions at her before she had put a foot into the warm feed room.

"Yes, Daddy," she replied.

"Now, Captain dear, and when has she ever forgot a thing

to do with pony or horse?" Mick demanded, bent over the buckets as he poured hot water on the bran. He winked at her. Ever since Mick had clipped Blister, he had been as good as his word, sliding in the occasional remark, the subtle praise to forward Catriona's cause. "Philip, now, Owen, too, even Artie, might not have his mind on your orders, but Catriona always does."

Michael Carradyne regarded his daughter with a frown— not an angry one, Catriona was quick to perceive, but a thoughtful one: the way he'd look at a horse to check its well-being. Catriona held her breath a moment, wondering if Mick wasn't laying it on a bit too thick.

"She's getting bigger, too, so she is. Longer in the leg. She's riding a hole longer in the stirrup." Mick had made marks on the feed room door to mark her growth, but if she was riding a hole longer in her stirrups, she hadn't grown more than an inch above the initial mark Mick had made.

Mick pushed a bucket at her with his foot. "That's Blister's, and this one's the Prince's."

"And you can help with Artie's lot," her father added. "He left early."

"Now, Mick, what's all that in aid of?" she heard her father ask as she went out. She lost the answer as the thick door closed behind her, though she could hear Mick's light tenor and her father's short baritone reply.

Then Blister was demanding her prompt delivery of his feed, stamping anxiously as she dumped his dinner in the manger.

"If you didn't gobble your hay so fast, it'd last you till tea-time," she told him, scraping the last of the warm bran and nuts from the bucket. He only had the one feed in the day, so he deserved to get every speck of it.

Usually she stayed, communing with him while he ate. Tonight she left him with an affectionate tug on one daintily shaped, furry ear and went on Ballymore Prince.

Her father was halfway across the yard, pushing the barrow with the feeds for the horses in the courtyard. As soon as she reentered the feed room, Mick told off the buckets.

"Emmett, Flirty Lady, Temper, Wicket, and the bay filly—and remember to watch Temper's teeth."

"Oh, no fear."

Mick chuckled at her fervent assurance as she hefted the feed buckets. Temper's teeth were legend in the main yard. He'd had that name since the moment he was foaled, kicking at the caul. He had squealed with indignation when he found he couldn't rise quickly to his stilty legs, and his wet hooves had scattered the deep straw of the foaling box in that first fit of temper. Frolic's new colt was just as independent and active as Temper had been at the same age, but he was far more of a gentleman.

Catriona fed Emmett and Flirty Lady, a fine hunter mare who was owned by the elegant, pretty Mrs. Healey and on livery at Cornanagh. Then Catriona ran back with the empty buckets to collect the other three feeds. Two buckets in one hand were awkward, but it saved her a third trip. With the sun well down now, the wind had got up, slicing coldly at her as she made her return journey.

After Wicket, she opened the stall door into Temper's stable. Actually, Catriona and Temper got on very well; he would even blow in her hand if he smelled the carrot or slice of swede that she often brought to bribe him to good manners.

"It's me, Temper, Catriona," she said quietly. "It's me, and I've your nice warm dinner." The excitable four-year-old snorted angrily, striking out at the door. "Get back now." She edged sideways into the stable, holding the bucket up, out, and in front of her, the first thing he'd go for. But she had a system: she gave him a quick dip into the mash and then, dropping the bucket away from his nose, could flip it into the manger and be out of the stable before he thought of any mischief. "There now! That's better, isn't it, lad?" He was already digging at the straw with an impatient foreleg in an ecstasy of eating.

"Any trouble?" Mick asked, looking up from the buckets he was rinsing at the tap outside the feed room.

"I never have any trouble with Temper."

"Some horses do better for girls, I gotta say that," was Mick's predictable response. "Even Seamus McGraw's hired a few."

Catriona grinned. "Then, when I'm old enough, I'll go work for Sam McGraw."

"Over your da's dead body!"

Catriona giggled, then took her turn to rinse out her buckets. By then her father had returned to the main yard with the barrow, and without a word all three began to wash the buckets from the top yard.

"No need to splash," her father admonished absently. She wasn't splashing, nor was Mick, but it was part of the evening ritual, and she'd've missed it. It meant they were nearly done. And there was a scrumptious tea waiting to ease the pain of several more hours of school work before she could go to bed. They piled the buckets, upended in the evening pyramid, checked to see that the grain barrel was tightly closed, and filed out, her father flicking off all but the gate lights.

"G'night now, Catie," Mick said, closing the iron gates and making sure the latch was tight. "G'night, Captain." And he touched his finger to his cap brim.

Her father waited until Mick had reached the gate to the drive before he turned off the last yard light.

"Good night, Mick, and thank you."

Catriona wondered why her father always thanked the men in the evening, and never one of his own children, especially when they often had done as many chores in the day. She sighed as she followed her father across the courtyard to the back door and the beautiful two-story window at the back of the house that overlooked the stable yard. In any other house, such a window would have been in the front where the view across the fields to the convent and the sea would have been worth seeing.

"Wash up now, Trina," her father said, giving her a gentle shove toward the kitchen while he went on to the stairs, up to the master's room at the front of Cornanagh House, which did have a view of the sea.

3

*I*t had been the most irritating of days for Isabel Carradyne. She had had to take three tablets to control the wretched tremors. First there had been that dreadful man from Aughrim with his mare, and Bridie chatting with him as if he were a long-lost relative. Alarmed by the noise of his thumping on the back door, Isabel had come to the landing. As soon as she had seen the old Wolsley and dilapidated horsebox attached to it in the courtyard, she'd known why he was here. She'd gone right back into her room and taken the first tablet. And stayed in her room until she was certain that his business had been concluded. That awful stallion of Michael's made the most terrible noises when he was doing *that*.

So Isabel hadn't been downstairs to take in the post when it had come. Eithne had, but then, because she'd had to offer a cup of tea to that wretched man—out of courtesy, she'd said—she hadn't brought it directly to Isabel. Surely Eithne must have seen that there were foreign letters—especially the one from Isabel's son, Jack, who wrote infrequently enough so that each letter to his mother was doubly treasured. There had also been a letter for Michael from his brother Eamonn in Connecticut, but the one from her dear Jack had commanded her attention.

And it had required the second capsule because she quite clearly felt his frustration and anxiety about the safety of his mission in Nicaragua. While Isabel had been terribly proud and pleased that Jack had chosen the Ministry of Christ for his vocation, she had always envisioned her son as Father John, serving an Irish parish. Clutching his letter in her hands, she had knelt at her prie-dieu in fervent prayer for his continued safety.

Then, just when Isabel thought she had conquered her agitation, Catriona had called to her mind a tidal wave of humiliating memories that she had tried hard to bury along with the mortal remains of her overbearing, reprehensible, flamboyant father-in-law. And to think that he still so dominated the inhabitants of Cornanagh House that his youngest grandchild would recall *him* as her first memory.

But she'd been too upset to insist that Catriona pick another topic. She'd gone to her room and taken the third dose. That and a lie-down had calmed her sufficiently before she had to dress for dinner.

Now she had her fingers on the zip when she heard her husband's tread on the stairs. She finished closing the dress. It didn't do to give him any cause whatsoever, she thought apprehensively, although lately he had abstained.

"You've a letter from the States," she said without turning as he entered the room. "From Eamonn."

"Have I?" Michael's voice sounded amused, and Isabel slewed around on her dressing table chair. "I wonder what he wants."

"Michael! Eamonn doesn't always have errands for you to do."

"That's true enough, but my suspicions are aroused."

He began to undress, and she turned her back on him.

"The letter's on your dresser," she said, hoping to distract him long enough so that she could slip from the room.

"I see it is, but I'll shower first."

Isabel knew that he was delaying just to irritate her. She heard him rummage in his drawers for clean clothes, then rattle the wardrobe as he got his dressing gown. He'd be starkers, she knew, if she glanced around. But she wouldn't. She wouldn't. Then she caught a glimpse of his long wiry horseman's body in the mirror of her table as he passed. She closed her eyes. Why couldn't he undress in the decent privacy of the bathroom, as she'd asked him often enough?

"I shan't be long," Michael Carradyne said as he always did, and left the room.

Isabel got to her feet, rigid with frustration. Why must the man be so obstinate? It just wasn't proper. And there was absolutely nothing she could do about it. She was married to the man and had always had to cope with his ways and whims, no matter how distasteful they were to her. She could not understand how someone from a presumably good background could, in private, be so disgusting.

"All men are," her mother had told the distressed new bride. "It's their nature."

"But he's a Carradyne," the naive Isabel had replied.

"He's a man," her mother had said scathingly as if that explained all. "Endure it, my dear, as we all must for the children we bear as our sacred Catholic duty."

Marriage, and its intimacies, had been a shocking revelation to the gently reared, convent-trained Isabel Marshall. She had been brought up by the placid nuns to believe good of all, except, of course, the Brits. Her family had been well-to-do merchants in Dublin, with a comfortable large house in Mount Merrion, and she had been educated to go as wife, mother, and chatelaine to a similar establishment.

Thus primed for her life's work, it had seemed only right that she marry someone exactly like the young and handsome Michael Carradyne. Isabel had been unable to believe her good fortune—all her friends had been green with jealousy—when Michael had proposed. He was everything that could please a young girl: the second son of a fine old County Wicklow family. They were Anglo-Irish, not Republicans, but they *were* Catholic.

Michael was tall, just over six feet, with curly black hair and eyes of a brilliant blue. He was a graduate of University College Dublin, had been a member of the Irish Equestrian Team, and his family's horses consistently won at the Royal Dublin Horse Show. Everyone encouraged her and applauded the match. Caught up by the universal approval, Isabel had been delighted. Until her wedding night. Even now, she took an alternate route to bypass St. Stephen's Green rather than go near the Shelbourne Hotel.

Nine times she had become pregnant, and she had raised six children, taking what consolation she could from her sacred Catholic duty. In her last pregnancy, something had gone seriously wrong, and she had had to have a hysterectomy. During the convalescence from that drastic operation, Isabel had been given a prescription for tranquilizers, and the capsules had made all the difference. Even when the man insisted on his conjugal rights—though he knew perfectly well the Church forbade *that* if it was only for pleasure, not procreation—the tranquilizers helped her endure him. Why did men have all the rights, she wondered, and women none?

Isabel was startled to hear the door opening to readmit her husband. He was even now pulling loose the cord securing his robe. Compressing her lips into a thin, displeased line, she rose and left the room. She tried not to hear Michael's laugh as she stalked down the stairs.

"Was the news from Jack good, Belle?" Eithne asked as Isabel entered the lounge. Eithne was, as usual, studying the classified section of the Irish *Times*.

Startled, Isabel stared at her sister-in-law a moment until she remembered that Eithne had seen the post first.

"And another thing, Eithne, I really do like to see the post as soon as it arrives."

"I am sorry about that, Belle," she said, smiling apologeti-

cally. "But there was Michael insisting that they were perishing
of the cold after standing in the sand menage—"

"Eithne!" Isabel said severely.

"Well, there was so much going on all at once that I just put
the post down and . . ." She gave a little penitent sigh and a
fleeting smile. "Well, so how is Jack? He hasn't had another
attack of malaria, has he?" Eithne's hand flew to her throat, her
brown eyes anxious on Isabel's face.

"No, nothing *physical* is wrong," Isabel said.

"Oh, dear. Here, have a glass of sherry and tell me."

Isabel accepted the sherry and assumed her favorite chair
by the fireplace, angled so the heat of the logs or coal would
not scorch her stockinged legs. Isabel was of medium height,
and her early convent training had left her with a very erect,
almost military posture. Her fine, light brown hair was now
mostly a gray and no longer softened her fine-boned face. A
weekly salon appointment kept it stylishly dressed, but Eithne
thought she really ought to have it touched up, especially when
so many people did these days.

"Jack is extremely worried," said Isabel. "He's tried to get
old Father Perez to admit that the mission is being used as a
depot, but the man refuses to believe that his parishioners
would jeopardize the infirmary and the school. And they
change governments so quickly down there! Jack's afraid that
things will be very different in the next coup. Why couldn't he
have been satisfied to do God's work right here in Ireland
instead of thousands of miles away from me?"

"I know, Belle, I know. It's all so worrying."

"I said three rosaries for his safety."

"Of course you did. And what did Eamonn have to say?"

"I don't know. Michael will tell us in his own good time."

Just then their preprandial quiet was disrupted by the sound
of a car charging up the drive.

"Eithne, when is Owen going to fix that exhaust? You know

what Michael said about the dangers of petrol fumes in cold weather. It's too bad of Owen!"

Eithne sighed dramatically. "I told him, Isabel, that he had to get that done immediately. But he will listen to nothing his old mother says."

Isabel gave her sister-in-law a trenchant stare. At forty-two Eithne could scarcely be termed "old" even by the disrespectful young.

Eithne Gavaghan Carradyne, married at seventeen to Michael's younger brother and widowed by the war three years later, was almost the antithesis of her sister-in-law. She was a neatly made, well-rounded feminine woman, an inch shorter than Isabel, with brown hair that she discreetly colored with an equally discreet reddish tinge. She was devoted to the Carradyne family for their acceptance of a young, frightened bride from County Longford and eternally grateful to them for giving her widowed self and two small boys the shelter of Cornanagh's charming mews house.

Eithne had had opportunities to remarry. Certainly Tyler Carradyne had presented one eligible young man after another. Isabel, however, had turned deaf ears to the pleas of both husband and father-in-law that she urge Eithne to accept one of her suitors. She would not be a party to forcing Eithne to marital degradation.

And Eithne was a useful sort, quite willing to help with the children when they were young. She had been indispensable during their father-in-law's last illness, nursing him tenderly and with great compassion, for Isabel had found the man more impossible than ever, trying to dominate his house, business, and family from his bed. Eithne was not, however, as firm with her two sons as she should have been. Fortunately for them, their grandfather, and more lately Michael, had supplied the necessary masculine discipline. Only Owen now lived at home.

The door into the lounge rattled and burst inward as Philip,

Isabel's favorite of her own children, was pushed into the room by his cousin. Both were laughing in that maddening fashion of men after an off-color joke. They had the grace to moderate their mirth, and each gave his mother a dutiful peck on the cheek.

"Owen, you are to fix the exhaust on that motor this week!"

"I'd've had it done today, Auntie Isabel, but the part hasn't come in."

"It's been more than two weeks since your uncle asked you to have that fixed."

"Yes, ma'am." Owen smiled placatingly at his aunt.

"Perisher of a day, wasn't it?" Philip said to the room at large as he made for the drinks tray. "Owen?" He lifted the Paddy's meaningfully, his very regular eyebrows raised above his still laughing blue eyes.

Isabel suppressed a surge of pride in this graceful and courteous son who was such a contrast to Owen's brash, almost insolent manner. Philip had never caused her a moment's worry, not from the day he was born. Once again, she pondered the advisability of sending him to Michael's brother, Patrick, who was doing so well in the advertising business in the States. She was certain that Philip would do very well there, even if Michael insisted that the murky depths of that particular American business were not a suitable environment for an unsophisticated Irish lad.

"Patrick's done so well," she had argued with Michael.

Michael had eyed her, one of his brows climbing just as Philip's now did, and snorted derisively. "Patrick has a truly devious Irish soul and a suspicious nature. I'd never buy a horse from him."

"He's not selling horses in America."

"Isn't he? Horses of a different color and form. I always wondered about Mother and that tinker friend of hers!"

Isabel had been so outraged by Michael's naughtiness, even

though she knew it for a deliberate diversion, that she had dropped the subject.

Philip, however, did know horses. She was positive that that was why Michael would not stir himself to better Philip's employment. Philip had been showing Cornanagh horses since he was sixteen. And recently, since the war wound in Michael's thigh had begun to plague him, he had yielded the show jump riding to Owen and Philip—until Owen had lamed a horse two years ago for reasons that had put him in Coventry and not even Catriona had spoken to him for weeks.

The worry about Philip was wearing on Isabel's nerves, even with the help of her capsules, and although she couldn't think what else Philip was fitted to do, anything would be an improvement over selling cars. Now, as she sipped her evening sherry, regarding her favorite son with detachment, the thought occurred to her that possibly Eamonn's letter had to do with Philip. Michael could have acquiesced to her constant requests to inquire about openings with his brothers. Yes, that was what the letter would be about, Isabel thought, and began to relax and enjoy her aperitif.

Michael came in and acknowledged everyone's greetings. He gestured for Isabel to keep her seat as she began to rise to pour his Scotch. He was wearing his blazer, which meant that he'd be out for the evening. She could almost bless that horse board thing of his that kept him so busy. She and Eithne could watch their choice of programs on the telly instead of having to endure more football or rugby. Not that there was that much on tonight. Just then the double doors leading to the dining room slowly opened, and Catriona, leaning on the knob, swung in.

"Bridie says dinner's ready. It's shepherd's pie with a gorgeous pud."

"There's no need to recite the menu when you announce dinner, Catriona," Isabel reminded her, sipping the last of her sherry before rising to lead the way into the dining room with Eithne. She winced as Catriona banged against her chair, knocking it into the table.

"Do watch where you put your feet, child. I don't know what the nuns are teaching these days. Doesn't anyone care about deportment anymore? Why, we had to—"

"We know, Mother," Philip said, interrupting the well-known story with a charming grin as he held out her chair for her. Then, pretending that he was balancing a book on his head, he paraded in a rigid-backed strut to his own chair. Catriona watched him, muffling a giggle.

Remembering that the letter might be about Philip, Isabel forbore to rebuke him. It would not do to prejudice Michael in any way right now. Isabel removed her napkin from its ring, her fingers sliding over the smooth jade. The ring had once held her mother-in-law's linen, the jade was a gift from one of her peripatetic brothers. That generation's priest, yet another Father John Carradyne, had been a missionary in China, a victim of the Boxer Rebellion. Isabel signed the cross in a quick gesture of memory for the man's martyrdom.

Then Bridie set the huge casserole in front of her, sniffing as she usually did when she served inferior dishes. Eithne bustled out to bring in the rest of the vegetables. Then Catriona had to be sent to fetch the butter, which she had forgotten to place on the table.

Eithne took her seat now, and Isabel began to serve the pie. Michael carved the roasts, but Isabel always served the less important entrées. As she pierced the crust—and it was Bridie's usual perfection—the steam rose, spreading its rich aroma.

"Catriona, it is impolite to sniff in that fashion at the dinner table."

Catriona bent her head, her forehead almost touching the plate.

"Well, it certainly does smell sniffing good, Mother," Philip said with an exaggerated inhalation.

"No one makes a shepherd's pie as good as Bridie's," Eithne added, and filled the silence while dinner was being shared out with a list of inferior meals she had had to endure, featuring the same dish. Michael's eyes became somewhat glazed as they often did when his sister-in-law bored him.

"How is your brother?" Isabel inquired with studied indifference when Eithne paused in her dissertation to take a forkful.

"Eamonn's fine," Michael replied blandly. "Shirley's well, and all the children."

Isabel waited through his pause, unwilling to give him any satisfaction by giving in to the suspense. Michael glanced about the table, his eyes pausing on Philip only briefly before he turned to his wife again.

"He was wondering if we'd mind having Patricia here for the summer."

"Patricia? Here?" Isabel had to reassemble her thoughts. She had been so positive that the letter concerned Philip. A wave of totally irrational fury surged through her, quickly suppressed. With as good grace as she could manage, she added, "Of course, but why Patricia?"

Michael gave one of his cryptic smiles and then looked at Catriona, who was busily eating.

"Trina?"

Fork suspended, she swung her head around to her father. "Daddy?"

"Your uncle Eamonn wants to send your cousin Patricia to spend the summer with us. She's only a year older than you are. I'm sure you'll be good company for each other."

Catriona slowly lowered the fork to her plate, her eyes unblinking on his face. Michael frowned. What response he had hoped for he didn't know. His youngest child was so self-contained. Or was she quiet simply because, as the youngest, her opinions and wishes were so rarely consulted?

"Your uncle Eamonn wants us to put some polish on her riding, bring her up to an Irish standard."

"She rides?" Catriona blinked, and some stirring of emotion crossed her face. Whatever was the child thinking? Michael wondered.

"So Eamonn says. She has won one or two equitation prizes." Michael's opinion of the source was not high.

"Can she jump?"

"I expect we'll find out. Isabel, please write Shirley tomorrow, will you, and extend the invitation?"

"Yes, yes, of course. She'll be here the entire summer?"

"Why not?" he said. "The Pony Show's mid-August, and if we can make any sort of rider out of her, Eamonn can boast about her Irish successes. You know how keen the Americans are to be international."

"The pony show?" Owen scoffed. "International? You must be joking, Uncle Mihall."

"If she's American," Philip chimed in with a glint of devilment in his eyes, "and we're across the ocean, it's international to America, isn't it?"

Isabel sniffed. At least Philip masked his disappointment well. "Catriona," she said, "it's impolite to stare so."

"I wasn't staring, Mummie, I was thinking."

"Then do so with your mouth closed. And can't you express some appreciation of your father's invitation to your cousin? It isn't always that you have someone to share your activities."

"What if she's cack-handed? And falls off all the time?" Catriona sounded aggrieved. "And who will she ride? You wouldn't let her ride Ballymore Prince, would you? Oh, Daddy, you couldn't?"

Michael regarded his daughter with some surprise.

"Don't worry, pet," Philip said with a sideways glance at his father. "Old Blister'll do fine for any Yankee cousin. Isn't it about time Trina graduated from that old soldier anyway, Father?"

Catriona's eyes widened as she turned to gaze adoringly at her brother.

"Well, Blister taught all of you how to ride. He can do the same for little Patricia until we can check her standard."

"There, now, petal," Philip said, leaning across the table conspiratorially to Catriona, "both Blister and the Prince are saved once more!"

4

*I*mmediately after Catriona had helped Auntie Eithne clear the table, her aunt said that she would help Bridie with the washing up, so Catriona was free to scamper to the library to find the box where her mother kept family photos.

Aunt Shirley kept her Irish connections supplied with photographic records of her family on holidays, anniversaries, birthdays, and Christmases. Owen had been heard to remark that there were more than enough pictures of the Connecticut Carradynes to make up for the lack of both the New York State Carradynes and the Marshall branches in Australia.

She found the latest photo of the Connecticut Carradynes, posed in front of their Christmas-card-bedecked mantel, everyone dressed as befit the occasion. Catriona squinted to see Patricia in her green A-line dress, her brown hair drawn in two ponytails, one over each ear, tied with wide satin bows. Her expression was brightly smiling, but there wasn't all that much to show Patricia's personality or, most particularly, to reassure Catriona's mind on the vital questions of how good were her cousin's hands and her seat in a saddle.

Auntie Shirley had on a shiny red dress, and she wore lots of jewelry. "Dressed up like a Christmas tree herself, she is," Isabel had remarked enviously to Eithne when the card had been examined last December.

"I suppose she has to now that Eamonn's the plant manager," Eithne had replied, placing the card carefully in a prominent position.

Auntie Shirley looked cute, Catriona thought, with short curly hair in a fringe framing her face. Uncle Eamonn, on the other hand, looked like a blurred photo of his brother, sort of sloppy on the edges. Eamonn carried more weight than her father ever would. He'd ride at seventeen or eighteen stone, Catriona found herself thinking. Well, Minister and Jerry were up to weight. Then she remembered that Eamonn hadn't liked horses, which was one reason he'd gone to the States as soon as he could.

Just then Owen swung into the room, grinning when he saw her kneeling by the shelf.

"Checking up on the cousins? Any hope in her?"

Catriona shrugged. She had never particularly liked her cousin Owen. In her opinion, he was a sneaky one. When he was younger, he used to get Philip and Andrew in trouble with their grandfather and father. But his real disgrace in Catriona's eyes had occurred two years ago when he had been hunting Harp, one of Tulip's more promising geldings. It had been a marvelous day, with several long gallops and some good fences. Owen had brought the horse in lame on the off fore. Any *horseman* would have felt the unevenness in the horse's going, pulled him up, dismounted, and carefully walked him home.

The worst of it had been that there'd been a German buyer about to shake on a deal for the gelding. Her father had been a long time forgiving his nephew for that day's work. Michael Carradyne was all too familiar with the nasty habit horses had of going unsound just when you counted on them the most, but riding a horse to ruin was something else again.

Still and all, Catriona had been impressed by Sister Mary Josepha's continuous lectures on forgiving trespasses and made a conscious effort to forget Owen's grievous sin. Especially since he would give her a lift to the top of the road in the mornings, if she was ready on time, which saved her the long cold walk to catch the school bus.

"She looks nice," Catriona said noncommittally, and put the picture back, her eyes on Patricia's smiling face until the lid covered it.

She went back to the lounge then, taking her usual place at the old table to finish her preparation for school. Her mother and her aunt were watching a TV program, but Catriona had long since learned to discount that noise. She did her Irish first because it was an easy assignment, then her French, and finally tackled the maths. Sister Conceptua had given them an awful lot of problems, and she didn't understand the method at all. She put down lots of figures in case Mummie wanted to look at her prep. It was as well her father had gone out: she couldn't have fooled him so easily.

Then she slid out the uncompleted essay. Five hundred words, Miss Prendergast wanted. Was she likely to check every word from her twenty-nine students? Diligently Catriona counted. Some sentences were ten words long and some fifteen where she had used a lot of the smaller words, but she was nearly a hundred short of the requirement.

Five hundred words was an awful lot to write about your first memory. How could you have much to say about it, when you were so terribly young at the time? Well, if she wrote larger . . . no, that was not a trick to use on Miss Prendergast. Maybe if she just made longer loops between the letters.

"Are you scribbling again, Catriona?" her mother asked. There was a commercial blasting about motor oil, and Isabel had remembered to check her daughter's progress.

"No, Mummie. I'm doing my essay out."

"Hold it up."

Catriona did, thankful that she hadn't been sketching and all her mother could see was handwriting.

"All right, but see that I don't have another unpleasant interview with Mother Immaculata this term."

"No, Mummie."

Catriona sat looking at the unfinished, but undecorated,
page, wondering how she could possibly enlarge it. Then suddenly she knew.

*I think that the reason my first memory is so vivid is because
it was about horses. Horses were my first memory because the
business of my family is breeding and training horses. When
I grow up, I hope to continue in this exciting work. I love horses
and anything to do with them, even mucking out. That is why
my first memory is about horses.*

Sixty-six more words. Still short of the mark, but she couldn't
imagine Miss Prendergast counting every word in twenty-nine
essays. It had taken her long enough to count one.

To have touched on that first conscious memory produced
a train of them for Catriona, every one connected with horses
and many linked to her irascible grandfather, who had not, in
fact, been so snap-tempered with her.

"Good blood in her, Michael, already has a feeling for
horses." She could hear her grandfather's husky voice. They
had been in the barn, her grandfather holding her up to peer
over the door at Frolic's latest foal.

"Don't be daft, Father. She's only repeating what she's heard
you and me say."

"Hmmm, but she's using it at the right time."

Catriona could not remember what she had said, but five
years later that colt had taken first prize as a medium-weight
hunter in the Royal Dublin Horse Show. She remembered that
she'd cried bitterly when the animal had not come back to
Cornanagh in triumph so that she could tell him how proud
she was of him. He'd been sold, at a very good price.

She looked down at the recalcitrant half-filled page and
gasped, glanced hastily over her shoulder at her mother, and,

relieved that she was engrossed in the news, surreptitiously scratched out the half-realized head of a horse that now decorated the sheet. The sketch would have been of the gelding but it clearly was not one of her first memories!

Catriona grimaced at her essay. She'd have been away in a hack if she could have added the sketch. Or the other extraneous thoughts that kept crowding into her mind.

Grandfather had taught her to ride, too. On Blister. First on the long lunge rein until she had developed some confidence and balance, then on the leading rein on the ride. She did remember the heated argument when her mother had seen her, sans leading rein, careering down the last stretch of the ride at full gallop, Grandfather on old Tulip beside her, shortening the stallion's stride to match Blister's pelter.

Her mother had tried to snatch her off the pony while she had held on to the reins, obeying one of her grandfather's many injunctions. Her mother had hurt her that day, slapping at her hands and her face to make her let go. She remembered screaming that she couldn't, she couldn't, until Mick was prying her fingers loose and trying to soothe her.

"She's well able, Isabel"—Catriona remembered the tone of contempt with which Tyler Carradyne had addressed his daughter-in-law—"and you will kindly not go into hysterics when the child is quite competent. As if she were on her own. I was right there beside her all the time. Now stop your carry-on, woman. I'll not have you prejudicing a good rider by your vapors. She's a rider, that one."

Catriona remembered being sent to her room. She remembered finding refuge under bedcovers to escape her mother's shrieking, her father's baritone bellow, and the almost continuous loud comment of her grandfather. She could not recall the upshot of that furor, but she distinctly remembered riding out the next day. She also remembered that her mother had been red-eyed and silent for days afterward, and that Catriona had been quite in a fret wondering how to appease her.

Well, she honestly couldn't think of anything to add. It would just have to do. And if Miss Prendergast rated her, she'd just say she must have miscounted somehow or other, or lost her place and counted one line twice, or something like that. That was only a little sin, a venial one. And it would be something to tell Father John in confession. He got very annoyed if you couldn't confess anything, for he wouldn't even allow that the Virgin Mary had been totally without sin, her being a woman and all.

She shoved her books back into the school bag and, kissing her mother and her aunt good night, left the warmth of the lounge. She dropped the bag where she could reach it on the way out of the house the next morning and took the steps two at a time to reach her bedroom. It was right above the kitchen and so generally retained some of the evening warmth. But she'd forgotten to close the curtains when she'd gone out for evening stables, and the room was chill.

She tested the foot of the bed and felt the lump of warmth that was the hot-water bottle Bridie would have put there. She blessed the woman as she made for the bathroom. That was warm, and she slipped off her clothes and changed into the pajamas she kept on the door hook. Then she had only to dash out into the cold hall and back into her room and shove herself under the covers. Her feet connected with the soothing warmth of the hot-water bottle, and she made her body relax.

Her last conscious thought was whether her smiling, pony-tailed cousin would be able for Blister. And if she wasn't, would the pony then be put down?

Michael Carradyne shrugged into his raincoat and left the house, pausing for a moment in the courtyard to listen. His keen ears picked up no unusual banging or kicking from the hunters or old Tulip. He walked to his left, stepping close enough to the main yard to take a second moment's listen, before he went through the iron gates to the drive, making certain that the latch had caught. This was an automatic habit, born of the incident when he'd spent half the night searching Cornanagh for the Hussy, a mare who specialized in undoing her stable door, no matter what sort of fastening they tried to keep her in with. They'd had an unwanted and unplanned foal from her that year—tinker in origin, if its broken color was any indication. So automatic was it for Michael to close gates and check locks that, were he to be asked a moment later if he had done so, he could not have sworn that he had.

Once beyond the yard gate he turned left again, to the graveled parking space where his Austin Cambridge sat by itself. Owen and Philip had gone off in Owen's banger, promising to arrange for the exhaust to be fixed on Saturday.

Michael had a curious affection for his old Austin: in the first place, his father had bought it new in 1959, swearing in his vociferous fashion that Austin knew how to build a motor to last. A sturdy car, it needed only regular servicing, unlike his wife's rather nuisancy little Fiat. Isabel was forever having to phone up the AA. He willingly paid for that service since it kept him from having to rescue her at ill-timed moments from Dublin or Kildare.

Isabel! He sighed, turning the ignition key and listening to the well-bred rumble from the Austin, a thoroughbred of a car. A fine thing when a man could feel more affection for his vehicle than for his wife. And why must the woman nag at Trina so much? He had, reluctantly, stopped giving Trina goodnight hugs or kisses since Isabel was certain such demonstrations might have a bad effect on her preadolescent daughter. Michael had been incredulous at first. Did the woman think him incestuous? Did she recognize incest at all, except as something to be prayed against? She'd not had the same fears about

Sybil when his older daughter was growing up, so where had she acquired the notion that he might "ruin" the child closest to his heart?

But when Isabel had reacted with even harsher criticism of Catriona those times he had forgotten and embraced the girl, he had stopped doing so. There were other ways he could show affection and approval. Suddenly he hoped that Fiona Bernon would be at the pub tonight.

He swung the Austin past Mick's cottage, noticing the blue TV glow and almost envying Mick his solitude and his freedom to retreat to his own uncluttered bastion. Yet Michael knew that was nonsense, even if Cornanagh and its horses seemed to fill Mick's life totally.

Michael Carradyne turned his thoughts to more positive matters, such as getting Jack Garden's active support for the Horse Board Bill. Garden was exactly the sort of small horse breeder that the Survey wished to encourage, with its premium schemes for mare, foal, and stallion. Jack might not see the merit of hanging on to a promising animal, breaking and schooling it, but he did understand the importance of putting good mares to good, and hopefully registered, stallions. Which brought the Chou Chin Chow gelding readily to Michael's mind.

He'd seen the animal in Jack's field—Jack had been sounding off about his most recent losses of newborn lambs to loose dogs. The gelding had been startled by their approach and charged off down the field, clearing the bramble hedge, five feet high and at least the same in width. Michael didn't buy many animals outside Cornanagh, so he'd have to go very carefully with Jack or the man would hike the price out of sight. Michael could point out that the gelding was on the small side, couldn't be more than 15.2 hands high. These days even sixteen hands was considered small for a show jumper. As if height had anything to do with innate ability.

Michael had a hunch about that chesnut gelding. He slapped the steering wheel with excitement. His father had been a great one for following hunches.

"They don't come often, Michael," he'd say, "not the real gut ones, so pursue one even if it seems irrational. I did when I paid two hundred pound for a little brown mare in foal to Cottage, and none of us have ever been sorry for that, I'd say." From that mare had come the Tulip and most of Cornanagh's current success.

Christ, how he missed the old man! Even his interfering ways and contradictory orders when Cornanagh was not running the way old Tyler had expected it to. Odd to realize that what he missed most about the old man were their arguments. Particularly on the subject of horses and their training. Now, what would old Tyler have had to say about his intention to get the Chou Chin Chow gelding?

"Depends on his price." He could hear a voice made gravelly by chain-smoking Woodbines. "And who've you got to show him? Philip'd look damned silly up on him, too long in the leg, make the horse look even smaller. That Artie? Now, he's good enough on the ground and a decent work rider, but he's got no style whatever. Have to show a horse properly, and you've no one to do that."

"Trina?"

"Too young. No point in feeding a horse for two, three years until the girl is old enough for him. You'll never make a profit out of this business, Michael, if you don't spin 'em off as soon as you can for whatever you can."

"That gelding can be made into a fine horse—a junior eventer, maybe. I've got a feeling about him."

"Then buy him, man, for not a shilling more than you have to give, and stop havering. I can't abide indecision."

Michael slowed as he reached the Willow Grove, noticing that Jack's car was already there. And Fiona's red Mini. He grinned. The evening could prove most rewarding. He went in by the side door, past the loos, and into the lounge. Buxom, redheaded Fiona Bernon was in a corner seat, chatting in her animated way with her friends. She gave him a friendly wave as she caught sight of him but didn't so much as take a breath in what she was saying. Looking to his left, Michael saw that Jack Garden was at the bar, one hip on a stool, turned sideways toward Bob Kelly.

"And here he is himself, just the man I need," Jack said cheerfully.

"And why do you need me, Jack?" Michael asked affably as he joined the two men. Michael nodded a greeting to the publican and signaled Tom to pour a pint for himself and two more for his friends.

"I've a problem only you can solve." Jack pretended mystery, taking a fold of Michael's raincoat sleeve to pull him closer. "Remember me sending the wife to America to visit her relatives? Well, yet another one appeared this week, combining a business trip with a chance to see the land of his fathers." Here Jack allowed a mock American accent to color his speech. "Only he's the most awkward one yet. He wants to ride to the hounds!"

"Can he ride?" Michael asked, grinning at Jack's discomfort.

"He says he can, but you know Americans. Problem is that I've nothing up to his weight. Grace has been wingeing that the family honor is at stake and all that shit." Jack gave Michael a look of piteous appeal. "That is, of course, if you didn't sell all your hunters abroad."

Michael ignored the snide remark—he had recently sold four horses to the Italians and some were still annoyed about it. He did some rapid mental revision. If he told Lycroft that he should have a change of mount, that would free Jake for Jack's guest. The bay was not only well up to weight, but he could be counted on to cope with an indifferent rider just as long as the man could stay in the pad. And the favor would put Garden under obligation to him. Not that that would go all that far in the matter of the gelding, but you never knew.

"I think I can sort something out all right. Bray's or Wicklow's?" Michael asked.

"Pffst, the man wouldn't be up to Wicklow's. He's a Yank, man, and has probably never seen a hound, much less rid to them! Thanks," he added in an altered tone. "I knew you'd see him right for me."

Michael frowned slightly, catching what Jack didn't say. "Won't you be hunting with him?"

"Don't you remember? My hunter pulled a shoulder muscle two weeks ago, and he's still unsound."

"I had forgot. Well, there'll be enough of us from Cornanagh to keep an eye on him. Philip and I will both be hunting. So will Catriona. If he's backward, she'll keep an eye on him."

Garden pretended to be affronted, but Bob Kelly found Michael's suggestion excessively funny.

"So when's the Yank coming?" Michael asked when Bob's laughter had subsided.

"Jaysus, he's here already. He and the wife are off to Dublin with mine for a bit of culture tonight at the Gate. Fortunately, I'd other business this evening"—Jack lifted his pint glass, slyly winking—"and regretted that I couldn't join them. He's done the entire bit, checking out his genealogy, to be sure he's Irish enough for his political aspirations." Jack rolled his eyes extravagantly and was rewarded with chuckles. "The lengths these Yanks'll go to prove an Irish connection!"

"And then there's Bord Fáilte demanding more funds to improve tourism," Bob Kelly said, always the conscience of the *Dáil* in Delgany. "First, they let all these artistic people in, and now they want us to cope with hordes of tourists, poking and prying. . . ."

"And buying," Michael said firmly. "We could use more of them, you know."

"Not satisfied with selling to Europe, you want to corner the American market, too?" Jack asked Michael, outraged.

"Your man isn't over here to buy horses," Michael replied, "but he *is* buying seats at the Gate, and tweeds, and Waterford glass, and good Irish whiskey."

They spent the rest of the evening arguing the pros and cons of increasing tourism in Ireland.

When Tom called, "Time, ladies and gents, time!" Michael glanced across the room to Fiona. She was looking in his direction and gave an almost imperceptible nod, smiling as she turned back to listen to what her friend was saying.

Michael downed the last of his pint, feeling a pleasant excitement. Sometimes, he thought, anticipation was the best part of these clandestine meetings. He couldn't raise more than a fleeting gratitude for Fiona's willingness, and he was reasonably sure she had more than one discreet liaison.

"See you, Jack, Bob," he said. "Last check on the horses!"

Garden grimaced forbearingly at Michael's habitual excuse. Without apparent hurry, Michael walked through the dark cool night to his car and quickly drove up the Altador road, pausing, as always, halfway up, at the entrance to the Castle. He hadn't long to wait before Fiona's little Mini came along, and when she had passed him with a flash of her lights, he followed her the rest of the way to her cottage.

5

Blister was in Catriona's thoughts the next morning when she heard her father thump on her door. This Friday's morning was clear, if cool, and there was a light breeze, which meant the ground would be just right for the hunt tomorrow—if it didn't rain in the night and spoil everything. She rose eagerly because there were only today's school hours to get through, and she could tell Mary Evans about her cousin's visit.

Once she got home from school, she'd have Ballymore Prince to ride. The pony had to be well exercised before Sean's lesson with her father on Saturday morning. Depending on how fresh the pony was, she might just have to ride him again in the morning before she helped with the hunters. So, really, the only bad part of the bright Friday was having to attend school.

Catriona dressed fast in her chilly room. She could hear Philip in the loo. She tried to get in there before he did because he took forever with shaving and all that, but he wouldn't shift until he was finished no matter what her emergency. She scrambled downstairs to the hall loo, even remembering to rub a towel over her teeth to get rid of the fuzz. Bridie might check.

But when Catriona entered the kitchen, Bridie just scowled, clattering her ladle against the porridge bowl and thrusting it at Catriona, who murmured her thanks, not meeting Bridie's eye. In one of these moods, Bridie might berate you for incidents that you'd totally forgotten. It put you at a severe disadvantage.

Bridie had been working at Cornanagh almost as long as Mick Lenahan. She had come with her husband, Barry, when he had been hired as cowman by the old Colonel. For all she was two inches under the five-foot mark, she had energy to spare in her oddly misshapen figure. Bridie was tiny to the waist and always wore her aprons tightly cinched, but her hips were out-of-proportion broad. She wore her thin gray hair tightly skewered in a bun at the nape of her neck, and her rather prominent nose drooped over her lips because she often left her false teeth in a glass in one of the kitchen cabinets, claiming they hurt her gums.

Philip had once suggested that Bridie's gums drove her to drink, and that her sour mornings invariably coincided with Barry's dart tournaments. Bridie drank, Philip maintained, only on those evenings when Barry was safely out of the house until midnight and she could finish a bottle by herself. For medicinal purposes, of course.

Catriona, who had encountered her brothers, even pious Jack, drink taken often enough, had argued that Bridie never reeked of drink as others she could name did. But she was ignored because Philip and Owen enjoyed the idea of stern Bridie deteriorating in a bout of solitary drinking.

Catriona inhaled surreptitiously as she passed Bridie but caught not a whiff of stale liquor or even mouthwash that would be disguising the lapse.

"D'you have a tissue, Catriona? Blow your nose. I can't abide a sniffling child," Bridie said irritably.

Catriona applied a tissue obediently before she slipped into her place at the table. Owen winked at her, jerking his head over his shoulder in Bridie's direction. Catriona dropped a knob of butter into her porridge and stirred cautiously for the lumps that often occurred when Bridie's mind was not entirely on her cooking. For a wonder, it was smooth enough, and she dug into her breakfast. Her brothers used to tease her because no child was supposed to like porridge, but Catriona even missed it when the weather turned too warm for Bridie to stoke up the Aga stove.

Owen was going quickly through his eggs, rashers, and sausage, alternating with bites of toast, his uneven front teeth making their unique impression on the slice. His hair was a dark brown, worn back without a part, and his eyes were a muddy color, not the rather brilliant brown of his mother's. He wasn't as tall as his brother, or cousins, and his clothes always looked a bit rumpled, though Catriona knew Auntie Eithne was forever pressing his suits and slacks and ironing his shirts. Owen could be very nice indeed, when he tried: it was just that half the time he didn't care to try.

Suddenly he rose, swallowing the last of his coffee and shoving half a piece of toast into his mouth.

"C'mon, Cat, we're running late," he mumbled around the bread.

Catriona swiveled for a glimpse at the kitchen clock and continued to spoon oatmeal into her mouth even as she rose from the chair.

"Catriona Mary Virginia!" Bridie shrilled. "And you're not any better, Owen Carradyne. No better than you should be on any score, and I'm the one as knows it."

"Did you put her in that mood?" Catriona asked as they hastily threw on their outer clothing on their way to the front door.

"Sure it's Friday the thirteenth, Trina. She's practicing to feel unlucky today. C'mon!"

As she plumped down on the cold leather of the Mini's passenger seat, Catriona breathed a prayer that the car would start first go. She had to get out and push when it didn't. When she was legally able to drive, she thought, she'd sit in the driver's seat and Owen would have to push it. But for a mercy, the Mini's engine turned over immediately.

"Thank God!" Owen said. "It almost never starts when we're late, does it, pet?"

The car had another trick in its repertoire—it bucked all the way up the drive, its exhaust making an awful noise. Catriona groaned, sliding down in the seat. She'd hear about that from Mummie when she got back from school.

And coming round the Kilquade turn is the red Carradyne Mini, Catriona thought as Owen, now in second gear, threw the little car into the curve and booted it up the road. They were still in second past the church and on up the long hill by the Russian village, into the S bend with Owen far too much to the right for Catriona's peace of mind. What if they should meet someone barreling down the road from Kilpedder? But it did no good at all to ask Owen to slow down or keep to his side of the road. He'd only tell her what good reflexes he had and ask, Didn't she trust her own cousin?

Actually, Catriona secretly enjoyed the exhilaration of Owen's driving. And he braked to a squealing stop most effectively at Mrs. O'Toole's shop where the Hagan boys were waiting. Catriona cast a hopeful glance down the road and saw the squat red-and-cream form of the Wicklow bus just rounding the curve from Fowler's garage. Reassured, she got out of the car and stood well clear of the Hagans, although what they could have done in the short wait for the bus, she couldn't imagine. They had endless variations of mischief.

Marty Byrne was driving the bus again this morning and gave her a cheery "Good morning!" He was better at keeping peace on the trip to Wicklow town than the other driver, who thought scowls and bellows ought to suffice. She gave him a grin, which widened as she saw that Mary Evans was saving her a place in the second seat back.

Mary was her best friend and lived only over the hill on the back road to Delgany. She was exactly Catriona's height, but she, too, wished to be tall and willowy like the owner of Flirty Lady, Mrs. Healey. Mary still had most of her childish plumpness, a pink-and-white complexion, and dimples in both cheeks. She was an uncomplicated child, as quick to laughter as to anxiety over trifling worries. She had very pretty green eyes and dark blond hair, which she wore in a Dutch boy bob with a fringe across her forehead.

"My cousin's coming to stay this summer," Catriona said, unable to contain her news a moment longer.

"Which one?" Mary tried to pretend that she wasn't envious.

"Patricia from Connecticut, Uncle Eamonn's girl. He wants her to learn how to ride like an Irishman."

Mary whooped, covering her mouth, her green eyes sparkling. "Well, that's a turn-up, isn't it? Your father won't put Blister down, then, will he?"

"Right!" Mary's ability to come quickly to essentials constantly endeared her to Catriona. Besides, Mary was the only other girl in her form who had a pony, who understood about horses, and was, in the words of Captain Carradyne, "not a bad little rider." "Will you be hunting tomorrow, too?" Catriona asked.

"Sure thing, with the hunt at Willow Grove. Mother said that isn't too far for me to hack over alone."

The bus heaved itself through the Newtownmountkennedy bend and halted in front of Nolan's to let the next gaggle of children on.

"Where'll your cousin sleep?" Mary asked once the bus started up again.

"In with me, of course," Catriona replied. "I'm going to ask Mummie if we can have the boys' old bunk beds."

"Bunk beds? That'd be super, that would."

Catriona nodded enthusiastically. "And there'd be enough space in the center of my room so we wouldn't be walking all over each other. I could store all my winter things and leave her space in the wardrobe."

"What's she like?"

Catriona shrugged. "All we've got are Christmas photos."

Mary made a grimace. "They're no good, really. Can't tell you what you need to know. What did she say in her letter?"

"Oh, Patricia didn't write. My uncle Eamonn did. To my father."

"Then you really don't know if she's coming."

"Well, I don't think Uncle Eamonn would waste time writing a letter to Father if he didn't mean her to come. He's a busy executive." But Catriona had a sinking sensation that maybe this was an American-type joke.

"No, I guess not."

"I should hope not." Catriona spoke in a somewhat repressive voice, much like her mother's, although she wouldn't herself have noticed the similarity.

"Who'll bring her over?"

"Uncle Eamonn didn't say, or maybe he did and Father just didn't mention it."

"Your auntie?"

"More than likely," Catriona replied with more confidence than she felt. Although all her American relations had come for Tyler Carradyne's funeral five years ago, she couldn't remember that much of the visit, since a seven-year-old girl child didn't attend many of the evening affairs.

"It could be a very good summer for us," Mary hazarded, trying to restore Catriona's good humor. "Maybe if Patricia isn't able for Blister, Mother would lend your father our old Patch. He's not good for much, but he taught Mother and me how to ride, and he's got a few more years left in him, Mother always says."

"Oh, Mary, could you lend us Patch?" Catriona felt relief wash over her. She couldn't have asked: one just didn't beg the lend of a horse—at least, the Carradynes didn't. "Hadn't you better ask your mother?"

"Oh, I will, but she will because I know your father's a stickler."

"For good reason." Catriona thought darkly of the time when an acquaintance of her father's, a man known to be a capable rider, had begged the loan of one of the hunters to keep in his own stable for the hunting season. The animal had been returned to Cornanagh with bowed tendons in both front legs.

"Sorry." Mary dragged out the word in exaggerated remorse.

Catriona gave her an elbow in the ribs, and the two subsided into giggles as the bus joggled around the fountain in the square and stopped just short of the Dominican School.

"Well, only today to go and the week's over," she said to Mary as they rose to leave.

That afternoon Catriona half walked, half jogged the mile from the bus stop to Cornanagh, her school bag banging against her back, as she looked forward to riding Ballymore Prince. All the dreads and deeds of the school day were forgotten, even Sister Conceptua's threat of a math quiz next week because no one had been able to finish the prep.

Such mundane matters could not afflict Catriona Carradyne with a weekend of Horse in prospect, a hunt tomorrow and Philip riding Teasle in a training show on Sunday. School was the necessary evil she tolerated as a bridge between weekends spent with Horse. And the weather had held fair. That was only a bonus, for Catriona cared nothing for the weather if she was working with horses. Except, of course, when too much rain canceled an event.

She closed the iron-strap gates of Cornanagh behind her and paused briefly as she crossed the ride, to test its surface. A little soft, but not boggy. Would her father ever find the perfect all-weather material for the ride and the lunge yard?

She passed the gate lodge where Mick lived, charged down the path behind Bridie's cottage and through the passageway, then ran full pelt across the cobbles to the back door.

Flinging her school bag to exactly the right spot in the corner by the boots, she began to shed her coat and jumper as she climbed the stairs two at a time.

"Catriona Mary, can you not enter the house like a lady?" Her mother leaned over the balustrade. "I will not tolerate such behavior. You're nearly a young woman, and you've the manners of a tinker. I shall have to speak to your father!"

"I'm sorry, Mummie, but there's only so much daylight left to ride in," Catriona replied as she generally did.

"I really *will* have to speak to your father," Isabel repeated, and, dismissing the incident almost as fast as Catriona, returned to the box room, where she was restoring order to the cluttered shelves.

What was she to do with Catriona? The girl was not the least bit like her older sister, Sybil: as different as chalk and cheese the two were. Sybil had been a biddable child, taking pains with her appearance, well mannered, dutiful, and not the least bit interested in horses. For which mercy Isabel had thanked the Blessed Virgin. It was enough of a worry that all the boys had had to ride up to the exacting standards of both Tyler and Michael. Injuries were so common in riding.

Irritably she pushed aside the box of hacking jackets, relics of Tyler's career as a show jumper, thriftily saved for future Carradynes. Well, Catriona would soon be a woman, and her mind would turn from horses to boys. Isabel gave a shudder. Sybil's one lapse from grace in her eyes had been her fascination with boys and her blithe marriage at nineteen to Aidan Roche.

Isabel had tried very hard to dissuade her daughter from marriage. Not that she could find argument against Aidan, who was already assistant manager in his father's shop in Dun Laoghaire. When Sybil had been adamant, Isabel had yielded, fumbling so badly in her attempt to explain the ordeal to come that she had only then been able to forgive her own mother's inability to discuss the subject. Consequently, Isabel had suffered a shock when, on her return from her honeymoon in Marbella, Sybil had winked at her mother and said, "Oh, Mummie, it wasn't as bad as all that."

Too bad Catriona showed absolutely no sign of a religious vocation, Isabel thought, dusting the tall Carradyne hatbox that contained the top hat her father-in-law had worn in dressage competitions. Now, if she could only be encouraged to prefer dressage to show jumping, perhaps there might be hope. Such excellent families on the Continent competed in the dressage arena at Goodwood.

Why, oh, why, did she constantly go back to marriage for Catriona? Maybe the girl's interest in horses should be encouraged as an alternative? Too bad that both Colonel Dudgeon and his marvelous old trainer, Mr. Mac, were dead. They had had world recognition as Ireland's leading trainers, and certainly Burton Hall had turned out top riders and successful horses. Why, the Queen of England sent her horses to be schooled there. Isabel would have felt more confident of the quality of her child's instruction if the colonel or Mr. Mac had been there to oversee it. It didn't occur to her at all that her husband was their equal.

Meanwhile, Catriona wasted no time changing into her jods, a thermal ski top, and two jumpers. It'd be cold on the ride. She padded downstairs in her stocking feet, hoping to be quiet enough not to attract her mother's notice again. In the front hall, she pushed aside her school bag and rummaged until she found her jodhpur boots among the clutter. She grimaced as she shoved her feet into the slightly clammy interiors. She had *meant* to put newspaper in them on Wednesday to absorb the damp, and now she was stuck with the result of her oversight. She grabbed up her hard hat and was out the door, giving Tory's ears an affectionate pull.

The farrier was in the yard with her father and Artie, who was holding Mr. Hardcastle's bay hunter.

"Good afternoon, Mr. Boyne," Catriona said, for she liked the blacksmith. He explained things while he worked.

"And how are you today, Catriona Carradyne?"

"Saddle up the Prince, Catriona," her father said without giving her time to respond.

"I quartered him for you, Catriona," Artie said in an aside as she passed him, and she smiled her thanks. With the pony already groomed, she could just saddle up.

"If this fella keeps on losing shoes," the farrier was saying, "there'll be no hoof left to set any nails in, Captain." He held up the bay's off fore and pointed to the series of old nail holes and the clinches torn out by the last loss.

"There're only two more hunts this season, John, and I've nothing else Hardcastle could manage on a hunt. A summer at grass will set the hooves to rights."

Catriona hummed as she got the Prince's tack down. She tested the string girth, selected brushing boots, and paused by the over-reach bells. But they were only going for a hack, not a jumping lesson. Though if no one came with her, she might sneak the Prince in for a run down the jump alley. Blister was nowhere near as exciting to jump as Ballymore Prince.

The Prince farrupped happily when she entered the stable and butted at her hand for the treat she usually had for him, but she'd been scolded for nicking stale bread.

"Those horses are fed far too well," Bridie had complained. "They don't do anything for us, but the hens'll lay better for a crust or two."

Catriona patted the Prince's arching neck and then unbuckled his rug, automatically folding it the long way before sliding it off into the manger. Then she began to tack him up.

Ballymore Prince was a bay, of that marvelous shade not quite "blood" and certainly not mousy, superbly set off by his full black tail and mane. He had beautiful conformation, this delicately boned miniature horse, being of quite different stock from the blunt Blister. There was considerable power in the Prince's hindquarters, deceptively so. The pony could clear a barrier four feet high and a bit or a six-foot spread without a bother to him. His head was his best feature, almost classic in its fine line and proportion, with well-set liquid brown eyes, often rolling white preparatory to some mischief, and rather large but shapely ears. When Catriona started to put the brushing boots on his hind legs, he messed about a bit, but then he always did.

"Stannup!" She growled it the way Mick or her father would, and the Prince stood. She buckled on her hat, took her gloves from her waistband, and led the pony out.

Without skipping a word of his reply to John Boyne, Michael Carradyne stepped over to check the saddled pony. He gave Catriona a brief smile and the nod to mount, watching her with slightly narrowed eyes. To a nervous rider or an erring groom, that look could be unnerving. Catriona checked her girth, hoisted it up one more notch now that she was mounted, and then waited quietly.

"A moment, John," her father said, placing one hand on the Prince's neck. "No canter work today, Catriona. Keep him at a good working trot, on the bit and rhythmic." He cocked his head warningly. "Three laps of the ride. You can take the jump lane tomorrow before Sean gets here, but today I want this pony between the aids and working hard."

"Yes, Daddy," she replied, and pressed her legs to move the Prince off.

He began to fuss instantly, and her hands resisted his attempt to career out of the yard. She was up to all the pony's tricks and only wished that Sean were, too. The Prince was so easy, really, to manage.

She heard her father take up his discussion with John, although she was aware that both men watched her until she turned out of the yard and right toward the ride. As soon as she had the Prince's full attention, she gave enough with her hands to set him off at the prescribed working trot.

The Prince was eager, and he tossed his head, resisting the conservative pace, his teeth clattering against the vulcanite bit. She could feel him gathering his hind quarters and checked him, gently. He'd get chucked in the mouth enough tomorrow when Sean rode.

The Tulip, hearing hooves on the ride, bugled a challenge and charged right up to the stud railing. He shook his head and great curved neck with its full black mane at the impudent pony passing his domain.

"Hello, Tulip, how's she cutting?" Catriona said, not losing her rhythm. She thought he looked gorgeous, even if his off side was muddy from a recent roll. He shook his head at her again, extending his neck and whinnying, stamping imperiously with a front foot.

The Prince tried to lengthen his stride, but Catriona kept a firm grip on the reins and her legs tight against him: she could almost see the white of his eyes. The Prince was terrified of the Tulip.

"He could eat the Prince in two bites," Mick was fond of saying proudly of the great old horse, "and that'd learn the little sod!"

Once past the Tulip, the Prince was willing to settle a bit. Despite his fractiousness and displays of terror, the Prince was a pleasure to ride, a challenge Catriona thoroughly enjoyed. He had a smooth even trot which was the result of many hours of work by Catriona and her father. Before they'd turned to face the sea, gun-metal gray in the waning afternoon light, the

Prince was on the bit and listening, aware that this rider could make him obey.

The Ride, as it was called, had been created by Tyler Carradyne and followed the perimeter of Cornanagh. It was a good track, nearly two miles long, from which the stones had been carefully pried, with a surface that changed from grass, to peat, to shavings for firm footing. Three smaller paths branched off the main ride on the longer northern side of the property. One of the smaller paths was dissected by a variety of jumps—some fences could be adjusted in height, others were fixed—and the small stream that flowed through Cornanagh Stud had been slightly diverted and dammed to provide a water jump a third of the way down the course. The longest of the extra tracks was a measured five furlongs. The shortest followed a zigzag up and down the natural ridge running parallel to the main ride.

Catriona and Blister had had many exhilarating afternoons chasing up and around the various tracks, sometimes with Mary, who would hack over on her pony. But today Catriona was riding work, and she was far too responsible a rider to alter her instructions. She held the Prince at the working trot speed, counting it out occasionally—one-two, one-two, one-two—to be sure of the rhythm. The sun was bright through the stark branches as she turned on the sea side of the ride, catching glimpses of the dull gray water through the bare trees. The Prince's ears twitched at the sunlight, but they were soon behind the thick ditch hedges again. One-two, one-two, one-two. She gave the jump track the merest glance as they passed its entry. The Prince reacted to the opening, but she pressed her left leg in, and he obediently yielded away from temptation.

"Tomorrow, fella," she murmured, and his ears wigwagged at the reassuring sound in her voice. One-two, one-two.

He leaned into the left again as they neared the ridge track and then dropped behind the bit a moment in disappointment.

One-two, one-two. One of her father's maxims was that you always schooled a horse even when you were just out hacking. What was the point of working a horse in the menage to achieve the perfect pace and gait if you let him go any which way on track or road? A well-schooled horse should always be on the bit, except for those moments when he was allowed to stretch at the walk, relieving his back muscles.

The most beautiful part of the ride, Catriona thought, was the beech alley, a double row of trees that must have been planted by the very first Carradynes, for their trunks were immense, their first branches twenty feet up. She felt very small on the fine-boned show pony as they swung up the ride under the massive beeches, past Mick's cottage, then Bridie's, toward the front of the main house now as they finished the first lap. So that the Prince would not get a mistaken notion that one circuit was their work for the day, Catriona reined him in only when they were well past the entrance to the stable yard. Then she slowed him to the walk, critically feeling for the smoothness of the transition from one gait to the next.

"Good boy, Prince, that's a good boy," she said, slapping the curved neck. She loosened the reins to give him a chance to stretch but kept the walk active. Not that that took much doing; the Prince was active under any circumstances. As proof, he began to edge to the left, putting as much distance between himself and the terrifying stallion as the track would allow. "And the Tulip's gone in, so you don't have to spook at his paddock." She straightened him.

6

The light was waning as they finished the third lap, and the pony knew he'd been worked. Just at the stable yard gates she dismounted and snagged a handful of the late winter grass as a treat for him. Munching contentedly, he walked obediently beside her back to his stable. With a swatch of straw she worked the saddle marks off his back before she rugged him up. He butted for a head rub: his left ear always itched. She complied.

"Catriona, we need help feeding," her father called, and she gathered up the tack to put it away before she lent a hand with the feed buckets. "You'll clean that tack before dinner?" her father added as he gave her the pony feeds. She nodded, wondering if there'd ever come a day when he realized that she knew the routine without reminders. But then he even told Mick what to do, so it wasn't as if he thought her especially feeble-minded. Catriona might not always understand why she did certain things in school, but around horses, her comprehension verged on the instinctive. She knew the wheres, whys, and whens of stable management.

However, cleaning tack made her arrive at the house just as Bridie was serving up the dinner.

"Where have you been, wretched child? Your auntie Eithne's away, and your mother only just back from one of her meetings, and no one to set the table, and the good plaice nearly burnt to a crisp with me seeing to everything all at the oncet. Didn't you know you was to help me?"

Catriona looked frantically at her saddle-soap-stained hands and dashed for the kitchen sink.

"Not there! Oh, spare me," cried Bridie, lashing out at Catriona with her dishcloth to drive her away from the sink.

"Now she's contaminatering my taties. Was there ever such a girl?"

When Catriona entered the dining room after a cursory wash in the loo, she found the table set and everyone in their places, waiting for her. She slid into her seat, keeping her eyes down. She just knew there was a frown on her mother's face. In fact, her mother gave a particularly authoritative sniff, but her father broke the silence first.

"I'll expect that tack to be well cleaned, Catriona, not skimped."

"I did it and took the mud off the brushing boots as well, Daddy."

"Michael," Isabel began, "you know how Bridie fusses if she's not helped with the tea, and Eithne had to drive to see her father. . . ."

"You were here."

"I was not, Michael. Mairead Sims called a meeting of the hospitality committee."

"I see," Michael Carradyne replied in the tone of voice that plainly said he wasn't to be bothered with domestic problems.

"Michael!" Isabel's soft protest told volumes about her dismay and her continued martyrdom to horses. She served the fish, showing her disapproval of her daughter by giving her the smallest piece, one with a charred tail.

Actually Catriona liked burned bits and ate them all, though she pretended to sulk about the penance. She'd probably have to do the washing up by herself, but the Prince had gone so well for her that she really didn't mind.

"The paper says that milk producers are to get an extra two

shillings a gallon," Isabel remarked to begin the evening's dinner conversation.

Catriona tuned out her father's polite reply and lost herself in wondering which route they'd take the next day at the Willow Grove hunt. It would be a scent drag because, as Mick was fond of saying, the real foxes were too smart to let the dogs catch them. Indeed, they hadn't started a fox in years. Billy Evans rode good lines—dragging a bag of rags redolent of fox spoor for the hounds to follow—so it could be a fast hunt even if they went through Calary Bog, where the going would be very heavy and slow everyone down. Not that that wasn't a good idea because it was a Saturday hunt and likely all the Grafton Street Harriers—as the locals contemptuously styled businessmen who hunted on the Saturday—would be out. There'd only be the St. Patrick's Day hunt on Tuesday left of this year's season. Then a few weeks' break, and the spring show-jumping season would get into swing. This would be her last hunt for 1970, so she wanted it to be an especially good one.

In a way, it was too bad that her cousin Patricia couldn't get here for hunting—at least to see a hunt move out, always a thrilling moment for Catriona, no matter how the hunt turned out. But perhaps it was just as well, for it wouldn't do for Cornanagh to turn out a rider who might disgrace them. She must remember to tell her father that Mary had offered her old pony, in case Patricia needed a bombproof mount.

She tuned back in briefly to the dinner conversation, but it had moved from milk to the Troubles up in Ulster, and she didn't like hearing who had killed whom and how the whole exercise was bloody useless.

Friday evening she was allowed to watch telly. Though there was seldom a program she wanted to see, she watched up to the nine o'clock news because she was allowed. Then she was glad to retreat to her room. That afternoon she had remembered to draw the drapes, and her room was warm enough for her to read for a little while. Mary had loaned her a new Pullein-Thompson book about horses: Catriona found non-horse books a real chore. She finished a chapter, turned out her light, and went to sleep. Tomorrow was going to be a busy day for Cornanagh's stables.

Saturdays—and Sundays, too, for that matter—Catriona was awake even before she heard her father thump on her door. One of these days she might actually open the door before he had a chance to knock, just to surprise him. Would he find it amusing? However, if Michael Carradyne found her prompt appearance at the breakfast table pleasing, he gave no indication, merely nodded at her. It occurred to Catriona, in a flash, that she hadn't realized before that her father was as given to significant nods as her mother was to sniffs and Auntie Eithne to sighs. When she got old enough to have such habits, which would she pick?

"Can I trust you to plait four hunters this morning?" he asked.

"Oh, yes," she replied eagerly as Bridie served her porridge. "Which ones?"

"Black Bess, Jacko, Flirty Lady, and Stormy. I want you to take the Prince out first, a lap at the trot and a controlled—mind you, controlled—run of the jump alley. Do not"—Michael Carradyne waggled an admonitory finger at his daughter—"do not let him out."

"I won't, Daddy, I know what he does to Sean if he gets the wind up."

Michael gave his daughter a long, appraising look, then smiled at her. "You're a good little rider, Kitten," he said with a rare display of affection. "That pony's wasted on Sean." He pursed his lips as if regretting his indiscretion.

Catriona grinned at him. "Don't worry, Daddy."

"Minx. What have you been doing to upset your mother? She says you've the manners of a tinker."

"Only on a horse, Daddy."

Michael Carradyne tipped his head back and laughed aloud. "What else does she expect of a Carradyne? C'mon. We've a lot to do before the hunt starts."

Mick and Artie were feeding the horses when father and daughter emerged from the house. Barry was bringing the trailer, hitched to the tractor to speed the mucking-out, as Catriona swung the Prince out of the yard. The pony danced, taking great exception to the tractor's menacing appearance, while Catriona, laughing, sat down to his antics. Finally she urged the Prince out and down to the Ride to give him his warm-up. The Tulip came charging up to the paddock rails to see them on their way.

They were barely back into the now tidy yard when Catriona heard the throaty sound of a heavy car, gearing down to make the turn into the yard.

"That'll be Sean and his father," Michael said, and Catriona was sure there was a trace of impatience in the set of his jaw. If Sean found his lessons with Captain Carradyne a trial, so did the captain. "Give him a bit of a brush before you bring him out, Artie."

Artie, catching Catriona's gaze, winked at her. They both felt sorry for the Prince on Wednesdays and Saturdays.

But she had hunter manes to plait. She got the mane comb, packets of rubber bands, and the old stool and started with Flirty Lady. The mare could be difficult, and Catriona wanted to be sure that the plaits were perfect because she was in awe of Selina Healey, Flirty's owner. Catriona knew that her mother was rather chuffed that Mrs. Healey, who had been Lady Selina Worthyn before her marriage, kept her hunter at Cornanagh. Such connections mattered to Isabel Carradyne.

What mattered to Catriona was that Mrs. Healey was a superb

horsewoman. Even her father said so. She had a deep seat, a light hand, and an instinct for her volatile mare's sometimes outrageous behavior. The woman never faltered in the field, no matter what the obstacle, even *the* ditch at Glenealy. Flirty Lady had never been known to refuse and was exceedingly clever in getting herself and her rider over any jump.

Catriona had never actually heard Mrs. Healey make a single remark to anyone. She would appear promptly at the hunt, accept a leg up from either the Captain or one of his sons, smile graciously, and move off. Consequently Mrs. Healey retained every ounce of glamour that Catriona accorded her. And, unlike some of her father's clients, Mrs. Healey's accounts were always paid by return of post.

So, Flirty Lady received Catriona's best plaiting effort. Despite the care she took with each, she was finished before Sean's lesson ended. And since Jacko and Stormy were in the top yard, some of her father's louder commands to Sean were completely audible. Occasionally she winced for the Prince's sake, as the orders confirmed her notion that the lesson was not going well.

"Stop chucking him in the mouth, Sean. Give with your hands. Small wonder the pony refused. Give! Give!"

That was more than Catriona could abide. She ducked into Auntie Eithne's side door, up the steps to the first story, and she had started into Auntie Eithne's bedroom when a strange sound caught her attention. The door to Owen's bedroom was open. She could see his naked back, and he was exercising in the strangest way, rocking back and forth. Whatever was he about? Then Catriona caught sight of the second occupant of the bed: a girl underneath Owen, her dark hair loose on the pillow and the oddest expression of concentration on her face.

Abruptly aware that she ought not to be here, ought not to be witness to what was happening in Owen's room with his mother away, Catriona abandoned her idea of overlooking the lunge ring from her aunt's room and slipped down the steps as soundlessly as she could.

She was busy grooming Blister when her father, Sean, and the sweating pony returned to the bottom yard. Sean was white and rebellious, and her father wore his firm-lipped look. He signaled for Artie to take the pony and with a motion of his hand indicated that the pony was to remain tacked up. Artie nodded, with a look of pity for Sean as he turned away. Then her father, one arm about Sean's shoulders, escorted him back to the main yard.

As soon as the high-powered Mercedes had left the premises, Father was back in the yard, calling for Catriona.

"I want you to take Prince over the fences in the lunge ring. Carry a stick and don't let him away with anything. Now, Catriona."

She nodded, not quite looking at her father because she could tell that he was furious. She knew perfectly well that he was not annoyed with her, but she hated her father in this sort of a mood. Equally, she disliked the damage to the Prince, undoing her careful schooling of the past week.

The Prince tried to run out at the very first upright, but she was waiting for just such an attempt and gave him a sharp crack with her stick. By the second fence he was on the bit again, reassured by her kind hands and firm seat. He actually enjoyed the last obstacle.

"That's enough, Trina," her father called from the entrance. He didn't sound quite so tense, and obediently she circled the pony.

At noon they all took time off for a bowl of Bridie's thick lentil soup.

"It'll keep you warm hunting," she said watching sternly until everyone had finished.

The first to appear for his horse was, as usual, Mr. Hardcastle.

No sooner was he mounted up and out of the yard than Jack Garden appeared with his American relative. Barney Camwell was appropriately dressed for a hunt, but all his clothes looked new and the boots so stiff it was a wonder he could walk in them at all.

Catriona watched as Mr. Camwell had to be practically hoisted into the saddle by the combined efforts of Jack Garden and her father, the man laughing all the time as if this were the greatest lark. Artie, who was holding Jake's head, shot her an exasperated look, which he quickly erased at a scowl from Michael. Just then the other owners arrived, and there was a bit of a scramble to get everyone mounted. Catriona barely had time to collect Blister and mount before the cavalcade started off, her father leading Mrs. Healey's mare, with the American paired off with Mr. Hardcastle and Philip on Teasle behind them. Catriona brought up the rear. Blister snorted and tossed his head. He knew perfectly well where they were going, and Catriona gave him an affectionate slap for his high spirits. It was a beautiful day, and it was going to be a good hunt. At least for herself, Catriona amended, watching the American bounce all over the saddle as they trotted up the road. Poor Jake. He'd be back sore tonight.

Mary was waiting for her at the pub on Champers, her black pony. They both dismounted to give their ponies' backs a bit of a rest while they watched the adults mounting up. The two daughters of Mr. O'Brien, the master of the hunt, who were assistant whippers-in, were collecting the cap money and chatting vivaciously with the better-known members.

Mrs. Healey arrived, parking her red Lancia sportscar just beyond where the girls waited with their patient ponies. As always, she was properly dressed for the hunt, her long blond hair netted neatly under her hard hat, her stock blazingly white with a pretty jeweled pin securing it, her jacket and jods without a speck on them, and her custom-made long boots polished to perfection. Mrs. Healey was also wearing a clear red lipstick and just a hint of blue eye shadow to emphasize that color in her gray-blue eyes.

Catriona and Mary were equally impressed by her smart turnout. If only one of them could grow up looking so elegant, so tall and willowy slender. . . . Then Michael Carradyne led up Flirty Lady, and Mrs. Healey, her head just visible above his shoulder, walked up to the near side. She gathered the reins quickly and took a graceful leg up into the saddle, smiling her thanks as Flirty Lady began her usual excited dance about the verge.

"It's a big field today," Mary said, surveying the assembly. "Over a hundred, I'll bet."

"Almost the last hunt of the year, and a fine day," Catriona replied. "What else would you expect?"

"You ponies," said a whipper-in, coming up to them on her big bay, "mind yourselves now, and don't get into trouble."

Catriona agreed meekly, but Mary muttered, "We're less likely to get into trouble than those Saturday experts. And she knows it, too."

"Isn't that what she means?" Catriona replied, giggling.

She swung up on Blister's back just as the hounds were released from the horse van and had to restrain the eager pony from rushing forward. Mary had a time holding Champers in as well, but eventually the hunt streamed away after the master and the whip, and they were able to let the ponies move out in the wake of the longer-legged hunters.

"Oh, great!" Mary cried as the hunt was led up the road. "We're going Calary Bog way."

Catriona was equally delighted, for there'd be some good runs across the high plateau fields behind Sugar Loaf Mountain. There'd be ditches, not as big as the ones on the Glenealy Hunt, but respectable and certainly easy enough for a poor rider like Mr. Camwell. Jake'd see him safe. If he lasted.

They went up the steep road and down the other side, right into the bog, and the hounds followed the drag yapping excitedly. As they reached the top of the road, the two girls could see the hunt field spread out below them, the master's red coat visible half a mile away and the white of the hounds' patches as they leaped low gorse.

Catriona looked for and found Jake, cantering along by her father and Mr. Hardcastle, Mr. Camwell evidently holding his own, though he rode like most Yanks, feet straight out in front of him, hands higher than they should be, and his reins far too long. Then Mary and Catriona had to concentrate on the course as the ponies went full pelt down the slope.

Blister was enjoying himself, too, on this clear, crisp March day to tell from his high blowing. He charged down the slope and took the first ditch out onto the road, falling back to a trot before banking the next obstacle neatly. Ahead of the two girls, horses were already flying the next ditches and out across the long field to the top of Calary Bog. Then down the far side, where the hedge row was thicker, and across another field, a trifle soggier going for the big horses so that the lighter ponies caught up with the main field. Mary grinned over her shoulder at Catriona for the pleasure of passing out adults. Catriona caught sight of her father well ahead, with Mrs. Healey to his left and Mr. Camwell, with little choice in the matter, hanging on to Jake's mane as the old hunter traversed the next ditch.

It wasn't as if she were urging Blister to noble deed and a faster pace, Catriona thought, exhilarated, as she and Mary passed out slower horses. The ponies were just more able for the ground, and it really wasn't fair to have to pull them back when they were going so well. Catriona gave Blister his head to jump the next ditch, and then they were off and running toward the next obstacle. She noticed that several of the big hunters had failed to take the ditch ahead of them and were circling for a second try. But, as she was only a couple of strides away from the ditch, she and Blister had the right of way. She heard Mary call out, but not what she said, and turned her head left to see what the matter was. She could feel Blister gathering himself to take off.

The next thing she knew she was thumped to the ground with the breath knocked out of her. Blister screamed, high-pitched and terrified, almost in her ear. She heard Mary cry out, and some instinct prompted her to roll as a horse came down just where she had been. The roll hurt her left arm terribly, but then Blister's continued screaming blocked out everything else. She got to her feet, still dazed, her eyes not quite focusing. Then she found Blister. He was trying to stand and couldn't. He was trapped in the ditch, trapped with both front legs broken. Someone began to scream, and it wasn't until much later that Catriona realized it was herself. She flung her body against Blister's neck to keep the valiant pony from trying to rise. She was only peripherally aware that another horse had crashed down into the same ditch but had struggled to his feet, reins flapping as he trotted away, his rider floundering after him.

Catriona clung to Blister's head, trying to reassure him, weeping bitterly because she knew there was only one thing that could be done for her lovely pony. Where was someone to do it!

"Hold his head steady, Catriona," she heard a voice order, and she turned her head away so that she would not see the pistol. The bullet might have thudded into her own skull, for she felt the impact through the pony's neck. Then Blister slumped, and she screamed again, for his head pinned her left arm to the bank.

Someone lifted the weight from her and began to ease her gently out of the ditch.

"There now, child, take my hand," said a crisply kind voice.

Blinded by blood and tears, Catriona tried to comply, but

her left arm wouldn't move and she couldn't see the proffered hand.

"For God's sake, Captain, leave the tack, man. Help your daughter."

Someone was mopping at her forehead then, and suddenly Catriona could see Mary, her round face pale and terribly anxious, and there were a lot of people crowding around her.

"It certainly wasn't the child's fault, Michael," the kind voice was saying. "She had the right of way. He rode right across her path. Lucky she wasn't killed, too."

Catriona wanted badly to lie down. She knew she was swaying on her feet.

"At times, Michael Carradyne, you are an insensitive bastard. Here, hand her up to me. I'll bring her to the road. Head wounds always bleed profusely. There. That'll hold."

Someone had bound up her head, and she was able to see better. Then suddenly, she felt her father's arms about her. She cried out because he caught her sore arm. The next moment she was seated across a saddle and pressed against someone who smelled faintly of lavender.

"Easy now, child. We'll have you safe and warm."

"You're Mrs. Healey," Catriona said wonderingly.

"Why, so I am," the voice said, laughter running through it. "And you're a very brave little girl."

"No, I'm not," Catriona said in a wail. "I've just lost my pony."

The horse began to move forward, and Mrs. Healey tightened her grasp on Catriona, inadvertently pressing the broken arm so tightly that Catriona fainted.

7

The only one who really could have understood how keenly Catriona missed Blister was Mary. And girls Mary's age weren't allowed in hospital . . . unless they were sick. And no one told Catriona why she was kept in hospital once they had put seven stitches to close the cut on the back of her head and splinted her arm. The doctor told her that it was only a simple fracture and would mend in next to no time.

The nursing sisters told her that her father and mother had both been in to see her the evening before, but she'd been asleep from the medication. Catriona was aware of several meaningful glances exchanged by the sisters, winks and nods, and she worried that she'd said or done something wrong.

That afternoon her mother brought in her schoolbooks. "As it's only your left arm you've broken, you can still write and do your preparation."

Catriona thanked her mother, but she had no enthusiasm for anything, much less schoolwork. She leaned back against the pillows and sighed.

"Your head doesn't still ache, does it, Catriona?" Her mother's tone was urgent, and Catriona felt her mother's moist warm hand on her forehead. "I should never have let your father take you hunting. I really am going to have words with him."

"Was he very angry?" Catriona winced, thinking of poor Blister. She could still feel the thud of the bullet.

"He was furious! Raging! I heard"—Isabel leaned forward

and lowered her voice since Catriona was in a ward with three other women—"that he had a terrific argument with Jack Garden. He oughtn't to blame him because his American relative was so inexperienced. Apparently, Mr. Camwell just got back on Jake and rode on, totally oblivious to what he had done to you and that poor old pony. Your father was livid. He took the horse away from him and made him walk back. Needless to say, that didn't set well with Jack Garden, either. I do wish your father would control his temper." She sighed.

Catriona rested her head back on the pillows, wondering if it was a sin to be pleased that Mr. Camwell had had to walk back down from Calary in stiff new riding boots. She still didn't quite know what had happened, and it was no use asking her mother.

"Did you know that Mrs. Healey came all the way into the hospital with you?"

Catriona opened her eyes in astonishment and noticed a little flush in her mother's face.

"Mrs. Healey?" Catriona was distressed. She'd have got Mrs. Healey all bloody.

"And the flowers are from her as well."

Catriona had noticed the little bouquet, bright with narcissus and orange tulips and some white blossom, but as she'd never been in a hospital before, she'd thought flowers were part of the services. Her mother located the card.

"Very kind of her, I must say. 'Be back in the saddle again as soon as possible,' it says," Isabel told her, sniffing as she handed her the card.

Catriona looked at the handwriting, which was not the sort of script she'd imagined for Mrs. Healey. The words were formed in a very neat but cramped hand. Not half elegant enough to match up with Mrs. Healey's appearance, Catriona thought, a trifle disappointed.

"Well, I am going to talk to your father about you being back in the saddle at all, ever!"

"Mummie . . ." Catriona sat up in protest, and everything spun. She clasped her head, groaning.

"I am not going to make a practice of visiting my daughter in hospital. I really do have some say in the rearing of my own— Whatever is the matter with you, Catriona? Sister! Sister! Oh, do come!"

Catriona couldn't tell the Sister why she had taken such a turn, but the result was that her mother tiptoed away to let her rest. Then she had to have her blood pressure taken, and the doctor arrived to flash a beam of light into her eyes and ask how often she had felt dizzy. Did her head ache? Spots before her eyes? Was her arm comfortable?

She responded meekly and truthfully, and then they all left her bedside, closing the curtains about her bed so that she was free of the kind and curious glances of her wardmates. She tried to sleep then, because she did feel terribly listless. Although her head didn't hurt, it felt hot and heavy on her neck, and she couldn't really get comfortable. The Sister kept looking in on her. More lights were shone in her eyes and more blood pressures were taken. When supper came she couldn't eat much of it, only the bread and butter and a bit of the creamed potato, which was of the instant sort that Bridie wouldn't have allowed in her larder. But the person who collected the tray didn't scold her for wasting food.

She heard the other women receiving visitors and was hoping against hope that her father might come. She framed an apology about Blister a hundred times so that it would come out without being stammered, but he didn't appear and she became increasingly fretful. He really was furious with her. How was she ever going to explain? And she couldn't really recall exactly what had happened. All she could remember now was Jake being circled before the ditch, Mary behind her on the left, several other adults crossing the field toward the ditch, and then . . . nothing more until she felt the impact.

She began to weep then, silently so as not to disturb the other women, and suddenly was so weak that she couldn't reach up to brush the tears away. Blister had been so marvelous: an honest pony, sturdy, reliable, genuine. She pictured his heavy pony head over the door of his stable, the neat Connemara ears pricked forward, the pink-and-dark-gray splotches on his muzzle, his velvety lips laid back so he could nibble at the palm of her outstretched hand. She couldn't remember a time when Blister hadn't been there in the stable block. Other horses had come and gone, but Blister, and the Tulip, had always been there. Had the knacker come quickly to take Blister's poor body from the ditch? She didn't like to think of the pony lying there alone and cold all night.

"Here, here, what's this?" a brisk voice demanded.

Through her tears, Catriona saw the Ward Sister approaching the bed.

"My pony! I don't want him lying out cold in the ditch!"

The tears streamed down Catriona's face, and then suddenly someone had brushed by the woman and was holding her in his arms.

"There now, Catie," Mick's rough voice reassured her, "I saw to it myself. Didja think I wouldn't? Didja think the Captain wouldn't? Now, don't you fret, Catriona Carradyne. Not that it isn't just what I'd expect of you, but sure we took care of it."

"Mr. Lenahan . . ." the Ward Sister began.

"You just leave us be, missus." Mick's face was suffused with red, almost masking the tiny broken capillaries in his wind-scored cheeks.

It suddenly struck Catriona that she had never heard Mick speak so firmly in her life. And he was speaking up for her. She clung to him, more reassured by his attitude than anything he could have said in comfort. And so her tears stopped.

A clean handkerchief, but one that nevertheless smelled heavily of Old Spice after-shave and horses, mopped her cheeks and then was patted against her forehead. Having completed that necessary ministration, Mick settled back into the chair at the side of her little curtained cubicle. He cleared his throat.

"I've only got a minute, Cat, because it's near the end of visiting hours, but when I heard that your father wasn't to go in because you'd turned queer, I thought maybe I'd better pop in. And I was right. You were grieving for the pony."

"Mother won't let me ride again, Mick."

Mick's eyes took on a challenging sparkle.

"You didn't ever believe her, didja, Cat? You've the best hands and seat of the lot, and once you get a bit of leg on you, there won't be anything in the yard you can't manage. As well as the Captain, or I don't know my bran and bridoons." Mick gave his chin a decisive downward jerk. "You don't worry about your mother. She's a good churchgoing woman, but she don't know about horses or riders, at all. Now"—Mick leaned forward, elbows on his knees—"as I understand it, you've got some stitches in your skull, but those things heal fast on a young body. And the break in your arm will be well mended before the spring show, so you'll be back, riding fit, for the summer."

"But now Father doesn't have anything for my cousin. . . ."

Mick cocked his head, grinning. "Don't worry about her, Cat. And don't worry that you'll not be mounted. You'll see."

The gong sounding the end of visiting hours reverberated down the hall. Mick was up on his feet instantly, his reassuring grin gone and his expression very serious.

"Don't you fret anymore, Catriona *alanna*. The pony went down doing what he loved best. No blame to you." Mick's jaw tightened. Then, to her astonishment, he grinned. "You'll see. All'll come right."

"But my father's angry with me!"

"With you? Whyever would he be?"

Mick had been about to add something else when the curtain was pulled aside and Ward Sister stood in the gap, her eyes on Catriona's face.

"Well, there's a trifle more color in her face after all. You were the tonic she needed, Mr. Lenahan."

"Of course I was," Mick replied. "I've known the girl since she was foaled." Then, with a salute to Catriona, he walked off, a jaunty arrogant tilt to his sturdy shoulders.

When Catriona returned to Cornanagh two days later on the Wednesday, she willingly allowed her mother to shepherd her quickly into the house. For the first time in her life, she didn't make directly for the yard. She couldn't bear to see Blister's empty box, for random thoughts of the pony brought quick tears to her eyes. Passively she allowed her mother to guide her into the lounge and tuck her up on the small sofa in front of the fire. Clyde Cat joined her immediately, delighted with the opportunity. Her mother, Auntie Eithne, or Bridie checked constantly on her.

Such solicitude, reminding her of her grandfather's last days, made Catriona uneasy, so she welcomed Mary's visit that afternoon with great relief. Mary was most satisfactorily impressed by the stitches in her scalp and the solidity of the plaster cast on her arm. And she took great pleasure in signing her name with a flourish, though the pen sputtered on the rough surface. The girls decided the splotches were artistic embellishments.

"Honest, Trina, I thought you were a goner when that idjit crossed you and—and Blister," Mary stammered, looking up quickly to see her friend's reaction to the name.

"I don't remember what happened, Mary. . . ."

"Well"—Mary settled down with enthusiasm for the account—"do you remember the field?"

"I remember Jake being circled."

"Well, you had the right of way over the ditch because that stupid Mr. Camwell was only circling. But all of a sudden, he gives Jake an unmerciful crack with his stick and jabs him with his spurs. I mean, the horse could do nothing except take off, with your man swinging out of his mouth. I'll say this, Jake tried to correct himself, but there was no way he could have avoided colliding with you. Sort of sunfished. Jake did his best, he really did, but he must have caught you with his forelegs and then Blister with the hind ones. You went down with such a thud, everyone heard it. Blister just dropped."

Both girls looked away for a long moment, and Catriona felt the tears pricking her eyes again.

"You should have heard your father going at Mr. Camwell! You really should have. What he didn't say to that man. . . ." Mary's voice was rich with satisfaction. "And did you know it was Mrs. Healey rode you off the field, and you dripping blood all down her and the mare. Me, I wouldn't have thought the mare would've taken it all so calmly, but Mrs. Healey's such a fine rider."

"She sent me flowers," Catriona said, pointing to the little bouquet, still fresh in the florist's plastic dish.

"She's not half as distant as she seems, looking so elegant all the time."

Catriona had to agree. "I hope the bloodstains come out all right."

"Oh, sure she's got a maid to look after her clothes, and she'd know how to do that."

Bridie came in then with juice and biscuits, frowning until she was sure that a visitor was not too great a strain on the invalid.

"Janey Mack! You're getting the royal treatment, aren't you?" Mary giggled.

"It won't last long," Catriona replied cynically.

"Enjoy it while it does!"

"I suppose I should."

"Suppose?" Mary was aghast. "Catriona Mary Carradyne, you are the most contrary person I know. Ungrateful! Here you're out of class—"

"I've ruined my perfect attendance. . . ."

"Catriona Mary, if you don't stop talking nonsense, I'll leave!" Mary leaned forward, putting her cool hand on Catriona's cheek, peering at her critically. "Headache? Mother says you could have headaches for days after the knock you took."

"No, no headache," Catriona replied irritably. And was instantly sorry.

"That's more like it," Mary said with an exaggerated sigh of relief. "D'you know what Marty Byrne said when he heard?"

"No, what?" Catriona was surprised that she figured in their bus driver's conversation. "Tell me."

And Mary did, in such detail that both girls were startled when Mrs. Evans appeared in the doorway to collect her daughter. Almost on her heels Michael Carradyne arrived, still in his riding clothes. He spoke pleasantly to the Evanses, seeing them courteously to the outer door before he returned to the lounge. He came right up to Catriona, bending down to kiss her cheek and stroke her hair lightly before he sat down beside her.

"Blister was a good pony, Catriona," he said, regarding the tip of his boot earnestly. "We buried him in the ten-acre field."

"Buried him?" Catriona was astonished. Her father never buried horses: the carcasses went to the Hunt pack.

"He was a small pony, and we'd that big hole in the hayfield where Barry took out the boulder . . ." Michael Carradyne's voice trailed off. He cleared his throat and began again more briskly. "The doctor says the stitches will come out in a few days, but it's three weeks for the bones to knit. Then, if we strap your arm, you'll be able to ride."

"But Mummie said . . ." Then her father's expression altered so sternly, she caught her breath.

"I don't believe for one moment that your fall or Blister's death has put you off riding, but if it has, and I am forcing you to participate in an activity repugnant to you, now is the time to tell me."

Catriona knew that her mouth had dropped open in surprise at her father's crisp speech. Then she couldn't help grinning. He must have been quoting her mother's exact words.

"Mummie never understands about horses, does she?"

Her father reached out to tousle her hair, but gently because of the bandage.

"No, Trina, she doesn't, but I had to clear the air. You be in the yard about three tomorrow. All right?"

Actually Catriona couldn't wait that long to get back into the yard. The next morning, thoroughly bored by the confines of the lounge, she took the first opportunity to sneak out of the house. Of course, she had had to wait until her mother and Auntie Eithne had gone shopping in Bray and Bridie was busy upstairs. Then she filled her lungs with the crisp fresh spring air, redolent with the stable odors she most enjoyed. She could hear Artie calling across the main yard and Mick's rather caustic reply. She noticed that the double horsebox was gone from its bay in the garage. Her father had probably gone to collect a mare for the Tulip. She could hear him stamping in his stall, a rhythmic banging. Or maybe the Captain was after a horse to be schooled. This was the time of year Cornanagh did a lot of breaking and backing.

She paused long enough to wrench a handful of grass growing through the cobbles. The Tulip could get most obstreperous if he wasn't offered something by a family visitor. She remembered being taken up by her grandfather onto the Tulip: a signal honor, and one she knew had never been given her brothers or Sybil. But then she'd never been afraid of the Tulip. She believed that he felt obliged to display and cut shapes, as he did now when he heard her step on the cobbles.

Snort, snort, whuffle angrily, and he was a blacker shadow against the dim light of his big, padded box stall.

"It's me, Tulip. Catriona," she said in the authoritative tone she knew he respected. "Here—" She pushed the grass through the bars of the door. They were immediately swiped away by the flick of a large pink tongue. The Tulip whuffled softly and stamped in a demand for more. With her eyes adapted to the dim light inside the stable, she could see the gleam of his eyes, wide set on his broad forehead. His forelock reached halfway down his aristocratic nose. He stamped again, impatiently. "Now, Tulip, you've had a treat. You mustn't beg," she said cajolingly. She didn't want him making too much noise, or someone in the other yard would wonder what had upset him. If her father had gone for a mare, the Tulip should be kept calm.

She held her hand up flat against the bars and felt the Tulip blow against it, identifying her smell. He licked at her palm, and she giggled because it tickled. He stamped again, whickering with more volume.

"I'd better go, Tulip, but I wanted to check in with you."

He whuffled once more; she thought he sounded lonely, though there were five other horses in the coach house to keep him company.

The moment she appeared in the yard, Artie dropped the body brush and came charging over to her, his thin face contorted with a glad welcome. He grabbed her hand and kept shaking it.

"I sure have missed you. I sure have missed you."

"Only because he's had to exercise the Prince," Mick said.

"Oh, no." Catriona covered her mouth with her hand to keep from grinning. "Your legs must be touching his knees, even if you are light enough to ride him."

"That makes it all the easier for him to stop the pony," said Mick. "Just has to drop his heels to the ground."

"Oh, Artie, is the Prince being very bad?"

Artie straightened up at the suggestion. "Not a bit. That pony is smart enough to know who's his rider, you know. He don't mess with me any more than he does with you."

"Should you be out, Catie?" Mick asked.

"No one said I couldn't." Then Mick gave her a stern glance. "Well, I just wanted to see . . ." Her voice trailed off as her eyes fell on the open door of Blister's empty stable. "I just couldn't stay in the house one more minute. It's stuffy!"

"And your mother and Mrs. Eithne are gone to Bray as well? Isn't Bridie minding you?"

"She's upstairs!"

"Well, you get back into the warm. Concussion's nothing to fool with," Mick said gruffly.

"It was the warm was giving me the headache. Has Dad gone for a mare?"

Mick chuckled, laying a finger alongside his nose. "That's for me to know and you to guess."

"Guessing will bring on the headache." Catriona shot a look at Artie, who was grinning from ear to ear.

"A mare or a gelding, I didn't hear which. Now, go back into the house afore Bridie finds you missing and gives me the rough edge of her tongue."

Dutifully she went because she was all too conscious of Blister's empty stall and couldn't feel easy in the yard. She had fallen asleep when the clock struck three and the Austin hauled the double horsebox into the yard, followed by a second, stylish vehicle.

As Mrs. Healey emerged from her Lancia, Mick and Artie converged on the horsebox.

"I don't understand why she isn't out here," the captain told Mrs. Healey.

"She was, Captain, this morning," Mick said. "As soon as she could sneak out. I sent her back in so's she wouldn't catch cold."

"No, Michael, I'll go," Mrs. Healey said with a smile as the Captain began a purposeful advance. "Just through the door here?"

"She'll be in the lounge, Mrs. Healey," the Captain said. "Last door on the right facing the hall."

Mrs. Healey found Catriona fast asleep on the lounge, a lean marmalade cat curled up at her feet, a Pullein-Thompson book dangling from one lax hand, the schoolbooks stuffed any old way into their bag. Catriona's face was slightly flushed, and Mrs. Healey looked down at the delicate countenance, wondering why she had never noticed the quality there, the fine bone structure, the promise of an unusual beauty. The child had seemed so frail in her arms when she'd carried her across the field to the road.

It had been an unusual experience for Selina Healey to hold a child. She and David had not been blessed with children, which, considering how seldom David had time for connubial bliss, did not surprise her. Until that moment, she had been grateful for such indifference. But suddenly a wave of regret had rushed over her. And she had experienced a second dose of that rare sentiment when she had had to leave the child with the hospital emergency staff.

Stirred by these unusual emotions, Selina Healey had not let the matter drop. The dead pony had been elderly but game, as ponies so often were. As her last pony still was. And then she recalled that neither that pony nor she herself were all that aged.

Conker couldn't be more than eighteen. He'd been bought for her at just three years old on her thirteenth birthday, a beautiful bright sorrel chesnut, 14.1 hands high, exceedingly well bred. She'd had three very good years out of him before her father had graduated her to a proper ladies' hunter. There was no reason for Conker to continue eating his head off when he could be of use. Especially to a rider of Catriona's standard. And a girl of Catriona's courage. For Selina Healey had been impressed that Catriona's first thought, despite her own injuries, had been for her pony.

She had told the Captain in a tone that brooked absolutely no refusal that Catriona was to have the use of Conker until she went into horses. She named time and place and ended the conversation with the stammering captain by hanging up the phone. Selina was well pleased with herself right now, thinking how much pleasure it would give Catriona to have Conker to ride. Then a cynical laugh started in her throat. So often the surprises you planned for people backfired in the most awkward fashion, such as her last dinner party. Her husband had not been pleased. Ah, well.

Now Selina shook Catriona gently by the shoulder.

"Wake up, it's three o'clock, Catriona, your father wants you."

Catriona stirred. Then her drowsy mind registered an unfamiliar voice, and, startled, she shot to a sitting position, sending Clyde Cat flying in retreat.

"Mrs. Healey!" She tried to untangle her feet from the rug. "I bled all over you, and yet you sent me the flowers. . . ." Catriona was torn between trying to stand up for an adult guest of Mrs. Healey's consequence and making sure to mention all the various kindnesses.

Laughing gently at Catriona's confusion, Selina Healey helped her get free of the afghan.

"The stains did come out, didn't they? Mary said you'd have a maid who knows . . ."

"My dear child, that was the least of my concerns, I assure you." Gently, Selina urged Catriona out of the room toward the yard. She could hardly wait to see the effect of her gift on this lovely child. "Now, wait. Which is yours?" Her hand went to the various outerwear hung on pegs by the door. When Catriona pointed, she took it down, and then they couldn't get the cast into the sleeve, so Selina draped it over the left shoulder, all the time easing Catriona outside. She was hoping that the Captain had not yet unloaded the pony, for she wanted to savor the scene to its fullest.

As they reached the yard, she realized she need not have worried. The Captain was waiting for them to appear. The ramp went down with a thump, and Conker squealed. Catriona's eyes widened, and she cast one startled glance up at Mrs. Healey. There was a thud, a kick against the box that made it shake, a muffled curse from Artie, and then he led Conker out.

"It occurred to me, Catriona, that it was silly to let Conker eat his head off in retirement simply because I've outgrown ponies. Your father has agreed to let you use him, and I'm sure you'll be very good partners indeed."

Selina joined the captain and the two stable hands as they watched Catriona awkwardly strip the travel rug from Conker, who never took his eyes off her, turning his handsome head to check on her efforts. He submitted to her gentling hand, let her blow in his nostrils, and then lipped at a stray strand of her hair. He blew delicately into her hand at last, after sniffing the cast with a snort for the antiseptic smell. Then he stamped, snorted, and regarded the rest of his admirers.

"Conker always did like an audience," Selina murmured.

"Oh, Mrs. Healey . . . Mrs. Healey . . ." Catriona stared at her, wonder and utter delight shining from her face. "Mrs. Healey . . ."

Selina chuckled.

"Surely you can do better than that," Captain Carradyne said with a frown.

"How could I ever thank her properly for Conker?" Catriona demanded, turning to the pony, who lifted his head proudly. "How could I, Daddy? There just aren't words."

"Those will do quite well enough, I assure you, Catriona. Now, I think we'd better settle him in," Mrs. Healey said briskly. "You get back indoors. And you must promise me not to ride until that arm is healed. Conker will need to be lunged a bit. He hasn't worked a day in at least ten years."

"Oh, Mrs. Healey! And after me bleeding all over you, too!" Catriona burst into tears.

Selina wanted badly to gather the child into her arms and experienced the most incredible surge of jealousy when Michael Carradyne did so.

"Catriona!" he said.

"Don't scold, Captain. Her reaction is completely sincere and natural."

"Please come in, Mrs. Healey."

"No, I really must fly."

"You must stop for a cup of tea, at least," Catriona said, mastering her emotions and remembering her manners.

"I'll take you up on that, Catriona, when you're riding again and I can see what progress you and Conker are making as a team. All right?"

Smiling courteously to the three men and Catriona, Selina Healey returned to her car and drove smartly out of the yard, wishing with all her heart that she could have stayed.

8

*F*irst thing the next morning, even before Mick and Artie had arrived in the yard, Catriona watered, fed, and hayed Conker.

"I want him to settle in quickly," she said when they showed up.

Artie grinned, but Mick gave a snort. "That pony settled in the moment he was fed," he said. "Horrid little sod!"

"He is not! He's very well bred, Mick, and he has excellent stable manners. He doesn't barge into you for his feed the way the Prince and the hunters do. And Temper!"

"Get back inside, Cat, it's freezing. Can't have you catching your death! Then where will you be during the holidays?"

Mick had a point, and Catriona dashed back to the house, planning to come out later to quarter Conker. However, when Isabel descended for her breakfast, she informed Catriona that they were going shopping for Easter clothes and would stop in at Grandmother Marshall's for tea.

"But, Mummie, I've missed so much school," Catriona replied. She hated shopping with the same intensity Isabel adored it. And her grandmother was always critical of her youngest grandchild and the manners of the younger generation in general. "Easter holidays start next week. Couldn't we go then?"

"No, because the shops will be far too crowded. It's high time you took some interest in your appearance. You'll be thirteen in a matter of weeks." Isabel glanced slyly at her husband, who was reviewing the post. He was ignoring the conversation, and she didn't see the wink he gave his daughter. "I really should have enrolled you for Irish dancing lessons when I wanted to," she continued. "You'd've done extremely well. You're very agile. And it's not too late for you to start."

"Oh, Mummie, have you ever looked at the dancers' legs? They have calves like . . . like rugby players."

"But the costumes are so feminine. Eithne could make you a stunning one. You know how good she is with the needle."

Catriona winced, and Philip didn't help by smothering a guffaw that earned him his mother's darkest look. It was yet another betrayal from her adored son. For when she had tried to wean him to her cause, he had been outright incredulous and then scornful. "Trina's the best rider of the lot of us, Mother. You're wide of the mark if you think you can change her. Give over! You'll never make it."

But his attitude only reinforced her determination. It was important that Catriona spend more time with her mother and learn the feminine side of life—with all its trials and tribulations. Isabel sniffed.

The trip into town was not a success for either mother or daughter. Catriona had no preferences about clothing that was not for riding. Discussions over this style and that color irritated her. If the dress or shirt or coat fit and served its purpose, she'd wear it. Generally one good dress sufficed her, being used for Mass, birthday parties, or the occasional family dinner.

This time, Isabel bought not only the new Easter outfit for her daughter, but several other dresses, moaning over the awkward cast. Catriona was so annoyed by all the changing into and out of and back again that when it came time to try on shoes, she did not pay proper attention to the salesman and failed to get the right fitting.

As expected, afternoon tea with Grandmother Marshall was a second trial.

"Girls who devote too much time to horses and ponies begin to resemble them," Grandmother Marshall pronounced, and bent a severe eye on Catriona, who choked on crumbs of the soda bread and butter she was trying to eat. "Catriona should join the Girl Guides. They do so much good work in the community. You really would enjoy the company of other girls, Catriona."

"I do, Grandmother."

"Oh?"

"Mary Evans is my best friend. . . ."

Isabel made a moue. "The father's an estate agent in Delgany. Does rather well, in fact."

"Not what I had in mind for you, Catriona. You must make eligible connections among the girls in your school."

"Mary goes to the Dominican."

"Don't be cheeky with me, young lady. I'm certain that the Delahayes live in Wicklow. They have a daughter Catriona's age, don't they, Isabel?"

"No, Mother, Sinead Delahaye has six boys."

"Well, it can't hurt to cultivate Selina Healey, Isabel. Do be sensible. It can't last long, this infatuation of Catriona's. She's nearly twelve, isn't she?"

"She'll be thirteen in April, Mother."

"I wouldn't have guessed to look at her. Well, let's see if there's any improvement when she's properly dressed. You may change in my dressing room, Catriona."

Catriona had been hoping that her mother and grandmother would get involved with who married whom and where they now resided. Then she could have made surreptitious inroads on the nice cream buns Grandmother always served with tea. But she knew better than to protest, even if she was sweaty and awkward with the cast on her arm. Then her grandmother complained that her underwear was totally unacceptable, and she doubted if the child would ever develop any sort of a figure. Both women decided that riding was the cause of her backwardness.

By the time the shopping expedition returned to Cornanagh, evening stables were over and the yard darkened for the night. Catriona felt cheated.

Over the next few days, her mother continually had activities planned that took Catriona away from Cornanagh and Conker. She had to parade about in the new clothes and get her feet rubbed raw in the ill-fitting shoes. Her mother took her along to morning coffees with her Irish Countrywomen's Association friends and afternoon teas with elderly relatives who didn't remember Catriona any better than she did them.

The only afternoon outing that Catriona half enjoyed was seeing Mrs. Healey on Tuesday at her superb Georgian home in Dalkey. For this occasion, Catriona's best manners were easily assumed, and she soon realized that her mother's conversational tidbits bored Mrs. Healey, who seemed to smile at Catriona almost conspiratorially.

"And how is Conker settling in for you?" Selina Healey asked at last, turning her attention firmly in Catriona's direction.

"Father's working him on the lunge, and he's turned out for a few hours every day."

Selina Healey nodded, smiling. "He's always been good at exercising himself. Don't worry if he takes off and laps the field. I've seen him racing round and round like that, for the pure joy of it."

Catriona laughed out loud. "Oh, that's just what he's doing. I've seen him myself. And then he clears the gorse bushes and jumps down the bank and wheels and jumps up it."

"He's got a super pop, Catriona. As you'll discover as soon as your arm is out of plaster. A very scopy pony. I wonder, is there still time to enter him in the Spring Show?"

"Oh, yes!" Catriona was pleased. "That is, if it's all right with you, and my father agrees. Entries for jumping competitions don't close until April twenty-seventh. I know because my father has to enter Sean Doherty on the Ballymore Prince."

"Would you be competing in the same class?"

"No, Sean's older'n me, and the Prince is in the fourteen-twos."

Isabel entered the conversation with effusive thanks for the use of such a valuable pony, then rose and said they had to be returning home. The Dohertys were good clients of her husband's but were certainly not in the same social sphere as the Healeys, she thought. Not for want of Aisling Doherty's trying. Selina, smiling kindly, caught Catriona's eye as she walked them to the door.

"Now, if you'd only act as natural and polite with everyone else," Isabel began as they drove home, "you'd be an asset."

"Mrs. Healey understands horses," Catriona said, knowing that was exactly the wrong justification to present her mother.

"Yes, but Mrs. Healey knows far more than just horses, Catriona, and it shows in that magnificent house, which I hear she decorated herself. She is socially active, goes everywhere, her husband is an important man—an associate of Mr. Haughey who will be *Taoiseach* soon enough. And Selina Healey knows how to dress well. I'm sure that dress of hers is an Ib Jorgensen. There's far more to Selina Healey than horses, my girl, and don't you forget it."

Not for the first time did Isabel Carradyne resent the fact that they had to live in Wicklow County. Now, if only they lived in Dublin, near her parents, there would be evenings when fascinating people would gather in her mother's lounge, people with keen interests in the world about them, in the theater, letters, politics. Nevertheless, it was time Catriona learned how to behave in society. And Isabel would say a special novena to the Virgin Mary to intercede for her and dissolve Catriona's resistance.

As soon as they reached the house, Catriona dutifully went

to change out of her good clothes but accomplished this with such speed that Isabel didn't have time to stop the child as she tore out to the yard and that wretched pony. Yes, wretched, even if it had been offered by someone as socially prominent as Selina Healey. Isabel gave a delicate sniff.

Michael Carradyne had no reservations about the unexpected gift. Ponies were generally selfish little beasts, but Conker already recognized Catriona's step and would be at the door whickering eagerly for her company. Michael was rather keen to see them working. If they could get the pony and Catriona fit, there was still time to put the pair in the Spring Show.

Already she fed him, groomed him to a shine generally only Mick could achieve, took him to and from the field. Michael had watched from a distance as the pony displayed his paces and ability by jumping every gorse bush and obstacle in the big field, almost as if he were promising Catriona what they would soon be doing together. Then he returned to lay his muzzle on her shoulder, blowing softly into her hair while she giggled from the tickling.

Conker also followed her about the yard without so much as a baling string about his neck. Michael had reprimanded her for that sort of carelessness.

"Head collar and lead rope, Catriona Carradyne. We'll have no sloppy manners in this yard."

Michael had decided to mend relations with Jack Garden. He recognized now that he had said things in anger to Garden that would have been better unsaid. But there it was! He'd lost his temper, probably any chance at the gelding, and possibly a good friend. Well, not "good," precisely, for Jack Garden was more a drinking companion than a friend.

Fortunately, Jack was well into the evening's drinking when

Michael reached the Willow Grove pub, and as Jack was a happy drinker, he was affability itself, accepting Michael's apologies.

"Sure the man was all wind and piss as far as horses. Hadn't a bog's notion about riding and didn't have the sense to know it. These Yanks. Full of shit most of the time. And you did me a favor." Jack gave Michael a sly glance. "I'd've had to tick him off if you hadn't. And that might have queered the deal we were doing. So I gave you the blame and took the credit!"

"Did you now?" Michael quelled the surge of anger that Jack had turned the incident to his own advantage. But then, Garden was known to be quick.

"How's the little girl doing?"

"Grand. She'll be riding again in a couple of weeks' time. Young bones heal quickly."

"I hear the Healey came up handsomely with a pony for her."

Michael nodded. "Very kind of Mrs. Healey. Totally unexpected."

"It's a good pony?"

"Very, and with Catriona on its back, likely to improve."

"Well, then, we're friends so?" And Jack held out his hand. Michael took it, thinking that perhaps he hadn't lost out in the matter of the gelding.

Then Bob Kelly barged in, wanting to know what people were about, spending so much money on a stupidity like this Eurovision song contest, and involved half the lounge in a discussion that became so heated, Tom had to act the referee several times. It was near closing time before Michael had a chance to inquire, casually, if Jack had thought about selling the Chou Chin Chow gelding in the spring.

"He's small," Jack said ruefully.

"Some three-year-olds grow right up to five."

Jack shrugged.

"I do have a buyer interested in that sort of breeding." That was sufficiently noncommittal. From time to time, Michael bought horses for clients. "What sort of money are you asking?"

"What sort of money has your client got?" Jack Garden had a horse trader's gleam in his eye.

Michael shrugged. "I was only asked to look out for Chou Chin Chows. Shall I bring them round?" In his mind he was turning over those of his acquaintances who might be asked to fall in with his scheme.

Michael left the Willow Grove feeling relieved by his conversation with Jack. He might even luck out if he were careful. The flaw in the evening's pleasure was Fiona's absence, but she had told him that she intended to watch the Eurovision contest. He hoped that the whole thing would be over by the time he got back to the house.

It wasn't, for the blue television light was visible through a break in the drapes. Also visible was the pale votive light in the master bedroom upstairs. He parked the Austin and went in by the front door, upstairs to the back bedroom, which he preferred to use when Isabel was at her interminable prayers. Easter Sunday should see the end of that.

Allowed to stay up for the song contest with her aunt, Catriona was actually paying little attention to it. She was sketching. With her mother upstairs, and her aunt engrossed in the songs, she could indulge herself. Her sister Sybil had always thought Catriona's scribbling was rather good and could be counted on to supply colored and drawing pencils for special occasions. Sybil had felt a broken arm qualified.

"Good job it was your left arm you broke," she said, teasing. "Don't let Mother see these. She's got the wind up again about you."

Now Catriona filled her margins with sketches of Conker in every attitude: looking out over his door in the yard, pawing the ground at the gate in the big field, curving his back in a beautiful bascule over the big gorse bush, scratching his nose on his knee, which showed off the curve of his neck as well as his broad forehead. Daily lunging was beginning to put a top line back on him and tighten up the grass belly.

Three weeks, especially when they included the spring holidays, were a very long time to wait to ride her new pony. It was depressing, Catriona thought, to realize that the cast wouldn't come off until Saturday, April 4th, and she'd have to be back in school on the following Monday. She'd only have one weekend to enjoy riding Conker. So, she decided to make the most of that.

Catriona also decided to be dutiful. She would ask to be allowed to join her mother for the Stations of the Cross because she knew how much the Easter observations meant to her. And Catriona could always pray for her arm to be completely restored. Easter was a time of revival, too.

Fortunately, the X-rays proved that the bone had knitted well, and as soon as they got back from the doctor's, Catriona fled down the ride to the big field, unable to wait any longer.

Conker came to a stiff-legged halt at the gate, and Catriona flung it wide. With dainty steps he came right up to her, snuffling into her outstretched hand. She grabbed a lock of his mane and vaulted onto his back. She felt his muscles stiffen and set herself for a buck. Then he nodded twice and awaited her aids. She squeezed her legs, and he moved forward, neck arched, poll high, dropping his head to obey a nonexistent bit. She squeezed a little harder, urging him forward with her seat on his warm bare back. He glided into a collected trot, a gait so smooth she hardly felt the movement.

"Oh, Conker, you're a dream! Oh, Conker, I'm riding you at last."

She slid off his back and opened the gate into the main yard.

"Catriona Carradyne, how often must I tell you to use head collar and lead with that valuable pony!"

Her father was standing right at the entrance, scowling at her. Could he have seen her dismounting? She tried to remember the angle of vision he'd have had.

"I'm sorry, Daddy. I just had to show Conker that the cast is off!" A very weak reply, she knew, and she grabbed at Conker's forelock. "But he never resists me. See?"

"Head collar and lead, Catriona Mary Virginia Carradyne."

What she didn't see was her father's tender look as she passed him by. He had witnessed everything and indeed would have been disappointed if she hadn't done exactly as she had.

9

Selina Healey drove her red Lancia coupé into the yard on Wednesday afternoon just as Michael Carradyne and Catriona were heading for the menage.

"Wednesday *is* half day," Mrs. Healey said as they walked to the car. "I remembered. And Catriona is going to school Conker."

"I've got my arm properly bandaged, too," Catriona said, displaying it so that Selina Healey could see the thickness of her left anorak sleeve.

"Good girl. May I watch the lesson? Or would it put you off?"

"Put me off?"

"Not much interferes with Catriona's concentration on a horse, Mrs. Healey," Michael said in the same instant. And all three laughed.

Selina Healey was oddly pleased by their deference and flattered by a sudden alertness in Michael Carradyne's expression. She had not quite appreciated what a handsome man the Captain was! So tall and dark. And his brilliant blue eyes were made even more compelling by a marked twinkle. Yes, the Captain was a very manly sort of man.

She pulled the Lancia up by the garage, behind the horsebox, but just as she was arranging a scarf about her hair, she heard someone screaming:

"Michael! Michael! I prayed for guidance, and the Virgin Mary has given it to me."

Startled, Selina caught the entire tableau in the rearview mirror. She could see neither Michael's nor Catriona's faces as Isabel ran up to them. But their bodies turned rigid.

Plainly Isabel was unaware of Selina's presence in the yard. She looked dreadful, her face very pale, her eyes deeply shadowed, waving the cross of her rosary as if it were . . . a wand, which errant simile sprang inappropriately to Selina's mind.

"Catriona is not to ride anymore. It is against God's wishes!" Isabel cried. "The Virgin Mary told me!"

During that one afternoon call, Selina had been somewhat annoyed by Isabel's arch manners, but there'd been no indication then that she was unbalanced. Now Selina took a deep breath and opened the car door.

"Isabel, I couldn't wait to come and see Catriona on old Conker," she said, smiling graciously as she picked her way across the cobbles. "I was telling my husband only this morning that I thought this could be a winning partnership. He'll be waiting to hear about today's lesson."

She included Michael and Catriona in her smile, ignoring their dismay. She must pretend that she had not overheard Isabel's raving. All the sparkle had gone out of Michael's eyes, and lines dragged his mouth down, increasing her resolve to assist. Catriona's face mirrored her distress and embarrassment.

For one long moment, her face turning blotchy, Isabel glared at Selina Healey intensely. Then, wheeling abruptly, she scrambled back to the house, slamming the door behind her. Catriona flinched and looked anxiously from her father to her patron.

"Yes, David actually is interested in seeing you make something of old Conker, Catriona." Selina pulled her leather coat about her, suppressing a shiver, and regarded them with polite inquiry. Inwardly she was exceedingly pleased to have routed Isabel. Whatever was the woman on about? "I think my husband," she said, "wants to brag about Conker and you to his friends!"

"Catriona," Michael said in a noncommittal tone, and his daughter signaled the obedient Conker to walk on.

The menage, the outdoor training ring, had once been a second old walled garden, with huge sycamores whose arching branches made it nearly rainproof. It was an irregular rectangle in shape, and constant work on the lunge rein had worn a thirty-meter circular track inside the rectangle. On the wider of the unmatched ends, jump standards, poles, and cavallettis were neatly stacked. It was here that Selina went to stand, in the one sunlit area of the cloistered menage. Catriona began to work the pony in: walking and trotting on both reins, making him turn around her inside leg in first twenty-, then ten-meter circles to make him supple to the commands of her leg and hand. There was no sound but the pony's rhythmic hoof beats on the ground, for the high walls kept out the sounds of infrequent cars on the road beyond.

Selina watched, oddly soothed by the intense concentration of girl, man, and pony. Conker was working very well, his ears twitching as he listened to his rider. Catriona, elbow, arm, and hand in the prescribed line to his mouth, wore a look of almost painful concentration, on occasion biting her lip as she lightly restrained the pony's eagerness, keeping him to the crisp, collected trot.

Catriona was just the right size now for the pony. A pity if she suddenly grew over the summer, Selina thought, but there'd be the Spring Show, certainly: she'd insist on that.

"Serpentines," Michael called, leaving the center of the menage as Catriona began to execute the exercise. "And bend him around your leg, Trina." He took a position beside Selina, arms folded across his chest, never taking his eyes from the working pair executing continuous S shapes from one side of the menage to the other.

Selina glanced up at him. The muscles of his face had relaxed again. Indeed, the little scene in the yard might never have happened, now that he was again in his element. He really was an elegant man, with fine strong features: those amazing blue eyes with unexpectedly long black lashes framing them. There were just a few flecks of white in his sideburns, and although his hair needed to be trimmed, he managed not to look unkempt, only more masculine. The mustache suited him. He was fit and lean, and there were none of the signs of dissipation with which she was far too familiar. But then, Captain Carradyne always had horses to tend and was unlikely to forget that obligation. Or any other. He made as if to speak, then relaxed with a little smile as Catriona anticipated the correction.

"That pony's quick," he said in an aside to Selina Healey.

"He used to drop me in a flash," Selina said ruefully.

"That's right, Trina," he went on, "keep the pace. Look where you're going."

"Well, she'd have a soft landing here," Selina commented, "if Conker drops his shoulder on her."

"He won't get Catriona off, Mrs. Healey." Michael turned to her. "She'll be ready for him, weak arm or not."

"She is a very capable little rider."

Watching Catriona put Conker through the suppling exercise was for Selina Healey like stepping backward in time to her own girlhood. Except for the fact that Catriona Carradyne was twice the rider she had been and had the dedication she had lacked.

When Selina had been studying at Burton Hall, Colonel Dudgeon had told her father that all she lacked to become an outstanding rider was the necessary dedication, and she'd be a match for Iris Kellett or Marian McDowell.

Her father, in a fit of pique at her indolent, party-oriented life, had taxed Selina with that comment. She had answered that learning to ride properly was socially acceptable for a woman, but competition was not. Of late, Selina had regretted not only that remark, but also the orientation that had made a good marriage and social prominence more important than any other achievement in her life.

This afternoon, just when Selina realized how much time had passed while she watched the warm-up, Michael left her side to set up a small jump grid, using six of the cavalletti poles properly spaced for the pony to bounce over. Catriona promptly transferred Conker to the other end of the menage and continued her ten-meter circling.

"This might produce some interesting results," he told Selina quietly as he came back to stand beside her. His rather charming smile reappeared. "I don't want to overdo Catriona on her first day back in the saddle, but they've earned a bit of fun in the lesson. The pony's been far too well behaved."

"Indeed he has! I've been thinking that old age had mellowed him beyond recognition."

Michael's grin broadened. "You're here. He's got his best foot forward. All right, Catriona, and don't let him—"

Catriona had turned Conker, the pony had seen the grid and had charged it with such speed Michael had not been able to finish his advice. The pony flew the grid, and Selina couldn't help but laugh at the startled expression on Catriona's face. She cut it off as the two came around again and she saw the flush of angry embarrassment on the girl's face. Her resemblance to her father had never been more apparent, determined jaw and sparkling eye.

"Circle him, Trina, and keep circling him until he's listening. Try the grid again in your own time."

Docile enough doing flat work, Selina knew that Conker turned into a different animal when he faced jumps, even ones barely a foot off the ground. She disciplined her expression, but there was now a definite element of excitement in the performance of pony, rider, and trainer. Patience and firm determination finally won out, and Catriona was able to turn Conker into the grid without having him charge for it.

"Once more, Trina, nice and easy," Michael directed as the pony, cantering collectedly, once more faced the grid and popped calmly through it. Michael intercepted the pair as Catriona halted Conker. Both trainer and rider slapped the pony's neck approvingly. "How's the arm, Trina?"

"My arm?" Catriona regarded her father blankly for a moment and then laughed. "I forgot."

"Well?"

"It aches, but just a little!"

"Well, don't take any chances," Selina said, stroking Conker's sweaty neck as she looked up at the flushed and delighted girl. "Conker can take a bit of a hold when he wants to. Take it easy for a few more weeks. Promise?"

"Yes, ma'am," Catriona said, grinning from ear to ear. "We just have to get a bit more used to each other, but oh, Mrs. Healey, he's such a splendid pony!"

"And you're rather a splendid little rider." Selina gave Conker a final pat and then turned away.

"All right, now, Catriona, take him in and let Artie give him a rubdown. Mrs. Healey's right. We must remember you're not completely sound."

"Sound? Your daughter's not a horse, Michael."

Michael looked down at her. "The term works as well for a human. Can we ever thank you enough for the loan of Conker?"

"Yes, if you and Catriona can contrive a few wins for me. Conker and I used to do all right, but I'll never be the rider your daughter already is. Or shouldn't I mention that?"

Carradyne frowned slightly, looking after girl and pony as they disappeared under the arch between the yard and the menage. Then he gave an amused little snort. "You are right to remind me. I sometimes forget that the rider is not merely a necessary encumbrance for a horse."

"What a boor you are, Michael Carradyne!"

"No"—the twinkle in his eye suddenly dimmed—"but all too dedicated to horses." His head turned just fractionally toward the house, and his wife.

"I prefer that sort of dedication to many others I could name," she drawled. "It has the merit of being unselfish and harmless."

"Harmless?"

"Oh, yes indeed."

They had begun to make their way from the menage, Selina drawing her coat more securely about her, for dusk was settling in, and the wind was chilly.

"Will Catriona be doing any roadwork with Conker?"

"Yes indeed. They'll both need to do a lot of it to get them fit. Is Conker traffic proof?"

"Cars, yes; even yappy little dogs. But he's not all that fond of tractors or air brakes going off behind him. If it isn't inconvenient, I'd like to hack out now and then with Catriona."

Michael seemed surprised. "By all means, whenever you will. I had thought to rough your mare off and turn her out for the summer. . . ."

"No, no, please keep her in a while longer. I'd like an excuse to ride more often. And Catriona and Conker have just provided it." He had escorted her now to the Lancia, and she extended her hand to him. "Saturday? Eleven? If that's convenient." And when he agreed, still slightly bemused, she added: "Thank you very much for a most enjoyable afternoon."

No sooner had the red Lancia swung out of the yard than Eithne came running out to intercept him, an afghan over her shoulders against the evening chill.

"Michael, whatever did you say to Isabel?"

Michael frowned at his sister-in-law, then grimaced, recalling Isabel's little scene with a surge of impotent anger. "I said nothing to her. Mrs. Healey was here, for which she should be thankful. . . ."

"Thankful? She's still in hysterics!"

"Hysterics?" Disgusted, Michael tried to move past Eithne.

"Michael, don't run out on me," Eithne said with unusual firmness. "Isabel is in a terrible state. . . ."

"Fortunately, I don't think Mrs. Healey heard Isabel's ranting, if that's what's bothering her. Isabel went too far this afternoon, Eithne, and you had better know it, too. I will not conduct my affairs according to prayerful messages!"

His sister-in-law regarded him in total perplexity. "What on earth do you mean, Michael?"

"Eithne, Isabel is not going to stifle Catriona's opportunities. Just look at the change in her this afternoon." Michael pointed to his daughter, skipping out of the yard, her cheeks red with exercise, her face alight. "Does she look unsettled? Unhappy? Abused? Have I ever forced any of the boys to ride against their will? Do I not take every precaution against accidents?"

Eithne hesitated. She and Michael were talking at cross purposes. Not that she had been able to understand clearly what had happened that afternoon to put Isabel into such a state.

"You don't understand, Michael—"

"On the contrary, I believe I do. Isabel has decided that her darling baby daughter is meant for bigger things in life than horses! Well, she has never been more wrong. Catriona has no religious vocation whatever. Surely you must agree with me in that?"

When Eithne's expression informed him that she did indeed agree, he went on heatedly: "I'm fed up with Isabel's religious fervor, Eithne. It's excessive to the point of being unhealthy—for Isabel as well as everyone else in the family. And you can convey that message to my wife." He controlled his expression as his daughter approached and signaled her to go ahead to

105

the house. "I trust she's immured in her room at her prie-dieu?"

"Actually, she is, but Michael, you just won't understand. It isn't just Catriona." Eithne moved to block Michael's way again. "Isabel is not well. She's not yet recovered from the shock of Catriona's accident."

"It was *Catriona* who was hurt. All Isabel had to do was visit the child in hospital. Surely that was not too strenuous a maternal duty for her?" He pushed past his sister-in-law. "Now excuse me. I have duties to perform."

"Michael, you just won't understand!" Eithne cried after him.

He gritted his teeth and walked on. He had yet to deal with evening stables.

If he was frustrated, so was Eithne. Well, she thought, if she couldn't get Michael to face the problem, she really would have to have a word with Dr. Standish. She didn't believe for one moment that he knew how often Isabel had been renewing that prescription. The woman took far too many pills. She looked poorly, too. And she had always been so careful with her appearance. It shocked Eithne to see Isabel looking so unkempt, no longer having her hair done as the weekly ritual. Her skin was dry, sallow, and suddenly she was looking her age, without a snitch of grace in the alteration.

More and more of the household management was devolving onto Eithne's shoulders, too. She was more than happy to take charge, although she and Bridie didn't get on all that famously together. But it was odd for Isabel to give up control.

Eithne sighed deeply as she reentered the house and slowly unwound the afghan from her shoulders. She glanced up the stairs to Isabel's room, sighed again, and opened the kitchen door. Bridie, soup ladle raised, was holding forth.

"Now your mum's not feeling well again, so don't you be wasting my time with Conker this and Conker that and Mrs. Healey's doings. You get in there and lay that table proper, like a girl should be doing." Bridie glared over Catriona's shoulder at Eithne, who was trying to signal her.

"What's wrong with Mummie?" Catriona asked anxiously.

"Nothing serious, dear," Eithne said at the same time Bridie answered in a dire tone:

"It's that time of life for a woman."

Catriona regarded her aunt in some perplexity. "She didn't sound like herself this afternoon. She said—"

"Just be a good girl and lay the table, Catriona." Eithne took the girl by the shoulders and gave her a little shove, shooting a quelling glance at the cook. "Now, Bridie, let's not saddle young shoulders with old problems."

Bridie snorted in disgust. "I'm only speaking the truth. And did you speak it to the Captain?"

Eithne sighed. "I did. I really did, but he's just like any other man. He simply will not listen to the truth."

"Whyever should he? He's got what he wants: a well-managed home, good food, his pleasures when he wants 'em. What he won't understand is why they won't continue as he expects." Bridie emphasized every point by banging another pot lid. Eithne held her breath, hoping the meal would not suffer from Bridie's agitation. "The Captain is too busy with his effing horses to know that the missus is real sick."

"Bridie!"

"And it's the only lot a woman can expect in life, so it is. And the sooner young Catriona knows it, the better it'll be for her. And that's m'final word!" She clamped her lips shut over her teeth and glared accusingly at Eithne.

"I'd better see that Catriona's laying the table properly," Eithne said in an apologetic tone, and retreated. She did in fact open the door into the dining room and heard Catriona humming to herself as she placed the cutlery. The child's face was still glowing with happiness. Eithne sighed again. It was so unfair to foist adult worries on young shoulders. And didn't she know from firsthand experience as a child in her miserly father's dreary house? She could at least try to make her niece's youth as carefree as possible. Why did Isabel have to be so awkward about the pony? Catriona had always been such a nice child, no problem really to anyone.

❧ 10 ☙

*I*sabel Carradyne stayed in her room for several days. Then, on Saturday afternoon, she emerged and required Catriona to come with her to confession. On the short walk to St. Michael's Catriona saw that her mother was terribly short of breath. Beads of perspiration stood out on her brow and upper lip.

"Mummie, are you all right?" she asked.

"There is nothing wrong with me that a dutiful daughter cannot cure."

Catriona lapsed into guilty silence, but by the time they reached the church, Isabel was having difficulty walking. When Catriona put out a hand to support her, her mother slapped it away.

"You must pray for forgiveness, Catriona. Now! For your hope of salvation. Pray to the Virgin Mary to melt your obstinacy and unfeminine desires!"

With relief Catriona noted that the church and confessional were empty, for her mother's voice was overloud.

"Pray!" Her mother pushed her into the nearest pew and to her knees. Then Isabel had to clutch at the next stall for balance before entering the confessional.

Catriona made the sign of the cross and launched fervent prayers for her mother's health. Then:

"Holy Virgin, you might not know much about horses; you only got to ride a donkey now and then. But you must know by now just how much I love horses, and ponies, and how much horses mean to my family. Surely it's not wrong for me to love them if my father does. And good people like Mick and Artie. And Mrs. Healey. How can there be any harm in horses? I want to be a good daughter, but not if I have to give up horses. Please make Mother see that."

Catriona usually waited much farther back, out of respect for the sanctity of confession. But from where Isabel had made her kneel, she could hear her mother droning on, answered with short bass bursts from Father John. How could her mother have so much to confess when she hadn't even been out of the house all week?

Suddenly her mother emerged and went directly to the altar, where she knelt abjectly. Catriona rose stiffly and entered the confessional.

When she left it, she was confused and upset. Father John had never required more than five Hail Marys and five Our Fathers when she'd had far more venial sins to confess. Her mother had already left, and Catriona dutifully began her penance. She'd have more prayers to say this evening and every morning.

She got back to the yard just in time to help with evening stables. When her father asked her what had taken her so long, she hesitated briefly. Well, she thought, one more little lie would not make much difference, so she said that she'd had to wait for confession. As soon as she could, she hunted out Auntie Eithne.

"Did Mummie get home all right this afternoon?"

"Yes, of course, she did, child. Why?"

"She looked just awful walking to church. . . ."

"She needs to get out more, that's all, Catriona. To get out and about and stop that fasting. It's made her light-headed. But don't worry. It'll all sort itself out soon."

Catriona let herself be reassured. Her mother's wild words on Wednesday were not easy to forget, but, good Catholic child though she was, she could not believe that the Virgin Mary would have spoken to her mother about something as trivial as her riding horses. Catriona Mary Virginia Carradyne in County Wicklow was too unimportant to bother with when there were people in the north who really needed God's help and the Virgin's intercession.

Until the show season started, Sundays were quiet days for the stables. Once they'd been skipped out, the horses watered, hayed, and fed, there wasn't much to be done. Today her father told Catriona that she was to come with him to look at horses that afternoon. Mrs. Healey was coming, too.

"First, though," said her father, "let's see if we can give Frolic's foal another leading lesson. He gave Artie a real chase yesterday."

Tulip's Son—as Michael had decided to name the little foal—showed astonishing strength as he first dragged Catriona after his dam, then propped both overlong front legs in total refusal to move at all. But this wasn't the first foal Catriona had put manners on, and gentle persuasion, as well as the nuts she had hidden in her hand, encouraged him to follow his dam quietly enough.

When Mrs. Healey arrived, Catriona had to excuse herself and wash her sweaty hands and face. As she came back into the yard, her father and Mrs. Healey emerged from the coach house. The Tulip had been duly visited.

She wished that her father'd thought to warn her that it was Jack Garden's horse they were going to see. The initial encounter was a bit awkward for Catriona since she couldn't help but associate Garden with Blister's death. However, all the drills in proper social behavior proved useful, Catriona realized for the first time. She had only to make the proper responses to get through the difficulty.

Catriona admired Mrs. Healey very much that afternoon. She

knew so much about horses. She could appreciate conformation and made some acute comments that drew respectful
glances from her father as well as Mr. Garden. How marvelous
it would be, Catriona thought, if she could grow up to be like
Mrs. Healey, poised, clever, and so pretty.

The conversation between her father and Mrs. Healey on
the way home puzzled Catriona, who was sitting in the
backseat.

"You're after the Chou Chin Chow gelding?" Mrs. Healey
asked.

"Was it that obvious?"

"You didn't give yourself away, if that's what you mean, but
then I was paying more attention to you than Jack was." Mrs.
Healey gave a low chuckle, and her father joined in. "For the
transition?"

"I had that in mind, but the timing's off."

"But not your horseman's eye for a potentially useful
animal?"

"That's it."

"If you cared for my opinion, I'd say buy. You've three years
in which to school him properly, and that young lad of yours
can show him."

"Philip's too big already."

"I didn't mean your son. I meant the lad in the yard. Artie?"

"Artie? He's all right exercising the hunters, Selina, but he's
got no give in his hands. He'd wreck a sensitive mouth."

"Then I'll ride him for you. If you'd permit . . ."

"Permit?" Michael was astounded.

"Actually, I did a lot of showing for my father before my
marriage. I was quite good. I even have an assistant instruc-
torship, though I think that the British Horse Society must have
lowered their standards that year. Still, it was what my set was
doing in their spare time."

"You trained at Burton Hall, didn't you? You ride like a Mr. Mac graduate."

"Is it still that obvious?"

"His training leaves an indelible mark."

"He was a dear! We all adored him."

Michael Carradyne chuckled at that. "And you learned to sit!"

"Indeed I did. As well as a few horse coper's ploys."

"My dear woman . . ."

"I'm not your dear anything, but I know a horse trader when I see one." She laughed. "Oh, I don't blame you. That gelding has a lot of presence and such natural balance! Have you seen him over poles yet?"

Michael Carradyne grinned. "No, but I saw him flying the ditches."

"Buy him. Break him, and I'll show him for you. A deal?" She pushed a gloved hand at Michael Carradyne.

"You may regret it. I'm a hard ridemaster, aren't I, Catriona?" And Catriona nodded vigorously, grinning from ear to ear.

"It's always the things we don't do that we regret," Selina Healey said in a low voice, almost to herself. "What are you planning to give for him?"

"I'll try three hundred." When Mrs. Healey made a funny noise in her throat, he added, "but I'll go to five if I have to. Though I shouldn't. I intend to lean on Garden's conscience."

"Are you sure he has one? All's fair in war and horse trading."

"Exactly!"

Tuesday afternoon her mother was waiting for Catriona and insisted that she say a rosary with her. Catriona tried to concentrate on the prayers, but her mother paused after each bead and stared so fixedly at her that she was unnerved. Especially as the one rosary was taking so much time and her father would be down in the yard waiting for her.

Wednesday, when Catriona again arrived late in the yard, her father demanded an explanation.

"Mother wanted me to say the rosary with her," Catriona began, stumbling over the words.

"Rosary indeed! There's a time and place for prayer! Give the Prince a lap or two until I join you." Face set, her father strode toward the house, slapping his stick against his boot leg.

When her father, riding Teasle, met her on the Ride, his face was expressionless.

"From now on, Catriona, you will come directly to the yard after school. Any prayers your mother wishes to say with you can wait until after dinner. Is that understood?"

"Oh, yes, Daddy."

He gave her a sideways look, his taut expression relaxing. "Well, prayer is all very well, but the time must be appropriate. Let's take that brat of a pony down the jumps. Keep your stick ready and don't lose the contact. Sean is always dropping the pony before a jump. Small wonder he runs out."

The Prince did not run out on Catriona: she made very sure of that. Her father was well pleased, she knew, though he said nothing. It was his way when satisfied. One heard quickly enough when he wasn't.

At night, once her father left the house on more business concerning the Horse Board Bill, her mother came to Catriona's room and began a session of ardent prayer, although the girl had not yet finished her school preparation. The prayers had to be ardent, for the room was cool, the floor hard, and Catriona had difficulty staying awake. The session ended only when the sound of the captain's returning car could be heard.

When Catriona's sleepiness made her late for the school bus on Thursday and again on Friday, Owen accused her of reading too late to get enough sleep.

"Is that true, Catriona?" her father demanded sternly.

"No, Daddy, I'm not reading."

"Then what keeps you up so late?"

"Praying," Catriona finally responded, her head down and her voice so meek that her father angrily asked her to repeat her answer. "Praying," she said.

"God in heaven, what is wrong with the woman?" Her father threw down his napkin and flung out of the kitchen. They could hear him charging up the stairs and then angry but indistinguishable voices.

"Now you've done it, missie," Bridie said, giving Catriona a fierce nip on the arm.

"What have I done?" Catriona demanded, tears coming to her eyes. "I told the truth."

"You've put the cat among the pigeons for sure, now. There'll be no peace in this house."

"There isn't much anyway," Owen replied. "C'mon, Cat," he added, rising. "I'll take you down to school. It's not your fault, but this is the last time I'm your taxi man."

"Who says it isn't her fault?" Bridie demanded at the top of her voice. "A daughter is supposed to be the comfort and support of her mother in her trials. A daughter—"

"Oh, stuff it, Bridie," Owen said, disgusted. "This is the twentieth century." And he hustled Catriona out of the kitchen, muttering under his breath about priest-ridden women.

"How is it my fault, Owen?" Catriona demanded, close to tears.

"It isn't Cat, It isn't. If you ask me, Auntie Isabel's gone soft in the head with all that Easter prayer and fasting."

If Catriona had thought the previous week's penance stiff, Saturday's was doubled. Again she had the treacherous thought that her mother had complained to Father John.

During Sunday Mass, aware that Father John glared in her direction far too often, she tried to squinch down beside her mother and began to feel very queasy. She was nervous about the end of Mass, for Father John had been known to publicly charge a sinner on his way out of church. She couldn't bear such an open humiliation. Fortunately, neighbors stopped to exchange greetings with her mother. She mixed in with all their kids and avoided any confrontation.

But walking home, the cramps in her stomach became severe enough to double her over. It was as if she'd eaten too many figs or fresh apricots, though she'd only had her usual porridge for breakfast. She got into the house and went straight to the loo, hoping to relieve herself. When she discovered blood on the paper, she sat paralyzed. That her mother's prayers had been answered was her first wild thought, abruptly interrupted by a curt knock on the door.

"Trina!" It was her sister, Sybil, who had been expected for Sunday dinner. "Don't take all day in there!"

"Oh, Sybil," Catriona said in a horrified whisper, "I'm bleeding to death!"

"Bleeding? Well, it's about time you did!"

Between reassurances and a wad of loo roll between Catriona's legs, Sybil ushered her sister up to the privacy of her bedroom.

"Mother vowed that she'd tell you all about menstruation, Trina. Don't tell me she opted out on that one, too?" Sybil said with some exasperation. "Well, evidently her words of wisdom did not sink in. Now you change, and I'll just get a pad from Auntie Eithne."

Sybil whirled out of the room, leaving Catriona not much wiser. Then she remembered that just before her last birthday, her mother had tried to explain something about becoming a woman and having to put up with a curse that was never to be referred to in public, let alone mixed company. It was part of a woman's lot, Isabel had said. And, while disgusting, it was better to have the curse every month than not to have it because that meant more trouble than Catriona could imagine and ended with children being born.

Then Auntie Eithne, her pretty face wreathed with smiles, came in with Sybil, carrying a small box and still looking jubilant, right behind her.

"Oh, my dear child! And I shouldn't call you 'child' anymore, now that you're a woman," Auntie Eithne began, hugging Catriona warmly and beaming at her as if she had done something immensely clever. "How happy we are for you! But I don't think we'll mention it to your mother just yet." The smile on Auntie Eithne's face dimmed a trifle, but she hugged Catriona all the more warmly. "Oh, what's the matter? Do you have cramps?" For a belly spasm had wrenched a gasp from Catriona. "Go get an aspirin for her, Sybil, will you, there's a good girl. And a hot-water bottle. Only don't tell Bridie why. At least not yet. Now, dear, I don't think Isabel quite explained it all last year, did she?"

With a hot-water bottle resting comfortably on her stomach and a tablet working internally, Catriona listened as her aunt and sister explained exactly what had happened to her, why, what she might expect, what she should be careful not to do.

"And I'll drop a wee word in Father's ear," Sybil added with a stern look, "to be sure he doesn't expect you to muck out or ride for hours when you're off color. Oh, don't worry, Trina, your father does understand about all this. He'll be glad for you, too, pet." Sybil dropped a light kiss on her sister's cheek. "I've a book for you that explains it all again.

"And I've an article to show Mother as well," Sybil added, glancing significantly at Eithne, who looked startled. "Well, in America they understand these things. Actually, I'm positive that what's wrong with Mother is all postmenopausal change. We get it on both ends of the cycle, Trina, but you don't have to worry about that! Yet."

"I've been trying to get Isabel to consult Dr. Standish," said Eithne.

"Standish? He's medieval. He wouldn't know a hormone from a harmonica."

"The change takes some women hard, Sybil."

"Well, it can take 'em, it doesn't need to keep 'em," Sybil insisted. "Especially when nowadays enlightened medicine proves that the problem can be corrected. I read all about it in *Reader's Digest*."

"*Reader's Digest*?" Auntie Eithne raised skeptical eyebrows. "They never tell the full story in a digest. But if Dr. Standish feels a specialist is indicated, I'm sure he'll recommend one."

"She'd improve a lot faster if he stopped her taking those pills. She's probably addicted to them by now, you know. I know she took a whole bottle before she married me off."

"Sybil, how dare you suggest such a thing?" Eithne desperately tried to signal Sybil not to discuss such matters in front of Catriona.

"It doesn't take daring, Auntie Eithne," Sybil replied, ignoring the gestures and making a face at her young sister. "It takes a bit of facing facts. Which Mummie obviously isn't. She needs a woman doctor, someone who won't just pat her on the hand and tell her that it's the will of God." Sybil briefly adopted a sanctimonious expression, then relented. "I know of one."

"Isabel prefers Dr. Standish. I don't think you could get her to go to a woman doctor."

"Then for God's sake, get her to Dr. Standish. She can't continue the way she is. There'll come a time, Auntie Eithne"—Sybil shook her finger at her startled aunt—"when Irish women will stop being mere chattels and start demanding their rights as human beings."

"Sybil! You didn't get those notions from the *Reader's Digest*."

"No, I didn't, but that doesn't keep 'em from being true. You might say my year in London helped finish my education. And you, little sister, if you want to stay on horseback for the rest of your natural life, you do it. Choose your own destiny. Break the mold."

"Really, Sybil," Auntie Eithne went on, "I've half a mind to tell your husband what sort of ridiculous nonsense you've been spouting. It's a mercy your mother can't hear you talk like this. It'd give her a turn!"

"Whatever do you think she's in now? She can't handle the truth, so she's retreated into prayer. She's making everyone suffer because she can't have her way with Trina. Well, she won't, if I have any say in the matter. You hear me, Trina? Whoops, I hear my kids creating." And she quickly left the room.

"Are you comfortable now, dear?" Auntie Eithne said solicitously.

"Yes, thank you."

"Well, if you'd rather stay up here, I'll bring you a dinner tray." Her aunt sounded slightly dubious, and somehow Catriona did not want everyone knowing "that she had become a woman." Particularly her mother.

"No, I'd rather go down now. I'm not showing or anything?"

She was quickly and kindly reassured by her aunt. "But Trina, there is one thing. I'd rather you wouldn't repeat what Sybil said about your mother, and that other nonsense. I don't know what's happening to young people today. I really don't." And Auntie Eithne ruined her fierce manner by sniffing. Then, with an affectionate arm about her shoulders, Eithne led her niece down to the Sunday dinner table.

On Wednesday evening, Sybil phoned Catriona to ask how she was getting along.

"Well, I've still got it, Sybil, if that's what you mean." The novelty had worn off, and Catriona was not all that pleased with the prospect of this carry-on every twenty-eight days. However, it hadn't interfered with riding at all once the initial cramps had eased.

"It'll stop in due time, Trina. It's only four days. Now, has Auntie Eithne got Mother to the doctor yet?"

"I doubt it. But no one tells me anything. Bridie's been moaning about all the trays she's had to carry upstairs and Mummie not eating more than a pick."

"Damn, you'd think Mummie enjoyed being ill." Catriona was a bit flabbergasted to hear Sybil say what Bridie had bitterly mentioned. "Well, I've that article about menopause and hormone therapy. Mummie is going to read it if it's the last thing I do." After inquiring how the new pony was going, Sybil hung up. Catriona knew that it was just a polite afterthought, but still, Sybil had remembered to ask.

And Conker was going great. He was almost fit after his long retirement, and most of his grass belly had been worked off. He acted more like a five-year-old than a staid and aged pony. The Spring Show was eleven days off, and with each session Catriona's hopes of winning improved.

On Friday when Catriona came into the yard, she was surprised to find the Chou Chin Chow gelding in the box next to Conker. The new gelding poked his head out the door at her, talking deep in his throat. She let him sniff her hand, blew in his nostrils when he raised his head, and then gave him a good scratch, right up to his ears.

"Let him get to know you, Trina," her father said, coming up behind her.

"I think he's super, Dad. Will Mrs. Healey really show him for us? She's such an elegant rider. She'll make a horse look even better. What'd you give for him?" Aghast at her cheekiness, Catriona waited for a rebuke, but her father only laughed.

"I stole him, Trina, as Jack Garden will discover when he starts winning!"

❧ 11 ❧

*M*ichael Carradyne felt the situation in his home keenly. He tried on three occasions to reason with Isabel, but she would begin to say a silent rosary, her eyes focusing on another dimension entirely. She rejected his appeal to see Dr. Standish by saying that a medical practitioner knew better than to meddle in spiritual matters.

Catriona and her father began to rise, breakfast, and escape the house before Bridie arrived to take charge of her kitchen. Catriona would quickly rinse their dishes so that Bridie could have no complaint. She'd be with her father in the yard, halfway through mucking out, before Mick or Artie appeared.

"Captain, you've no call to be doing that now," Mick would complain, his face as dark as peat with outrage. "Artie and me're to do that. You get on with the riding, see?"

"Mucking out's soothing, Mick. Clears the sinuses" was her father's rejoinder, but he would relinquish the fork to Mick.

There was plenty to do in the yard all day. Mrs. Healey appeared every morning to help break and back the Chou Chin Chow gelding, whom she had named Charlie Chan. Michael had been commissioned to break and school five three-year-old horses. And Sean arrived every afternoon, now that the Spring Show was nearly upon them. With Catriona on Conker in the lead, the Prince settled more quickly and worked better.

"Maybe I should always work them with you, Trina," Michael had remarked on the second occasion. "Sean's actually relaxing."

"The pressure's not on the boy all the time," Mrs. Healey said. "Really, I have no use for such parents. That child is not a natural rider. I suspect, though, that he does very well in either cricket or football."

"However did you know?" Catriona asked, surprised, because she happened to know that Sean was on the St. Andrew's cricket team.

"A lucky guess," Mrs. Healey replied. "It doesn't take money to play cricket or football, which, at Sean's tender age, add nothing to the family status."

Catriona did not quite understand that, but she thought it would be great if Sean and she could change mothers. And why couldn't her mother be as keen and helpful and knowledgeable about horses as Mrs. Healey? Then everything would be all right at Cornanagh. And, not because Father John had given her such penances, but because she wanted to, Catriona was praying every evening: praying that her mother would get better.

She really needed the solace of Mass, but she dreaded the approach of Sunday and another encounter with Father John.

"Cat, you shouldn't oughta worry about your mum so," Artie surprised her by saying as they were sweeping the yard on a Thursday evening. "M'mum says women get sort of silly daft, but they always snap out of it."

"It's not Mummie. It's . . . it's . . . ." Artie nodded encouragingly, and suddenly she had to tell someone. "It's Church, and Father John. He gave me awful penances because I'm not a good daughter. . . ."

Artie stared at her for a long moment, then swallowed, making the Adam's apple in his thin neck bobble. "There's some as are saying she's being a touch hard on you when you've finally got a cracker pony. And if you're getting the business from Father John, go to Kilcoole. They've an early Mass, too, and it's not that far if you go over the fields."

When Catriona's doubt was obvious, he added, "The sin is in not going to Mass, not where you go, Cat, and you need the comfort."

Catriona wrestled with the ethics of such a solution all Friday. St. Michael's was her parish church, Father John her regular confessor. But even Sister Conceptua, adroitly questioned, admitted that it was by no means compulsory to attend the parish church if, for a valid reason, it was impossible to do so. Nevertheless, Catriona felt almost guilty as she slipped across the fields, soaking her shoes and socks, to reach St. Anthony's in Kilcoole. Her prayers and participation in the Mass were sincere, and she returned home much refreshed by the familiar and comforting rite, and delighted with this new option.

On Monday, as soon as she climbed on the bus, Mary Evans thrust a flat-wrapped package at her. "Happy Birthday, Catriona!" she said with a shy smile of anticipation on her plump face.

"You remembered?" Catriona blinked back sudden tears. Bridie hadn't said a word this morning. Owen never did remember, until dinnertime when everyone had had a chance to remind him, and she'd seen neither her father nor Philip.

"Of course I remembered, Trina! As if I would forget. Open it," Mary urged, for she was eager to see Catriona's reaction to the present, purchased with considerable thought.

"Oh, Mary, *National Velvet*! A copy all my very own." Eyes shining with delight, Catriona clasped the paperback to her chest with both hands. "Oh, you are such a dear, dear friend!" With uncharacteristic effusiveness, Catriona hugged her friend, mindful of the book's safety.

"*Now* you look happy," Mary said, well pleased.

"And so I should. I'm thirteen today."

"Well, you've been awfully glum lately." Mary was firm. "You haven't fooled me, but I know you, clam face. With your mother sick and all, it can't be fun."

"How do you know my mother's sick?"

"Everyone knows that by now," Mary replied. "I knew something was wrong, and it couldn't be Conker because you would tell me that. So, what's wrong with your mum? You can tell me, you know. I can keep my mouth shut as much as you can."

"I don't think anyone knows what's really wrong with her."

"It must be grim," Mary said. "Is your mum better that you look happier?"

"Not really." Catriona could not admit to Mary that she hadn't seen her mother at all over the weekend. "It's just that the Spring Show is next week, and both Conker and the Prince worked really well over the weekend." She giggled. "Sean's finally learned how to relax. He might even win this year if he keeps his head in the ring, and the Prince doesn't spook at the crowds."

"Well, you know you can always come over and visit me if things get too rough."

"Thanks, Mary, you're a real friend. And when I've finished *National Velvet*, I'll give you another read of it." Catriona squeezed Mary's hand gratefully. She stroked the cover of the book, rewrapped it, and put it safely in her book bag. "I think Bridie's planning a cake for tea. She was that way, you know, this morning."

"Will your relatives be coming over for tea?"

Catriona hesitated before replying. She almost didn't want to see any of them, except Sybil, because all anyone talked about was her mother and her illness. She earnestly hoped that Grandmother Marshall would stay away: she ought to be spared *that* on her birthday.

"Sybil will come," she told Mary.

"More colored pencils?"

"No, I asked for chalk pastels. You can get a lot more shading and contrast with pastels."

"Speaking of relatives, have you heard anything more from

your cousin?" And when Catriona regarded Mary blankly, "Your American cousin, Patricia? Is she still coming this summer with your mother sick and all?"

Catriona did not know. In the fuss and furor over her mother, she had completely forgotten about that proposed visit. She asked her father while they were doing evening stables.

"Yes, she's coming," he said. "June fifteenth, to be precise. You'll like having someone your own age, won't you?"

"Yes, but we don't have Blister for her, and . . . and we don't know if Conker would be too much for her."

Her father gripped her shoulder affectionately. "Jack Garden has a pony that he'll lend if it's needed. Or I'll take Mrs. Evans up on her offer of old Patch if that's all your cousin can manage. Don't worry your head about a pony for her, Trina." For the first time in ages, her father grinned, his eyes twinkling. "I hear Bridie's giving us a special tea tonight."

Now that he had referred to her birthday, she couldn't be accused of wheedling. "Wasn't it super of Artie to give me a body brush with Conker's name burned on the back of it? That way he'll always have his very own."

Michael Carradyne ruffled his daughter's hair. He'd made a special trip to Kilcullen to Berney Brothers' saddle shop from which he always bought the riding equipment Cornanagh needed. What had been adequate as a bridle for old Blister was not appropriate for a pony of Conker's caliber. He found himself anticipating the look on Catriona's face when she held up the new bridle. And the hell with Isabel.

Actually, his wife elected to stay in her room as usual that evening, although she called Catriona in to visit her on her way down to tea. Catriona appeared in the lounge, looking sadly pensive, and dutifully displayed the new rosary. Her birth date and initials had been inscribed on the silver cross.

Michael was delighted with her stunned reaction to the bridle.

"This is because you don't get to wear a bridle," Owen said, grinning as he handed her his gift, a gold locket that opened. "To preserve Conker's photo," he added with an embarrassed grin when she threw her arms around his neck and kissed his cheek.

"Hey, I've got something for you, too," Philip complained in mock jealousy. His present was a blue lightweight anorak jacket. "To keep away the wind and the wet when you ride out this spring."

"And it's got pockets I can reach from both sides. Oh, Pip!" He was awarded an equally ardent embrace. "You're the best brother a girl ever had."

Then Eithne entered the lounge to announce tea. Catriona had been excused from her usual household chores on her birthday and allowed to open the family's gifts before the evening meal, so the table was already laid out. Bridie had outdone herself with a roast chicken stuffed with sage and onion dressing, roasted and creamed potatoes, mushy peas about which Owen complained, and braised celery, Catriona's special favorite.

Just as they finished the meat course, Sybil arrived with her husband, Aidan, and her two children, a sturdy five-year-old boy and a tiny girl who had just discovered how to walk. She demonstrated this, round and round the dining room table, tripping up on the rug, righting herself, and toddling off again under indulgent eyes.

From Sybil and Aidan, presented by Catriona's young nephew, was a riding shirt, complete with high collar, a stock, and a pretty tie pin.

"With room to grow into," Sybil said with a wink as Catriona held the slightly large shirt against her.

When Eithne gave Catriona a large flat package that was

shortly seen to contain one hundred different shades of pastel sticks and a block of special pastel paper, Eithne and Sybil had a laugh together. Generally it was Eithne who thought of clothes and Sybil who provided drawing materials.

"Oh, this is the very best birthday I've ever had," Catriona said with a sigh of tremulous joy.

"And she hasn't seen Bridie's cake yet," Eithne told the gathering.

"Let's see if she needs help lighting all those candles," Philip told Owen, and the pair headed off to the kitchen. They reentered immediately, Owen holding open one of the double doors, Philip the other, as Bridie, a smirk of great satisfaction on her face, marched in holding the Spode plate on which rested a truly splendid cake. It was festooned with roses and wreaths in a pale pink, with an appropriate inscription on top and candles all alight.

"Oh, Bridie! You must have been making it for weeks!" Catriona cried with delight, and hugged the diminutive cook after she had placed the cake on the table. "It's . . . it's . . . absolutely spectacular!" To which everyone else loudly agreed and her little nephew wanted to know couldn't he please have a big piece because he'd eaten all his tea.

"Well now," Bridie began, smoothing her apron with a semblance of modesty, "I did put a bit of extra effort into it, being as how you're thirteen now, Catriona Mary Virginia." She paused, scowling a bit at the Captain and then raising her eyes to the ceiling beneath her mistress's bedroom. "What with all that's been happening and you becoming a woman and all. Here!" she said hastily, seeing the grim expression on the captain's face. "Cut it and see if all me work's worth me time and effort."

She handed Catriona the old silver cake knife and matching spatula and gave her a little push toward the table. With an intent expression, Catriona made two neat incisions in the white perfection of icing, oohed appreciatively at the depth of the marzipan layer, and again at the double cream between three layers of light yellow sponge, and, while everyone held their breath, managed to transfer the slice to the plate that Eithne held under it.

"That's for Mother," Catriona said with suitable gravity. "I'll take it up to her in a minute."

Once she had served everyone else, she took the cake to her mother. She found Isabel asleep, her hands twined about a rosary that was identical to the one she had given her daughter. Catriona hesitated, wondering should she leave the cake or take it back for Bridie to keep. It would be a shame to let such a superior cake go stale. Finally she left it on the bedside table, moving aside the brown plastic bottle half-full of capsules.

On Wednesday, as Catriona was riding leading file in the sand menage, Conker kicked a beer bottle that had been lobbed over the wall. The moment she heard the ominous crack of glass, Catriona pulled him up, but it was too late. She was off his back the next moment, yelling at Sean to turn to the center. Her father was equally quick, the first to lift the pony's foot and assess the damage. A shard of glass was imbedded in the sole at the toe. Father and daughter exchanged glances.

"Steady him, Trina," Michael said, and jerked the thin shard out. Blood welled up instantly. "Sean, find Mick and have him ring the vet. Tell Artie to bring me gamgee and bandages. We've got to keep the wound as clean as possible."

When Sean clattered out of the menage on the Prince, Conker nickered and pulled at Catriona's restraint. She soothed him so that he wouldn't jerk his foot out of her father's hand.

"I should have checked," said Michael. "I should have had Artie check. Those yahbos are always turfing bottles over the wall. Of all the times in the world, I should have been extra cautious right now."

"See, he knows to stand quiet," Catriona said, stroking Conker's neck as her other hand securely held the cheekpiece of the splendid new bridle.

"You work and school, and do your damnedest, and what happens? The bloody horse goes lame just when he has to be sound! I don't know why I stick to horses! I really don't."

Catriona had never heard her father sound so bitter, so defeated.

"There'll be other shows, Dad. August isn't that far away, and the pony classes in the Horse Show are much better than the spring ones. Anyway, a true Carradyne can't stay away from horses. That's what Grandfather always said."

Michael Carradyne looked up at his daughter's earnest face. He gave a short, affectionate laugh. Just then Artie, with Sean on foot and Mick close behind them, came flying into the yard. Conker whickered nervously at the commotion and tried to pull his foreleg out of Michael's hand.

"Steady there!" The admonition was as much for the rush of assistance as for the startled pony. "Don't you know better than to charge at an injured horse?" he demanded of Artie, who held out the gamgee and rolled bandage. Artie started to stammer, but then Mick brushed by him, bending to peer at the injury.

"Sure, I've seen worse. It's a long way from his heart. Vet's coming. Caught him at the surgery."

Catriona surrendered her position to Mick and stood back beside Artie and the wide-eyed Sean as the two men applied first aid to the wound.

"It's all right, Artie," she told him, noticing that his face was beet red with humiliation.

"Will he be all right for the show, Catriona?" Sean asked in a subdued whisper.

She shook her head.

"Gosh, what're you going to do, then?"

"Watch you, Sean, and don't you and the Prince dare put a foot wrong, you hear me?"

The bandage secure, the two men began leading the crippled pony back to his stall.

"C'mon, Artie, let's get up all the glass," said Catriona. "Sean, go get us a spring rake and the skip."

That task kept the others from seeing the tears streaming down her face. And she stuck to the search long after the others left, until she heard the throaty sound of the vet's Merc as it shifted down for the turn at Kilquade Road.

"I've seen worse," Finbarr O'Sullivan said, smiling encouragingly. "When did he last have a tetanus jab?"

Michael regarded Finbarr for a moment and then sighed. "Not since he got to this yard. I'll give Mrs. Healey a shout." He strode off toward the house.

"Sure, I should have checked the menage myself this morning," Mick said, shaking his head slowly. Then, when he saw Artie regarding him with a fearful expression, "No, lad, it's no fault of yours. But with the Show only a few days off, we should have known something could happen. And hasn't it just?"

"It'll take more than that slice to do this fella in," the vet said soothingly as he began to fill a syringe from the upheld bottle. "D'you have any penicillin, Mick?"

"No, sir, we used up the last we had when the brown mare had that cough."

Conker stood quietly while the vet gave him the first injection.

"He's not had tet in at least five years," Michael said, reappearing. He slipped an arm about Catriona's shoulders, smiling down at her reassuringly. "She understands, Trina. Don't fret. But I think from now on, Artie, your first job every morning is to check the menage for bottles." Artie flushed and scuffed his toe in the shavings. "I should have thought of doing it on a regular basis long before this," Michael added ruefully. "Artie, off you go now and clear up that glass. . . ."

"We already did that, Captain," Artie said, his Adam's apple bobbing in relief. "Cat and Sean and me."

"Thank you, and would you saddle Teasle up for me? I think Sean and I will go down the Ride today." Then he turned expectantly to Finbarr.

"He'll be grand when that heals. Keep poulticing with the antiphlogistene. You know the drill, Michael. Ten cc's of penicillin for the next five days. Call me if there's any heat in the hoof or swelling in the leg. Though I don't think there will be." Finbarr closed up his medical case and, after shaking hands with the Captain, went on his way.

Catriona watched while Mick stripped off Conker's horseshoe, and once the antiphlogistene had been heated on the little stove in the feed room, she helped him apply the poultice. Conker was behaving beautifully, and he'd even allowed Mr. O'Sullivan to give him the injection without more than a hand on the head collar. Then they rugged him up, made him a deep bed of straw and a warm bran mash.

It wasn't until the necessary had been done to ensure the pony's comfort that realization hit Catriona. She slid the bolts on the stable door and leaned against it, turning her head from Mick so he wouldn't see her distress. It wasn't that she wouldn't be in the spring show. It wasn't even that Mrs. Healey would be disappointed; she was a horsewoman and knew these stupid accidents could happen. It hurt Catriona because Conker had been injured, through no fault of his.

"Go have a cup of tea, Catriona," Mick suggested, his voice rough. He gave her a little push toward the house. "With lots of sugar. Artie and me'll finish up here. Sure it's a long way from his heart."

"Thanks, Mick," she said, and obeyed. She'd check Conker

131

later this evening, to be sure he hadn't shed the poultice or twisted his rug. And this evening, no matter what Bridie said, she'd bring him a treat. There were apples in the bowl in the lounge. Surely an injured pony could have one.

As she stepped into the kitchen, Bridie began:

"I told ya. I warned ya. And now you've been punished. Pray, Catriona Mary Carradyne, pray. Repent, and this trial will be taken from you. For God's way is not to be gainsaid. His laws shall not be mocked. You have not honored your mother!"

Catriona stared at Bridie a moment, then wheeled and slammed out of the kitchen, sobs tearing out of her. She pounded up the stairs with such a clatter that her aunt, who had been sitting with the invalid, came out to investigate. Catriona gave her one fearful glance and fled to the dubious safety of her room. She turned the key in the lock. She flung herself down on her bed, covered her head with her pillow, and abandoned herself to tears.

She was aware, though she told herself she didn't hear anything with her head under the pillow, that Auntie Eithne knocked, then pounded on the door, calling for admittance.

Then the knocking began again.

"Catriona Mary!" It was her mother's voice. "You have reaped the only reward for your obstinacy. You must come to the Virgin Mary in humility and pray with me for the salvation of your immortal soul."

"Then why wasn't the glass in my foot? Why should God punish an innocent pony?"

"God is not to be mocked, Catriona Mary."

"You are the mocker, Mother, pretending to know what God does and wants and says. Go away."

"Open this door, Catriona Mary. Open this door to your mother so that I may pray for your immortal soul."

"No, no! *No!*" Catriona screamed. "No, no, no. *Never!*" Then she rammed the pillow over her head, pressing its sides down against her ears. In a voice loud enough to drown out her mother's, Catriona began to recite the Hail Mary. When she realized what she had unconsciously chosen, she writhed on the bed and shouted out the multiplication tables. Then her mother stopped abruptly. Catriona paused. The suddenness of the silence unnerved her.

She uncovered her left ear and listened. Then Bridie's unmistakable keening broke the silence.

"Stop that this instance, Bridie Doolin," came the clear, angry voice of her Auntie Eithne. "Phone Dr. Standish. Which is what ought to have been done any time since Easter. Then get Mick or Barry or whoever's about to help me." There was a moment of silence, and then Auntie Eithne began in a different tone altogether. "Belle? Belle? Can you hear me? Isabel? Isabel?"

Terrified, Catriona crept slowly to the door, unlocked, and opened it. Her mother was crumpled on the floor, her face a ghastly white. Auntie Eithne was chaffing one hand.

"You're a good girl, Catriona. Bring me your blankets and pillow. We'll try to keep her warm. They always say that's the first thing to do."

Catriona could not move. She could only stare at her mother's limp figure. She had done this. She had been just as willful and awful a child as Bridie said she was.

"Catriona Mary, don't look so stricken. This is *not* your fault. Not even saints fast forever."

The contempt and disapproval in her aunt's voice did more to reassure Catriona than her words. She darted for the blankets and pillows, half stripping the sheets in the process.

"It's all so very ridiculous," Auntie Eithne said, more to herself than to Catriona, as they tucked the blankets about the still form. Then, "There, there, now, Trina dear, your mother's simply not herself." She patted Catriona's shoulder and gave her a tender smile.

Just then the courtyard door was yanked open, and both could hear the tramp of men coming to their assistance.

"Eithne?" Michael cried, and he was first up the steps, followed by Mick and an ashen-faced Artie.

"She just collapsed, Michael," Eithne said. "Did you reach Dr. Standish, Bridie?"

"Oh, the dear, the poor darling!" Bridie howled.

Michael bent over his wife's still body, feeling for the pulse with one hand as he pulled up an eyelid with the other. Then he rose and, leaning over the balustrade, told Bridie to stop her banshee wail and answer the question.

"Yis, yis, he's coming, and why wouldn't he with the mistress dying on the cold floor!"

"She's not dying. . . ." His opinion, pronounced in such a firm voice, made Catriona reel with relief. Michael saw her reaction and drew his daughter to his side, smiling down at her with reassurance. "Not our day, is it, Trina? She's just fainted. All the fasting and prayer caught up with her, I shouldn't wonder."

"Exactly," Eithne said. "If only I had ignored Belle and sent for the doctor long ago. . ."

"I ought to have insisted."

"If *you* had, Michael, she wouldn't have seen him if she'd been at death's door," Eithne said tartly. "Now, let's get her into bed. Dr. Standish may be coming, but who's to say when." As the three men lifted Isabel, Eithne leaned over the balustrade. "Bridie, you'd better wet the tea. We'll all do better for a cup."

"Tea? At a time like this?"

"At a time like this, tea is exactly what is needed."

🍃 *12* 🍃

*D*r. Standish arrived promptly and set everyone's worst fears to rest: Isabel Carradyne had only fainted, although her blood pressure and heart rate caused him such concern that he phoned for an ambulance to take her immediately to St. Gabriel's in Cabinteely.

"Isabel's piety could be the death of her, Michael," he said with a disapproving stare.

With her bedroom door a trifle ajar, Catriona could see the landing and hear the conversation.

When Michael merely shrugged, Eithne intervened nervously. "Dr. Standish, I've been wanting to call you for the past three weeks. Michael has begged me to get her to see reason." She ignored her brother-in-law's disavowing snort. "And then there're those pills. . . ."

"What pills?"

With reluctance and embarrassment, Eithne handed him the brown plastic bottle Catriona had seen so often on her mother's bedside locker. The doctor frowned as he read the label.

"I prescribed them myself. Valium's entirely suitable for a woman at Isabel's time of life. It's certainly not as harmful as this continual fasting."

Eithne twisted her handkerchief through her fingers. "But she's been taking a lot of these lately. Surely that's not good."

Dr. Standish patted Eithne on the arm reassuringly. "Not to worry, Eithne, though your concern does you credit. We'll give her a thorough check-up in the hospital and sort it all out. I want to be sure extended fasting hasn't done any damage. There isn't a pick of flesh on her. I'm not against prayer, mind you," he added hastily, "and fasting can be good for the flesh as well as the soul. I'll ring you, Michael, as soon as I've studied the test results."

Catriona was weak with relief that she had not killed her mother.

On the bus the next day, Catriona told Mary that her mother had been taken to hospital. Mary was properly sympathetic, which perversely only made Catriona feel worse. Especially as she then had to report Conker's injury.

"But that means you won't have anything to ride in the Spring Show!"

" 'Pride goeth before a fall,' as Bridie would say."

"Catriona Mary, don't be so stupid. It wasn't your fault."

"In a way it was." Catriona slumped in the seat, as Mary gave her a wide-eyed stare of disbelief.

"How could it be? *You* didn't litter the menage with bottles."

"Yes, but we know people throw things over the wall, and we should have been checking, especially right now, just in case!"

"I don't understand you, Catriona Mary Carradyne. Do you *want* to feel guilty about it?" Mary had considerably more to add to that argument, and the result was that, by the time they got to Wicklow town, Catriona had been roused from her gloom, although her conscience continued to nag her. If she had not been so naughty, if she had opened the door, her mother would not have been so wrought, would not have fainted. But then, she argued with herself, Dr. Standish would not have been called, and her mother would have continued to fast.

"For want of a shoe," as her grandfather used to say about a chain of events, each leading into the next. Thinking about

Grandfather was oddly comforting. So was the school routine that would take up the rest of this day.

When she returned to Cornanagh, Auntie Eithne, still wearing a house coat, with a scarf over her hair, met her with the news that the doctor said her mother was only rundown, suffering from malnutrition.

"And I couldn't actually tell him how long she'd been fasting this time, but if we hadn't caught her, it could have been disastrous. She was terribly dehydrated." Catriona had never known that dehydration was a disease, but her aunt patted her shoulder, smiling with both relief and reassurance. "So she'll be in hospital for a week or so, pet. And after she's put on a bit of weight and is sleeping and resting normally, we'll be able to visit her—maybe even by Sunday."

Catriona nodded and shrugged out of her jacket, taking an appreciative look around her.

"The house smells nice and fresh and clean, Auntie Eithne," Catriona said.

"What a good child you are, Catriona." Her aunt beamed. "A good airing on such a lovely fresh day does a world of good, I think. Now, you go up and get changed. Your father's waiting for you."

"But Conker—" Catriona broke off and ran upstairs. After all, there were more horses to be cared for than her precious pony.

What Auntie Eithne had forgotten to tell her was that Mrs. Healey had come the first thing that morning and stayed till noon.

"She got into an old pair of Philip's jods and wellies," Artie told a delighted Catriona, "and helped Mick change the poultice, and she knows a thing or two about vet'rinary, she does. Then, because she was dressed for it"—Artie's eyes widened with remembered delight—"she helped the captain with the Charlie Chan gelding. She laid across him an' all. She's done that afore, I'd say. Tomorrow she's going to come back and help again."

"Then she's not mad about Conker?"

"Not a bit of it. And first thing I did this morning was check out the menage. Dirt clean!" Then Artie made a face: he made very funny faces without half trying, for he was a bone thin, gawky adolescent. "The Prince's saddled," he added. "Don't worry, Cat, Conker'll be sound soon enough."

The Prince could wait a moment. She had an apple for Conker that she had filched from the bowl. Endearingly, he nickered when he identified her step on the cobbles of the yard. With delicate bites, he eagerly reduced the apple to moist crumbs, which he then licked from the palm of her hand.

Saturday, her father had her riding Teasle as leading file for Sean on the Prince. Catriona had ridden Teasle the odd time or two and had actually been the first human weight on his back. Nevertheless, it was an unusual but not unpleasant sensation to have so much horse under her after Conker and the Prince.

She didn't notice that Mrs. Healey was watching the lesson until it was nearly over. She was dressed for riding, wearing a blue quilted Husky instead of a hacking jacket, but contrived to remain as elegant as ever.

"Teasle works well for you, Catriona," Mrs. Healey said.

"Thank you, Mrs. Healey. If you're here to ride Charlie, may I watch?"

"Turnabout's fair play, isn't it?" she replied, smiling up at Catriona as she patted Teasle's damp neck.

Just then Mick came up, Charlie ambling placidly behind him, a bitless training head collar festooning his head and the old breaking saddle on his back. Catriona thought that in deference to Mrs. Healey, they could have used a slightly better saddle. That one was hard as bricks to sit in for any length of time.

Mick took Teasle as she was heading for the stable, and, thanking him profusely, Catriona ran back to the menage. She slowed as she reached the end of the passageway and sidled quietly to the corner, out of the way.

Mrs. Healey stood beside Michael Carradyne in the center as he began to lunge the horse, paying out the wide-webbed lunge line until Charlie was on a thirty-meter circuit, the line taut to the ring on the cavesson nose-band.

The process of breaking and backing a young horse had always fascinated Catriona. She remembered standing quietly by her grandfather in this same spot during other introductory sessions. Of course, in those days, she had had no real understanding of what she was watching, though she still remembered some of the spectacular sessions with the Tulip's high-strung progeny.

For a young horse, Charlie had an amazing sense of balance, his hocks well engaged so that he was already using himself properly, a knack many horses had to learn through long and tedious drills. He was moving from behind, and his strides were so easy that he seemed to be gliding effortlessly, with that subtle little extra flick to his fetlocks, an innate grace that was certain to please show judges. Although her father's plans for Charlie had not been discussed with her, she knew what would be routine for the young horse over the summer and for the next year, for it was the sequence that Cornanagh followed with all its animals in the hope of attracting buyers and extracting from them a premium price for the "made" horse. One day someone would offer her father the money he wanted for Charlie, and he'd be sold on, as Teasle hopefully would this summer, maybe even this spring at the show, if he showed to advantage. Abruptly, Catriona realized she did not want to see Charlie sold on. If she could only grow some leg over the next few months, she'd be able for Charlie.

She caught her breath and bit her lower lip. How could she be so disloyal to Conker? But Catriona had learned to be a realist about horses, and Conker *was* getting on in years. It wasn't fair to make horse or pony work past its usefulness. And oh, the Charlie horse would be a dream to ride.

Her father began to talk Charlie from trot to walk and then to stand. Charlie had already learned not to turn in to his handler and stood, head turned to watch for commands, perfectly square on the track. Collecting the broad lunge line hand over hand, Michael Carradyne walked to Charlie and patted his head, murmuring encouragements. Then he led the gelding to Mrs. Healey.

"Trina, come here. We'll want an extra hand, just to be on the safe side."

But Charlie never moved as Michael Carradyne gave Mrs. Healey a leg up. She lay over the saddle for a long moment while both she and Michael slapped Charlie along the flanks and sides and moved the stirrups against him, all motions designed to familiarize the animal with human activity around and about him. At a word from the trainer, Mrs. Healey slipped back to the ground and praised Charlie.

"Up and over this time, Selina. Hold him steady, Trina."

Again an unnecessary command, for even when Mrs. Healey sat up properly straight in the saddle and slipped her booted feet into the stirrups, Charlie just stood, ears pricked, eyes ahead of him, relaxed and completely unperturbed.

Catriona and her father walked beside the gelding as he was led back and forth in the center of the menage. Then her father began to pay out the lunge line.

"Give him a leg aid, Selina, get him used to the pressure. Trina, walk at his head on the outside now. Don't let him swing in."

After two full circuits, Catriona was dismissed from that duty as Charlie was gently persuaded to trot. All he did at that command was to snort a bit, toss his head, and quicken into the trot.

"He has the loveliest movement," Selina Healey said, a delighted smile on her face. "Like silk. Oh, he's going to be a joy to show. I've been riding hunters too long. And just look at him arch his neck. Michael, this horse is a consummate ham."

Walk. Trot, walk again on the other rein. Trot, walk, halt, walk, trot.

"That'll be enough for today. His back needs to strengthen up but he's coming on a treat, Selina. A real treat!"

No sooner had Mrs. Healey dismounted than the older Doherty appeared in the archway, wanting principally to be reassured that Sean had a very good chance of winning the Wednesday class. Then, after he had been adroitly handled, Barry appeared from the potato field to say that the cattle had broken the fence at the stream, the farrier had arrived for the weekly shoeings, and Sybil was on the phone, wanting a word with her father.

"Doesn't the man ever have any time off?" Selina Healey asked as she and Catriona led Charlie back to the yard.

"My grandfather used to say that you never had time off if you worked horses: only the horses did."

Selina smiled down at Catriona. "C'mon, I said that I'd change Conker's poultice."

As Artie had noted, Mrs. Healey did know a thing or two about veterinary. She and Catriona fixed the poultice and rebandaged Conker, the last part under the approving eye of Michael Carradyne.

Her father ran expert hands down the bandaged foreleg, then asked, "Catriona, would you pull the Prince's mane? It'll be too thick to plait neatly. And give him a good grooming. I want his coat to shine."

"Let me help," Selina Healey said.

"My dear Selina," Michael began, pausing only when he saw the eager look on his daughter's face and the entreaty in Selina's.

"No, really, Michael. David's away north, checking over his holdings there in case the banks actually do strike. Do you think they will?"

Michael shrugged. "If they do, they do, though it's an idiotic notion considering the Republic's finances."

"Got all your money in the mattresses?"

Michael stared at her a moment and then, throwing back his head, roared with laughter. "Even the tinkers use banks, you know."

"That's what I like in you, Michael. You get on with the job at hand and let tomorrow take care of itself."

"If you work with horses, that philosophy saves you a great deal of needless worry."

"C'mon, Catriona, I need a mane comb."

The Prince had a thick mane, the tough strands able to inflict thin, painful wounds. Mrs. Healey made her use a glove on her right hand and showed her a trick of snatching a few strands only. Then they also thinned his thick tail, considerably improving his general appearance.

"Do all your brothers ride?" Selina Healey asked Catriona as they worked.

"Yes and no. My grandfather taught all of us, and my cousins. Harry's the best competition rider, but he's working down in Wexford and can't always get time off. Philip is very good, and he generally gets a good show out of a horse. He's not quite as effective over jumps."

Selina Healey muffled a laugh. "Sometimes, my dear, when you're talking about horses, you sound a hundred and one. There, now, don't hang your head. You *do* know what you're talking about. I've noticed that. What else does Philip do? I haven't seen him around the yard during the weekdays."

"He has a very good job as a salesman," Catriona said, "with Crawford's in Dun Laoghaire. My mother thinks he'd do well in advertising, and she wants him to go live with my uncle in Long Island."

"Would you?"

"What? Like him to go to America?" Catriona was unused to having her opinion sought. "I'd miss him," she said slowly. "He's such fun. He knows a lot of jokes, and he has a good seat and hands."

She didn't understand why Mrs. Healey chuckled again and patted her shoulder.

Mrs. Healey joined them for dinner at noon, and Bridie out-did herself with a thick hearty lentil soup, freshly baked bread, steak, chips, and a cream sponge cake. Nor did Mrs. Healey mind that Mick and Artie sat down with the family. In fact, she coaxed Artie into the conversation and chatted with Mick about old Mr. Mac, whom they had both known. Philip told some jokes that had Mrs. Healey drying tears of laughter from her eyes, and Michael laughed as loud as anyone. Indeed it was the most pleasant meal that Catriona could remember in months.

"It's only about time that someone got praise due them," Bridie said as she and Catriona cleared the table. The cook was chuffed by Mrs. Healey's compliments on the meal and her apologies for adding to Bridie's work. "And she meant it. Every word of it. Lovely woman, Mrs. Healey."

❧ 13 ❧

*M*ichael Carradyne felt a curious sense of anticipation as he and Selina swung out of the yard, she easy in the saddle of Flirty Lady, who was far better behaved as a hack than as a hunter, and he on the four-year-old brown gelding Emmett, whom he was shaping up for the August Horse Show.

They went up the road to McBride's lane, the gate open since Evans was working the big field. In a companionable silence they rode down the farm lane and on to the grass path bordering the stream. Michael reminded himself to send Artie down here with clippers, for some of the branches had grown from nuisance to hazard. They trotted from the farther gates past the farms and halted only briefly as they came on to where the old Delgany road was interrupted by an unpaved but graded stretch of the new dual carriageway. Catching Selina's glance, Michael nodded and they set the horses to a controlled canter down the wide, curving road. They slowed in mutual accord just before the barrier that closed off the unfinished carriageway and turned the horses back, reins loose as the horses blew.

Hoping to prolong the outing, Michael turned the gelding up Blackberry Hill, and Selina's laugh challenged him as Flirty Lady trotted energetically past, up the steep slope. He encouraged Emmett, and the gelding obediently lengthened. Then the two were in stride together, the mare laying her ears flat back, only her rider's firm control preventing her from swinging her head to bite the gelding for his attempt to pass her out. They reached the crest of the hill and, again in accord, pulled up the sweating horses.

"What a heavenly day!" Selina said, removing her hard hat to ruffle her damp blond hair. "I don't know why I stop when the hunting season ends. This is clearly the best time of the the year to ride."

"Well, this year, at any rate," Michael replied, grinning, and her eyes danced back at him, appreciating the whimsies of their climate.

"Any chance that the good weather will hold for the Spring Show?" Selina asked.

"If it happens, I'll enjoy it."

"Is that your philosophy in life, Michael?" She glanced at him sideways.

"As a soldier, I learned to live from one day to the next, expecting only what happens. That way one isn't disappointed."

"Oh, dear, that's a rather grim way of looking at life, isn't it? Or maybe it isn't," she went on before Michael could answer. "We're always advised to live each day as our last. Such a bleak notion, that this day could be my last." She gave him a determinedly gay smile. "Stupid, really, since I fully intend to live to a ripe and graceful old age, like my granny, who was as wise as she was beautiful, even at eighty-seven."

"That's a grand age."

"She always said it was because she had good bones. She didn't suffer from whatever it is that makes people's spines curl up. She always stood, and sat, ramrod straight. She rode sidesaddle until she was eighty, you know, and only quit because her favorite mare died and she never reposed the same confidence in the replacements Daddy found."

"My father knew your grandmother and had the greatest respect for her."

"Everyone did. Catriona has good bones, too, as well as an

astonishingly mature outlook. I'm impressed with the way she has taken the disappointment of not riding in the Spring Show."

"Yes, she took that well."

"She'll be a beauty when she grows up. And frankly, I think she'll stay in horses." She noticed Michael's frown and misinterpreted it. "Oh, I know most girls her age are crazy about horses, but sometimes it's not a passing fancy, and I'll wager that'll be the case with her. Now what have I said?"

Michael made an effort to clear his expression and gave Selina a quick reassuring grin. "Sorry. I agree with you, actually, though it's not really a good life for a girl."

"Why not? Look at Iris Kellett. Or Marian Mould and Liz Edgar in the UK. If Catriona has your backing and Cornanagh horses, she could do famously. It's not as if she'd be stuck in some hunter yard, having to cope with idiotic beginners and cack-handed adult novices. She's got a fine standard right now. How many Pony Club tests has she passed?"

"Actually, none," Michael said. "She's not much on group activities. Tends to stay at home—"

"Shouldn't you say, in the yard?"

"—with the exception of the little Evans girl."

"Well, she should get out more. She's too intense at times. And mixing's good for her social development. . . . Now what have I said?"

"I do apologize, Selina." And Michael was sorry—sorry that the conversation had taken a turn that could only remind him of Isabel.

"No, I think I should apologize," she said, and, leaning across the small gap that separated their horses, touched his arm contritely. "I have no business discussing your daughter."

"On the contrary, you have her interests at heart." Michael tried to keep the bitterness from his voice. "You appreciate her ability and her real needs. And you are right. She should get about more, and the Pony Club ties in with her interests, at least. Her cousin, my brother's daughter, is coming to spend the summer here. She rides, but how well I don't know."

Selina gave a rude snort. "Yanks!"

"Both Catriona and Patricia can join the Pony Club. I'll speak to the Secretary. She'll be at the show."

They rode on in harmonious silence again as the horses negotiated the slippery mud of the down slope and came out onto the Delgany-Pretty Bush road. Once past the left-hand bend, they trotted up to the T junction. The children at Pretty Bush were playing a ball game in the middle of the road and, squealing, scattered to the sides of the road as the horses walked by. The sea spread out to their left, glistening blue in the sunlight. All too soon for Michael, they turned in Cornanagh's gates.

The yard was empty; Mick and Artie would be out checking the field horses and yearlings.

"That was the nicest ride I've had in years, Michael," Selina said, swinging her right leg over the pommel and kicking her left foot free of the stirrup.

Michael dismounted and reached up to assist Selina. She clasped his forearms as his hands circled her waist and smiled down at him as he lifted her from the saddle. He caught the scent of her light perfume, and the curve of her smiling mouth begged to be kissed. How he wanted to. Then, all too aware that he still had his hands about her waist, he released her abruptly. He stepped back and busied himself with the stirrup irons and undoing Emmett's girth, but his hands still tingled from the feel of her. He told himself not to be an old fool.

"Just leave Flirty Lady in her stable, and I'll get the tack," he said.

"What? Mr. Mac would turn in his grave. And think what a bad example it would be to Catriona." She led her mare to the tack room, ran the stirrup irons up, and stripped off the saddle, handing it to him.

"Just leave the bridle outside the stall, Selina. I'll collect it. And thank you for all your help today."

"It's been my pleasure, Michael. It's been a lovely day!"

He smiled back at her and wished that he weren't quite so out of practice in gallantries. With a final wave, she left the top yard. He let out a sigh for the fleeting moment he had held her in his arms, then shook his head and opened Emmett's stable door.

There had been nothing untoward in spending an afternoon in her company, he thought. But he reminded himself sternly that he was married, fifty-two, and had a grown family. Selina was also married and not yet thirty. He had never had much respect for men his age who got involved with younger women.

When he heard Selina's Lancia leave the yard, he roused himself and returned to the house, going at once to the small room on the ground floor that he used as an office. He had those bloody tax forms to complete. A self-imposed penance, he thought with a rueful grin. He must send in a cancellation for Conker, too. Because of the injury, he'd get a partial refund of the entrance monies. Every economy helped. Now, if Teasle showed to advantage and attracted a buyer, and the gelding should, he'd keep his bank manager happy as well.

Breeding and training horses was never a profitable occupation, though it could be: it should be. If only others would wake up to the potential of the Irish horse, establish standards, get decent facilities in which to show and sell the young stock, thoroughbred as well as three-quarter. Employ trainers to improve rider performances. And establish internationally recognized horse shows, with prize money amounting to six figures, instead of a miserly hundred pounds and a tacky trophy, to attract more of the top show jumpers and monied sponsors.

Then there'd be a reason for young people to choose horses as a career.

The problem with us Irish, he thought, is we're all chiefs with no indians. Can't work together toward a single goal like the Horse Bill, because everyone defines the goal differently and fights over the definition till Kingdom Come—Ulster being a prime example of that psychology.

He took down the heavy account ledgers, the manila envelope stuffed with notices from the tax collectors, found a pen that still had ink in it, and began his tedious calculations.

He was halfway through a column of figures when he heard the phone ring. And ring. He ignored it, wanting to finish, but the phone continued to ring. Where the hell was Bridie? Could the woman do nothing on her own without Isabel to prod her? Abruptly the ringing stopped, and a minute later someone tapped at the thick door, fortunately just as he finished the column.

"Yes, what the hell is it?" Michael knew that his temper frayed when he was forced to cope with figures.

"Daddy?" Catriona's voice quavered a bit.

"Yes, pet?"

"It's Mrs. Healey. For you."

As he opened the door he saw Catriona's anxious expression, so he ruffled her hair as he picked up the phone.

"Michael, I feel a right fool, but I think I've left my clutch bag there. Probably in the dining room"

"Not to worry," Michael replied, more pleased than he should be to hear her voice so unexpectedly. "Trina'll pop into the dining room and see if there's a spare purse lying about." And Catriona ran eagerly off.

"I changed rather a large check at the bank yesterday," Selina went on, "and I've been half-afraid the purse might have dropped out of the car when I got petrol. David called yesterday to tell me to be sure to have enough on hand because he's certain the banks'll be out next week."

"Will they so?"

"He has a weird habit of being right."

"We'll be in trouble if they do. Ah, yes, Trina's found it, Selina."

"What a relief!"

"I'll drop it in to you, shall I?" The offer was made before he was aware that this was an excuse to see her again, this almost magical day. He held the purse Catriona had given him as a talisman.

"Oh, would you?" She laughed. "I don't deserve such courtesy."

"Why not? About eight-thirty?"

"Grand! Most considerate of you, kind sir."

He replaced the phone and, damning himself for being all kinds of a fool, went back to the office and worked on taxes until almost tea time.

He showered and dressed, taking special, but not too noticeable, pains with his appearance. He had, he decided, not lost to age and weather the looks that had allowed him to cut quite a figure in the army. But then, Carradyne men aged well. His father had still been a very handsome fellow up till his death.

The evening meal was a pleasant one with only himself, Catriona, and Philip to enjoy the excellent shepherd's pie. Was it sheer coincidence that Bridie served them a strawberry fool for the sweet course? To be sure, Catriona was delighted and went through three helpings.

"It's never any good the second day," she said to excuse her greed.

The child—no, he must really start thinking of her as a girl, if not a young woman now—was in the best of spirits, and he found himself proud of her, as Selina was, that she'd been so resilient over her disappointment. He would give her a note to be absent from school three days during the Spring Show anyway. He needed her to work the Prince. Sean would only make a hames of it as he had last summer when his father made so much of bringing his friends to the Royal Dublin Show to watch his son ride. Catriona would keep the elegant pony light and relaxed until the very moment the class was called.

He'd deliver Selina's purse, he decided, come back to Willow Grove, have one drink, and then go home. An early evening, even an early Saturday evening, would do him no harm. And if Fiona happened to be there, well, that would solve that problem.

At first, standing at the door of the Healeys' rather splendid Georgian home, he thought that she might have changed her mind. But the outside light was on, so he was expected. He used the knocker the second time, in case the electric bell was out. He was about to give another stroke when the door opened and a rather breathless Selina stood there.

"I thought I'd heard the bell," she said, one hand appealingly at her throat. "Television!"

He handed her the purse, noticing that her dress was the right shade of red to accentuate her delicate complexion. Then he wondered if she always dressed so elegantly for an evening watching the tellie.

"Oh, do come in, Michael." She reclaimed the purse and gestured him in. "Or may I buy you a drink?" She waggled the purse as her bonafides to stand a round.

Michael hesitated, then hoped that moment's reluctance wasn't visible. He would have liked to come in the house for that drink, to be in her environment. But all things considered, discretion must prevail.

"By all means," he said affably, remaining where he was on the threshold.

"I'll just get a coat." She pulled open a cloakroom to the right of the front door. He stepped in then and took the camel's-hair coat. With a flick of his hand, which he was pleased to see he remembered, he arranged her shoulder-length hair to the outside of the coat. It was very silky, almost as fine as Catriona's. Yes, Michael, remember Catriona, home alone because her mother is ill in hospital. Remember also, Michael, that you live each day one at a time. And this is a remarkable day.

"Where's your local?" he asked as he handed her into the Austin.

She gave a little laugh. "I don't really have one in Dalkey. D'you? Or is the Queen acceptable?"

"Noisy. What about the Coliemore? Good view of Goat Island." He grinned at her, determinedly putting aside every reservation.

"A pub with a view! That's for me."

The Coliemore parking lot was crowded, but Saturday night was always a busy time for pubs. As he turned down a line, looking for a space, he suddenly spotted Eithne's little car. He braked in surprise, for she had distinctly told them she was going to her father's in Longford. She had even had an overnight case with her. But that was her car, dinged wing and all.

"This may be too crowded to get a drink," he remarked easily. "I'll just check." He gave her a fleeting grin and, leaving the gear in neutral, got out.

He entered the pub, its air blue with cigarette smoke, and scanned the crowd, looking for his sister-in-law. The car could have been stolen. Then he spotted her, seated at the far end of the bar, laughing with unusual vivacity with her companion, a rather stocky man. This, apparently, was not the time to find out what Eithne was doing here.

"Not a space anywhere. Sorry, Selina." He got back in the car and began to reverse.

"Where away now?" she asked.

"The Castle?"

"Grand!"

It was only a short drive up the road to the old Castle, during which Michael tried to assimilate the fact that Eithne, who was supposed to be in County Longford, dancing attendance to her impossible old father, was very definitely in County Dublin, being danced attendance on by a presentable man. Despite his slight embarrassment over finding Eithne out, he had to grin. That cagey minx. He wondered how often indeed she had gone dutifully to County Longford. How very convenient it was, too, that Gavaghan was far too miserly to be on the phone and thus accessible. Clever Eithne! And he'd never suspected. Nor, he was very sure, had Isabel.

There were plenty of spaces in the Castle parking lot, as the old place was not in vogue at the moment. Nor was the air in the lounge as tainted with smoke. They settled themselves in an empty booth.

"May I have a Carlsberg?" Selina asked, cocking her head at Michael.

"Of course."

"David says it's a plebeian drink, but I really enjoy a good lager."

"Then I'll join you."

When the barman returned with the lagers, Michael was so astonished to see Selina Healey put a five-pound note on the tray that he spluttered for a moment.

"Michael," she said in mock reproof, "I owe you a drink for saving my pelf that way."

"Saving your what?" He took the offending note and put it in front of her, reaching for his wallet. She stopped him, smiling up at the amused barman.

"When a lady offers to pay, she should be allowed the privilege, right?"

153

"Fine by me, lady," the barman said, grinning apologetically at Michael.

"Really, Selina . . ."

"Really, Michael!" She mimicked him perfectly, even to deepening her voice to his baritone level. "You shout for the next round. But a lady always keeps her promises!"

Rather than cause a fuss just then, Michael subsided until the barman had left.

"Is your male ego bruised?" Selina's eyes were sparkling with such devilment that he decided not to give her satisfaction and shook his head. "That was a rather nice sort you were riding this afternoon," she began. "Did you breed him?"

"Yes, he's another of Tulip's by a three-quarter-bred mare my father bought. Her last foal, in fact, which might account for why he is rather slow to develop."

"Big horses do take time to grow into themselves, but he's got a marvelous front on him. Does he jump?"

"Easily enough, but I've been concentrating on the flat work first."

"You are probably one of the few trainers in Ireland who do, outside of Sylvia Stanier."

"Loyal to Burton Hall?"

"Well, I *know* that crowd. I never got in with the Mespil Road people. What're you going to do with the gelding?"

"Bring him on this spring, put him in the Horse Show, and see if I can spin him off to the foreign buyers."

"Tut tut! Selling Ireland's best natural resource out of the country?"

"To the people who will give me a decent price for a made horse."

"My, we are touchy."

"It's a case, my dear Selina, of being damned if I do and broke if I don't. You know how people are: if you're making money, they carp about how unfair it is that you're making money and they're not. But if you're not well off, they criticize you for dossing about all the time."

"It's odd. I never have understood it."

"Have you had to?"

"Now, that's unfair, Michael Carradyne!" Then she saw that he was teasing her in turn. "Let's not have any more arguments," she growled at him. "What other youngsters are you breaking and making? Every time I've been down there recently, there're new faces staring at me over stall doors."

Michael was perfectly willing to talk about horses and their prospects, including those he was breaking for others. But he knew his own young stock best, the ones the Tulip sired. Cornanagh had five brood mares, though Frolic remained his own personal favorite, and most years there were five new foals to be reared. He generally sold them off as made horses at four and five; sometimes he kept an especially promising show jumper as an advertisement. Also as an abrasively consistent winner at the smaller shows to remind his detractors that Cornanagh bred the best in County Wicklow.

He told her about attending the *Dáil* debates on the Horse Board Bill, and his hopes for it.

"Actually," Selina said. "My father has always thought it was a pity something wasn't organized in Ireland to improve the standard of horses."

Michael grinned at her, signaling the barman for another round, and talked on. Until time was called, he was unaware that she had been adroitly encouraging him to continue with comments and questions.

"I am sorry, Selina, waffling on like that."

"Why? Because we talked horses all evening?"

"Because *I* talked horses all evening!"

"But I asked you." Her surprise was genuine. "I wanted to know. I hadn't properly realized just how involved you are. Oh, I knew from Tom Hardcastle that you kept one of the best livery stables in Wicklow, and I've certainly had no complaints about Flirty Lady in your care. Why, you're worse than Catriona. And she might outgrow it all. You haven't."

"It's a Carradyne failing." Michael tried to keep the bitterness out of his tone, but she caught it and quickly covered his hand with hers.

"I don't think it's a failing, Michael Carradyne. And I'm sorry to hear time called." She stood up, and he helped her with her coat.

They stepped out into the crisp spring evening and silently made their way to the car. As they drove back to Selina's house, Michael kept thinking of clever things he would like to say. But he could articulate nothing. He caught a glimpse of her profile in the streetlights and thought she looked sad or distant. He wasn't sure which and didn't want to chance his luck. He didn't drive at his usual clip because of his reluctance to end this day, to leave her company.

All too soon he had to turn the Austin into her driveway. He could, and did, escort her to the door, taking her keys to unlock it. He pushed it open, then put the keys back into her hand and held it.

"This has been a wonderful day, Selina."

She smiled up at him, starlight catching a gleam in her eye. "Yes, it has, Michael. Thank you." Before he guessed her intention, she stood on tiptoe and kissed his cheek, whirling away and into her house. "See you tomorrow!" came her cheerful call through the door.

Laughing to himself, shaking his head, but immeasurably pleased by her sauciness, he returned to his car. Once he had it straight on the road, he touched the spot on his cheek and smiled all the way back to Cornanagh.

A giggle penetrated Catriona's sleep. She'd lain awake a long time, listening to the house. She had never noticed how many noises the old house made at night when there was no one in it but herself. She wasn't nervous alone. She was thirteen and quite old enough to be left. She'd rather enjoyed having the telly all to herself and getting exactly what she wanted from the larder without needing to ask. She had felt very grown-up.

The giggling continued, and Catriona, clutching her quilt about her, went to the window. There was enough light for her to see Owen's Mini in the courtyard and two people making a very unsteady way to the mews house. The girl's idiotic laughter continued until closed off by the door. Then Catriona remembered Owen and a girl in bed, the day of Blister's last hunt. Auntie Eithne had been away on that occasion, too.

Catriona wasn't disturbed as she turned back to her bed, merely puzzled. But she knew that Owen was obviously doing something not quite on. It had to do with the whispering that went on among the fourth and fifth formers at Dominican. It had to do with why girls her age weren't allowed to read some books and why she wasn't allowed in the yard when the Tulip covered a mare. But she'd seen that anyhow and really wasn't much wiser.

She padded back to her bed, shivering at the cooled sheet and hugging herself until it had warmed up enough to lull her back to sleep.

❧ *14* ❧

*T*he ringing of the phone roused Catriona. She glanced
at her alarm clock, knuckling her eyes because she
couldn't quite believe the reading: six-fifteen?

She heard rapid footsteps and low cursing. Her father
wouldn't be best pleased awakened so early on a Sunday. She
yawned and snuggled back into her covers, but she was awake
now. She was also rather curious who would have the temerity
to ring Cornanagh when everyone knew that Sunday was a
morning to lie in.

She was compelled to get out of bed and go to the head of
the stairs. Her father replaced the receiver, missing the cradle
the first time. She couldn't see his face, but there was something about the way he stood that worried her.

"Daddy?"

At her soft voice her father looked up, and she could see
that the call had upset him. Sort of absently he tied the belt
of his robe and then began to climb the steps to her. Something
was terribly wrong. She wanted to ask him but didn't dare.
She just stood where she was, waiting for him. When he was
nearly to the top, on a level with her, he pulled her into his
arms. He hadn't done that in a long time, and she wasn't sure,
considering his expression, if she should embrace him.

"That was St. Gabriel's, Catriona. Your mother died just before six o'clock."

Catriona heard what he said, but the words did not make
sense.

"But Daddy, how could she die? She wasn't really sick. Everyone said so. You said so."

Her father, still holding her tightly, sat down on the top step
and gently transferred her to his lap. He pushed back her sleep-
tousled hair and stroked her cheek.

"They suspect a heart attack, Trina. They don't know yet for
certain. But all that fasting left her in a very weak condition.
She died in her sleep."

"Without the last rites?" Catriona was appalled, knowing how
much the sacrament would mean to her mother.

"No, she had those. And Father John had anointed her only
Thursday, and she'd taken Communion. She died in a state of
grace."

"But she died!" And suddenly Catriona had to believe this
awful news. Her mother had died!

The sobs came now, and she flung her arms about her father's neck, clinging to him as if never to let him go.

"What's going on?" demanded a sleepy Philip. "I wanted a
lie-in."

"Your mother died this morning, Philip."

"Oh, my God!" Philip sat down by his father. "How? Why?
She wasn't that ill, surely?"

Catriona barely heard what her father said, for all she could
think of was the door that she had not opened. She cried the
harder. She was still crying when her father carried her downstairs to the kitchen, where Philip made tea. Bridie was there,
weeping and moaning, alternately using her apron to dry her
face and smoothing its wet splotched surface over her hips.
She kept repeating, "Oh, the poor dear, the poor darling," as
if it were a litany.

Catriona managed to choke down the tea, but she couldn't
eat the porridge Bridie set before her. It had lumps, and Catriona pushed her spoon around in it, knowing she couldn't
get them past the lumps in her throat. By then Mick had arrived,

looking extremely ill at ease and clearing his throat constantly. He patted Catriona's shoulder in awkward sympathy. Then he finished a cup of tea so quickly she knew he burned his mouth.

"The horses," he said cryptically, and got out of the kitchen.

He'd need some help, Catriona thought, for Sunday was Artie's day off.

"And where are you going, Catriona Mary?" Bridie demanded as she slipped off her chair to follow Mick.

"To help Mick feed."

"Feed horses?" Bridie's words came out in a screech. "And your poor mother not even cold?"

"Bridie, for Christ's sake!" Philip shouted.

"If you'd been a proper daughter and done as your mother wished," Bridie went on, shaking her fist at Catriona, "she'd be alive this morning!"

Catriona stared at Bridie for one long, horror-stricken moment. Then she spun out the door and up to her room. Bridie knew! Bridie had said it aloud! Catriona had killed her mother.

She flung herself into her bed, writhing. If only she'd opened the door. Why hadn't she opened the door? She pounded at the bedclothes and pillows, wanting to tear them, howling and twisting. A hard hand connected with her cheek, and stunned, she lay there, panting, hiccuping over the sobs building up in her throat, staring up at her brother. Philip's face was pale and grim, the tears wet on his unshaven cheeks.

"Catriona Mary Virginia, you had nothing to do with Mother's death. Bridie's grief-stricken. She doesn't know what she's saying. I thought it was wonderful of you to remember that Mick would need help today."

Philip gathered her up in his arms, patting her and pushing back her tangled hair. "I'm sorry I had to slap you," he said, "but you'd gone hysterical."

"I should have opened my door, Pip, I should have. She wouldn't have collapsed like that. If she hadn't collapsed, she wouldn't have had to go to hospital. If she hadn't gone to hospital, she wouldn't have died. People die in hospitals."

Philip took a corner of her sheet to mop her face, and then his. "Catriona, Mother wasn't well. You did not cause her death!"

"But I didn't see her after. She didn't want me to come to see her."

"She wasn't seeing anyone, pet. Not just you. Not even Grandmother got to see her. The doctor said she had to have complete rest and quiet for a few days, remember?"

Neither heard the quick steps on the stairs, then Sybil erupted into Catriona's room. Seeing her sister, Catriona broke into fresh sobs.

"Thank God, you're here, Syb," Philip said. "I can't say anything to comfort her. She thinks she's responsible for Mother's death."

"How on earth can she think that?" Sybil eased her sister into her arms.

"Because I didn't open the door. I couldn't open the door. Oh, Sybil!"

"There now, Trina, there now, baby. Cry. We'll all cry together."

But Catriona couldn't stop. Finally, in desperation, Sybil phoned Dr. Standish, and he attended the limp and sobbing girl.

"I've given her a mild sedative," he said when he emerged from the room. "She'll sleep. Let her. It's the best way to ease the shock she's had. You've all had." He put his hand on Michael's arm, shaking his head. "While Isabel had seriously debilitated her system, there was absolutely no indication of serious heart or circulatory problems. There was nothing that would lead us to believe there would be complications. We now suspect an embolism. The autopsy will provide conclusive proof. All that lying in bed, no exercise." He shook his head again. "I'm sorry, Michael, truly sorry."

Between them, Michael and Philip informed everyone who would need to know. The most difficult was Mairead Marshall, who simply refused to believe that her daughter had died.

"What do you want to bet that she phones St. Gabriel's?" Philip asked, for he had kept his father company during that call.

"Nothing."

By now it was ten o'clock, and Michael sent a telegram to his son Jack in Nicaragua. He stood for a long moment then, his hand on the phone, wondering if Eithne would be at the Coliemore Hotel. He needed her help.

Then he heard a car in the courtyard and glanced out the window to see Selina's red Lancia. He took a stern hold on the jump of pure pleasure he felt. Yesterday's tranquillity belonged to the past and could not be reclaimed. But Selina might be able to sort Bridie out and console Catriona when she awoke. Just the sight of her slim figure in riding clothes heartened him.

"Oh, Michael, it's so awful," she said when she heard his grim news. She embraced him gently, kissing both cheeks and resting her hand lightly on his face in sympathy. "How's Catriona taking it?" And then Bridie set up a new crescendo of wailing. "Well, *that* won't help."

"I tore strips out of the woman when I heard what she said to Catriona, and she hasn't been quiet since. Do what you can, will you, Selina? The doctor's just been and given Trina a sedative. The poor child's shattered."

"Oh, she would be." Selina gave his hand a quick reassuring pressure before she strode toward the kitchen.

Michael decided to let all the horses out for the day, and Philip and Owen came out to help.

Wasn't it just like Isabel, Michael thought as he led the Tulip out to his paddock, to die two days before the spring show? He was appalled at the blasphemy, but he would not indulge in hypocrisies, he thought, in his own mind. Beside him, the Tulip, who usually cut shapes in the air on his way to pasture, walked with quiet dignity. He'd known when old Tyler had died and been subdued for weeks. Isabel would not at all appreciate being mourned by a horse! Michael opened the paddock gate, led the stallion through, and unclipped the lead rope. The Tulip walked on a few steps before he lowered his head to graze.

"They know, Captain dear," Mick said, nodding his head slowly as he came back from turning the ponies out. "They've a way of knowing. Sure they can do with a day out, exercise themselves."

He cast a sideways glance at his employer.

"Oh, we'll be at the show, Mick," Michael said. "Teasle and the Prince both have Wednesday classes. And for Trina's sake, I'm not drawing the funeral out any longer than I have to."

Mick made an affirmative noise deep in his throat.

Somehow, Selina had dealt with Bridie, and there was food on the kitchen table when the men came back into the house. By noontime, all his family in Ireland had arrived at Cornanagh: his oldest son, James, with his wife; Andrew in fatigues, having obtained emergency leave from his regiment to Curragh Barracks; his son-in-law, Aidan Roche, to help Sybil. His sister, Margaret, came, saying that her husband and children would pay their respects later in the day.

Owen had phoned his brother, Harry, but when he had tried to locate the phone number of John Gavaghan's nearest neighbor in Longford, Michael said that there was no point in upsetting Eithne with a long drive ahead of her. She'd be back by evening, and that was soon enough to know.

A subdued and sniffling Bridie helped Sybil, Margaret, and Selina serve the meal. Michael didn't feel like eating, no one did. Dr. Standish phoned after dinner to say that he had been able to arrange the autopsy for Monday and agreed that there was no reason to prolong matters past Tuesday.

Michael was speaking to his brother in the States when the cream-colored Mercedes of Robert and Mairead Marshall turned into the courtyard. He saw his mother-in-law step out, dressed all in black even to the veiled hat on her white and stylishly dressed hair.

"The Marshalls just drove in, Eamonn," he said quickly.

"Christ, Mick, I don't envy you that," Eamonn replied. "Look, I'll come, and I'm sure Paddy will. I'll ring him. Save you another transatlantic call. See you tomorrow."

"Dad?" Philip bounced into the hall, jerking his thumb over his shoulder.

Michael handed him the receiver. "Try the Australian Marshalls again, Pip. Eamonn at least will be coming."

Mairead Marshall accused her son-in-law of causing her daughter's death. He had neglected a fine woman—loyal, Christian, devout, the pillar of the Irish Countrywoman's Association, the instigator of all good works in the community, the most devoted mother and most maligned wife, struck down in her prime, a tragedy of tremendous proportion. Michael endured it, though several times he had to catch Sybil's or Margaret's indignant glance as one or the other started to come to his defense. He recognized Mairead Marshall's need to vent her sorrow and blame, and it was preferable she do it now, in the privacy of the immediate family, rather than during the funeral.

Nothing the woman accused him of could restore life to her daughter, his wife, and he excused her to himself, knowing how close she had been to Isabel. Far too close for their marital relationship to have had any chance of improving. Isabel was—had been—very like her mother in so many ways. Michael sighed. Some very clever man had said one could see the daughter in the mother, only Michael would never have believed the truth of it during his courtship of the charming Isabel Marshall. She had been such a lovely girl. And it had seemed important for him to have her as his very own before he marched off to war. In truth, he had never had her, though she had spent thirty-three years as his wife and had borne him six children. And that was the pity of it all.

"Michael, attend me when I'm speaking to you." Mairead's voice cut through his wandering thoughts.

"I'm sorry." He waved his hand in a helpless gesture. "It's hard to keep my mind on anything."

"I asked you, Michael"—her voice had softened,—"what plans have been made."

Michael exhaled. "The usual. Autopsy tomorrow . . ."

"Autopsy? On my daughter?" Good old Mairead, defending her daughter's sanctity and the family honor to the last. "Why, I've never heard such nonsense."

"The exact cause of death has to be established," he said wearily. "Dr. Standish has at least been able to arrange it for tomorrow so that Isabel can be buried on Tuesday."

Mairead's eyes bulged and she half rose from the straight-backed Victorian chair. "On Tuesday? That is unseemly! Are we to be given no chance to mourn our dead? Why, her brothers in Australia could scarcely get here by Wednesday."

"They can't come in any case, Grandmother," Philip said, speaking for the first time since he had entered the drawing room. "I phoned all the uncles. They send their deepest sympathy, and there'll be Masses said for Mother."

"Nonetheless, Michael Carradyne, Tuesday is out of the question."

"Tuesday it will be, Mrs. Marshall," Michael replied with quiet authority. "I'm not having Catriona endure more than is necessary."

Mairead suddenly sat even more erect than ever, glancing about her. "And just where is Catriona?"

"Asleep, Grandmother," Sybil said almost defiantly. "Dr. Standish gave her a sedative."

"I do not approve of giving sedatives to children."

"Neither does he," Sybil replied, "but we all felt it was better than hysterics. Trina is inconsolable."

"And so she should be, losing her mother at such a critical age. I shall give her future considerable thought."

"And why should you do that?" Michael asked.

Mairead Marshall fixed her son-in-law with a hard stare. "She will need sensible guidance from a mature woman over these next few months."

"She will have that at Cornanagh, where she shall stay." Michael spoke emphatically. "Eithne is devoted to Catriona."

"So am I," Sybil said, sitting as erect as her grandmother.

Just then Selina appeared in the doorway, with an apologetic smile to the assembled family. "The phone, Michael. It's Murphy's of Bray."

It would be almost a relief to talk to the undertaker, Michael thought as he excused himself from the room. Once the door was closed behind him, he caught Selina's arm. "How's Catriona?"

"Still asleep."

"Selina, do me a favor? Stay with Catriona. I'd rather she didn't see her grandmother right now."

"Wise of you," she replied, and, drying her hands on a tea towel, went softly up to Catriona's room. She had crept up to see her before the noon meal as well, and had almost burst into tears.

Catriona was curled up on her side now, sheet white and vulnerable, one tear lingering on the long fringe of lashes, so black against the pallor of her skin. Selina thought she seemed to be sleeping more peacefully. A car drove into the courtyard, and Catriona moved restlessly at the noise. Selina heard the house door open and the low voices of people offering condolences.

She sat down at Catriona's desk, idly scanning the titles of the few books on the shelf, smiling that all of them were about horses. She ran a finger down the spine of *National Velvet*, already well used though she knew it had been a birthday gift. Idly Selina took down the Pony Club Manual next to it. The binding was broken, and the book fell open to a page, much embellished by pencil sketches of horse hooves from various perspectives. Surprised and delighted, Selina riffled through and found that the beginnings of each new chapter, having more white space, featured remarkably accurate line drawings of horses.

She glanced over at the sleeping girl. Catriona sketched? And she was talented. Biting her lip against an invasion of a young girl's private things, Selina removed the sketch pad from under the schoolbooks on the desk.

She stifled a gasp at the drawings within, for most were of a clearly identifiable Conker: his head from many different angles, half a dozen sketches of him peering over his stall door. With an economy of line, Catriona had captured the essential inquisitiveness of the pony, the bright mischief in his eyes and his elegance. There were many more sketches of him cavorting in the fields, soaring over the gorse bush or standing at the field gate, neck outstretched for a treat. Selina felt a pang of regret when she came to blank pages and flipped through to the end. She was rewarded by two more sketches.

These must be of Blister, for she remembered the delicate Connemara ears of the dead pony. The pencil lines were not as decisive as those of Conker. Almost as if—as if, without the model, the memory of the loving eye had faltered.

Oh, dear Catriona, dear dear Catriona, Selina thought, pressing the sketch pad to her chest and rocking it as she would have liked to rock, and comfort, her young friend.

Catriona began to stir, muttering and moaning a bit in her sleep. "I'll open it. I'll open it!" Selina rushed to Catriona's bed. The girl sat up, staring around her with frightened, unfocused eyes.

"Mrs. Healey?" Tears welled immediately into Catriona's blue eyes.

"I'm here, pet." Selina put her arms about the thin body.

"Mother didn't want to see me. I never saw her again!"

"Catriona, none of us know why people are suddenly taken from us. Sometimes it doesn't make sense at all. But your mother is dead, and not all the tears or all the earnest prayers of the world can bring her back to life. I didn't know your mother well, but I'm sure she wouldn't want you to make yourself sick with grief."

"She wanted me to give up horses. That's why she was fasting." A sob shook Catriona, and Selina hugged her more tightly.

"Catriona Carradyne," she said, giving the thin shoulders a little shake as she held the girl from her, "she may have, believing that she knew what was best for you. But you're not at all like your mother. You're your father's child, a child of Cornanagh and all it represents. That much I do know. I also know that it is wrong to force someone into being what they are not. I'm positive that your mother would have come to recognize this in time."

"No, she wouldn't have." Catriona's voice was sullen. "She hated horses. She didn't understand anything about horses. She didn't like me."

Selina gave her another shake. "Don't say such things, Trina. Your mother did love you, or she wouldn't have worried so about your future. She may not have liked horses, but she loved *you*. And she'd have come round. Really, she would. I would have helped there all I could. I want to help you now. And I want you to stop thinking of all the things you didn't do and didn't say to your mother. I want you to think of the good things and happier times you shared."

She caught the angry expression on Catriona's face. "And don't, for God's sake, Catriona, go on blaming yourself for something you didn't do." Selina spoke almost sharply, remembering keenly her own feelings of remorse when her mother had died. She'd been older than Catriona was now but equally unable to deal with the loss.

"Catriona, I'm going to ask you an unfair and difficult question. If your mother came to the door right now"—she was appalled by Catriona's sudden rigidity—"if your mother asked you to agree never to sit on another horse as long as you lived, what would you say?"

Catriona stared up at Selina, her eyes wide. She swallowed and slowly began to shake her head. Then she collapsed against Selina, weeping with a quiet desperation, her fingers digging into Selina's arms. Selina rocked her slowly, stroking the fine soft black hair.

When the sobs began to ease, she held Catriona away from her.

"Now, wash your face, pet. And we'll have no more 'what ifs' and 'if onlys.' There's no time for them now. There are several very difficult days for you to get through. I'll help you all I can, but a lot of it you have to do for yourself, mostly by recognizing that your mother has died and that there is nothing you can do to change that."

❧ 15 ❧

W hat Catriona remembered most about the next few days was the endlessness of it all and the headache she had from so much weeping. And so many people, few of whom she knew or remembered, coming in and out of the house. She heard Auntie Eithne remark constantly what a consolation is was that so many people called to pay their respects. Catriona only fretted, having to be available to receive the condolences, and the pitying glances, the deep sorrowful sighs. But she learned the responses expected, even that a sad "thank you" often sufficed all by itself. Either her Aunt Eithne or Selina were with her: Auntie Eithne in the house and Selina in the yard. And Selina had asked her to use her Christian name.

She had some time with Conker and had to ride the Prince, for he had to be exercised each morning before he was taken into the RDS. Bridie had compressed her lips in a thin disapproving line when she saw Catriona dressed in riding clothes Monday morning, but a look from Michael had quelled comment.

The horses were worked early in the morning before anyone was likely to call in with condolences. Buoyed by Selina Healey's reassurances and her presence, Catriona had been able to ride without qualms. The exercise had done her good, to which even Bridie had sourly agreed, for there was color in Catriona's face and more animation. She was also able to eat a full bowl of smooth porridge.

On Monday afternoon when her mother's body was brought

home and the coffin installed in the drawing room, Catriona
was accompanied by the entire family to pay her last respects.
Seeing her mother laid out, her face smoothed by death, Catriona felt oddly relieved. She'd never seen a dead person
before; she hadn't been allowed to see her grandfather. Her
mother looked so peaceful, hands clasped over her chest, the
rosary twined in her fingers. Her mother looked asleep or
deeply immersed in prayer.

Prayer hadn't done her mother much good, had it? The
thought came unbidden to Catriona's mind, and she burst into
tears. Her father led her out of the drawing room and into the
lounge, where he held her in his arms until her weeping
stopped.

"Here, pet," he said, handing her one of his big white hand-
kerchiefs to mop her face and blow her nose. "That's over with
now."

"You mean, I don't have to—" she faltered, "to go in again?"

"Only if you want to, Trina. Only if you want to."

Philip returned from the airport with his uncles and, despite
the sorrowful occasion, the atmosphere in the house lightened.
They were full of the tale of having to fly through London as
the Aer Lingus flight direct to Dublin had been booked solid.

Uncle Eamonn was indeed a blurred, slightly smaller, and
definitely plumper copy of her father, thought Catriona. He
had an odd habit of swinging one foot, twitching it almost
constantly, and he smoked cigarette after cigarette.

Uncle Patrick wasn't as fat as Uncle Eamonn. He had the
same Carradyne black curly hair, but his eyes were more gray
than blue. He wore a continuous half smile as if everything
amused him slightly. And the things he said! Catriona couldn't
believe her ears and didn't know if she was supposed to laugh
or not. Philip did, and so did Selina and Eithne, and occasionally her father smiled.

She liked Uncle Patrick, but she didn't feel as comfortable

with him as she did with Uncle Eamonn. Catriona also urgently wanted to ask her uncle Eamonn something, but she didn't because she was afraid of the answer she would get. Her cousin Patricia's visit this summer seemed tremendously important to her now, and she didn't know why.

The next day, Tuesday, the fifth of May, was one of the worst days of Catriona's life. What she remembered most about it was the mountains of flowers. She would always associate their almost sickening scent with her mother's funeral.

She and her father, Mick, Harry, and Philip had ridden out at six and set the yard to rights. "Before anyone could possibly be up and about," Philip had said, trying to lighten the sadness that permeated the yard and house.

Catriona walked beside her grandmother Marshall behind her mother's coffin from the house to the church. Her father was on her other side. Her grandmother took her hand and held it in a grip that seemed to tighten with every step nearer the church. Catriona did not dare complain, especially after she saw her grandmother's face. Tears streamed down an otherwise expressionless countenance and dripped unregarded onto the black silk front. Catriona looked down, at the tarmacadam road, at her feet, at the tight toes of her Easter shoes. They had already raised raw blisters. She let the pain of her feet overcome the pain of her clasped hand. It wasn't a long way to walk.

As they filed up the aisle behind the coffin borne on the shoulders of her brothers and uncles, her grandmother released her hand to cross herself. The next thing Catriona knew, Eithne was gently pushing her to follow Sybil into the front pew, and she was separated from her grandmother. Her brothers and her uncles filed into the pew behind her, and that was comforting. She knelt with everyone else but could not pray. She didn't know what to pray. Nothing seemed suitable.

She didn't look around her, but she could feel the press of people and knew that the church was crowded. Obscurely this comforted her. Then the solemn Requiem Mass began. She followed the first part, but a terrible pounding started in her head, and the heavy scent of the flowers began to nauseate her. She had to concentrate very hard to keep from being sick. There was no way she'd be allowed to leave the church during her own mother's Requiem Mass. She swallowed and swallowed and found a prayer: not to be sick here, now.

Then it was time for Father John to give the eulogy, and although at no time did Catriona dare look at him, he didn't sound as formidable as he had a week ago. As he praised the selflessness of Isabel Virginia Catriona Marshall Carradyne, her indefatigable energy, her charity, her contributions to the church and the community, tears began to trickle from Catriona's eyes, and the headache eased a bit.

Finally it was over, and Catriona stood squarely behind Auntie Eithne so that she didn't have to watch them carry the coffin back down the aisle. Then Sybil, who was crying quietly, touched her shoulder, and she realized that Auntie Eithne was already in the aisle, following her grandmother, grandfather, and her father.

She was in a sort of daze now, walking with her head down. She could hear subdued weeping around her and sighs, and the shuffling of feet. She looked up involuntarily when they emerged into the overcast day. She was astonished to see people standing about the old graveyard beside the church and people out in the road and in the parking lot. She had never seen so many people, not even for Easter or Christmas Day.

They carried the coffin all the way to the new cemetery on the hill near Cornanagh. She watched the first time the bearers changed and was amazed that no one lost step, nor did the coffin, with its blanket of flowers, so much as tilt. It would have been simply awful if someone had dropped the coffin and her mother had spilled out. Catriona gasped and began to cry because these weren't at all the sort of thoughts she should be having today. She felt someone's arm about her shoulder, and a clean handkerchief was offered.

And then they were right by the open grave with the coffin laid on the ropes that would lower it out of sight. There were masses of flowers, and despite the open air, the scent brought on her nausea again. She concentrated on her throbbing feet and made it recede.

She wasn't at first aware of Father John's voice. It was only when her brothers and cousins stepped forward and began lowering the coffin into the ground that she realized she ought to have been listening. They were putting her mother in the ground, and that grave would not be opened again until Judgment Day. Not opened as she had not opened her door!

At that point all strength left her legs, and she sank to the ground, sobbing.

Someone picked her up, and she was hurried through the crowd, which parted instantly. Then she was being handed into a car, and she heard her Auntie Eithne telling the driver to take them back to Cornanagh.

"Selina!" her aunt cried when they came to a stop in the courtyard and Selina, who had decided not to attend the interment, appeared in the door.

Together they carried Catriona into the lounge and laid her down on the red leather couch.

"I don't think she fainted, Selina, but it was just too much to ask of the child."

"Oh, my God!" Selina exclaimed because she had removed Catriona's shoes. "Will you just look at this?"

Catriona opened her eyes.

"You idiot! Why on earth didn't you tell us those shoes were too small?" Selina glared down at her.

"But those shoes are new," Eithne said. "Isabel bought them just before Easter. Catriona, why ever didn't you say something?"

"I don't know," Catriona replied, rather surprised that her two supporters had become so angry at her.

"Listen to me, Catriona Carradyne," Auntie Eithne said, her face stern as she pointed severely at the bloody toes. "If those blisters have anything to do with a self-imposed penance or something stupid like that, I'll take you across my knee!"

"Penance?" Selina asked.

"There's been enough of that in this house," Eithne said, "and we're having no more. Not while you're in my care, young lady. Now, you just work off those socks while I get the plasters."

When her aunt had left the room, Catriona grinned.

"And what's so amusing?" Selina demanded.

"Auntie Eithne can't stand the sight of blood."

"Well, I can. You lie back. This will hurt." Then Selina added, with a ripple of laughter in her voice, "Regard it as a penance for your folly."

By the time people began to return to the house for the cold meal Selina and Bridie had laid out in the dining room, Catriona had soft socks and house slippers on, the afghan tucked around her and orders not to leave the couch. She was brought a cup of tea and a plate of sandwiches. Her uncles and brothers came in to see how she was doing, and Andrew stayed with her. Mother hadn't liked him much, either, because he'd insisted on joining the army instead of going into law. Catriona tucked her hand through his arm when people stopped in to talk to them.

After four cups of tea, Catriona had to excuse herself. There was someone in the downstairs loo and, when she crept painfully up the stairs, someone occupying the bathroom. Her need to go was severe, and as there was no one in the hall, she managed to get out of the house undetected. She made a bee-line for the yard and the first empty stable and relieved herself in the straw.

In the yard she hesitated, not wanting to reenter the house, not while there were all those people trying to console her. She left the yard and slipped down to the Ride gate and out, avoiding the worst of the mud to keep her house slippers dry.

The Tulip came charging up to the fence as she passed his paddock. He waggled his head from side to side, nickering, plainly asking why she had neglected him these past days. She pulled several handfuls of grass from the unmowed verge and presented them to him.

Conker was waiting at the field gate, a burlap sack and plastic protecting the injured sole.

"Did Tulip warn you I was coming?" she asked him, holding out her hand for him to blow into. Lovingly she straightened his forelock and finger-combed his mane to lie all on the one side.

He blew into her hand again, not looking for food as much as saying that he had missed her.

"Not as much as I have, Conker," she said, and buried her face against his mane.

He stood quietly then, though she could hear the flick of his tail.

"You know something's wrong, don't you? Mother's dead, Conker."

She cried once more, against the neck of her patient pony, clinging to him. Then suddenly she felt prickly hairs on her arm and the warmth of breath. Startled, she looked up and saw Tulip's Son beside her.

"Hello there," she said softly, gulping back the last of her sobs and slowly extending her hand to the colt.

He snuffled into it and then tried to bite her flat palm, his hairs tickling it.

"Don't be cheeky now," she said reprovingly. Ears flattened against his head, he made to bite the air and, with a flick of his scut of a tail, wheeled and charged back to his mother.

Catriona stayed with Conker, fussing with his mane until Mick came to check on the field horses.

❧ 16 ❧

For once the weather cooperated and the Wednesday of the Spring Show 1970 was blessed for the most part with sunny skies. The few showers did not dampen the general public and certainly had no effect on the competitors. Early that bright morning, Catriona went in to the Royal Dublin Society grounds with her father, her brother, and Mick. They'd been up since dawn, setting the yard to rights, which, as Philip had said gaily, was not a chore on such a gorgeous day.

Artie and Mick had brought Teasle and the Prince in on time on Monday evening, and they had passed the veterinary with no problem. Artie was staying with the horses, a job Mick had happily resigned in his favor. As it happened, both the Prince's and Teasle's competitions were scheduled for the same hour, ten A.M. Her father muttered all the way in about which competition to attend until Philip reminded him that he was quite capable of showing Teasle well, so there was no real dilemma.

"On the other hand," Philip went on, grinning delightedly, "young Sean is scareder of you than he is of either the pony or his father. Maybe you'd better leave him to the tender mercies of Mick and Trina. The Dohertys will be none the wiser."

Catriona and Mick held their breath for the reply, but Michael Carradyne said he'd wait and see.

Because of the early hour, Michael had no trouble finding a parking spot on Simmonscourt Road close to the turnstile entrance at Gate H. Just inside the gate there was a bustle of activity as grooms and handlers were emptying their wheelbarrows and muck sacks into the loader to be taken from the grounds before the general public arrived. To their left was Sandymount Hall, where three-year-olds and Connemara ponies were stabled. Ballymore Prince was in the Anglesea Stables, underneath the main stands overlooking the Jumping Enclosure.

Following his son's advice—"for the first time," Philip added, with a grin—Michael Carradyne and Philip turned off at Simmonscourt Hall, where Teasle was, while Mick and Catriona continued on to the Prince.

They passed the jumping exercise ring, where three horses were being schooled. Across the walkway was the timbered elegance of Pembroke Hall, loud with bawling cattle, the famous RDS clock on its northeast corner. To the left was Ring Number Three, smaller than One and Two, where the major showing classes were always held, and generally set aside for warming up the show class entries. Then came the Tudor-style Industries Hall.

Catriona vowed that she'd visit there today, because for the first time she was considered old enough to go by herself. She touched the zip pocket of her birthday anorak and felt the comfortable bulge of her small hoard of shillings and pence. Then she and Mick turned into the Anglesea Stables.

Artie's smile was somewhat hesitant, but when he saw Catriona's cheerful grin, he brightened.

"They're watered, fed, hayed, mucked out, and I lunged the Prince like the captain told me."

"How long didja lunge 'im?" Mick was not about to give out any compliments.

"Thirty minutes, just like I was told."

"Have you had any breakfast yet, Artie?" Catriona asked, thinking that he sounded testy.

"Too busy."

"Ya gobshite, go get something in your belly," Mick said,

thrusting a ten-shilling note at him. "Now, Cat, we'll get this pony slicked up."

It was such a relief to Catriona to be busy again after the enforced idleness of the last three days. She pushed away the sad thoughts that threatened to bring the ever-ready tears, picked up the body brush, and began to groom the Prince. By eight-thirty the pony was plaited, mane and tail, and his dark bay coat glowed silkily—by using elbow grease, not the furniture polish the lad across the aisle had sprayed on his pony. The Prince's hooves were polished and the white of his fetlocks immaculate. So Mick sent Catriona down to look at the F course, which was still being built when she got to the main Jumping Enclosure.

Between shows, she forgot just how immense the main arena of the Royal Dublin Showgrounds really was. Daunting, and beautiful. The variegated privet hedging was neatly trimmed, and there were displays of spring flowers around the edges. She smiled to herself as she walked out on the springy grass surface. Her grandfather had always had a chuckle about the RDS hedging since privet was poisonous to horses and not all the fools knew it.

The various stands, the Anglesea to her right was newer than the Grand Stand Enclosure on her left, where the notables sat, and the members stand was beyond it. Across the end were the elevated private boxes, where the embassies would hold parties during the August Show, especially on the Friday of the Aga Khan Challenge Trophy. She felt a shiver for remembered excitements, then turned her attention to the course being laid out, every pole gleaming with fresh paint and the rustics set with evergreens.

She could see that there'd be some racing to do between fences, for the course was spread out over the three-hundred-foot length and one-hundred-and-fifty-foot width of the enclosure. There was a treble halfway through the sixteen fences and a double. That was to be expected. However, she didn't feel that the obstacles would be all that difficult, even if spaced out; certainly they were well within the Prince's abilities, for he had a good deal of scope. That wretched stile gate was just like the one the Prince had refused last May, but they'd been schooling him over narrow obstacles, so he ought not to balk this year.

The final wall, beautifully decorated with urns full of flowers, was deceptive. And high. She went up to it: it had to be four feet, for it was as high as her shoulder now and would probably go up for the final round. Oh, well, she had often jumped Prince that height.

Others were now inspecting the course, and she watched those who were pacing between the fences. She counted their strides, checking her own assessment.

"How's the course?" Mick asked her when she returned.

"Well." Catriona thought it over. "Nothing that the Prince hasn't jumped at home. Just in a different order."

"Then where's the lad?" Mick grumbled. "The Captain told him nine sharp so they could walk it twice if need be. And he'd need to."

There was now considerable activity about them in the boxes of all the jumping ponies. Catriona craned her neck towards the entrance, looking for Sean's stocky figure. What she did see pleased her far more: Mrs. Healey, stylish in an elegant gray wool suit, coming their way between her father and another, heavyset man. The man was walking with his chin up so that he was looking down at everything. Her father, his tweed hat at a jaunty tilt, was smiling at something Mrs. Healey had just said. That made Catriona feel even better. Maybe this would be a good show, and Teasle'd bring a big price. Cornanagh needed a bit of luck today.

"David, this is Catriona," Selina Healey said. "Catriona, this is Mr. Healey."

He gave a brief smile, looking anywhere but at her. "My sympathies, Catriona, on your terrible loss."

Catriona murmured something polite and felt obliged to curtsey.

"I told Mr. Healey how very grateful we all are for Selina's help over the last few days," her father said, placing a gentling hand on his daughter's shoulder.

"Very grateful," Catriona murmured.

"The least I could do," Selina said, smiling reassuringly at her.

"Well, now, Selina, Carradyne, I've an appointment." David Healey glanced at the very expensive gold watch on his wrist as if to prove that he had to leave. "This damned bank strike! Hope you prepared for it, Carradyne?" When her father nodded solemnly, he plowed right on. "Calm heads are needed, sensible compromises. Could go on for months. Obstinate bastards. Ruin the country. Well, I must be off. Keep an eye on her, Carradyne." He favored them all with a quick smile before he leaned down to kiss his wife's cheek—just the way her mother had always kissed her father in public, Catriona thought.

Selina turned to them and brightened as he strode off. "Oh, you've got the Prince looking splendid, Catriona, Mick."

"I caught Artie leaving the cafe, Mick, and sent him to help Philip," her father said. "There've been two people inquiring about Teasle."

"Teasle looks marvelous today with all the show polish. Not that he's a patch on the Prince." She winked at Catriona, then dropped her voice. "Ah, and here is young Sean, the sheep to the slaughter."

"Selina!" Michael said.

She reorganized her expression but winked again at Catriona. "Oh, Lord, will you look at the delegation?"

They all turned and saw the gaggle of fashionably dressed

adults that followed Sean. Catriona made herself as invisible as possible to one side of Mrs. Healey. Mr. and Mrs. Doherty, whom she knew, the grandparents, and three business gentlemen beamed and looked about them as they proceeded down the aisle. There were loud guffaws as the entire party had to wait for a fractious pony to be led out.

"Trina, as soon as I've taken Sean to walk the course with me," her father said in a low voice, "take the Prince to the practice ring and work him in. Got your hard hat?" She nodded, for she was dressed properly in jods and boots and a white shirt, wearing her new anorak. Her father wouldn't permit jeans even if she was only work-riding the Prince. Then the Doherty contingent was upon them.

Catriona had to endure yet another spate of condolences and Sean offering her his moist and fleshy hand to shake, muttering something about being so sorry for her.

"Well, and how's the Prince today, Carradyne?" Mr. Doherty said, rubbing his hands together. "Going to make us all proud, eh, Sean?"

Catriona wished she could like Mr. Doherty because he always paid the livery bills on time, but he had an alarmingly florid face and thick fingers like sausages. He looked stuffed into his tweed jacket. His wife was indulging in light conversation with one of the businessmen. He looked as if he were afraid a horse would drop something on him, and Catriona sort of wished that one would.

"As you see," Michael Carradyne gestured toward the pony, who was ducking his head, trying, Catriona thought, to get his tongue over the bit. The dropped nose band Mick had just tightened made that impossible.

"He's so elegant," Mrs. Doherty said. "That should impress the judges."

Her father gave Mrs. Doherty a reassuring smile, forbearing to mention it was performance that mattered.

"Sean is number twelve, and they'll be jumping in numerical order. Sean, we'll be off to walk the course. This way, Bob, Aisling, gentlemen." Thus her father began to shepherd the group out of the stable block.

Giving the others a head start, Catriona and Mick then led the pony down, one on either side of his head. He went quietly enough.

There were by now a respectable number of spectators strolling about the Show Grounds. Catriona could see her father's tall figure, Sean and Mrs. Healey beside him, as they made their way to the pocket entrance of the Jumping Enclosure. Then Mick was giving her a leg up, and she could feel the tension in the pony.

"Nice and easy, Cat. Don't let him get flustered. Sean'll do that right enough." Mick always sounded disgusted just before a competition: his way of warding off evil. Once in the practice ring, she began to trot Prince quietly around the outside track, sparing a glance for the other ponies. She recognized some of the northern riders now, and they were really the ones Sean must beat. The Prince was behaving, Artie's lunging had helped settle him. She indicated she wanted to take the jump next and trotted him up to the crossed poles, gave with her hands as he jumped it, then let him canter on a few strides afterward before bringing him back to the trot again.

Someone came out to raise the top pole, but the next jumper rolled it off. His rider gave him what-for, but Catriona thought he'd dropped the contact two strides out, so what else did he expect?

The clock on the tower was a tick away from ten. Teasle's class was about to start, too, in Ring One, and Philip would be warming him up.

She put the Prince back into a trot and then, in her turn, took him neatly over the fence, changing the rein and coming back over the fence the other way. Then she saw her father and Sean, just the pair of them at the rails. She reined the pony in and nodded to Mick to open the gate for her.

"He's grand and easy today, Sean. Artie lunged him good this morning. You'll do just fine," she said.

Sean swallowed, jerked at his right sleeve where his number was tied, then took the reins she offered him.

"Catriona's right, Sean, you'll do just fine. Those fences are just like the ones you've been jumping all spring on the Ride." Her father gave him a buffet on the shoulder and held the Prince's head as Sean mounted.

Catriona was not the only one to see the pony prick his ears forward at the change of riders. Please, Prince, she thought, give Sean a break for once.

"Just trot him around, Sean, and then in your own time jump the practice fence," her father said.

"Isn't it pretty big?"

"No bigger than the one you were jumping Saturday. All the open space here makes everything seem bigger than it is. Just pretend you're jumping down the alley."

As Sean nudged the Prince forward, Catriona noticed Mick's raised eyes and her father's almost imperceptible shake of his head behind the lad's back.

"Captain"—Artie was beside them, pointing toward Ring One, where the horses were now filing in—"them men want to know more about Teasle."

"The Italians?"

"Well, they're foreigners. Phil says would you come. And your brothers is here, too."

"Damn!" Her father looked at Sean, trotting collectedly around the practice ring.

"Sure, go on, Captain," Mick said. "They're only up to number six. Catie'll beckon you when we're called."

Her father went off with Artie, and Catriona crossed her fingers for Teasle. She saw her uncles over at Ring One, leaning on the rails by Mrs. Healey and her cousins to watch Teasle's class.

Oops, the Prince was bucking. She heard Mick's swift intake of breath and held her own, but, for a miracle, Sean managed. He wasn't really such a bad rider, she thought; all he lacked was self-confidence.

Then the steward was calling number twelve, and Sean looked about him with frantic indecision. Mick gestured for her to go fetch her father and went to the Prince's head, walking beside the pony into the pocket, to be ready for his turn to jump.

When she found him, her father excused himself to the Italians. They looked very prosperous, festooned with binoculars and cameras, and she also thought they were horsemen, the way they were focusing their attention on horse bodies and legs rather than on riders.

She and her father got to the pocket in time to see Sean trotting the Prince into the ring. Catriona stole a look at the intense concentration on her father's face. She felt the same way.

Sean did remember to salute the judges, though the nervous bob of his head was far too quick to be proper. He remembered to canter the Prince in a wide settling circle until the starting bell. He seemed to remember the course with no hesitation, looking on to the next fence each time he landed. He even managed to check the pony as they came round to the treble, and he didn't chuck him in the mouth once as they came down the final stretch. It was then Catriona realized Sean had a death grip on the pony's mane. And his eyes were closed.

Her father moved forward as the steward flung the gate open, and the pony dived for a familiar face.

"You did very well, Sean, very well indeed, a good clear round," her father said, clapping the Prince on the neck in approval. "Good lad." Catriona wasn't sure if her father meant the pony or the boy.

Then Sean opened his eyes, his face white.

"Down you get now."

"I gotta go. Where can I go?" The last word was slightly anguished, and her father, one hand about Sean's shoulders, guided him quickly out of the pocket.

Mick ran the stirrups up and threw the sheet over the pony, who was still dancing about with excitement. "Walk him, wouldja, Cat? I'll just pop round and see how it's going for Philip with your father occupied so."

Catriona walked the Prince, patting his neck and telling him what a grand fellow he was to take Sean about so cleverly, and he was to do it again. Mick returned, grinning broadly.

"Them Italian characters don't look at any other horse. I watched 'em good. Now, up you get on Prince and back into the practice ring. If he starts to charge, collect him. You know how he tends to flatten over fences at speed."

By the time Mick signaled her to bring the Prince out, her father was again in deep conversation with the Italians.

Philip was just being pulled up in second position when Mick signalled her to bring the Prince out. Sean, waiting in the pocket, still looked awfully white.

"Sean, that was such a great round. I knew you could do it. Go in there and show 'em all!" She grinned up at him.

"You'll do just great, Sean," Mick added.

"I don't see the captain." Sean glanced wildly about him.

"He's coming, Sean, he's coming, but you have to go in now," Mick said, and gave the Prince a whack on the rump. The pony spurted forward, leaving his rider behind in the saddle, and then they were in the Enclosure once again.

Catriona wrung her hands together as the Prince charged past the starting line; beside her Mick was groaning. She wasn't sure what happened then because she could only see Sean's back and the Prince's high-held head as they went over the jumps. Sean must be glued to the reins, chucking the pony in the mouth over every obstacle. Then the pony came across the arena for the treble, and she could see that she was right. But the Prince was jumping, and he wasn't going to let a little thing like a paralyzed rider stop him. Sean did remember to steer a bit, enough to keep the Prince in the proper direction. Otherwise the pony did it all. He clattered back into the pocket, looking exceedingly pleased with himself.

"You did it, Sean, you did it." Catriona was jumping with relief and delight, slapping the Prince's neck as Mick hauled him to a stop. "I'm so proud of you, Sean."

"Open your eyes," Mick growled, and Sean unsquinched his face enough to peer about him.

"What happened?"

"Another clear round, that's what happened!"

"Shit!" Sean said in a half wail, finally dropping the reins and clapping his hands over his face.

Mick clouted him on the knee. "No need for language, boy."

"Oh, shit!" Sean said much more softly as Mick led him and the pony to the right of the pocket gate, behind the huge number board. Catriona followed. Sean slipped out of the saddle and was promptly sick in the corner.

Mick was utterly disgusted, but Catriona glared at him so fiercely that he didn't make any comment. Mick threw the sheet over the pony, keeping him between Sean and any observers, but most of the pocket's occupants were far too interested in ponies jumping in the Enclosure to notice them. Catriona heard the cheers and the applause and saw Brian McConnell come cantering back into the pocket, a huge grin on his face.

"Can I get you something, Sean?" she asked. He was still leaning against the wall, his shoulders hunched. Then he heaved again, and she looked away. "Everyone is so proud of you. Two clear rounds, that's the very best you and the Prince have ever done."

Sean's reply was to vomit again, and she could see that he was shuddering violently.

"Mick," she said softly, pointing to the retching boy. Mick mouthed words, the sort he wouldn't ever say out loud, and looked urgently over his shoulder as yet another pony returned to the pocket.

Then the announcer informed the audience that there were seven clear second rounds, and the next one would be against the clock. He listed the fences involved in the jump-off and added that the final jump would be the wall, now at five feet two inches. Would the first contestant please enter?

"Christ, what'll we do?" Mick demanded, regarding the shaking boy. "He couldn't even hang on." Suddenly Mick looked very hard at Catriona. The next moment, he had circled the pony in by Sean. "By God, you're tall enough. Quick. Take his jacket off. A mercy you've jods and boots on. Here. Stuff this in your front." Mick thrust a wadded stable rubber at her. "You're much thinner than he is."

Catriona had long been accustomed to obeying Mick, particularly Mick giving crisp and unequivocal orders. Sean had not soiled his hacking jacket. She wrenched his jacket off and threw her wind cheater over his shoulders. The stable rubber took up some of the slack in the front of the jacket, and when she buttoned it, it fit well enough. Just then number twelve was called. Mick whipped off the sheet, swirling it over Sean, lifted her up into the saddle, and again walloped the Prince on the rump.

Catriona moved forward with the pony, past the gate steward at such a clip he hadn't a chance to notice the change in riders, and then into the arena. She remembered to pause and bow, remembered also to make it a nervous bob of her head, and then she circled the pony, frantically trying to recall the fences named for the jump-off. Fortunately the discarded ones had flags across them. At the sound of the bell, she aimed the Prince at the starting line and dug in her heels.

It was exhilarating to be astride the willing Prince, with a good springy turf under his hooves, the sun warm on her back, and all the space in the world to ride. Then the Prince was charging. She let him, knowing this round was for speed, and that she had him well in hand. The elements of the double were separated by two strides. She was glad she had watched the course being built. Then into the turn, and she and the pony were almost horizontal as she steered him around. His hooves scattered as he gained impulsion for the spread of the oxer. Then she lined him up for the triple, one stride and then two, and the pony galloped for the last three fences and the wall. It did look big! She had time to straighten him, and then they were up and over.

Catriona didn't stop him as they scattered back into the pocket, though she managed to avoid a collision with the pony and rider waiting to enter and still head the Prince to the corner where Mick waited, shielding a sick boy.

As if they had practiced the maneuver a hundred times, Mick spread the sheet over the Prince while Catriona, simultaneously hauling the stable rubber out of her shirtfront, slid from the saddle to the ground. She had her wind cheater on and was draping Sean's jacket over his shoulders when her father jogged up to them.

"I couldn't leave right away," he apologized, looking from Mick to Catriona. "I heard the time, Sean, great. . . . What's the matter?"

"He charged over here, Daddy, and only just made it to the wall," Catriona said, brandishing the stable rubber because she suddenly realized that the hard hat had sweated up her forehead. Fortunately her father was so concerned about Sean that he didn't notice.

"Sean, that was a great round! Great. Excellent time. You'll be placed. I know it. We're all proud of you!"

Sean groaned and rolled his eyes, still shuddering.

"Catriona, go get some water. Easy there, lad. I've sicked up myself a time or two. Excitement, that's all. And you did great!" she heard her father saying as she scooted off on her errand.

When she got back, Sean was looking far less green. He was walking between the two men. Mick had a very odd expression on his face, and he kept his arm about the boy. To keep him from blurting out the truth, Catriona was sure. Then the last contestant had jumped, and the announcer gave the results. Anne Lowry on Popcorn had the fastest time, but—and here Catriona could not suppress her whoop of delight—Sean Doherty on Ballymore Prince was second. In fact, she didn't hear the rest of the line-up, she was cheering so loudly.

"You're second, you're second, Sean! You've done it. You've done it!" Under the guise of congratulating him, Catriona gave him such a fierce look that Sean almost recoiled from her. "You've done it, Sean," she kept repeating.

"That's enough, Trina," her father said, grinning, while Mick, nodding his head up and down, winked at Catriona.

Then Sean had to mount up to receive his rosette, and she pinched him when he opened his mouth.

"Enjoy it," she urged him. "Enjoy it, Sean. You're second."

As if something had just clicked this information into place, Sean sat more erect in the saddle and gathered the reins in steady hands to shorten them properly. This time Mick did not swat the pony on the rump, so the pair entered at a dignified trot in the van of the other winners.

"Now maybe they'll sell the pony and give the boy a break!" her father said.

"Sure and that's what they ought to do," Mick agreed, at his most amiable.

"Trina, c'mon." Her father grabbed her hand and hurried her toward Ring One.

Here the winning horses were cantering around. Catriona and her father could see Philip's back as he and Teasle moved down the long side.

"Teasle gave both judges a good ride," her father said, half jogging, half limping in his haste. "He showed to advantage, yes, he did. He's got first!" And her father slowed as he caught the flutter of the first-prize red ribbon streaming from Teasle's double bridle. "The Italians'll like that!" He stood on tiptoe, peering over the crowd to the far side, and grinned. "They do. C'mon, Trina. Selina's doing the pretty along with my brothers."

The Italians did the pretty as well, for the deal was struck and the sale made on the way back to the Simmonscourt Hall. Vendor and buyer were deciding where to go for a drink when the Doherty contingent arrived. This reinforced the need for refreshment. Sean was wearing the second-place blue ribbon, looking both scared and proud, his father's arm about his shoulders and his mother still a bit weepy from her child's success.

Quite probably, Catriona thought, Mrs. Healey's hand in hers as they followed the others to the members' lounge, this was the very best show she'd ever been in! Then she thought of the day before, and her mother "not yet cold in her grave," and she moaned a little.

"Catriona Carradyne," Selina Healey said in a stern voice, glaring down at her, "don't you dare! Cornanagh deserves today! You do, too."

17

A s it turned out, Catriona spent the afternoon wandering about the exhibits in the Industries Hall escorted by her uncles. She had the suspicion that they were pretending to enjoy themselves far more than they did because of her recent loss, but she was quite willing to fall in with the deception. The two men joked a lot and made her laugh. And they wouldn't let her spend her pennies but bought her small boxes of Chez Nous chocolates and bonbons, and larger boxes for Eithne and Bridie.

Although they'd had the full luncheon at the members' dining room, they purchased buns at Johnson Mooney & O'Brien's stall, and pounds of coffee and tea in pretty canisters, and queen cakes at Bewley's.

"Christ," said Uncle Pat, "doesn't this take you back, and the colonel roaring at us not to fill our guts?"

They had their Guinness while she dawdled, with many great sighs, before the main saddlery booths, Callaghan's and the Beirne Brothers, ogling the magnificent saddles, bridles, and full-leather boots as well as the more plebeian rubber imitations, not to mention the gorgeous wool stable rugs with initials and the racks of fine bridles and arrays of bits.

"You're as bad as my Pat," Uncle Eamonn said when they had finished their pint. "Bugging your eyes out over boots and saddles."

She saw them exchange mildly exasperated glances over her head and wondered if she dared ask about her cousin. They were both in such good moods after their pints: maybe they were enough like her father . . . It came out in a rush.

"Uncle Eamonn, is my cousin still going to come over?"

Surprised, her uncle touched her head in a brief caress and smiled down at her.

"Yes, she is. Your aunt Eithne saw no reason why she couldn't cope with two horse-mad girls. You'll have company for the summer. You'll like Patty. You've a lot in common."

"Horses!" Uncle Patrick said, but he grinned at her. "Thank God, my boys are into baseball!"

"I knew I'd find Trina near the saddlery," Philip said, suddenly appearing before them out of the crowd. "How's she cutting, Sis?" And he tousled her hair. "Look, Dad phoned Eithne to tell her the good news, and she told us the bad. Bridie's taken to her bed." Everyone groaned, but then Philip brightened. "Actually, that's good, too. Now we can eat out!"

"So." Eamonn rubbed his hands together with anticipation. "Where do we dine?"

"All the places near the RDS are booked out, but don't worry, Uncle Patrick, we won't let you down." Philip saw the hopeful look on his sister's face and pulled her to his side for a quick hug. "And you're coming, too, Trina. You're part of Cornanagh's success today: that pony never would have got round that course without all the schooling you've done with him."

Catriona felt her heart skip halfway through Philip's sentence. She didn't think Mick would mention the switch to anyone, and she wondered if she'd have to mention it in confession on Saturday. Mick would never make her do something sinful, or something that would harm Cornanagh's reputation. And what would it be a sin of—pride? No, because she couldn't admit to having done it. Covetousness? No, because she hadn't had time to envy Sean. Mick had just made her change clothes. It certainly wasn't a sin to follow the orders of one's elders. Mick was even older than her father. So she hadn't committed a sin. Possibly a transgression, but she only had to confess sins so she wouldn't mention it to Father John. Relieved, she put the whole matter to the back of her mind.

"I think we ought to stand young Philip a drink for the glory he brought Cornanagh today," Eamonn said.

"Not to mention a fat price for the gelding," Patrick added.

"If you don't mind, I'd like to go see the jumping," Catriona said wistfully. It was nearly three, and the big show-jumping competition of the day was about to start.

Even Philip laughed, but they told her to meet everyone back at Teasle's stable at six.

Only the Glenview Hotel just down the road from Cornanagh could accommodate so large a group that evening. The management arranged their table across the bay window that overlooked the lovely garden and the cut through the mountains that was Glen o' the Downs.

To Catriona it was a splendid occasion: all her favorite people were here, for Selina had accepted Cornanagh's invitation. Her husband had left a message that he'd had to go North. Auntie Eithne was waiting for them at the hotel, dressed in a lovely garnet wool suit that Catriona didn't remember seeing her wear before. Of course, the men all wore black mourning bands on their coat sleeves, but they, too, looked so handsome and so big! She counted: seven Carradyne men, all with the same crisp black curly hair, most of them with blue eyes, if not the exact brilliant hue as her father's, which she thought was the best shade ever.

Her uncles insisted that she sit between them. It embarrassed her at first, but Uncle Eamonn was so kind and Uncle Pat kept making such ridiculous comments that she soon relaxed. She was even served a Shirley Temple cocktail. This was a special treat for Catriona, who had never eaten out at a such an elegant, adult restaurant before. She was relieved when the waitress took away the silver she wouldn't need from the rather impressive assortment on either side of her plate. She also watched what Selina and Eithne were doing so as not to make any mistakes, determined not to disgrace her family.

And Uncle Eamonn told her all about her cousin Patricia, that she went to a boarding school now and had a boyfriend, which astonished Catriona because none of the fourteen-year-old girls she knew were allowed to keep company with anyone in particular. Patricia haunted a nearby stable that specialized in gaited saddle horses, and she'd managed to talk herself into riding them in local shows.

"She's got a couple of thirds and fourths," her uncle confided, "and I don't mean to poor-mouth her, but"—he sighed deeply—"well, I know Americans ride differently, but it's not the way your grandfather taught me to ride. So, you and your daddy are to make a proper rider out of her, and then maybe she can get firsts. But she's all Carradyne—horse crazy."

"Her mother doesn't mind?" The question caused her uncle to give her a very sharp look.

"No, her mother doesn't mind." He seemed about to add something else and then cleared his throat several times. "Do you win many firsts, Trina?"

"Me?" Catriona swallowed abruptly. "No, I'm to have my first show this summer. Blister wasn't a show pony, and besides, Dad doesn't approve of children competing too early. He says it spoils them for riding horses. Ponies can give you very bad habits."

"They can?" Eamonn appeared surprised.

"Well, for instance, Ballymore Prince is a right sod at times—" She broke off and covered her mouth because she'd used an improper word. She wasn't quite prepared to hear both uncles burst into fits of laughter.

"Chip off the old man's block, this one," Eamonn finally

managed through tears of laughter. "Did you hear her, Mike? Ponies can be right sods. And doesn't that bring back Father?"

Catriona never got to expound on ponies, which, she decided, was just as well because her uncles and her father reminisced about their father. That brought back many memories to Catriona, too, and she thought how much she missed her grandfather and how pleased he would have been today. *He*'d've had a great laugh over her switching with Sean and coming in second. So she ate the roast lamb placed before her with great relish.

Even when she was so tired she could barely keep her eyes open, she didn't want the evening to end because it was such fun being allowed to stay at the table while the adults were enjoying liqueurs and port. Mostly, she didn't want this day to end.

"Look at Trina, Michael," Eithne said finally. "You lot can stay on if you wish, but I'm taking her home."

However, everyone was willing to leave, the overseas Carradynes feeling travel fatigue and the younger Carradynes faced with work the next day. There had to be some organization to get everyone into the cars available, especially as Selina didn't have transport. But with a minimum of crowding, Eithne and Philip managed the Cornanagh group so that Michael could drive Selina directly home to Dalkey.

"God, I'll be asleep the moment I hit the sack tonight," Eamonn said as he ducked into the back of Philip's Kadette. "Jet lag!"

Michael found himself obscurely pleased at the way things had worked out. He had been exceedingly conscious of Selina all day. Conscious of her smart and fashionable appearance, of the oddly spicy perfume she wore, of the way she had handled the D'Albrettis, who had bought Teasle. The son had been very much attracted by her, but she had deftly avoided his attempts to detach her from the others at the ringside, pretending not to understand Italian. "And, Michael," she said after lunch, "it took a great effort of will not to give them a proper farewell . . . in their own language. But they had paid such a good price for Teasle, I was afraid they'd renege."

"Oh, you needn't have worried." He grinned at her. "Philip cashed their bank draft promptly."

"Michael Carradyne!"

He hadn't liked David Healey, nor the proprietary way he treated Selina. In fact, he thought, there was something . . . not quite sound about Healey. If the man were a horse, Michael would be wary in the saddle.

Now, as Michael handed Selina into the Austin, he was wondering just how slowly he could drive to Dalkey without being obvious. She smiled as she sank gratefully onto the leather upholstery.

"This has been quite a day," she said as he got into the car. She put a quick hand on his arm. "And Cornanagh deserved it. Did you see how much more animated Catriona was?"

"You mean when she folded into Eithne's car?"

"No." Selina pretended exasperation. "I still don't understand how that Doherty boy managed to come second."

"Pure fluke, and hours of Trina's patient schooling."

"Will she be all right?"

Michael gave her a quick look, gratified. "We'll see that she is. And did I hear her calling you Selina today?"

Selina raised her eyebrows. "She and I made a pact the other day. A special one between us."

"Eamonn wants to send his daughter Patricia over for the summer. She'll be another friend for Trina. I'm to teach Pat how to ride."

"But you don't *like* teaching people." Her voice rippled with good-humored mockery.

"Sure, she's a Carradyne and horse mad, or so my brother

tells me. And it'll be very good for Trina to have company this summer."

"Those brothers of yours! You Carradynes are a law unto yourselves," she said, shaking her head. "It was a very good thing that Trina was half-asleep. Eithne didn't miss much, though, did she? Does she know many Americans?"

"I shouldn't think so," Michael replied, puzzled. "Why?"

"Well, she understood a lot more of your brothers' slang than I did. She got the punchline of that outrageous joke Paddy told while I was still struggling with the translation from the American."

Michael chuckled, for that particular joke had been not only hilarious but bawdy. He gave Eithne full marks.

"Is a way with a joke another talent of the Carradyne family?" she went on. "Philip has some beauts. Even surprised your Madison Avenue brother."

"We're full of hidden talents, we Carradynes. Perhaps I should ask Patrick if he can find a spot for Philip in the States."

"Which reminds me, Michael, Trina did some lovely sketches of Conker and a heartbreaking one of poor Blister. Were you aware of how good she is?"

"I'm aware that she was called to task by the Mother Superior for scribbling in her school notebooks. Her mother was furious."

"Did you never *look* at what she does?"

Michael felt his jaw clenching. "I found it advisable not to interfere with Isabel's discipline of Catriona in domestic and school matters."

"Sunday Trina said that her mother hadn't liked her." Selina's voice was stern, and all the comfortable friendliness between them had disappeared. "I assured her that her mother had loved her."

"I don't think she did," Michael said slowly. "She hadn't wanted another child, and she had a very difficult pregnancy with Catriona. I always thought that was why she was so hard on her. My father complicated matters by making a special pet of Catriona while he was alive. But children don't notice. . . ."

"Catriona noticed!" Selina said bitterly. "She's a very perceptive child."

"I can't thank you enough for all you've done for her."

"I intend to go on doing for her. I warn you."

He grinned at her for her fierceness. "You should have children of your own, Selina."

"If I could be sure of having a son first, I might risk it," she said in the affected tones of the bored society woman, a pose she didn't often assume at Cornanagh. "David would be mortified if I produced a girl."

Michael winced at letting the conversation get out of hand. "So, I'll borrow your Catriona to assuage my frustrated maternal instincts. Now, tell me, when will Conker be sound again? Or would you put her up on Charlie as a special treat?"

Michael was immensely relieved to discuss Conker's injury and the possibility of putting Catriona up on Charlie, or perhaps one of the quieter horses he had been training for a neighbor. He had by no means exhausted the possibilities by the time Selina handed him her front-door key and they walked up the shallow steps to the deep crimson door, with its intricate fan light and well-polished brasses. He opened it for her, returning the keys, sorry that the evening was over.

"A nightcap? Or is jet lag contagious?" she asked with an odd half smile on her lips.

Tired though he was, a jolt of elation lifted him as he followed her into the house. They'd all be asleep at Cornanagh. And Isabel was dead. He owed her no further loyalty.

"Make yourself at home," she said, gesturing to the beautiful salon at the left of the front door. "I'll just get some ice."

"Make yourself at home," his mind echoed as he entered the room and thought that he could be, in a setting as charming as this. The room was done in light, soft blues and grays with little touches of brighter blue and a vivid amethyst. The chairs and three-seater couch were upholstered in the sort of covering that would not wear well at all in Cornanagh with dogs, cats, and riding boots. There were elegant prints on the walls, again in soft pastels, and an oil painting of a watery landscape over the Adam fireplace. He sank onto one corner of the couch, legs crossed at the ankle.

"Don't you dare get up!" he heard her say. She put an ice-keeper on the drinks tray. "You look far too relaxed. Which you need to do more." From her light tone, she had evidently forgiven him, and he was grateful. "There's lager if you'd prefer that, but I brought the port. It's an excellent vintage. My father sends it over every August to be sure it's drinkable by Christmas. I've a fine brandy, too. What would you like?"

She stood in front of him, her head slightly cocked to one side, a gently inquiring smile on her face. She'd taken off her jacket, and the silk shirt she wore outlined her upper body. He knew exactly what he wanted, what he needed.

He got to his feet before she realized what he was doing and pulled her to him. He heard her gasp of surprise, but not denial, and quickly bent his head to kiss her slightly open mouth. His left hand cupped a silk-covered breast. He felt her stiffen and would have released her had she not, in the next instant, melted against him, her hands reaching up to his neck.

He could feel passion flaring up, so abruptly that it startled him. To get control of himself, he forced himself to release her, but she clung and buried her head against his chest. He allowed himself the luxury of holding her closely, feeling her slender, vibrant body pressing against him.

"Selina . . ." He was desperate not to say the wrong thing.

"Come," she whispered, abruptly releasing her hold to take his hand and lead him up the stairs.

He needed no further invitation, and then she was beside

him on the silken cover of her bed, her warm, naked skin against his own with no memory of having stripped, so great had been their urgency. Michael hadn't known how keenly he had needed sexual relief until he had plunged into her willing body. To his delight, her rhythm was as fierce as his own, seeking, seeking, seeking the release that broke over them both, so exquisite he cried aloud with the pain of it. Her voice joined his.

He was strengthless when it was over. When he had recovered enough to move away, her arms held him.

"I'll crush you," he whispered.

She shook her head. But, mindful of having bony hips, he moved just a bit to one side and propped himself up on his elbows so he could see her face. She looked beautiful in the soft light of the May evening, a marvelous smile lifting the corners of her mouth. She reached up and ran a finger lightly over his lips. He kissed the searching finger, and her smile deepened.

Thought or speech seemed unnecessary until they both became aware of the cool breeze coming from the open window.

"I had better go," he said in a reluctant whisper.

"Thank you, Michael, for a marvelous day," she said, the innocuous phrase contrasting with a grin of pure sensuality.

With a laugh he embraced her once more, able to kiss her lightly before he rolled to a sitting position. As he reached for his scattered clothes, he felt her hands caressing his bare flesh, and he gently but firmly lifted them off.

"I have got to leave, Selina."

She gave a low sensual laugh but did not interfere again. When he had dressed, he turned to look once more at her naked slender body, stretched in an alluring pose on the bed.

"Good night, sweet wanton. It was a marvelous *evening*, too."

Her laughter followed him down the stairs and out of the house.

℘ 18 ℘

When habit roused Michael the next morning, light was streaming into the room, which was unusual as Isabel always kept the heavy brown drapes pulled shut. It took him a moment to realize that they were not Isabel's drapes. They were, however, familiar, and his sleepy mind managed to identify them: the old cream-and-crimson-striped drapes from his father's tenancy of this room. He flipped onto his back, now aware of the empty space on his left, and, stuffing the pillows behind his head, looked about him.

He smiled as he noticed other changes. How very considerate of Eithne. She had taken down all the religious pictures, even the heavy wooden cross. He was most grateful to see that the prie-dieu was gone. Isabel's dressing table had been removed as well and his press repositioned between the windows. He must remember to thank Eithne. He hadn't realized just how much the room had depressed him.

He lay for another moment, listening to an aimless whistle: Mick walking down the Ride to the yard for the beginning of the day. Resolutely he thrust back the blanket, then swore under his breath.

He'd have to take the brothers into the airport this morning, right about the time Selina was likely to arrive. And he very much wanted to be here and gauge her mood. Jesus, but last night had been marvelous! And a surprise. He hadn't intended to chance his arm that way: not with Selina Healey. But God, it'd been good. She had been as eager as he. Pulling on corduroy slacks, Michael frowned. Why had she been as eager? Was Healey a cold bastard in bed as well?

He shaved quickly, for once managing not to nick himself in his haste. Then he looked at himself in critical appraisal. Well, he didn't look as dissipated or cynical as Paddy, nor had he developed Eamonn's jowls. In fact, he looked younger than they did. Clean living, lots of exercise, fresh Irish air, and not many opportunities for the high living his brothers enjoyed. But was it enough to attract a woman who was—and he made himself think it—younger than his eldest son?

Michael cleared his throat, amused and slightly dismayed by the tenor of his thoughts. Yes, he was attracted to Selina. Who wouldn't be? But last night, he told himself, Selina was kind to you, responding honestly to a creature need. Leave it at that. She certainly will.

He splashed after-shave on his face, winced at the sting, and dried his hands. He heard Philip coming down the hall and opened the bathroom door. Philip wasn't there. Surprised, Michael heard the faintest creak of a door being opened. He peered around the corner and saw Philip checking quietly on Catriona.

"Sleeping?" he asked quietly.

"And looking a lot better, Dad." Philip smiled with relief, sleepily scratching at his head. "The uncles saw she had a good time yesterday."

"You gave Teasle a great show, Philip, a great show!" He gave his son a friendly slap on the back before he went on his way down the steps.

Michael reminded himself to get Teasle's papers and vet records from his office. He could drop them off to the D'Albrettis on his way back through town and check to see if Artie had taken good care of the gelding and the pony. He had no doubts that the boy had, but it was up to him to check.

"You're to eat in the dining room, Captain," Bridie said with a mild sniff. "There's too many of you cluttering up m'kitchen."

"In good form today, are you, Bridie Doolin?"

"No better'n I should be." She sniffed more emphatically.

"G'win with ya. *She* can pour your coffee."

Michael gave a mental twitch: so Eithne was not in Bridie's good books today. If his sister-in-law had been disturbing Isabel's ordering of Cornanagh, that was to be expected. Maybe now was the time to get in a proper housekeeper. Last Christmas Isabel had been saying that Bridie was getting on and really shouldn't be asked to do more than the cooking.

"Is Catriona awake yet, Michael?" Eithne asked, looking up from her perusal of the *Times*. "I really don't think she should go back to school this week at all. She was exhausted last night."

"Everyone was," he began carefully. "And let me thank you for rearranging"—he hesitated only briefly, still unaccustomed to Isabel's absence from his life—"my room. It can't have been an easy task for you."

"Well, it had to be done, and I felt that the sooner the better," she said, looking both troubled and grateful as she poured his coffee. "I've given most of her clothes to St. Vincent's: easier that way. But I saved out some of her lovely jumpers. Catriona will grow into them. That child *is* growing, Michael. Anything personal I've put together for you to go through—later on. Did Isabel leave a will of any kind?"

Michael shook his head. "I doubt that it ever occurred to her."

"Any word from Jack?"

Again Michael shook his head: he was beginning to worry. At that point Bridie arrived with his breakfast, and Owen appeared, yawning mightily.

"You'll be late, dear," Eithne said, glancing anxiously at the clock on the breakfront.

"Ah, sure, the old man'll be understanding today. Got to wish the uncles a safe trip, you know."

Eamonn and Patrick reached the dining room just as Philip left for work, with "safe trip home" to the uncles and a cheerful "God bless" to the entire room, and Catriona appeared shortly after.

"Trina," Michael began, "when Selina comes, would you ride out with her?"

Catriona started to agree, then stopped. He suppressed a smile because his question had completed her waking up. "Who? I didn't think Conker was sound yet."

"No, I'd like you to ride Charlie this morning."

"You mean it, Daddy?"

"I mean it," he said, smiling broadly now at the delighted surprise on her pretty face. It had suddenly occurred to him that Catriona was pretty: certainly now, when she was so animated at the prospect of riding Charlie. "Emmett needs a good long hack, and I'd rather Selina had company. You're elected. I'm taking your uncles to the airport, and I'll have to stop off with Teasle's papers. . . ."

"Oh, Daddy, say good-bye to him for me." Catriona's face reflected her regret.

"I will, so if you and Selina can take some of the edge off the two geldings, we can get back to some real schooling tomorrow."

"The leg pond hill?" Catriona asked, brightening again, for that was one of her favorite long rides. When Blister's shins had been bucked, she often walked him over to the little stream, standing him in the pool, which, most seasons, was knee deep for horses. They could nibble cress on the banks and would stand quite quietly while the running water soothed their legs.

"And see if you can trot both horses to the crest." He glanced at the ormolu clock on the sideboard. He hated the thing, a wedding gift from one of the Marshall relations, but it kept the most accurate time in the house. "C'mon, brothers. Traffic across town can be heavy."

While Owen went up to collect their luggage, Michael had a chance to speak to Eithne.

"I think we ought to pack away Isabel's knicknacks, too, Eithne," he said. "Mrs. Marshall has so often told us how valuable they are. Perhaps she'd like to keep them."

Eithne met his eyes squarely, her own startled. "Why, I think that's a very good idea, Michael. I didn't want to suggest . . ." She faltered.

He touched her arm. "Eithne, I'll support any changes you care to make here at Cornanagh. And d'you have any idea where those hunting prints of my father's disappeared to? I'd like them back in my room."

"Yes, I can certainly do that," she said with a quick smile. "They're in the attic. The whole house wants a good turning out."

Michael drove out of the courtyard with his brothers, while everyone sent them on their way with good wishes and God blesses. Eamonn was in the passenger seat while Patrick sprawled his long legs across the back.

"I don't think I've had a chance to mention it, Mike," Eamonn said as they turned up the Kilquade road, "but the old place looks great. The father would be pleased."

"His ghost makes certain I do a good job," Michael replied, gratified that Eamonn, at least, had noticed.

"Any word yet from Father Jack in Central America?" Patrick wanted to know.

Michael shook his head. "It'll hit him very hard indeed. He adored his mother."

"Ah, sure he can say a daily mass for the repose of her soul for the rest of his life." Patrick had never been devout and considered the priesthood an escape from reality.

"On the subject of my sons," Michael said, glancing in the rearview mirror to see Patrick's reaction, "I noticed you and Philip talking a fair bit over the past few days. It was one of Isabel's hopes that perhaps he could do better for himself in the States. Would you have any ideas on that score, Paddy?"

"As a matter of fact, Mike"—Patrick leaned forward—"I was very much impressed by Phil. He's got all the family charm and most of the looks. Said he didn't get much of a challenge selling cars for Crawford's, especially as the son would take over when the old man retires. Did you make enough out of horses to send him to college?"

There was just a faint tinge of bitterness in Patrick's voice. He had never forgotten, or forgiven, old Tyler that after the war there hadn't been enough money to pay college fees.

"I did. He went to UCD and took a second in liberal arts. Lord, Paddy, he doesn't have to go into advertising. There're plenty of horse farms out on Long Island. . . ."

"And plenty of rich and useless young female equestriennes, too, riding all kinds of mounts," Patrick said. "Is that what you have in mind for Phil?"

"God, but you're American," Eamonn said, rather disgusted.

"I'd rather he and Owen had more opportunity than they have here in Ireland, and what else are well-placed relatives good for?" Michael grinned into the rearview mirror.

"Phil, yes," Patrick said, "but Owen, no." He leaned back again. "I have enough people sucking up to me in the office. I don't need it from my relatives, too. Now Phil has a lot of charm and I expect he has sufficient chutzpah to do well. Nephew Owen comes on too strong."

"It's because he's a posthumous baby," Eamonn said, mimicking Eithne's breathy, apologetic tones. The brothers all chuckled.

"I'll toss it around a bit, Mike, and see what I can do for

Phil," Patrick said, and his older brother was content to leave it at that.

"Speaking of Eithne," Eamonn began, clearing his throat as one does before introducing a delicate subject, "is she staying on?"

"I certainly hope so." Michael shot a quick concerned look at Eamonn, who appeared embarrassed. "Why? She's settled at Cornanagh, and where else would she go? Longford and that father of hers?"

"It's not that, Michael, it's . . . well . . ."

"Something your mother-in-law, that bitch, let fall," Patrick finished what his brother could not.

"What do you mean?"

"About how convenient it was now for Eithne and you."

"What!" The Austin swerved suddenly, but he recovered with a deft adjustment of the wheel. "Eithne lives in the mews house," he said crisply.

"Sure, sure, Mike, we know that," Eamonn said soothingly, "but I did notice that Eithne's still a damned attractive woman. And you're now single."

"Christ, man, the flowers on my wife's grave are still fresh! You can be sure I'm not thinking of marrying for a long time."

Patrick gave an appreciative snort. "Just to warn you."

"Did Eithne hear this?"

"I suspect Mairead Marshall took pains to see that she did."

"Damn!" Michael slapped the steering wheel in frustration. He had been very naive to think that his mother-in-law had gone out of his life. "I'll get a housekeeper. A woman of un-assailable virtue. She can even lock me in at night, but I am not asking Eithne to leave Cornanagh, not after everything she's done for the family all these years."

"And everything, might I add, that the family has done for her," Patrick murmured. "Wicklow is a touch better than Longford."

"God, you are cynical, Paddy," Michael said.

"Pragmatic."

"Sorry, Mike, but we thought we ought to warn you," Eamonn said unhappily.

"I'm glad you did. Damn that woman!"

"Just don't let her get her hands on Trina," Eamonn went on.

"You're not changing your mind about sending Patricia over, are you?" Michael shot his brother a frown. "Trina's counting on it, and I don't want her disappointed."

"Hell, Mike, of course she's coming." He hesitated.

"G'wan, tell him," Patrick said, grinning slyly at his brother's hesitation.

"Tell me what?"

"I've decided to file for a divorce," Eamonn said quickly, and then glanced at his older brother. "Shirley's got a serious drink problem, and she's ruining the kids' lives. That's why Patty goes to a boarding school and why I asked you to take her for the summer."

Michael glanced back at Patrick and saw from his expression that he knew all of this and approved of Eamonn's decision.

"I hadn't any idea it was like that," Michael said, seeking a diplomatic response.

"Legal divorce is just another advantage of living in the United States," Patrick said.

"The divorce proceedings may be dirty," Eamonn went on, shooting a quelling glance at Patrick. "Shirley will contest it. Once I've got Patricia off to you, as soon as school's out, I'll file the papers. But I don't want Patty in the middle of the mess. I know she'll be safe and happy in Ireland. Is that okay with you?"

"I see no reason to change my mind. You're lucky you can get a divorce, Eamonn."

They were in the center of Dublin now, the brothers keenly

interested in the changes they noticed. They reached the airport with sufficient time to spare for a quick farewell pint. Patrick was particularly pleased to sink one more Guinness.

"God, if it only tasted as good when it gets across the Atlantic!" Wistfully he turned his pint, admiring the foam and the deep rich brown of the stout. "What a campaign I could mount!"

"You'd be stones heavier in no time," Michael said, giving Patrick's incipient paunch an affectionate punch. He had to keep a light touch in conversation or he'd get maudlin. He'd forgotten how much he liked his brothers and how easily they had reestablished old bonds, and arguments. He was more grateful for their support the past few days than he could ever express.

"Oh, a couple of saunas and few games of handball, and I'll have that all worked off." But Patrick's hand stayed at his middle, and his eyes flickered to Michael's trimmer figure. "Leg give you any trouble, old man?"

"Only when I laugh!"

At that old tag line all three laughed, just as the departure of the New York flight was announced. With masculine dignity, they embraced, thumping each other soundly.

As Eithne went back into the house with Catriona, the girl said, "I'll be with Conker, Auntie Eithne." She was still joyous over her father's permission to ride Charlie, but Eithne was worried about her. She didn't believe that Catriona truly realized yet that her mother was dead. Even Michael, she thought, had a sort of dazed look this morning.

"D'you need the paper, missus?" Bridie's question recalled her to her own reality.

"Yes, please, Bridie, and weren't the boys delighted by a real Irish breakfast to start them on their way home," she said, determined to be pleasant. Of course, Bridie had not been upstairs yet, and she could expect another spate of wailing when she'd seen what had happened. "Patrick was so pleased to have that extra loaf of soda bread to take back with him."

Bridie gave her a long look as she handed her the paper and only grunted.

"I'll just do the upstairs, Bridie," Eithne said. She kept a firm smile on her face as she placed the last of the delft on the sink and walked out. Could Bridie have overheard Mailread Marshall's insinuations? she wondered. Not likely. Mairead would not parade her opinions within earshot of staff.

She went upstairs and began stripping the beds in the guest rooms. She found herself listening and realized that her ears were tuned for sounds coming from Isabel's room. Oh, dear. Quick tears came to her eyes, and she brushed them away on the pillowcase she was holding.

She was most relieved that Michael had not been upset about her adjustments. And what a relief to get rid of the figurines and vases and dishes that cluttered every surface in the drawing room! She'd felt very shamefaced about suggesting that, but after so many years of dusting them, and some of them not worth keeping, really, their absence would be a blessing. Now that Eithne had begun to appreciate genuine antiques, she was appalled at how worthless some of Isabel's little "treasures" actually were. Isabel had had odd notions about decoration, and Eithne had been surprised to find so many really fine pieces acquired by generations of Carradynes stacked in the attics.

She'd have to tell Michael about Davis Haggerty soon, she thought, and invite him to Cornanagh. Davis wanted to be open and aboveboard, as he put it, which confirmed her own hopeful suspicion that he might be very serious indeed about their relationship. His appearance wouldn't offend her male relatives, but she had known that Isabel would have taken it all up in the worst possible way. And really, she had been devoted to Isabel and very grateful for all her kindnesses when she'd come to Cornanagh as an anxious young country bride.

As she finished tidying, Eithne decided that her next task had better be shopping. There wasn't much left in the larder after four days of extra family, despite the quick trip Selina and Catriona had made.

"Hello!"

Eithne nearly dropped the bundle of linen at the sound of Selina's cheerful call.

"Captain's taking the brothers to the airport," she heard Bridie say.

"Trina's in the yard," Eithne said, leaning over the balustrade.

"Where else?" Selina said, grinning as she craned her head about to spot Eithne on the first story. "See you later."

Selina was both relieved by Michael's absence and unaccountably depressed. She almost hadn't come, except that she knew he was shorthanded and very much behind in schooling the young horses. It would have been churlish of her to stay away. She hadn't meant to go to bed with him last night, although she'd thought of that interesting possibility off and on for the last several weeks. But when she'd seen the look on his face as he'd risen to his feet, when his hand had so longingly cupped her breast and his lips had touched hers, no other outcome had been possible.

And he had been an absolutely splendid lover. She could have forgiven him much because she was so attracted to him, but Michael Carradyne had totally and unexpectedly fulfilled her. She had been sorry when he had left so soon afterward. But perhaps that was for the best. He had had an urgent need of solace, she had provided it. She put all that out of her mind as she turned the corner into the yard and saw Mick and Catriona bent over Conker's hoof. "Is it improving?"

"Selina!" Catriona looked up, no longer stumbling, Selina

noticed, over her Christian name. "Daddy wants you to hack out Emmett, and I'm to ride Charlie!"

"He's feeling very generous today, isn't he?"

"I wouldn't call it that, Miz Healey," Mick said, touching his cap to her, "not when that gelding's in need of good hard roadwork. He can take quite a hold when he's fresh."

"Well, I take it as the Captain's vote of confidence, then."

Mick gave her a long look and then grinned. "Tell me after you've ridden. Leave the pony, Catie, I'll get him after. You tack Charlie up."

However, Mick wouldn't permit Selina to saddle Emmett. He had to be sure it was on right. He put on a martingale as well, for Emmett could be a bit strong even for a rider as capable and experienced as she.

He led the gelding into the yard just as Catriona emerged with Charlie, her face glowing under the hard hat.

"Jist lemme give Miz Healey a leg up," he called to her.

"Nonsense, Mick," Selina said, taking the reins from him. "I've leg enough. You mount Catriona." And she swung up onto Emmett. He sidled a bit at the light weight, but she checked him with authority, and immediately he stood still.

She did not miss Mick's ritual checking of Charlie's girth and bridle with Catriona all but dancing on the cobbles in her eagerness.

"Okay, up you go." He tossed her lightly onto the amiable Charlie. "Now, let's just see how much leg you've put on since November," he said as he adjusted her stirrup leather length. Then he grinned up at her as he measured the stirrup iron against her extended leg and corrected the length. "I'd say you're riding two full holes longer these days."

"Oh, Mick, really?"

"Whatcha think, missus?" Mick appealed to Selina.

Selina smiled, appraising the look of Catrina on the gelding. She was longer in the leg, to be sure, but her body was still immature, and she looked small in the saddle, her head no higher than the horse's. But Catriona sat with such style and confidence that she looked just right on Charlie.

"You two suit each other. I fear"—Selina gave a mock sad sigh—"that I'll be done out of showing him."

"Oh, no," Catriona said, dismayed. "I'd never be able to show Charlie the way you do."

Emmett backed now and pawed at the cobbles, eager to be moving.

"I wouldn't bet on that, Trina. You've got the Carradyne style on a horse. So, which way are we going today?"

"Daddy said to do the leg pond hill. At the trot. If they can make it," Catriona said, now the serious work rider. Then she turned Charlie to follow Emmett out of the yard. "Oh, Selina, he's light as a feather under you. And he's nowhere near as wide through the shoulder as I thought he'd be."

"It's about time you got weaned from ponies," Selina said as they turned out of the courtyard and onto the Kilcoole road.

For Catriona, it was another unforgettable afternoon. She hadn't actually hacked out on a horse before, though she'd often worked one under her father's eye in the menage, and while she half-suspected that her father was just being very kind to her right now, she hoped that riding Charlie would not be a on-off treat.

He had an active but smooth walk, and she could feel his hindquarters moving under her, the muscles of his side rippling with every long stride, so different from Blister's or Conker's or even the Prince's. Best of all, she could feel through the reins the very light contact with his mouth. He was right there, between her leg and her hand, and his ears were twitching to show that he was ready to accept any command she gave him.

"How can you bear to let anyone else ride him, Selina?" Catriona said.

"I'm generous, too, Trina," Selina said teasingly.

She looked as elegant as ever, Catriona thought, glancing to Selina on her right. She was dressed now for the warmer weather in a short-sleeved knit shirt, open at the throat, her arms already lightly tanned, and open-backed riding gloves. She was also concentrating on Emmett, who was eager to move on at a faster pace. He was a more massive animal than either Charlie or Flirty Lady, and from the rolling of his eye, Catriona guessed that he was trying it on his lighter rider to see what he could get away with. She could see that Selina was sitting deep in the saddle, her hands playing lightly with the reins, getting his attention.

"Let's trot, shall we? Work the fidgets out," Selina suggested, and the words were no sooner out of her mouth than Emmett attempted to charge up the slope by Kilquade House. She laughed as she restrained him, and Catriona, delighted at her skill, brought Charlie up alongside Emmett so that the two horses swung up the incline, their strides matching perfectly. Charlie seemed to flow up the hill, his trot so smooth she didn't need to rise.

They kept at the working trot until they got to the Y turn where the Kilcoole road branched off to the left. In mutual accord they slowed, because the next bit of road to the right was winding and narrow, with the high stone wall on the right and people apt to drive down the road like the clappers.

Selina kept a firm contact on the reins, but Catriona let Charlie relax his neck and back a bit on a longer rein. She gave him several approving slaps.

"Charlie, you're absolutely marvelous. You're like glass to ride. Smooth and steady."

"He is, isn't he," Selina agreed, keeping her right leg tight against Emmett's side to keep him to the left of the road. "He reminds me a bit of a mare that Colonel Dudgeon had. She was a joy to ride on the flat but a devil in her if you were jumping. Have you ever been to Burton Hall? Yes, well, do you know the piano jump? She flew it! And I did, too, only not with her. She unseated me halfway up." Selina chuckled as she remembered how terribly embarrassed she had been as she was sprawled on the jump while her mount ran back to the stables. Then she saw Catriona's expression, not quite sure if she should join in the laughter and perhaps, Selina thought, a bit disappointed. "Heavens, Trina, everyone comes off a time or two. Even your father."

"Not often," Catriona declared stoutly, and then, catching Selina's twinkling glance, began to laugh at herself.

They were able to trot both horses to the top of the long slope and let them blow a bit before they started back down. By then, Catriona was positive that Charlie was the best horse now in Cornanagh, bar the Tulip, of course.

❧ 19 ❧

Selina and Catriona heard Tory's furious barking just as they reached the beginning of Cornanagh's garden wall. Abruptly Tory's angry voice became muffled.

"They've locked him up," Catriona said. "I wonder who's there. He doesn't usually carry on like that."

They broke into a trot, swinging quickly into the courtyard, where a white Fiat van was parked. With Mick's help, Michael was propping blocks against the garage door to keep the agitated dog inside. Michael grinned and waved at the two riders, then gestured to the van's occupant that it was safe to emerge.

"It's Johnny Cash," Catriona told Selina as the man, with a wary eye on the bucking garage door, stepped out of the van, holding the door, shieldlike, in front of him. If Selina found it very odd that Michael Carradyne welcomed a tinker in his yard, for it was obvious to her that the new arrival was one of the traveling folk, Catriona seemed delighted at his arrival, grinning and waving at him.

"How's she cutting, Johnny?" Michael was saying cheerily.

"Not so bad, sor, not so bad. Those are fine animals the ladies is riding," he went on courteously, touching his cap brim to Selina and grinning back at Catriona. "Have you given up riding the ponies, *alanna*?"

Mick came forward between the two horses, his expression sour as he held them for their riders to dismount.

"A good ride, Trina?" Michael asked.

"Charlie was marvelous, Daddy, and we never even paused on the way up the leg pond hill. At a good working trot, too."

Michael gave Catriona's shoulders a quick hug. "Emmett behave himself?" Though he looked at Selina, Catriona answered.

"Of course he did, with Selina riding him. Not that he didn't try it on, but she was up to his tricks."

"He worked well, Michael," she said, relieved that their first encounter today was in such easy circumstances. But then, Michael Carradyne had a great deal of presence in any situation.

"Well, now, Johnny, what can I do for you this fine day?" Michael asked. "Are you buying or selling?" He didn't like to rush the man, but he'd only just lunged Temper, and there were three more to be worked today.

"I've a right problem now, sor, and it's only yourself could help or for sure the filly'll die."

"Another one of those, huh, Johnny?"

"Well, now, sor, she's a fine filly, good blood in her, as you're sure to see yourself once you've clapped eyes on her." He hesitated, glancing at Selina to judge her reaction. "We only found her t'other day, up in Baldoyle, racked up at a fence and near dead o' thirst. Oh, sor, she's in a desp'rite way. Terrible deep gash in her near fore and cuts along both stifles."

"The pony races?"

Johnny nodded, took a drag on his cigarette, and threw it to the ground, twisting it firmly into the cobbles with his boot heel. Selina noticed that his clothes were tweeds, good once but unmatched and well worn.

"She's not more'n three year, and she was raced something wicked, sor. I've no place to put her, and there's no hay to be got at a daycent price this time o' year. But you get her right for me, and she'll make a good price, so she will. She'll die otherwise." Johnny included Selina in his appeal, and she found herself unexpectedly moved by the plea in those amazingly blue eyes.

Michael sighed, rubbing at his forehead. Then he shrugged. "All right, Johnny, bring her in. I'll see if I can do anything for her."

Catriona gave a hoot of relief.

"Ah, you're a grand man, so you are, sor, a grand man." Johnny quickly reseated himself in the van, closed the door, touching his cap brim between each movement. "I'll be right back, sor. She's not far away."

"Stashed in his box at the churchyard, I've no doubt," Michael murmured as Johnny reversed the van handily and flew out the gate. Only then did the mewed-up dog stop barking.

"Captain Michael Carradyne dealing with a tinker?" Selina could not resist taunting him. Suddenly she was completely at ease with him again. He grinned at her, and she wondered if he was as relieved as she. Sometimes it could be so awkward the next day.

"With Johnny Cash, yes. And Ned and Miley. Especially when they are also willing to take unreliable horses that I won't sell under the Cornanagh name."

"The Ned Cash who show jumps? Are they related?"

"I doubt it. Johnny never claims kinship, but the Cashes are a large clan."

"Tinkers tend to be."

"Ah, but"—Michael's grin chided her for her intolerance—"you don't see many ill-treated tinker horses, Selina."

"They're so common they wouldn't show it."

"Not all, not by a long chalk. Johnny's a useful man to have on your side, especially if someone inadvertently leaves open the gate to the field with your promising young stock."

"Really?" Selina felt a burst of anxiety.

"Selina, you'd never believe," Catriona piped up, "just how many horses there are, sort of hidden away behind gorse bushes on empty lots all over Dublin. But Johnny helped Daddy find two yearlings that we never would have found in a million years."

Michael nodded. "I've had occasion to be very grateful to Johnny Cash and quite willing to help him in my turn. He doesn't always bring me something I can buy from him, but he never sets me up."

"But this filly . . ."

"Was undoubtedly stolen, raced to the point of foundering and then left, much as Johnny just told us. Generally, the ponies are let loose and either find their own way home or are impounded by the Gardái. I'll find out if there's an alert out on her, which I can do with none of the embarrassing questions Johnny would be asked. First, let's just have a look at her." Michael saw the eager expectation on Catriona's face and smiled. "Johnny also has produced several legitimate, very good animals for me: unlikely lookers at two or three that were sloughed off to the tinkers, who have a keen eye for potential. One of the horses I sold to Italy last year I got from Johnny Cash. He needed only to be fed properly and have a chance to grow into himself."

"Baggins?" Catriona asked.

Michael nodded. "He was a spindly 15 hands when he came into the yard. He went out, a year later, at 16.2 and a bit with an astonishing leap in him. He'll make an international grade-A show jumper." Michael sighed. "I'd planned to hang on to him until the horse show, but once they'd seen him doing the jump alley, they offered more money than I could refuse."

Selina's doubts were fading when Johnny Cash drove back into the courtyard with his battered open trailer. In it was as sorry a looking sight as Selina had ever seen, and she echoed Catriona's groan of dismay. The filly was badly tucked up; every bone showed through her muddy, torn skin. Head drooping and ears lopped to the side, she was brambles and mud from head to toe, pieces of hoof missing where front shoes had been torn off. Dried blood caked her stifles and all four legs, though some effort had been made to clean the worst of the lacerations. The filly was trembling, from weakness and starvation, Selina thought, appalled at her condition. Then she looked at the whole animal and saw what the tinker had seen, the unmistakable look of breeding and, despite her condition, a rather elegant conformation.

"My God, can you do anything for her, Michael?"

"I'm committed to try," he said, but his tone was dubious. "I always try, don't I, Trina? Johnny, would you just pull into the yard?"

Selina followed with Catriona, and they both gasped with alarm as they saw the filly stagger in the box even though Johnny Cash was driving very carefully. Michael was shouting for Mick now, and he sent Catriona to check that the little stable next to Conker had a deep clean bed of straw and fresh water. He told Selina to put the kettle on in the feed room and bring him his veterinary box. She ran to do his bidding and emerged from the tack room to see Michael, Mick, Johnny, several youngsters, and a woman, all of whom must have been in the van, lifting the filly out of the trailer.

An hour later, after Finbarr had examined her, stitched the worst laceration, and given her appropriate injections, Selina wouldn't have recognized the creature. Catriona was feeding her judicious handfuls of a bran mash, for she was almost too weak to raise her head to the manger in the small stable. The worst of the mud had been removed in order to assess her injuries. To Selina's astonishment, honey had been applied liberally to the minor cuts.

"Best thing in the world for healing, Selina," Michael said cheerfully, washing his sticky fingers under the yard tap. "Rarely leaves scars and almost never changes the hair color over a wound. That's the real benefit." He stroked the pa-

thetically thin rump, his final pat the barest caress so as not
to unbalance the little thing.

"Will she make it, Michael?"

"We'll know tomorrow. If we've caught her in time, she
should pick up noticeably. Johnny was right, you know. She's
well bred."

The filly turned her head slowly, as if she knew she was
under discussion, and regarded them with patient, question-
ing, slightly furrowed eyes, deep hollows in the brow exaggerated by her emaciation. Her ears twitched, managed a more
alert stance, and then fell back loppedly as if the effort of holding them pricked was too great. She turned back to lip up
Catriona's palmful of bran.

"Just as if she were being polite," Selina murmured, her
breath catching in her throat at the valiant courtesy of the little
horse.

Michael crouched, running a light, knowing hand down the
tendons of her forelegs, shaking his head and sighing.

"She's a tough little thing, though, and the tendons are tight.
Luck, pure luck."

"Pure luck for her that that tinker talked you into taking her
off his hands," Selina remarked sardonically.

Michael grinned and gestured for her to precede him out
of the small stable.

"We'll see. I've been lucky with Johnny's offerings before
now, and I've an idea about her. But first I'll check in with the
Gardái. Trina, that's enough bran for now. We'll let her rest.
Can I rely on you to nurse her?"

"Oh, yes, Daddy!"

"Then you're to keep track of how much she's drinking, how
much she's eating, and she's to get little feeds at three-hour
intervals." He glanced at his watch. "Another at five o'clock.
God, where has the day gone?"

"Any way I can help?" Selina heard herself asking to relieve his frown of exasperation.

"You only signed on to show Charlie for me, Selina," he said, eyeing her. "I have no intention of imposing on your good nature."

She gave him a long, thoughtful look. "I enjoy riding in this yard, Michael, and"—she let her voice fall into a social drawl—"it's ever so much more interesting than my usual routine."

"Hmmm." Now there was a glint of mischief in his eyes. "Yes, well, all to the good. Mine."

"So what have you in mind?" At that he gave her such an outrageously roguish grin that she said hastily, "The horse, that is."

Another grin, and he reverted to his professional self. "I've that gelding of Morton's to work, and I'd completely forgot that Artie's still in at the show. I need a light rider. Are you game? He's too stupid to have any vices yet."

"Artie?"

"Don't be cheeky with me, missus, or I'll make you ride with no stirrups."

"Oh, fate worse than death!" she replied, holding up both hands to ward it off.

"Well, he's a far cry from Charlie," she said an hour later, trying to mop her sweaty face with a soggy handkerchief. Michael dipped one of his own in the trough and, wringing it out, gave it to her, an unpenitent grin on his face.

"C'mon, I'll buy you a cup of tea."

She was more than willing. Michael was an exacting trainer, but one with incredible patience for a stupid horse like the brown gelding. Unlike Charlie or Teasle, the brown horse had not yet developed any sense of balance with a rider on his back and had a choppy, unrhythmic trot, all of which made him an uncomfortable ride. She had had moments of regret that she had agreed to help but remained determined to see it through.

At the end of the session, she actually could feel an improvement: his trot had achieved some basic rhythm, and he was beginning to engage his hocks, lightening a bit on the forehand and acquiring a modicum of balance. The session had also shown her a new dimension of Michael. It was relatively simple to get a willing, intelligent horse to do what you wanted: horses generally had an innate desire to please. But to school a stupid, unresponsive horse took considerably more skill and a firm determination to make it submit. As Michael had.

"Well, he'll be no more than an adequate hunter," Michael was saying, "which, fortunately, is all Morton wants of him. Sometimes, though, the doting horse owner exceeds his steed's native ability." He grimaced. "You know that dapple gray? Well, Connolly is certain that he has placed the successor to Morning Light in my keeping. Bridie, is the tea wet?" He poked his head into the kitchen.

"In here, Michael," cried Eithne, coming to the door of the lounge and beckoning to them. "Bridie's only just brought it in."

As Selina entered the lounge she paused, staring about her. There was a subtle change in the room, and she saw that Michael was aware of it, too. Catriona, seated on the couch and stroking the marmalade cat, grinned.

"Isn't it marvelous? Auntie Eithne and Bridget have been at it hammer and tongs since the uncles left, Daddy, and everything's all bright and airy."

"Well, as I told Bridie, we really need Bridget to come in more," Eithne began, looking embarrassedly pleased. "Those drapes haven't been cleaned in donkey's years. And those old chintz ones are really most suitable for summer."

The windows were open to the spring afternoon, and the

floral curtains billowed in the breeze, lightly caressing the half-moon table now standing between the windows. On it was a huge old jardiniere, filled with weigela branches, some showing the pink and red of the blossoms. There was another vase on the heavy old refectory table, sporting some late tulips, and Eithne had resurrected pillows covered in the same chintz as the curtains.

"Isn't that table a Sheraton?" Selina asked, pointing to the half-moon table with its slender legs and delicate inlay.

"Yes, and in excellent condition," Eithne replied.

"And is that bowl Staffordshire?"

"Yes, but I had to turn a chip to the wall so it's not noticeable." Eithne looked gratified by Selina's implied compliment.

"It's ever so much cozier now," Catriona said, pushing two pillows behind her back since she was not quite long enough in the thigh to sit comfortably on the deep couch.

"Are you interested in antiques, Eithne?" Selina asked.

"She knows who made everything in this house, and when," Catriona said, quite willing to put her aunt in the best possible light to Selina. "She gets books and books out of the library at Greystones and studies antiques."

Michael regarded his sister-in-law with veiled surprise. He had often seen her with her nose buried in large awkward volumes, but he'd never noticed their titles. He was intrigued when Eithne blushed a bit and became very intent on pouring tea for Selina.

"Well, yes, I've become more interested over the last few years, especially when I took a closer look at some of the things stored in the garret. Did you know that there is a Peninsula chest up there, Michael? It's initialed MCC."

"Another Michael Carradyne," he replied, taking the cup she offered him. "One of the military ones." He addressed Selina. "Carradynes have three professions open to them: horses,

army, and Church. There's rarely been a generation of Carradynes without sons in all three."

"That's more English than Irish, Michael," Selina teased.

"Some of the best Wicklow families *are* more English than
Irish."

The dining room clock struck four loudly.

"Oh, I'd no idea how late it was. I've got to run." Selina
drained her cup, thanked Eithne, complimented her again on
the room, and, with a smile for both Michael and Catriona,
departed.

When Selina turned into her drive, she had to jam on the
brakes: the gravel courtyard was well tenanted. She recognized
the blue BMW, which belonged to Declan Murray, and grimaced. The 220 gray Mercedes was unfamiliar to her, but it
bore Dublin plates. The Ford Cortina belonged to David's accountant, and the other Jag bore northern plates. Somewhat
relieved, for the accountant would not have been present at a
social occasion, she squeezed the Lancia up on the lawn, being
careful to leave plenty of space for the larger cars to maneuver.

Fortunately the men were all in the dining room. She could
hear their voices and see the cigar smoke billowing a blue
haze into the hallway. David would not be pleased that she
hadn't been home when he arrived, although how she could
have guessed his early return was moot, but she'd change first.

"David, I am sorry. I'd no idea you would be down this
afternoon," she said, smiling graciously when she made her
appearance in the dining room five minutes later.

Her smile wavered as she saw the overflowing ashtrays, the
litter of sandwich remains and used cups of coffee, one pushed
dangerously near the edge of the mahogany dining table. She
rescued it, smile intact.

"You've been out all morning, or so Kathleen said," he said
coldly.

"I do apologize, gentlemen"—she ignored his tacit rebuke—"for my tardy welcome, although I see that Kathleen has managed to supply you with some refreshments." She noted that they had gone from sandwiches and coffee to alcohol. "Let me just freshen your drinks. Yours is Scotch and soda, isn't it, Martin?" she said, smiling at the vice-president of a merchant bank with which David had dealings. He was probably supplying David with all the cash he needed for his payrolls.

"We've just about finished," David said, sighing weightily.

"Well, then, my timing is perfect, for I'm never any use to you when there's business to discuss."

It didn't please Selina to note that only Declan Murray caught the barb in her light words. But she went through the motions, getting more ice from the freezer, asking Kathleen to fix canapes. The woman was very relieved to see her employer, and soon the men were resettled in the lounge, drinks in their hands and hot cheese puffs to eat. Selina perched on the footstool near David's wing chair, smiling and pretending interest in cryptic comments that apparently summarized their meeting.

They were becoming more and more concerned at the number of troops the British were sending to Belfast. Troops could only mean trouble, and trouble meant property damage.

"The way tempers are flaring in the North," Martin said, "soon no one will stop to question the religion of those in their way."

"Ach," said one of the northerners in his clipped, half-chewed accent, "ye kin tell a Catholic by the look of him."

"But not the building he owns," Declan Murray said.

"But you'd know by where the building was," came the quick reply.

Selina kept her smile in place, but she did not like sitting at the foot of her husband just then.

The casement clock in the hallway bonged five times, and abruptly the men began to rise, straightening their suit jackets and making their farewells. They must have accomplished something, for they had the air of men who have made decisions as they shook hands with David and edged toward the front door.

"Why on earth didn't you let me know this morning that you'd be down?" Selina asked as David closed the door on the last of them.

"I rang at ten-thirty, and the woman said you'd only just left. She expected you back."

Selina knew that Kathleen had seen her leave, dressed for riding, and she wondered why Kathleen hadn't told David that she'd gone to Cornanagh.

"I'd errands to do, and they took longer than I'd expected," she replied, shrugging. "You know how it can be," she added, seeing his frown. "But I managed. Are you in for dinner tonight? If so, I must tell Kathleen."

"I'm in, I'm in," he said testily, waving at her.

"I knew you'd be in the yard, Trina," said Mary Evans, appearing in the open stall door. "Oh, who's this?"

"Oh, Mary, just look at her," Catriona cried, oblivious to the fact that she hadn't seen her best friend all week. The filly was nibbling the warm bran mash from Catriona's open palm. Catriona had made Mick add an egg for strength. "Isn't she the most pathetic thing you've ever seen! Come on in, easily, though I don't think she has the energy to be scared of anything right now."

"Johnny Cash?" Mary asked, knowing a good deal about Cornanagh's affairs.

Catriona nodded. "The Baldoyle pony races."

"How can people be so mean?" Mary gently stroked the thin,

scarred neck, smoothing a wisp of mane. "And she looks a real dote. Is your father keeping her?"

"At least until we get her well."

"Can you? She looks so awful."

"Well"—Catriona regarded her charge dispassionately—"we'll know tomorrow, Daddy says. She should pick up. If she's going to. Did you bring me homework?"

Mary's expression changed. "Oh, Trina, we were all so shocked about your mother! The Mother Superior led a special novena on Tuesday. I wanted to come to the funeral, but Mum and Dad said that they'd represent the family. Did you see them?"

Catriona held out another handful of the bran mash, and when the filly started to lip it up, she turned to her friend. "No. I don't think I really *saw* anybody."

"No, I expect it was a bit much," Mary said in quick compassion. She was a bit nervous meeting her friend; she didn't really know what she was supposed to say. "Mum said that half of Wicklow County was there: even a representative from the president, and all the *T.D.*s. And the floral tributes covered just acres."

"The flowers smelled." Catriona felt her backbone seized by a fierce tremor. "That's what I remember most. The flowers."

"Oh, Trina," Mary murmured, bending toward her friend and patting her awkwardly on the shoulder, "don't cry. Please don't cry." And she started to weep in sympathy, leaning her head against Catriona's, the two clinging together.

The filly nickered, a soft querying note, and instantly Catriona recovered herself to the task at hand, brushing away her tears with a bran-smeared fist.

"Oh, look what you've done," Mary said, gulping back the last of her tears and managing a tremulous smile. "You're all bran."

"Yes, and I'm supposed to get it into the filly," Catriona said with a little laugh. "I can do something about *you, alanna*," she said to the filly, and Mary just knew that her friend was being terribly brave about her loss and admired Catriona all the more.

❧ 20 ❧

*S*urprisingly enough, there had been no report of the theft of an animal. Michael asked the Gardái to check with the nearby counties, for the filly could have been nicked farther afield than County Dublin. Meanwhile, care of the newly named Orphan Annie was Catriona's first concern every morning, then Conker because, as she said, Conker was nearly better and didn't mind all the attention she was giving his stablemate.

"She might not have *absorbed* it all yet, Michael," Eithne confided as the adults indulged in their customary evening drink. "I worry about her."

"A sick horse always has priority with Trina," Philip said with a chuckle. "Johnny Cash couldn't have picked a better time to bring a charity case into the yard."

Eithne nodded slowly, then began, "It was so thoughtful of Sybil to invite us all to dinner Sunday. But, if you don't mind, Michael, I think I'll give it a miss. That'll give the family a chance to be together."

"Since when aren't you family, Auntie Eithne?" Philip drew himself up as if affronted.

"Oh, Philip, you know what I mean. And . . . well, I have had a long-standing invitation which I just thought I might like to take up this Sunday." She blushed prettily.

"Do tell," teased Philip.

"Nothing, really"—Eithne was flustered—"just a collection of antiques that I rather wanted to look over. It's the final viewing, you see, and last Sunday, of course . . ." Her voice trailed off apologetically.

"The secret can now be told: our Auntie Eithne's a closet antique dealer," Philip said.

"You deserve a day out, Eithne," Michael said warmly. "Don't let these young idjits tease you."

Catriona came in from the dining room, a grin on her face. "A good tea and the most scrumptious pud for afters!" Then she looked guilty and hunched into her shoulders.

"*And* a good pud?" Philip said, quickly bridging the awkwardness. "I'm starving of the hunger, but I'll know better than to fill up."

As they were rising from the table, Michael said that he was going to the pub later to change a check. Did anyone else want some cash? "Tom'd rather take our checks than keep all that money lying around. The Gardái report a spate of robberies."

"There would be, wouldn't there, with the banks shut tight," Eithne said anxiously. "How long is this to go on, Michael?"

"Can't last long. The country'll be ruined." Owen rose on that definitive statement and left the room, his mother looking after him in helpless amazement.

"Well, he's right, you know," Philip remarked amiably.

After a depressing hour going through a pile of sympathy cards and notes, Michael felt he deserved a pint or two at the Willow Grove. As he entered the pub, he caught sight of Fiona Bernon, seated with the Mulvaneys in her usual corner. For the first time, she waved openly, even calling the Mulvaneys' attention to the new arrival.

Jack Garden and Robert Kelly greeted Michael warmly, their voices tinged with solicitude for his bereavement. Michael realized, with a little surprise, that every one of the regulars in the Willow Grove had been at the funeral, including Tom and Fiona.

She came up to the bar now to express sympathy, briefly resting her hand on his arm, her fingers tightening in an unspoken message. Thanking her, Michael deftly withdrew to accept the pint that Tom had pulled for him, but Fiona tossed her long red hair and seated herself on the empty bar stool beside him.

Jack Garden gave Michael a knowing wink. "I heard you got a record price for that gelding of yours."

"Yes, I'm happy to say."

"The Eye-talians, again?"

Michael nodded, then took a long pull on his pint. How was he going to detach himself from Fiona? He was grimly aware that there had been many times when he had been grateful for her discreet willingness, but right now bedding her was the last thing on his mind. For a variety of reasons.

"Say, is that gray of Connolly's half as good as he's making out?" Jack asked, pulling Michael toward him conspiratorially.

"He's got quite a pop in him over poles on the lunge," Michael agreed, ever the diplomat. "Good strong animal, but it's early days. Hell, we've only just backed him. As you and I know so well, anything can happen with horses."

"Yeah, pity about the glass in the menage. Pony sound yet?"

"Next week should see him right."

"Hey, Fiona, are you dry there, girl?" Jack said, looking beyond Michael's shoulder at her. "Michael, it's your turn to shout—since you've got pockets of shillings selling horses to the Eye-talians."

Michael vowed that he would repay Jack Garden somehow. In the meantime, this was scarcely the place, or time, to make too much of a fuss. He smiled and joked with Jack, Fiona and Bob, and Tom behind the bar; exchanged greetings with all the regulars. Later he found the appropriate moment to have a word with Tom, and the man was quite willing to change his check, returning with the notes in a brown envelope.

"Got a sick horse," he announced when they'd all bought a round. It was ten-fifteen: not early enough to give offense, but too early for Fiona to leave unnoticed.

Fiona gave his arm a quick sympathetic squeeze, then glanced at him sideways.

"A little thoroughbred filly injured at Baldoyle . . ." Michael eased himself away from Fiona without meeting her eyes.

"Did they nick one of yours?" Jack Garden was alarmed.

"No, but I've got to repair the damage done her. Catriona's doing the hard work. Well, g'night and God bless."

Waving impartially at all, he left the pub, reaching the safety of the Austin.

When he drove into the courtyard, the yard light was on. He walked quietly to the corner and heard Catriona talking to Conker as she filled his water bucket. The little filly had her head over her stall door and was watching.

"So, if she continues to eat and drink, and she feels safe here with us, she ought to do just fine, Conker. You don't mind. It isn't as if I'd neglect you."

Michael smiled as he walked quietly across the courtyard to the Tulip's stable for his late night check.

"I'm right, aren't I, Tulip?" he said as he reached the stallion's box. "Catriona's a horse Carradyne at heart."

The black stallion farruped quietly; his eyes, reflecting light from the single overhead bulb, were all that was visible of him in the shadows of his stable. Michael opened the door, and the Tulip politely walked back a few steps. The water bucket was brimming, and Michael wondered if Catriona had filled it. Well, she was the only one of his children who'd dare. Even Philip was wary of the Tulip. He gave the stallion several affectionate slaps on his heavy neck.

• •

Sybil had invited them for one o'clock on Sunday, which allowed them time to ride out, get the yard to rights, and shower
and dress appropriately. Michael had heard about Catriona's
blistered feet and asked Eithne to be sure of the fit of a new
pair of shoes, a task the two had undertaken on Saturday afternoon. Isabel had had good clothes sense, and Catriona, her
dark hair unbraided and swinging down her back, looked quite
fetching in a simple blue dress that matched the color of her
eyes.

Sybil and Aidan lived in Mount Merrion, on North Avenue,
in a semidetached, well-built four-bedroom house that had
been constructed in the building boom after the war. Michael
had always approved Sybil's choice of husband: the Roche family had a solid business that was steadily expanding, and he
got on very well with Aidan's parents. It was obvious that he
and Sybil were happy together, and they had two fine children
to add to their happiness. Isabel had had some queer notion
that Aidan might turn mean to Sybil, but there had never been
any evidence of that.

Right now, his daughter and her husband welcomed their
guests at the door, and little Perry and Ann came bouncing
out of the lounge, shrieking with glee at the appearance of
Grandda. Michael swung them both up and carried them into
the room.

"Have you heard from Jack yet?" Sybil asked when everyone
had been served their Sunday drinks and were seated in the
lounge.

"No, although Patrick said he would contact both the Nic-
araguan embassy in the States and the Order's office in New
York State."

Sybil frowned. "I do hope they haven't had another coup
or revolution or whatever."

"That would have made at least a mention in the papers,"
Aidan replied.

"In any event, I managed to get a letter off to him, with a clipping from the *Times*," Michael said.

"That was a very nice article," Sybil murmured, and bent her head, dabbing at her eyes and nose with a tissue. "I honestly didn't realize that Mother did so much community work. . . ." After a moment's silence, she began afresh, lightening her mood with determination. "How's that little waif of yours, Trina?"

"She's come on a treat," Catriona replied. She glanced at her father for confirmation and grinned as he nodded. "We caught her just in time. Another day and she'd've been too far gone. Poor thing. And she's so sweet, despite the way she was treated. Some horses are like that, though, genuine, honest, kind."

"Unlike Temper," Philip said with feeling. He'd had a hairy ride on the gelding that morning.

"He's one of the stubbornest animals we've ever bred," Michael agreed.

The phone rang, and Sybil excused herself while Aidan courteously complimented his brother-in-law on his success in the show. When Sybil returned from the phone call, her eyes were a trifle reddened.

"Dear," she said, "Nualla Fennell has called a meeting for tomorrow evening. Is that all right?"

Aidan grinned, teasingly proud. "This one's following in her mother's footsteps, doing community work."

"What? Not my mother's." Sybil rolled her eyes and grinned at her father. "She'd've had a fit if she knew I was assisting battered wives." She clasped her hands in an attitude of prayer and gazed soulfully heavenward. "It is a wife's duty to submit to her husband's will, even if it results in black eyes and lacerations!" She gave a snort of disgust. "Well, some of those gurriers are going to find that the worm is turning in Ireland!"

"I'm starved, Syb," Aidan said, noting the surprise on his father-in-law's face and rising to his feet.

"That's right, change the subject. Ohhhh, you men!" Sybil said with mock fierceness. She gave Aidan a quick kiss on the cheek before she started for the kitchen. "Trina, would you give me a hand? And Perry, you can be useful, too." She beckoned to her son, who obediently descended from his grandfather's lap to trot after mother and aunt.

"What's she on about?" Philip asked as Aidan ushered them into the dining room and pointed out their seats.

"Mind you, having heard some of the tales she brings home from these meetings"—Aidan lifted his daughter into her high chair and began to fasten a bib about her neck—"I agree that something should be done. I don't entirely hold with some of Sybil's more radical notions, but it's to her credit that she's willing to do what she can to help."

Sybil entered the dining room, proudly carrying the roast on its wooden platter, while Catriona followed with two heavy dishes of vegetables.

It was an excellent meal, complete with Yorkshire pud, done to perfection, three veg and creamed and roast potatoes, and a large apple tart with whipped cream for sweet. After the dinner, Sybil took her two children up for their afternoon nap while Trina and Aidan, who coaxed Philip in to dry the delft, coped with the washing-up. Michael had been ensconced in the lounge with a glass of excellent port and was feeling quite relaxed.

"Daddy," Sybil began when she rejoined her father, closing the lounge door behind her, "how is Catriona taking Mother's death?"

"Eithne thinks she hasn't quite realized it yet."

Sybil sat down on the footstool beside Michael's chair and gave her father a determined look. "I think she's terribly relieved and doesn't dare admit it," she said. "Mother was just beastly to her, you know, and there wasn't anything you or I could do about it, was there?"

Michael shook his head, feeling a surge of relief at Sybil's candor.

"Oh, I loved Mother, Daddy, for her good qualities: she never shirked an unpleasant task, and she was really very good managing the ICA and Church affairs. But she simply had no understanding of Catriona at all. I always thought it was because she didn't *want* Catriona." She gave her father a penetrating stare. "I was quite old enough, at fourteen, to understand."

"Sybil!" Michael was startled, and the glass of port tilted in his hand, splashing him. Absently she offered him a tissue from her apron pocket.

"Well, I don't hide from truths, Daddy. That's one reason Aidan and I get along so well." She giggled unexpectedly. "You'll never believe the twaddle she told me before I got married. Poor Mother! Poor Daddy!" There was a knowledge in her eyes as she patted his hand that astonished Michael. "You've been loyal to a fault and with precious little to compensate—except the horses. That's why I nearly cheered when you came down hard on Grandmother's notion of bringing Catriona up 'suitably.' Her notions are what made Mother so impossible. And Daddy, I really tried hard"—Sybil put both hands on her father's arm, her eyes beseeching him to believe—"to get Mother to see reason and shed her medieval notions of woman's position in Ireland. But there was Grandmother, always supporting the opposite point of view!"

"Sybil," Michael said, covering her hands with his, "don't blame yourself. You did try. Isabel didn't want to hear."

"Emotional blackmail." Sybil nodded knowingly. "Only it backfired on her." Sybil gave a sniff and retrieved the port-stained tissue to blow her nose briskly. "Well, Catriona is not going to be as ignorant as Mother was brought up to be. Not

if I can help it. She's going to *know* what her options are as
a woman. And you're going to see to it that she makes a mark
as a horsewoman—Cornanagh's first!"

Michael burst out laughing at his daughter's aggressiveness
and caught the finger she was waggling at him in an affectionate
grip, grinning back at her so amiably that she relaxed and gave
him a sheepish smile.

"So, we're agreed," she finished, less militant now that she
knew her father was on her side. "Grandma Marshall is out,
Cornanagh and horses are in, and I'll be over to check on
Catriona whenever I can. When's the cousin coming?"

"Eamonn said he was sending her over as soon as her school
was out. June fifteenth or so."

"Wants to get the child out of the house before he files for
the divorce? That's wise."

"How did you know?"

"Oh," Sybil said airily, "I picked up a few things that Uncle
Pat let drop. We could use divorce here in Ireland. . . ."

Trina, Aidan, and Philip entered the lounge at that point, and
the conversation turned to more general topics. At three-thirty
Michael ended the pleasant afternoon by reminding his daughter that he had horses to tend. But he had genuinely enjoyed
himself and embraced Sybil with great affection at leavetaking.
It had been a most instructive afternoon.

Eithne had managed to slip away in her car while the others
were all out riding. She had been so grateful that Sybil had
invited them to Sunday dinner in Mount Merrion, leaving her
free for the day. Davis Haggerty would be leaving for the States
on the Monday plane, and they'd had so little time together,
what with Isabel's funeral and everything.

So far, with the exception of Bridie, no one suspected that
Eithne's interest in antiques was anything more than a hobby.
Ever since she had become friendly with Davis, she had felt

obliged to practice discretion. In the beginning she had not wished to offend Isabel, and now . . . well, she felt it was a very poor time to spring any more surprises on Michael or upset Catriona so soon after the loss of her mother. She had been racking her brains trying to find a solution, and bless him, so had Davis.

The thing of it was that their association had all started so innocently three years ago. She and Meg Kelly had been schoolgirls together, and Isabel had certainly never objected to Eithne going out for an evening with Meg. It wasn't as if Eithne had been *looking* for male companionship, but Davis Haggerty had been so completely respectful, even at the beginning when he'd chatted up Meg and Eithne, more out of loneliness than from any lascivious motive. He had such an infectious chuckle, and a really charming smile, and told such interesting tales of his travels about Ireland, that it would have taken someone considerably more hard-hearted than Eithne, or Meg, to discourage him.

And he'd been quite candid. In the very first hour, he had told them all about himself—that he was divorced, had a son in college, that he'd been in the army in the Pacific, that he worked for a very respectable decorating firm in Houston, Texas, and came to Dublin twice a year looking for antiques. His firm "did" houses all over the state.

"That's why I need so much stuff," he had told them. "In Texas we use space because we've got it, and we like to spread out. Why, we've got as much oil as those Arabs, and that means money, which means we can charge as much as the traffic will bear when we get the things home. All it has to be is old. Preferably big, to fill up our Texan spaces. We don't try to put anything over on our customers: they get value for their money."

"The original owners don't, though," Eithne had pointed out.

"Well, honey"—his habit of addressing her as "honey" in that charming drawl of his always delighted her—"you know as well as I do, now, that they don't value what they've got. We pay more than they would get at an auction, if anyone could get some of that heavy old stuff *to* sales rooms. We get fine old furniture, they get money, and everyone's happy. That's good business."

Meg had liked him, too, and never discouraged him from joining them. It had been Meg who had told him about the furniture auction in Aughrim, which she'd seen advertised in the *Wicklow People*. And it had been she who suggested that Eithne act as his guide. Which Eithne had done. And she had enjoyed the outing tremendously, as much because he turned out to be so knowledgeable about antiques as because he was a most agreeable companion.

She had been his driver that spring on several excursions and had promised—rather surprised at herself—to keep an eye out for any especially tempting auctions over the summer. He sent her a checklist of items that his firm would be very eager to obtain and willing to pay her a "finder's fee." He came over several times to secure a purchase which Eithne discovered for him. At no time had he pressed her for details about her family circumstances, and he had always respected her request that he not appear uninvited at Cornanagh. In every way he had been the perfect gentleman.

By the end of the following year, their friendship had developed considerably. Eithne missed him more than she had expected to and anticipated each return with an eagerness that surprised her.

She had become valuable to Davis as a contact, although she didn't think of herself in such terms: she was only helping a friend, after all. She knew the county families in Meath and West Meath from her girlhood years there—her mother had come from a very good old family in Louth. From Isabel's involvement in the Irish Countrywoman's Association, she had become familiar with many lovely homes and estates in Wicklow, Waterford, and Wexford. To learn more about the various periods of furniture and their originators, she had started taking out books from the library at Greystones, ordering special volumes from the vast Trinity College Library. Gradually she began to appreciate the finer points of the different schools of furniture designers and to understand instinctively what would suit the needs of Davis's clients.

She began to watch out for the sales of county estates, and once or twice she had acted on her own, securing a few pieces she thought Davis could use. Davis had complimented her instincts and had insisted on giving her the finder's fee and expenses. Eithne had been somewhat embarrassed, but the money had come in handy, and she had been grateful for the windfall. Actually she found that she had enjoyed the search, the challenge, and certainly the thrill of auctions, outbidding contenders without going over whatever price she had initially set herself. Davis had given some invaluable pointers.

"You figure out what sort of money is tops for the item. Then you bid up to that point, and quit. That way you're never burned. People are funny in an auction situation. They'll bid out of sight for the worst crap imaginable, simply to keep someone else from getting it. Crazy!"

Just after the Spring Show, she had seen the stark public notice announcing that creditors to the estate of Desmond Comyn of Rathderry House, Wexford, should contact his solicitors. Remembering how impressed she had been with the decorations and furnishings at the Georgian house when she and Isabel had attended an ICA tea there, Eithne had phoned his widow, Elizabeth Comyn, and set up an appointment, which was to take place in a few hours. If the estate was up for sale to satisfy creditors, the furniture was likely to be sold as well—

and through Davis, Mrs. Comyn could get a far better price for some of her possessions than other dealers were likely to offer.

Now she drove into the Coliemore Hotel parking lot, empty this early on a Sunday morning, and parked next to Davis's rented Cortina. He had obviously been watching for her, for he emerged from the door of the hotel as she got out of her car.

"Gee, honey, I thought you'd never get here. Time's a wasting, and we've a fair piece to go," he said as he ushered her into the Cortina and settled himself in the driver's seat. He contented himself with a brief pat on her leg, a familiarity that always struck Eithne as affectionate. Davis liked to touch things—furniture, china, people—as if to assure himself they were solid, not illusion.

He was wearing the tweed jacket she had persuaded him to buy the previous autumn. It was a lovely mixture of heathery blues and grays that enhanced his Texan tan and his light blue eyes. Davis was nowhere near as handsome as her Owen had been, but his face had character; his irregular features also suggested a transparent honesty that was not assumed, though it often stood him in very good stead in his bargaining. He was only a few inches taller than she was and of stocky build, but he was quick and deft in his movements, never appearing clumsy or awkward.

"How're things, honey?" he asked solicitously, stealing a glance at her.

"I honestly don't think even Michael has recognized Belle's death," she said with a sigh. "He's been so marvelous. Of course, it's partly the horses: you have to carry on. You can't just leave them to themselves, and Michael has several three-year-olds in to be backed."

"I sure would like to see an Irishman break a horse, Eithne," he said with a sly grin.

"Now, Davis, I've told you that I'll invite you to Cornanagh as soon as I feel the time is right."

"That'd mean so much to me, Eithne honey. I don't like this hole-in-the-wall nonsense. You know how much I love you."

"But I can't leave Cornanagh now, not when everything's so muddled up. It won't be much longer—I promise."

Davis glanced at her, then nodded, a smile twitching at the corner of his mouth. "So, brief me about Rathderry. If it was a James Hicks satinwood desk you saw, it'll be a find. But will she know how valuable it is?"

"Quite likely. Elizabeth Comyn had everything displayed to perfection in her house, with just the right accessories. And she served us tea in a lovely old Royal Doulton set."

"Then how come she's so broke the creditors are selling it all up?"

"You wouldn't understand men like Desmond Comyn, Davis," Eithne said, and she was glad he didn't. "As long as he could live the way he wanted to and put off his creditors, he didn't think beyond the present. And then he died of a heart attack, with no warning whatsoever. The paper said there wasn't even a will . . . . You *will* give Elizabeth Comyn the best possible price you can, won't you, Davis?"

"Sure, sure, honey. What else do you remember she had in the living room? If we could get ol' Brat Comstock one of those fancy sideboards he's been yakking about . . ."

"Well, there is a massive one in the dining room. It was probably built in the house from the look of it. But I don't know if that's what Mr. Comstock has in mind."

Davis gave a snort. "I don't think *he'll* know until he sees it."

"Then you'll simply have to make him believe that the Rathderry one is it. Really, won't it impress him to know it had to be dismantled and shipped in sections? And that it was crafted under the eye of the master from timber seasoned especially and assembled in the very room in which it has stood for nearly three hundred years?"

Davis chuckled and reached over to pat her thigh. "I swan, honey, you've picked up a real good spiel from listening to me, haven't you?"

❦ 21 ❧

"Wretched hour to be hanging about an airport," Michael Carradyne muttered as he paced outside the customs hall in Dublin Airport, awaiting the arrival of his niece's flight from New York. It was nine-thirty of a Sunday morning, when any decent working man should be having a lie-in.

Catriona regarded her father surreptitiously. He wasn't usually bad-tempered, but yesterday Mr. Connolly had not been happy with Father's opinion of his gray gelding and had removed him from Cornanagh. There'd been quite a few loud words in the yard. Then Temper had lived up to his name, shedding Artie casually three times before her father had yelled for Philip to get up. Philip had lasted longer, but then he, too, had come off. He had climbed right back on, of course, and somehow stayed in the saddle long enough to prove to Temper that he couldn't just discard riders at will.

Afterward, as their father led a sweaty but completely unrepentant Temper back to the yard, Philip grinned at her as she walked by on Orphan Annie. He gave the filly an appraising glance.

"You wouldn't know her for the wretched rack of bones that Johnny Cash brought here four weeks ago, would you?"

Catriona beamed happily. Careful feeding and nursing had put pounds on the now graceful little filly, and her coat gleamed with health. She was so much improved that Michael had decided a little gentle exercise would firm up her muscles.

247

She hadn't actually been lamed, so she was sound enough to be ridden. Annie had cooperated, even to dipping her head to accept the light snaffle bit. Everyone agreed she was a real dote, and even Auntie Eithne was following her progress with keen interest.

"The flight's in, Trina," her father announced, breaking into her thoughts. She looked up excitedly.

The board was indeed blinking, and both father and daughter rushed to the window to see the plane as it taxied back up the runway. It seemed another age before the passengers started to emerge from the customs hall. Catriona tried to spot her cousin; she'd practically memorized Patricia's Christmas photo.

"Hi," said a cheerful voice at her elbow. "I'll bet you're my cousin!" A luggage cart swung erratically into Catriona's shins. "Whoops. This thing's got no steering or brakes."

Catriona stared at the young woman who stood there, grinning from ear to ear. The ponytails were missing, and she was several inches taller than expected, but there was no mistaking the Carradyne grin and the dark blue eyes.

"You—you're so grown-up!" Catriona blurted out.

"Hell, I'm an American," Patricia replied, then grimaced and snapped the fingers of her one free hand. "Damn, I told Daddy that I'd watch my language. Don't want to shock you, do I? Hey, isn't that my uncle Mihall?" She pointed unerringly at the perplexed and searching figure of Michael Carradyne.

Catriona nodded. "Yes, that's my father."

"Gee, he's like a slim version of my father. I know I'll like him. Who's he looking for?"

"Well, the stewardess escorting you, I think."

"Stewardess?" Patricia burst out laughing. "I travel to boarding school all the time by myself. What trouble could I get into on a plane across the Atlantic, for heaven's sake?"

Catriona had to admit that she'd have taken her cousin for

a much older girl, she was so poised and self-assured. And she wore the smartest trouser suit, with a scarf knotted casually at her throat. She had a navy-blue coat over her left arm, a big handbag over her shoulder, and several shopping bags hanging from her right hand. She shifted them now and turned expectantly toward her uncle.

Catriona waved an arm to attract her father's attention. He approached her, frowning impatiently at his daughter's summons, then caught sight of her companion and stared in amazement.

"Hi, Uncle Michael. I spotted Catriona . . . ."

As Michael hesitated, trying to decide whether or not to embrace this self-possessed young woman, Patricia threw her free arm about him and gave him a kiss on the cheek.

"I'd know you anywhere," she said. "You're the spit of my dad . . . if he'd only lose some weight." She hooked her free arm about Catriona. "And we could almost be sisters, couldn't we?" She giggled. "I always wanted a sister. Anything would be an improvement on those brothers of mine."

"Is all this luggage yours?" Michael asked, eyeing the trolley.

Patricia grinned. "Daddy had to cough up twenty bucks for overweight"—she pointed to a small metal trunk—"but I wouldn't come without my boots, and I thought I'd better bring my own saddle because it fits me right. Daddy said I was silly because you'd have scads of tack, but if I was going to bring all the rest of my camp stuff, it seemed sillier not to bring my saddle, too."

In something of a daze, the two Irish Carradynes led their American relative out to the car park.

Everything was fascinating to Patricia on the way across Dublin. She commented on the "funny-looking" houses, the "absolutely super" Georgian windows, the American embassy ("positively weirdo"), and the Royal Dublin Showgrounds ("Is that where you sold your horse, Uncle Michael?"). And she was properly impressed by the clear view of Dun Laoghaire as seen across Sandymount strand with the tide out. She had a hundred questions, and the answers given were often lost in the next spate of queries. Catriona almost exhausted herself trying to keep up with her. But her father chuckled several times at Patricia's reception of well-known landmarks. "Groovy" was the ultimate accolade, to be uttered in breathy wonder.

"Oh, I'm going to love it here!" she cried exuberantly at one point. "Oh, you're so good to let me come." And she threw her arms about Michael Carradyne's neck and gave him a moist kiss on the cheek.

"Easy now, girl. I've got to drive, you know," her uncle exclaimed gruffly but with a laugh in his voice, and Catriona, sitting in the back, grinned to hear it.

Patricia bounced about to kneel on the front seat and hung over its back to speak to Catriona again. "I brought a lot of things—you know, little things that Daddy said you might not have in Ireland. I gotta bottle of some great bourbon for you from Daddy, Uncle Mi— Can I call you Mike or Mihall? Uncle Michael sounds so formal, and it's a mouthful."

"I'd prefer Mihall to Mike, Patricia."

"Oh, for God's sake, call me Pat. Patricia is so . . . so . . . icky." Then she covered her mouth and made her eyes go wide. "Oooops! I promised Daddy that I'd moderate my language. Please don't tell him that I goofed my first hour in Ireland."

To Catriona's surprise, her father laughed.

"How much farther is it to Cornanagh? Daddy has told me just everything about it. It sounds absolutely groovy! I mean, just living in a house that's two hundred years old!"

"Two hundred and seventy-two, to be accurate. The mews is older than that."

"Wow!" Pat's eyes widened again, and she giggled. "That's

older than most of 'em in Boston or Hartford and the old wrecks near us that the state restored as tourist attractions— Oh, look! . . ."

It became almost as much a trip of discovery for Catriona, seeing old, familiar things take on a new allure through Patricia's enthusiasm. Her cousin even "adored" Sugarloaf.

"I've never seen such a perfect mountain. Wow!" She steepled her fingers into a cone shape. "Boy, are you lucky living in Ireland, Cat. Can I call you Cat? Then we'll be Pat and Cat." She roared with laughter at that. "I like it, I like it! Cat and Pat."

The enthusiasm and vitality of the new arrival infected Cornanagh. Even Bridie could not resist Patricia's ebullience.

"My dad told me all about the super suppers you've fed him, Bridie, and about your soda bread, and your puds, and how you gave him the best breakfasts he's had since he left Ireland." The compliments, delivered with sincerity, actually brought a flush of pleasure to Bridie's face, and she flapped her apron about, a sure sign of embarrassment.

Pat was sympathetic with Owen, who was sullen with hangover, and whipped him up what she said was a sovereign remedy for "overindulgence." She vied with Philip in telling American versions of jokes, and some that were confided quietly in a corner had Philip covering his mouth against bursts of laughter. She won Mick over in the course of a few minutes because she had not only brought him a fancy hoof pick but proceeded to demonstrate its various uses with a skill born of considerable practice.

After the initial introductions, Patricia wheedled a willing-enough Philip into lugging her metal box down to the stables. Thus the first personal item that the visitor unpacked at Cornanagh was her saddle, which she stowed carefully on the rack Mick indicated. He cast a judicious eye over it when she removed its waterproof cover and did not miss the proprietary way Patricia stroked it before she began an enthusiastic tour of the stable with Mick and her cousin.

"My God," she exclaimed at her first sight of the Tulip. "My God, what a lot of horse! I'm far too used to Standard Breds."

Before either Catriona or Mick could caution her about the Tulip's little ways, she had extended her hand, palm up, and with grave dignity he delicately nibbled the sugar cube with which she was bribing him.

"And you breed all your own horses from him?"

"Most, not all," Catriona replied, rather pleased with the Tulip's effect on Pat.

The whole tour was punctuated with exclamations and American expletives of amazement, yet Catriona heard nothing false in Patricia's unstinting praise, and she noticed that her cousin had already gained Mick's approval.

"This is all *so* different from the place where I ride. I mean, Cornanagh is a real live working stable!" Then, with a shake of her shoulders, "This is going to be the neatest summer of my life."

With an unusual burst of spontaneous affection, Catriona flung her arms about her cousin. "Oh, it will, Pat. I know it will!"

Only one odd note appeared to mar the success of the tour: Patricia was merely polite about Conker and the Prince. But she became quite excited about Orphan Annie and stroked the filly's neck affectionately. "She's lovely, even if she is the smallest horse you've got."

"She's just on the 14.2 mark," Catriona said, "so she's a pony."

"Well, she looks like a horse," Pat cried so vehemently that Catriona wondered what her cousin had against ponies.

Patricia said all the right things when they got to the fields to inspect the horses let out for day and the young stock. It was when she was watching the antics of Tulip's Son and the other foals that she made her most endearing statement to Mick.

"You know, I can sit on a horse and do most of the proper things to make one go, but I don't know much about horses at all."

"Well, now, in that case, you've got the right attitude to learn," Mick said, nodding his head in approval.

The day went from peak to peak for Catriona. She and Patricia went to late Mass, and her cousin thought the church was "just marvie" and Father John the most impressive priest. They were late back for Sunday dinner, but Bridie said it didn't matter: the roast wasn't destroyed, and the pud would keep.

Dinner was enlivened by Patricia's enthusiasms over all she'd seen and the questions that indicated a genuine desire for enlightenment. At one point she remarked, "Oh, Gawd, Daddy doesn't call me chatterbox for nothing, and I did swear on a stack that I'd behave myself. I guess I'm not, am I?" It was said with such ingratiating charm that everyone spoke at once to reassure her, even Owen.

She insisted on helping with the washing-up, even though Auntie Eithne said that she and Catriona could do it. But Patricia was adamant.

"If I'm family, and I am, then I do everything that Cat does. I'm not a freeloader, I can tell you that."

Once the chore was done, Auntie Eithne urged Catriona to help her cousin unpack. Catriona thought that perhaps her aunt had found Patricia a trifle wearing. She herself wondered if Pat ever wound down, and then she felt guilty for the thought.

Pat unpacked the first of her cases and then decided that she had to try out the bunks. Catriona politely gave her first choice, as both beds were freshly made up.

"I think it'll be groovy sleeping way up here," came the answer as Pat crawled up the ladder. "Hey, this is just great, Cat! Your house has such high ceilings. You could have put in three floors instead of just two and had space left over. Oh, bliss! The worst thing about airplanes is that you can't get stretched out with your feet *up*."

Catriona was hanging Patricia's clothes in the press, so she didn't notice the silence from the upper bunk at first. Then came an audible, if delicate, snore.

"Pat?" she called softly. If Patricia was really asleep, Catriona didn't want to wake her. To be sure, she climbed up the ladder. There was her cousin, arms flung over her head, fast asleep.

The next morning, because she could not expect to be excused from school even if she had a house guest, Catriona went off as quietly as possible, to let her cousin have a good long lie-in.

It was hard to keep her mind on her schoolwork because she kept wondering if her father had already put Patricia up to ride or if she had been allowed to help Mick with such stable chores as she could manage. But the school day finally ended, and she flew down the Kilquade road to Cornanagh. To her delight, Patricia was swinging on the gate, waiting for her, and they fell into each other's arms as if they'd been separated for years instead of a few hours.

"I rode a pony, and I got thrown four times!" Patricia cried, grabbing Catriona's book bag and dancing about her, swinging the bag wildly. It was only then that Catriona noticed the scrape on Patricia's chin and another along her arm.

"Which pony?" she asked, aghast.

"Conker. But you see, I've never ridden a *pony*"—her tone was slightly derogatory—"in my life, and there just wasn't enough under me to hang on to. I was mortified! And I didn't even have any control because Uncle Mihall had me on a lunge and I had to ride with my arms folded for hours at the sitting trot. And I kept losing my balance, and whoops! There I was on the ground, staring up at Conker, and he, the beast, laughed at me!"

"Conker wouldn't do such a thing!"

"Well, he did. Four times. Twice, I admit, while I was jumping him, and I wasn't even allowed to hold the reins then because Uncle Mihall said I had to develop an independent seat. But at the end I made it over a grid without falling off!" She shook her head in awe. "Boy, your father's the best instructor I've ever had. Really the only one, if you get right down to facts. Certainly the only one who *knows* what he's doing. When I told him that I'd never even ridden a pony before, he practically dropped his teeth. So then I explained that I'd been riding show hunters and why I wanted so desperately to come to Ireland and learn how to ride properly. Your father said that if I really work at my position and hands, he thinks I'll be able for Annie. I'm light, and she's gentle. You don't mind my riding your little horse, do you? It was the most super morning I've spent in simply years!"

By this time they had entered the house and Catriona had changed out of her school clothes and into her riding things.

"No, I don't mind at all, Pat," she replied. "She's genuine and much too honest to pull a fast one on you."

Patricia hugged her and rattled on amiably. "Then we had lunch. Bridie made the most delicious soup, and I made a pig of myself on her brown bread. My God, how good the butter tastes over here! The stuff at home leaves an icky film on the roof of your mouth. I can see what Daddy means about Ireland." The two girls started down the stairs. "And you're to ride the Prince, and I'm supposed to watch because your father says I'll learn as much watching you ride as I would riding myself. Are you that good?"

Unable to reply to such a question, Catriona hurried down the stairs and toward the yard, Patricia trailing behind her.

For once Catriona's notable concentration on horseback failed her. She was acutely aware of Patricia standing in the corner, watching her—and even more keenly aware that she consciously wanted to impress her cousin with her equestrian ability. To compound matters, neither her father nor the Prince was in the best frame of mind. She could understand the pony: he often reacted to his rider's mood. Her father's irritability was harder to understand.

"Catriona, will you concentrate? I expect that sort of thing from Sean, but not you! Now, settle him. Circle at the trot until he's back on the bit. You Americans don't use as much contact with your horse's mouth as we do here, Patricia," he added in a more conversational tone. "Notice how Trina keeps her leg just behind the girth: you ride with your leg more for-ward—out the front, we'd call it. All right, now, Trina. Turn him to the outside track. And don't let him quicken. Notice how Trina leans forward from the hips and gives with her hands as she jumps so she doesn't chuck the pony in the mouth. That's right, Trina. On you go!"

"Jumping! Gee, I never thought I'd be able to jump at all. You don't get to do that in the States until you're real advanced."

"Really?" Michael was surprised. "I don't think Catriona re-members when she couldn't. My father had her jumping on old Blister by the time she was five."

"No wonder she's so good!"

Catriona heard such a gratifying note of respect in her cou-sin's voice that she almost dropped the contact; but for the warning kick she gave, the Prince would have tried to run out as she finished the course. She hunched her shoulders, antic-ipating her father's reprimand.

"Don't slouch in the saddle, Trina. Head up, shoulders back, and I want a smooth transition into the walk. That'll be all for the Prince, but I want you to give Annie a half hour's exercise. And just a little trot."

He gave her a smile as she drew up beside him, slapping the Prince on the rump as she walked him out of the menage.

Pat jogged beside them back to the yard, grinning up at her all the while.

The next morning Catriona carried a note from her father to the Mother Superior, asking permission for Patricia to attend the Wednesday half day of classes. To Catriona's delight, permission was duly granted. On Wednesday an excited Patricia was introduced to Mary Evans on the bus, and Mary was suitably awed by the American's vivacity and friendliness. During the school sessions, Patricia was a model of propriety, but on the bus home she was her exuberant self again, asking hundreds of questions about school, work, and teachers.

"You guys have to work a lot harder than we do," she finally said, heaving a deep sigh. "I'm glad I only had to go one day. Boy, when I tell my gang, maybe they'll stop griping. They never had it so good!"

When they got to the house, the girls found that Bridie had made a special lunch. There were freshly baked ginger biscuits and a sponge cake for the dinner sweet, with a bowl of strawberries picked from the garden.

"Mind you, it took me all morning what with the art'ritis in me knees paining me, but they've got to be picked. Mrs. Healey and that aunt of yours"—Bridie scowled so that Catriona knew Eithne was still not in her favor—"are in the lounge with your father. Now that you're both here, Pat, you go tell them to come eat their lunch. Catriona, you can help me put it all on the table."

Fortunately she turned to get a platter from the fridge and didn't see Patricia mouthing, "What's up?" to Catriona, who simply motioned for her to go to the lounge.

Catriona was bringing in the butter and salad cream when Selina Healey and her aunt bustled in with other bowls and platters.

"Now, you just give your poor knees a rest, Bridie," Selina

was saying over her shoulder, and then she grinned conspiratorially at Eithne, Michael, and the girls.

"Are you riding with us this afternoon, Selina?" Catriona
asked.

"I've been asked," was the smiling reply, "and it's such a
beautiful day, I can't refuse."

Michael turned to Catriona. "I think we'll have to let Pat ride
Conker out—with Selina's permission, of course." Selina inclined her head graciously and winked at Catriona. "He's really
the only choice for her at her present standard. . . ." Pat
groaned, and Michael gave her a long look until she subsided
with a meek, "Sorry." "And I think she'd enjoy a hack after two
lunge lessons from me."

"Shall I ride the Prince, then?" Catriona asked, her voice
carefully neutral.

"No, Sean'll be riding him. I want you to hack Charlie out."

"Charlie!" Her brief surge of resentment at having someone
else ride Conker vanished in delight. The adults smiled back
at her.

"Selina's leading file on Flirty Lady, and I'll be rear guard
on Emmett. We'll have a nice long hack."

"Down to the beach at Greystones?" asked Catriona. When
he nodded, she asked, "Could Mary Evans come with us, too?"

"I don't see why not," her father agreed, smiling.

"And the Cornanagh Cavalry rides out again," Selina said
with a laugh.

An hour later, everyone rode out of Cornanagh in keen anticipation of a fine hack. Selina Healey on Flirty Lady led with
Mary just behind her on Champers; then came Pat on Conker;
Sean, already acting the maggot on the Prince; Catriona, radiant
with being on Charlie's back again; and Michael Carradyne on
the sturdy Emmett.

As they trotted up the short hill toward McBride's Lane and

she experienced the smoothness of Charlie's gait, Catriona sighed in sheer delight. Oh, he was heaven to ride: even better than Conker. She felt a twinge of disloyalty and glanced ahead to see how Pat was faring on her former favorite. She was rising easily to the trot—in fact, better than Sean, who seemed to get an extra bounce every other stride. They had to halt while Selina opened the gate to the lane, and as soon as the horses began to string out behind their leader, once again the Prince fussed to overtake Conker. Pat looked back nervously.

"More contact, Sean," her father called from behind her. "You're not to pass the others out."

Then everything happened at once. Flirty Lady shied at the bullock, who put his head through the hedge on the left. Mary's pony had more sense, but Conker, with an unfamiliar rider on his back, sidled away from the apparition. And that was all the excuse the Prince needed. He began to buck.

"Sit back! Sit back!" her father cried as the boy leaned forward, trying to get the pony's head up.

Instinctively Catriona reined Charlie to the left as her father urged Emmett forward. Selina responded by pulling her mare across the track, and Mary Evans pushed her pony up the left-hand bank. The Prince, having pulled the reins from Sean's grasp, stopped bucking long enough to scramble through the brush into the field, where, with another massive explosion, he pitched Sean right over his head, depositing him heavily on the ground. Freed, the pony sped up the hill, cutting a track through the new green of the field's crop.

"Get the pony, Selina!" cried Michael Carradyne, groaning as he saw the damage being done to the new growth. Even as he spoke, Selina was in pursuit, and though he permitted himself a moment's admiration for her quick-wittedness, he was more acutely aware of the boy, sprawled unmoving on the ground. "Here, Trina, hold Emmett. You all stays here!"

Following the pony's path through the undergrowth, he

raced to Sean's side, willing the boy to move. Then he saw the crooked angle of the right leg, although—thank heaven!—he could feel no injury to the spine as he ran careful hands down Sean's back.

He sent Catriona to Cornanagh to phone for the doctor and send Mick back with blankets. A few minutes later Selina returned with the recaptured pony.

"Is he badly hurt?" she asked.

"Broken leg at the least."

"Serves him right," Selina said, "considering how he's been acting ever since the spring show."

"You'd noticed?"

Selina gave a snort. "Just as if he won that red ribbon all by himself." Then she sighed. "Eventually his parents will have to recognize that the boy is, at best, only a passenger. Or one of these days he will do himself—or his mount—an even worse injury."

Sean had not recovered consciousness by the time the doctor arrived, but the boy's color was better. When Dr. Standish found no evident spinal injury, Sean's leg was jury-splinted for the trip to hospital. Once the boy was in the Austin, Michael turned to the politely waiting children.

"Trina, up you get on the Prince and *ride him*! He's not to put his nose out of line once. Pat, this hasn't put you off?"

"Oh, no, Uncle Mihall!"

"Good girl. Mary, you'll go on, won't you? Show Mrs. Healey the rides through your land, why don't you. Off with you now. Enjoy yourselves!"

As he turned to climb into the Austin, Michael Carradyne was already planning how to turn this latest mishap to his advantage. If he handled the matter tactfully, he might contrive to secure Ballymore Prince for Pat to ride through the summer. She had a long way to go to be as good a rider as Catriona, but at least she was fourteen and eligible to ride the Prince in registered shows. She'd come off a time or two, the Prince being what he was, but she had plenty of nerve and considerably more incentive than Sean had ever had. He could improve her riding to the point where she'd be able to show the Prince so the Dohertys could still brag about their winning show pony.

22

"*I*'m sure that everything you say is true, Selina," David said, and put his napkin to his lips, "but although I'm delighted you've found a suitable hobby, I regret that I cannot share your interest in horses."

Selina regarded her husband with a smile of spurious courtesy. Damn the man! she thought. If she had the grace to feign interest in all his financial and political observations, he could at least return the compliment.

"I was simply making conversation, David, since evidently you cannot comment on your current activities." He raised his eyebrows, mildly surprised. "Or hadn't you noticed that you haven't said a word to me throughout dinner? Perhaps it was the fault of the meal?"

"No, my dear, dinner was excellent," he said blandly, and gave her a reassuring smile. "It is true that I have been distracted." Abruptly his expression altered to one of outraged frustration. "This damnable strike. How dare they! Don't they know that it's ruining the economy? The banks will bankrupt this country, and only a few of us care!"

"Oh, dear, I had no idea that things were that bad."

"No, why should you," David replied, "when I do my very best to keep sordid realities out of my home."

"And here I am, boring you with my trivial pursuits," Selina said, dutifully playing out her long-established role. "Do please forgive me, David. But as your wife I want to assist you in every way, and you know I'm discreet. If talking it out would provide any relief . . . ?"

David thawed visibly and, reaching across the broad table, patted her hand. "Now, then, what sort of a man would I be if I dumped my problems in my wife's lap? As if you could help me."

Selina half closed her eyes. "I could listen sympathetically, David, provide you with a sounding board. Father always said—"

David interrupted with an irritated wave of his hand. "You just continue to see to my physical comfort, and the rest will take care of itself." Wiping his mouth on his napkin, he rose and stood behind her chair to pull it out for her.

For a moment Selina could not believe her ears. Had the man no sensitivity at all? To discount her interests as trivial because *he* cared only for pounds, shillings, and pence . . . To dismiss her as incapable of sharing his concerns simply because she was his wife—a woman—qualified only to cater to his physical comfort . . . "Physical comfort"? indeed! She couldn't remember when they had last had intercourse. And now the very thought of it was abhorrent to her.

In that moment, Selina Healey hated her husband—and not simply for his insensitivity or his preoccupation with making money, but for his smug complacency and all the archaic conventions he represented.

Struggling with her fury, Selina rose and, with the barest of nods for his courtesy, stalked from the room. She continued on to the front door, pausing only long enough to collect a light coat, her handbag, and the car keys. She had to get out of the house or she'd explode.

She guided the Lancia out of the drive and through the tight little streets of Dalkey, onto Vico Road and south, along the sea road in Greystones, before she realized that she was heading for Cornanagh. And Michael.

Abruptly she turned into the parking space by the railway bridge. She would *not* go any farther on a road that led inexorably to Cornanagh, she told herself. Not in this state of mind.

She rested her head briefly on the steering wheel, gripping it until she could feel her nails dig into the heels of her hands. She tried to calm the agitation in her belly with deep breaths and stern self-chidings.

There were only two other cars parked, dog owners walking their animals on the shingle. She got out of the car, felt the stiff sea breeze on her face, and, wrapping her coat tightly about her, walked under the bridge and out onto the sand, heading down the beach, away from dogs and their owners.

I'm overreacting, she told herself sternly, trudging carefully along the rocky strand. One should only have *crises de nerfs* when appropriately garbed for long hikes. She sat down on a convenient large boulder, winding her coat about her against the chill of the breeze.

I can't possibly be in love with Michael Carradyne, she thought. True, he's a fine man, and we always have so much to talk about. And I haven't felt so alive and energetic in years. But he's old enough to be my father! I must come to my senses, get my emotions under control. It's only that David was being so abominably pompous tonight. And he is under a great deal of stress. I should be sympathetic and forbearing, like a good wife.

"Hello there," said a low voice, and she whirled around so quickly, she lost her balance on the rock. "What's wrong, Selina?"

Michael put out a hand to steady her, his expression concerned. "I saw your car." He pointed vaguely over his shoulder. "I was down having a look at Joe Delahunt's new stallion."

She stared up at him, thinking, Sometimes you don't have a choice: some decisions are thrust upon you.

Michael took note of the brooding look in her eyes. "If you'd rather be by yourself . . ."

"No," she said, rising to her feet. "I'd much rather be with you."

A smile, charmingly hesitant at first, pulled at his mouth and made his eyes glow. One step closed the distance between them, and then he gathered her into his arms, smoothing her hair to rest his chin against her forehead. They stood that way for several moments before she tilted her head to meet his lips.

They exchanged a long and very gentle kiss, neither asking nor answering. Then, with one arm about her shoulders, her body held tightly against him, Michael Carradyne turned her to walk with him down the beach.

There were times when Catriona found her cousin's incessant curiosity and loquaciousness wearing on the nerves. Being the youngest in her family, she'd never had a constant companion and now occasionally found her loss of privacy a severe trial. But such moments were fleeting enough, and the periods before her lazy cousin woke up were still all hers.

What she did resent, and knew no way of protesting, was Patricia's assumption that Catriona share *everything*. Her cousin was forever asking what Cat was thinking, how she felt about this, that, and the other. Catriona was unaccustomed to sharing her thoughts—indeed, found it difficult to voice opinions on the myriad topics Patricia introduced. She didn't really care what was happening in the North, except that she had been taught to believe murder for any reason was a mortal sin whether a Protestant was killed by a Catholic or vice versa. And she had no opinion at all about the arms trials, the bank strike, Elvis Presley, or the dissolution of the Beatles as a rock group.

"Don't you do anything else except watch the telly?" Patricia cried in frustration with her uncommunicative cousin one evening. "Don't you ever go to the movies? Or dances? Gawd, even in boarding school we had dances!"

"That's not the Irish way," Catriona replied a bit primly. That phrase had become her refuge.

"And Daddy knew *that* when he sent me here." Patricia's bitter tone attracted Catriona's attention, and she stared at her cousin in surprise. "Oh, don't be an ass. I'm still a virgin, but I can't wait to try it myself. When I'm a little older, of course. I don't approve of promiscuity at fourteen. Not that that stops some of my classmates!" Catriona was aghast and far too shocked to make any response. Patricia stopped, caught by the expression on her cousin's face. "Haven't you any curiosity about sex?"

Catriona gulped, having recalled the strange behavior of her cousin Owen. She wanted to say yes but didn't dare.

"Didn't your mother tell you *anything*? About conception and stuff?" Patricia was becoming concerned. "I mean, you are having periods, aren't you?" Catriona nodded, for this was an occurrence she couldn't very well keep secret as she was living in the same room as Patricia. "Well, didn't your mother tell you anything then?"

"I read the book my sister gave me. She and Auntie Eithne, even Bridie, made a fuss about . . ."

"How you could now be fruitful and multiply?"

"Really, Pat!"

"Well, do you know that you can get pregnant now? Did they tell you that?" When Catriona shook her head, Patricia drew herself up to her full height and gestured imperiously.

"Sit down, Cat. I consider it my duty as your elder to inform you—and don't worry about me getting it all wrong. We had a whole term of sex education in my school, and my facts are not lost in religious babble and superstitious mumbo-jumbo. . . ." And with considerable alacrity, Patricia proceeded to lecture her fascinated cousin on the fundamentals of biology and procreation.

"It may be rude to say so," she concluded fifteen minutes later, "but I think the Irish way of bringing up kids is pretty damned silly. No wonder they have to advertise homes for pregnant girls in the paper. It's dangerous to be ignorant. Plain dangerous. I'm glad I'm American. Now, have I shocked you totally out of your tiny mind, Cat?"

Catriona heard the concern in her cousin's voice and managed a reassuring grin. "I don't think so. But I suppose I'd've learned when I got married."

"It's too late by then. Too late."

"But you're supposed to be . . . chaste"—Catriona could not quite manage to use the term "virgin" as easily as her uninhibited cousin—"when you get married."

"Chased, yea," Patricia replied, grinning mischievously. "Look, Cat, do yourself a favor. Stop thinking Catholic about sex. Think sensible, and you won't get into trouble. Because there'll come a time when your body's going to respond to some guy, and you'll want to go the whole way. And if you're all seized up in your head about being virgin, and saving yourself for your husband, you might miss the best things in life." Then, as if she sensed that she had dwelt on the topic long enough, Patricia announced that she was going to see if there was enough hot water for her to have a bath.

Catriona was intensely grateful for the respite and pretended to be asleep when Patricia returned from her bath. She had quite enough to think about; Patricia's explanation kept going round and round in her head, and it was some time before sleep finally overtook her.

Fortunately they were so busy during the day schooling the ponies for the Mount Armstrong show that there was no time for another "heart to heart" conversation; at night, Patricia usually fell asleep the moment she hit the upper mattress.

The Dohertys had yielded to Michael Carradyne's persuasions, so Patricia was to show Ballymore Prince while Sean was disabled. Michael had given Patricia some intensive training and was well pleased with her willingness and determination, and especially her good nature when the Prince planted her during the jumping lessons.

"She's a bit hey-go-mad, isn't she?" Selina remarked after one particularly difficult morning. The Prince had dropped Patricia no fewer than ten times in the jump alley. Each time the girl had bounced to her feet, dusted herself off, and swung back up on her mount.

"Contact, Pat, remember your contact," Michael had shouted encouragingly.

"With the ground?" Pat had quipped back, shortening her reins and repositioning herself in the saddle. "I've had more than enough of contact!"

But at last she managed to jump the entire alley without a run-out or a fall. She was justifiably pleased with herself and quite gratified by Michael's "Well done, Pat."

Suddenly it was Friday, and time to make sure all was ready for the show the next day. As the Mount Armstrong show had many classes that qualified the winners for the August Horse Show, it was an important event. It was especially important for Catriona, since this was her first real competition (she couldn't count that chance ride at the Spring Show, even in her most private thoughts). And, of course, all of it was "to die for" exciting to Patricia. Among the adults, Selina was leading Charlie as a three-year-old likely to make a small hunter, Philip was to ride Emmett in the Middle-Weight Hunter, and Michael and Mick were showing Tulip's various foals and their dams. Even Owen had to help, with so many animals to be led. The big lumbering horse lorry would have to be used as well as the two-horse box, and Barry and Mick tinkered with machinery all through the day, checking the wiring and the partitions.

June 29th dawned clear and bright with a light breeze, and though Patricia thought it absolutely incredible that the sun was halfway up the heavens at a mere five o'clock, she set to work with a will to groom and plait the Prince and then two of the brood mares. She was neat and quick, and it was easy to believe that she had prepared Standard Breds for American shows.

At seven, with most of the horses groomed and plaited, Bridie served them a huge breakfast, for they weren't to muddle their insides with "chips and sausages made of who knew what offal" at the show grounds. By seven-thirty she had breakfasted them, provided each with a packed lunch and Thermoses of coffee and tea, and seen them out the door.

Loading took a little longer than anticipated because young Tulip's Son refused to follow Frolic and finally had to be carried into the lorry by Mick and Barry. Then one of the yearlings turned obstinate and had to be wound up the ramp by means of a lunge line tucked about his rump. But time had been allowed for unexpected hitches, and they were ready to roll out of the yard by quarter to nine.

Michael Carradyne led, his Austin pulling the horsebox containing Emmett and Charlie, Philip as his passenger; then came Mick, driving the lorry with Artie and Owen beside him, while Selina brought up the rear in her car with the two girls.

They met little traffic on the back roads through Tallaght to the Naas dual carriageway and reached the show grounds by ten o'clock, just as the stewards had organized some semblance of order from the early morning chaos. After some minor confusion about parking, they were bumping across the field to set down among the horse vans.

The 12.2s were the first of the jumping classes to be held in the pony ring, so Michael Carradyne immediately sent the girls down to the entries caravan to register and collect their numbers. Then they were to stay by ring A until either he or Selina came to get them. That was easier said than done, Catriona discovered, with her ebullient cousin in a perfect frenzy of curiosity. By the time she had managed to haul Pat to the ringside, both her father and Selina Healey were there, trying anxiously to spot the wayward girls.

"I just had to see everything, Uncle Mihall. This is the grooviest place in the world!"

"Groovy it may be, Patricia, but when you're riding for me, you obey my instructions. I'm certain Catriona conveyed that message to you?"

"Yes, but she's *been* to these places before. I never have."

"You may never again, either, Patricia Carradyne, if you do not follow orders." He paused until Patricia assumed a properly penitent expression, then placed one hand on his niece's shoulder, giving her a little shake. "Now, I had a word with the course builder, and it's essentially the same, except in height, for all the ponies today. So study it well. Trina, when the second round of the 12.2s begins, you warm Conker up. We'll be busy with the in-hand classes, so it's up to you girls to be on time for your own. Is that understood?" Both girls nodded solemnly.

"Will we have time to see Selina and Charlie?" Catriona asked.

The Tannoy blared out an almost indistinguishable announcement about mare and foal classes.

"Just listen!" Michael set off for the trailer at a run, with Selina beside him. "It's Frolic's turn," he called back over his shoulder, and Catriona waved good luck.

Several minutes later she saw her father and Owen leading Frolic and Tulip's Son toward their ring and dragged Patricia away from the 12.2 competition. They found seating on a spare bale of hay at the ring's edge.

Tulip's Son had shed most of his foal fuzz by now, and his very dark brown coat was almost black in the sunlight, gleaming with health and good grooming. He was certainly behaving himself with Owen holding the lead and even assumed a drum horse stance, thrusting his hind legs back from his sturdy little body, his brush of a tail flicking at the flies and his ears constantly wigwagging. Catriona watched him avidly, for his good manners were the result of her patient work, and she felt maternally proud of him.

But the class was large and the judging process nowhere near as entertaining for Patricia as the 12.2 jumping. She began to entreat Catriona to return to the pony ring. Knowing that she had better not let her cousin wander around without her, Catriona reluctantly left before Frolic and Tulip's Son had been put through their paces for the judges.

However, it was Patricia who first saw the men leading the mare and foal back to the horsebox. She tore shrieking across the fields in her pleasure at seeing gaudy first-prize rosette ribbons streaming from the head collars of Frolic and Tulip's Son. Catriona followed after her, her face red with embarrassment, wondering if there was any way she could divorce herself from her cousin.

"Don't shush me, Cat! Aren't you proud, too?"

"Of course I am! But you don't go screaming around horses or carrying on like that because we've won. It just isn't done in Ireland."

"Too much isn't done in Ireland from all I see," Patricia said with considerable heat.

"Then why did you bother to come?"

"I was invited—by your father. Oh, fer Gawd's sake, Cat, what's got into you? Oh, all right, then. I'll behave like a well-brought-up Irish girl. But"—she waggled her finger in Catriona's face, a smile beginning to tug at her mouth—"only because it upsets you when I come on loud American . . . and only for today!"

Then the second round for the 12.2s began. Following instructions, the two girls hurried back to the lorry to collect Conker. Michael was not there, having gone to watch Emmett's performance in the middle-weight hunter class. Mick watched with a critical eye while the two girls tacked Conker up and Catriona redid a loosened plait.

"Your dad knows you're fifth to go, Cat, so he'll be there," Mick said while she mounted. "Work him in in that field above the practice jump, nice and easy. Just like you was at home an' all." Mick sent her off with an affectionate slap to the pony's neck.

"I'm so excited, Cat," Patricia said, trotting along beside Conker. Her eyes were shining, and her face glowed with anticipation. "Oh, this is a marvelous day! We're going to come home just loaded with firsts!"

Catriona sincerely hoped so and only wished she had half her cousin's self-confidence. Then, as she bent Conker around her left leg toward the practice field, where other 13.2s were being worked in before their competition, things suddenly fell into perspective: Conker, though his pricked ears indicated his excitement, was instantly obedient to her leg aid. He was too professional a pony to let her down today. Thus reassured, Catriona dismissed her qualms; after all, she could only do her best.

Conker worked well for her at trot and canter and popped neatly over the practice fence, even when someone's father put it up to the four-foot mark. She and Conker flew over it, but the next rider crashed into it, and it wasn't put up as high again. Then it was time to walk the course with her father. The first round was the same height as the final one for the 12.2s and a snap for a pony like Conker. She was fifth to go, and the round was over before she knew it: an ecstatic Patricia awaited them outside the pocket entrance, creating as if they'd already won.

Cornanagh certainly had.

"Selina got a first with Charlie," Patricia told her excitedly, "and your brother a first with Emmett.—The judges thought him a really top-quality animal. Owen's in the ring now with one of the yearlings and your father with the other. Mick says the judges are having a helluva time making up their minds."

❧ 23 ❧

*I*t was a long wait between the first and second rounds, but Patricia remained uncharacteristically well behaved as the two girls watched the other competitors. At last the Tannoy announced that twenty-two clear rounds were to go forward. If the next round failed to provide a clear winner, there would be a third one against the clock. Catriona began to understand just how badly one's stomach could roil in such circumstances and had more sympathy for Sean Doherty. She was much relieved when Selina and her father appeared at the ringside.

"You're the second to go in this round, Trina," her father told her. "I'm sorry we missed the first one." He gave her a proud smile and squeezed her hand. "C'mon, up you go and give him a couple of pops over the practice fence."

As if she could read the anxiety in Catriona's eyes, Selina Healey walked over and patted her knee. "You and Conker are a team, Trina, remember that!" she said, her voice low. "A great team!"

Catriona's tension eased miraculously, and, reassured, she urged Conker forward. In his turn, Conker cleared the fence effortlessly, and the two were back at the pocket in no time, waiting for their number to be called. The first contestant of the second round flew out of the ring so close to Conker that Catriona felt the wind of his passing. That speed had cost him four faults.

When the steward called her number, Catriona trotted Conker into the ring.

From the moment the bell sounded until she pulled him up outside again, Catriona concentrated only on the next fence or combination to be jumped. And Conker carried her fluidly over one obstacle after another. He wasn't at all like the Prince had been in the RDS; he was calm and listened to her the entire time.

"You did great, Cat, just great!" cried Patricia when it was over, slapping Conker's neck enthusiastically.

"We haven't won yet, you know."

"But you're that much closer!" Pat was undaunted. "And look, that bay's just clobbered himself! One more competitor gone."

"Pat!" Michael said, fixing his niece with such a stern eye that she subsided. "Walk him now, Trina. Don't let him stiffen up. You're doing just fine."

"I told you you were a great team," Selina said, smiling up at Catriona and giving Conker's ears an affectionate pull.

As the round went on, with more riders coming to grief, Catriona found that concentrating on Pat's babbling curiosity kept her from worrying too much about the final speed round.

"Now, Pat, it's time to warm up the Prince," Michael announced, turning to his niece. "He gets excited with all the other horses and riders around, so listen to Mick and do exactly what he tells you. Don't think you've learned everything you need to know about riding ponies."

"Uncle Mihall, I'm wounded to the quick," Pat replied, laying a hand across her chest and bowing her head in dismay. "And you told me only yesterday that I'm a vast improvement on Sean in the saddle."

As Michael stared in surprise, Selina laughed. "Pat, you are a complete hand! Go, get the pony, but listen to Mick! We all remember the Prince shedding Sean in that field."

Patricia rolled her eyes in agreement and scurried off.

"You never know what she'll do or say next, do you?" Michael remarked.

"No, and that's half the fun of her, isn't it?" Watching her hurry away, Selina asked anxiously, "Those fences aren't going to be too much for her, are they? She hasn't done any competition jumping before."

"They're no higher than the jump alley, and she's gotten down that without coming a cropper."

Catriona caught the slightest note of doubt in her father's voice and sighed, for Pat's sake this time. Then she saw her cousin on Ballymore Prince, with Mick at his head, walking to the practice field. The Prince was fidgety, but Patricia was sitting deep in the saddle and seemed totally unconcerned by his antics. She really had improved, thanks to hours on the lunge line and going without stirrups.

"Trina!" Her father's voice alerted her. "Nine clear rounds, and you're the first against the clock." He squeezed her knee encouragingly. "Move him on, but don't lose your rhythm. And watch the planks. They're the bogey fence at speed. The wind can almost knock them out of the cups."

At that moment the steward beckoned her to enter, and Catriona kneed Conker forward. The pony seemed to sense her urgency and entered at the canter, light in her hands but bouncing forward. Then the bell rang, and Conker knew what that meant as well as she did. They took the first fence before she was aware that they had. Rhythm, rhythm, she kept telling herself as they maneuvered at speed around the course. Conker never lost his impulsion, flowing as he surged up and over each fence, and then they were flying out of the ring with scattered clapping to tell her that she'd done well.

"That's a good time, Trina," her father said, holding up his stopwatch.

"Trina, I was never as good on Conker as you are!" Selina

said, all smiles. "You seemed to ooze around the course like the pro you are!"

"I could have made a few more seconds if we'd taken the turn tighter between the treble and the oxer. . . ."

"Don't analyze it all now," Selina said, grinning at Michael. "You were clear, in a good time, and no one could fault the jumping."

"Yes, it was a very good round, Catriona," her father said, "considering this is your first real competition against the clock."

"Her first?" Selina was astonished and looked at Catriona with wide eyes. "But I thought she'd been show jumping for ages."

"Blister?" Father and daughter regarded her with similar quizzical expressions.

She gave a rueful laugh. "No, Blister was an old dear, but not a competition pony— Whoops, Michael, Pat's having a rough ride!"

A quick look at the practice field showed the Prince bucking and switching in his usual manner. And even as Michael loped off, Patricia was deposited neatly on the ground. Fortunately there were enough onlookers to capture the pony before he could gallop off, and Pat scrambled to her feet and remounted before Michael could reach her.

"You've just lost another rival, Trina," Selina said as the next contestant, on a rather headstrong gray, flew off to land on his feet at the other side of the garish wall of paper bricks.

Philip arrived then, with a sweat rug for Conker and congratulations for Catriona's excellent round.

"Save the congratulations until Conker's won," Catriona said soberly, watching the next contestant. She had to wait through seven more rounds, and this latest rider looked to be just flying around the course.

"Look, pet," Selina said, putting her arm around Catriona,

"you and Conker went brilliantly. No one can take that from you even if you don't win. I know it might sound trite, but how hard you try is more important than winning each and every time. It's getting there that's the challenge. If you won every competition, it wouldn't give you as much pleasure."

Just then the final rider burst across the finish line. Even before the announcement was broadcast, Catriona knew that he had won. But she and Conker were second, only a second behind the winner: the second she could have made up by taking a closer turn into the oxer. And being second qualified her and Conker to compete in the August Horse Show. Catriona managed a big bright smile for Selina, who hugged her fiercely, then she swung up on Conker and entered the ring to receive the blue second.

Astonishingly enough, it was Patricia who managed to collect another first-prize red ribbon for Cornanagh that afternoon. Michael insisted that he was a few hairs grayer after those three rounds. Half a dozen times in the first round alone, he was sure that Patricia would come unstuck or that the Prince, taking corners on one leg, would slip.

"Patricia, you were not against the clock in that round," Michael said in a flat tone, barely controlling his anger.

"Honest, Unk, I tried to hold him in. It was all I could do to steer him, but, after all, we did go clear," she replied with wide-eyed innocence. "Such a good boy he is!" she added, slapping the pony's neck affectionately.

In the second round she seemed to go faster, if anything, but she also appeared to be just a fraction more in control of the pony. She and the Prince finished without a fault and careered out of the ring to a round of applause.

"Patricia!" Michael glared at her, his lips compressed to hold in what he would not say in front of a large audience.

"Honest, Uncle Mihall, I tried to go slower, but he can take quite a hold when he wants to!"

"If you hurt yourself, your father would never forgive me."

"Well, I don't intend to come off," Patricia said, absently smoothing her left buttock. "Again. Once a day is enough. That pony doesn't scare me."

"I wish something could," Michael muttered.

"Well, you've only yourself to blame." She grinned and cocked her head as she looked up at him. "All those hours of lunge work have really improved my seat."

Michael held up a stern forefinger. "Pat, I'm warning you. You take any more chances with yourself and that pony, and this is the only show you'll be in this summer. D'you understand me?"

During the third round, Patricia did not fly hell-bent around the course. And she had listened dutifully to the comments of her uncle and Mick as they watched the other competitors and nodded as her uncle had told her exactly how to ride her round. What she did do, however, was to cut every corner she could, at a very respectable speed, never so much as checking the pony once. When the Prince soared over the final wall, which now stood at a daunting five feet four, a wave of applause followed horse and rider over the finishing line. There was no doubt of the winner in this competition.

"By God, Pat, you're a Carradyne for sure," Philip cried as they all gathered around to congratulate her. And Patricia, her eyes catching Catriona's, became almost as modestly self-effacing as the other Irish competitors.

On the trip home, she proceeded to review every one of her errors until Selina, in desperation, turned on the late news. They all heard that an emergency had been proclaimed in the North, with special laws for the Royal Ulster Constabulary to enforce. Five hundred and fifty extra troops were being flown into Belfast, and the situation in the Falls Road and the Shankill areas of the city was considered explosive.

That sobered the occupants of the Lancia until Patricia's curiosity reasserted itself in a series of questions.

"My daddy says the whole thing's religious, Selina."

"I wouldn't say it was," Selina replied carefully. "Though it has been proven that an individual's religion in the North often limits his job opportunities."

"But why?" Patricia asked almost petulantly. "That doesn't make sense. A man's religion can't keep him from a job in the States. There's a special law to see that it can't."

"It can in Ulster, though not in the Republic, I'm happy to say."

As soon as they reached the yard—for they were well ahead of the horse van and the Austin—they started to make up the feeds. Eithne appeared in the feed room door, back from her own day's outing and dressed in what Catriona thought of as her Longford clothes. She was suitably impressed by the ribbons the girls showed her and the success of all Cornanagh's entries.

"Maybe we should eat out again tonight, to celebrate," she said brightly, "because Bridie has done nothing toward tea. I really don't know what's got into her. She's sitting there in the kitchen moaning and keening, and I can't get a sensible word out of her."

"I'll go in with you, Eithne," Selina said, her expression determined, "and see just what she's on about. We can trust the girls with the feeds."

When she and Eithne stepped into the kitchen, Selina could see that Bridie had at least started dinner preparations, for the potatoes were peeled and soaking in cold water and a casserole stood ready. There was even a tart on the sideboard.

"Now, Bridie, what has got you in such a state?" Selina crouched down by the old woman, who was rocking back and forth, hands crossed over her breast, her face reddened but bare of tears.

"Sure it's only the first of the visitations upon him. Only the first! God will not be mocked!"

"What visitation?" Selina asked, holding Bridie's small, strong hands in hers to make the woman look at her.

"Go see yoursel'. In the field. It's there to be seen. True retribution. The first, but not the last, mark my words."

Selina rose, staring at Eithne with real concern. "We'd better check the fields," she said, and hurried her out the door.

Just then Michael's Austin drove into the courtyard, the horn blowing in triumph. Selina raced to his door.

"Quickly, Michael, something's happened in the fields," she said.

He and Philip were out of the car in a flash. Michael grabbed her hands. "What's happened?"

"We don't know. Bridie's not coherent, but something has."

Michael cursed, glancing at the Austin with the horsebox hitched to it, then began to run toward the strap-iron gate that led to the ride. Patricia and Catriona appeared from the yard and followed.

They were just by the copse when they saw Barry running toward them.

"Oh, Captain, Captain, thank God you're back. There was nothing I could do, nothing!" The man's face was distorted with grief. "Nothing to be done, Captain!"

Michael stood, his face expressionless, while everyone else looked at Barry, afraid to hear the news he bore.

"It's the Tulip, Captain. He's dead!"

❧ 24 ❧

"**H**eart failure." Michael spoke tersely into the phone, and Selina suspected that he was fighting to keep his voice steady. "His age. He was rising twenty-four."

"Oh, Michael!" It was such an inadequate response that she gritted her teeth, trying to think of more comforting words. The commanding brown stallion had been a part of Cornanagh for almost a quarter of a century.

"Are you alone?" Michael asked.

"Yes. David was called to a meeting, something to do with troops in Belfast. Please, come over."

She had been reluctant to leave Cornanagh after the sad discovery. But David had been due home and generally cut up quite stiff if she weren't there to greet him. Lately he'd made the odd dig about her hobby taking up a lot of her time. So it had been infuriating to find him gone, and not even the note he'd left—announcing that his presence had been requested by several important *T.D.*'s—did much to pacify her. She had had no appetite for the dinner Kathleen had prepared and, with apologies, had sent the woman home.

Now Michael had phoned because he needed her. Selina blessed those *T.D.*'s who had required her husband's presence and left her free to minister to Michael's comfort. She ran up the stairs, stripping clothes off on her way to the bathroom. She showered quickly and was struggling into a housecoat when she heard the front-door bell.

Michael was standing on the top step when she cautiously

cracked open the door. She flung it wide enough for him to enter, and he closed it behind him, leaning against it as he drew her into his arms. He held her tightly against him, his face buried in the curve of her neck, his fingers gripping her fiercely.

They stood that way a long moment. Michael was not sobbing, but the tremors that ran through his body betrayed the self-control he was exerting. She wanted to tell him that crying would help, but she didn't know him well enough yet to make that kind of suggestion. And the knowledge was saddening.

Finally he released her and held her away from him, looking down at her with a weary sadness in his eyes.

"A drink?" she asked softly.

"Several drinks have not helped. . . ." His words ended on a hesitant note.

"Come, then," she said, taking his hand and leading him to the stairs.

A long, loving time later, when she had comforted him sufficiently to relax his lean body, Michael lay with his head on her shoulder, staring at the ceiling. Selina particularly liked his lean warm body resting against hers, the weight of his right leg as it lay across hers.

"Would talking help?" she asked.

He shrugged, the bony point of his shoulder nudging her ribs. "Talk will not put life back into the Tulip."

"It might put some back into you."

He gave a short snort and then, turning from her, stretched out, his arms under his head, still gazing at nothing.

"I just never imagined Cornanagh without the Tulip." He sighed heavily and then began to speak in a quiet voice, so altered from his rather crisp tones that she turned her head to catch other changes. "The Tulip was my father's horse, I think from the moment he was foaled. A case of eyes locking and a rapport developing all in an instant. Tulip always went to my dad first. Even before he tried to suckle his dam, he had nibbled my father's fingers. I was only just getting fit again,"— he scratched his scarred leg absently—"but my father swore that I'd be able to ride the Tulip when he was ready." He gave a soft chuckle. "I wasn't to get that chance for some years.

"As it happened, the bond between my father and the Tulip grew so strong that he refused to let anyone else break and back him. Oh, we raced the Tulip, had to, to be able to get him any mares. My father used to half die at every race, swearing all the time under his breath that he wouldn't ever again risk the stallion. But he did, because it had to be. And it was an education to listen to him instruct Eddie Newman, who piloted the Tulip most of the time. With the exception of his first race—and he was third in that—the Tulip won everything he was ever entered in."

Michael's eyes were wide now with cherished memories. "Every morning Father would go to the back door—Tulip was always in the coach house stallion box—and roar good morning to him. And the Tulip would bugle right back." An infinitely tender smile curved Michael's lips. "On the one or two days my father might oversleep, the commotion from the Tulip was enough to rouse the dead." A tear trickled from the corner of Michael's eye, but his smile widened. "There are few true partnerships between man and mount. They are to be treasured. And now he's gone."

"He's still there, in a way, isn't he, in his foals, in Tulip's Son?" Selina asked, her voice gentle.

"He's only a half bred."

"Still, good half-bred stallions will qualify for registering when this new horse board scheme comes to pass."

"*If* it comes to pass."

"Well, all those intimate little conversations you've been having with the *T.D.*'s ought to bear some fruit. You told me that you and your father felt that registration of half and three-quarter breds would benefit the whole industry. Why not prove it by standing the colt? He won at Mount Armstrong. Put him in the Horse Show, and any other show going; let him be seen and get him known."

"It's not as simple as that, Selina," he said with a smile, and then his eyes grew thoughtful. "He has got good conformation, and he'll make a big horse. If he's inherited half the potential of sire or dam, he should jump. Only stallions aren't usually show-jumped."

"Why not? I mean, he can be trained to behave around mares. And if he's as good as he ought to be, he won't go mashing himself over fences."

Michael contented himself with a low laugh. "Well, not more than once or twice. Damn, why did I geld Racketeer?"

"That three-year-old bay?" Selina shook her head and replied matter-of-factly, "Well, what's done's done: balls or breath."

"Selina!" Michael propelled himself up to one elbow, staring at her in astonishment.

She laughed. "There, there's more life in you now. You know, I do believe that you're more upset about the Tulip than you were about your wife."

Michael gave a harsh bark of laughter. "Isabel was never a part of Cornanagh as the Tulip was, and is. And no, I don't mourn her. That would be sheer hypocrisy." He let out a long sigh and began to stroke the contour of Selina's face. His eyes were obscured by shadow, but the wondering touch of his fingers kindled a fire within her.

"Michael . . ."

"Sssh, no, Selina." He kissed her lightly. "Not tonight. We don't have nearly enough time. Please."

And because she, too, was suddenly unwilling to put into words the conflict he aroused in her, she acquiesced and willingly returned his caresses. There had been a certain satisfaction earlier in giving him comfort, but she herself had not had a release. Now Michael made absolutely certain that she was fulfilled. She was still languorous when she felt him sit up beside her.

"Michael?" She reached out a hand to detain him.

"I have to get back, Selina. We must be discreet. I parked up the road."

She could hear him pulling on his clothes, covering the long leanness that was so unexpectedly sexy to her. She wanted very much to share more than these few illicit moments. But what about Michael? Had his earlier reluctance to talk stemmed from a desire to keep her at arm's length—to enjoy their brief affair until it palled?

The bed sagged as he sat to put on his shoes. Perhaps this really was nothing more than a short *affaire,* she told herself. Like a romantic fool, she had been trying to build something out of nothing—a brief flare of mutual attraction to fill the void left by her sham of a marriage. Michael had just lost a wife he hadn't loved; he wouldn't want another entanglement. And yet. . . She hunched her shoulders into the sheet just as he rose.

Suddenly he bent over her, kissed her cheek and stroked her shoulder in a lingering fashion, for all the world as if he were very reluctant to leave. It threw her into further confusion.

"God bless," he said, and left.

Selina buried her head in the pillow and writhed in frustration.

Somehow, even though it was Saturday night, Mick had got the knacker to remove the Tulip before Michael got back to Cornanagh. Mick had been listening for the sound of the Austin, and he flagged Michael down at the turn into the drive.

"Captain, it's done," he said, ducking his head down to his chest.

"Thanks, Mick." He shifted gears, but Mick's hands tightened on the open window. "Yes?"

"He's not gone, so to speak, Captain dear," Mick went on hurriedly. "That colt foal now, he did us proud today. Should we not be showing him more? He's as like his sire as two peas in the same pod. And haven't we been calling him Tulip's Son all along?"

Michael smiled wryly at the thought that his two major comforters had offered the same consolation. "That's a good notion, Mick. Thanks."

All the way up the drive, Michael mulled over the colt's strengths and faults. He parked the Austin and carefully opened the strap-iron fence, still lost in thought. Then, from nearly a quarter of a century of habit, he started to cross the courtyard to check on the Tulip—and stopped, overwhelmed again by an intense feeling of loss.

Catriona was lying in bed, still tearful over the Tulip's death; when she heard her father's soft curses, she wept anew—for him, for the Tulip, for Cornanagh. Then she crept out of bed, found her sketch pad, and rummaged in her pencil case as quietly as she could for a sharpened pencil. Pastels would just not do for the Tulip.

Curling up by the window to get the benefit of the long summer twilight, she began to draw the Tulip, head over the railing of his paddock, with her father beside him, outstretched hand under Tulip's nose. She felt she had to get it down before the Tulip faded from her memory as Blister had. There were a few tear splotches on the bottom of the page when she finished, but they would dry out, she knew.

The next morning Michael listened for the old stallion's welcoming whinny. You could regret the death of a useful animal, he told himself, but you shouldn't grieve for it, and it certainly wasn't on to mourn your stallion. However, the concerns of Cornanagh intruded once again when Barry met him at the kitchen door.

"With the weather so good and all, Captain, we ought to be thinking of cutting the hay. Too good a chance to miss, whatever else." It was Barry's way of expressing his understanding of Cornanagh's loss.

Selina phoned at ten-thirty on Sunday to tell him that she wouldn't be riding this morning and could he turn her mare out for the day? From the way she spoke, Michael knew someone was listening, and he grimaced over the need for such subterfuge.

"Isn't Selina coming over today?" Patricia asked at noon as they were finishing dinner.

"It's Sunday," Eithne said, "and that's generally a family day in Ireland, dear. She does have other obligations."

"Gets a day off for good behavior, huh?" Patricia grinned at her uncle. "She sure was great yesterday."

"Indeed she was," Michael remarked neutrally, looking up as Bridie entered the room.

"A *person* is here to see you, missus," she said, glaring at Eithne. Without waiting for a reply, she turned and left the room.

"Oh, dear," Eithne said, plainly dismayed. "He wasn't supposed to come today."

"Auntie Eithne has a secret admirer?" Philip said teasingly, and was totally unprepared to see his aunt burst into tears. "I'm sorry, Auntie Eithne, honest. I was only teasing."

"Eithne . . ." Michael went to her, crouching by her chair when she refused to look at him. "Eithne, what's the matter? Any friend of yours is certainly welcome at Cornanagh."

"Oh, Michael, it's not what you think." She lifted a tearstained face to him and then, with a gulp, dissolved into sobs, this time against his shoulder.

"There, there, Eithne," Michael said soothingly, patting her tear-streaked face with the napkin. "Here, take a drink of water. I'll go to the door and we'll sort this thing out for once and for all."

Eithne placed an urgent hand on his arm. "Wait, Michael. Not yet—not until I've told you what I ought to have told at least you, a long time ago."

He looked at the two girls. Patricia's ears were all but flapping with curiosity.

"No," she said, anticipating him, "they have to know, too."

Owen, looking both disgusted and puzzled, reentered with Philip, whose eyes were dancing with amusement.

"I beg to report, missus," he said, tugging at an imaginary cap brim, "that your consignment of antique furniture has just arrived from County Laois. Mr. Riley found that, after all, he could do a nixer better on Sunday than Monday."

"Oh, dear!" Eithne seemed about to dissolve into tears again.

"Really, Eithne, it's nothing to weep over," Michael said soothingly, despite a slight impatience with his sister-in-law's inexplicable tears. "Though I must say you gave us all the impression that Cornanagh had more than enough valuable things gathering cobwebs in the attic without taking on someone else's jumble."

"But it's not jumble, Michael. Some of it is very valuable," Eithne managed through her sniffles. "And oh, we can't just let him unload those things. They might get damaged. And then they won't be worth a penny." She struggled to her feet, wiping her face with the napkin. "Will you help me, boys? Michael, I was going to ask you if I could store them in the old shed. Just until they can be shipped."

"Shipped?"

"Explanations later?" Philip suggested helpfully. "Mr. Riley doesn't strike me as a very patient man. And he has his hand out of his pocket—and not to shake with."

"Oh, dear. I've got to give him cash."

"Do you have it, Eithne?" Michael asked, his patience restored but his curiosity as keen as Patricia's.

"Yes, yes, in my handbag."

"Trina, get your aunt's handbag, and the rest of you come with me."

The transfer from van to shed was completed with none of the questions that were bursting to be asked. While Philip and Owen worked, Catriona brought Mr. Riley a cup of tea to which Michael added a noggin of something to ease his labors, greatly improving the sour old man's temper.

When Mr. Riley finally trundled out of the courtyard, Michael turned to Eithne.

"You were right about those things being valuable, Eithne, but why did their arrival reduce you to tears?"

She compressed her lips, and sighed as she looked at the ring of inquisitive faces. "You see, Bridie has taken it up all wrong."

"What has Bridie to do with your sudden interest in antiques?"

"She thinks . . . she's certain . . . well, she did overhear my conversations with Davis, but she had taken the very worst interpretation, and I certainly don't want to put more on your plate right now, Michael." She paused, then took a deep breath and went on, "All I'm doing is acting as a consultant for a very nice, respectable buyer for a reputable interior decorator based in Houston, Texas. Of course he phones me from time to time when they need something in a hurry. Of course I have gone with him to special auctions. But there is nothing wrong in that at all."

"Not a thing," Michael said, glancing significantly at Owen

and Philip, who quickly added their approval. "So, now that Eithne's secret is out, you girls get on with the washing up."

"Daddy, will you be needing us this afternoon to help with the hay?" Catriona asked.

"Not today. Barry's only mowing, and the boys and I can spell him on the tractor. Why?"

"Well, Mary Evans wants us to hack out with her."

"Go right ahead. But no tricks, Patricia!" Michael waggled a finger at her, and she took on her most innocent expression. "No, I mean it. We've another show, and I don't want the Prince lamed for it."

"Okay, Unk, I'll behave."

As Patricia pulled Catriona about to head back to the house, Michael turned to his sister-in-law. "And now I think I'd like a little fuller explanation, Eithne. Let's go into the lounge."

"I'm coming, too," Owen said firmly.

"Come on, Auntie Eithne," Philip said, taking her free arm and marching her between himself and his father toward the house. "Confession is good for the soul, and you've been holding out on all of us."

It was a relief to Eithne to reach the lounge and settle herself on the couch with Philip beside her, Michael in the armchair, and Owen perched on the arm. Philip had been right: it would be good to clear the air once and for all.

She told them about her chance meeting with Davis Haggerty three years before, of how their friendship had developed to the extent that she acted now as his business liaison, searching out antiques between his trips to Ireland.

"And how long have you been doing that?" Owen demanded when she concluded her explanation. He waved vaguely in the direction of the old shed.

"Well, that's the first time, really, all on my own for so many pieces, but when I saw the auction advertised and found several items that I know are needed urgently, I phoned Davis, and he said I should go ahead. He trusts my judgment, you see." She flushed prettily.

"But, but . . . all that stuff cost a bundle!" Owen exclaimed. "Wherever could you get that kind of money?"

"Oh, Davis's firm sent a letter of credit for me on the Citibank in St. Stephen's Green. The auctioneer was quite delighted because, you see, what with the bank strike, it's been very hard to get the prices—in cash—that their clients expect."

Philip let out a whoop. "So my clever auntie strikes while the iron is hot! Good on you!"

Owen's expression turned forbidding. "But what if what you bought was no good?"

"Don't be such a gombeen, Owen," Philip said, giving his cousin a friendly push. "Auntie Eithne's been reading up on antiques over the past several years, I'd say. She's a clever boots, isn't she, Dad?"

"She certainly is," Michael agreed.

"And just what do you get out of this?" Owen continued, apparently determined to find some flaw in his mother's scheme.

"Well, I didn't want to accept anything. I mean, I've had fun going to the auctions. It doesn't seem right to accept money for something you enjoy doing anyway. But Davis insisted on paying me a finder's fee. And yesterday, because I was working on my own—Davis usually comes over, but he'd just been so he couldn't—he sent me a guide on the top price I was allowed to pay. So it's really quite simple." Eithne looked brightly at the three men, who were regarding her in various degrees of amusement and amazement.

"I think you're simply great, Auntie Eithne," Philip said, giving her a congratulatory pat on the back.

"I do, too," Michael remarked. He chose his next words carefully. "I think we've been exploiting you, Eithne, and unfairly. It's about time Cornanagh stopped imposing on your kind disposition."

"Oh, but Michael, you don't impose!" Eithne protested.

"Certainly Bridie has. I'll just sort her out now, today."

Eithne's look was dubious but not overly hopeful. She still hadn't quite told Michael everything. And she would have to be completely candid now; Davis would expect it of her.

Perhaps only Michael caught the shadow on her face and decided that she had discreetly withheld some information. He cleared his throat. "All right now, boys, you'd better spell Barry on the tractor. I'll join you presently." Dismissing them with a wave of his hand, he turned back to Eithne.

"Michael, how *are* we going to sort Bridie out?" Eithne asked when the boys had left the room. "I mean, she's going to think I've been complaining about her. And while we all know she eavesdrops, we can't come right out with that sort of an accusation!" She sighed. "After all, she is Cornanagh!"

"She is also getting on. We'll just have to get in a housekeeper."

"Can you afford one?"

"I think so. And I would like you to be able to go on with your . . . uh, antique hunting. I realize that your Fund doesn't stretch as far as it used to . . ."

Eithne gave a dismissive wave of her hand. "It isn't as if I need as much now, with the boys on their own—"

"And Owen with his hand out to you every time he runs short." Michael acknowledged her generosity with a tolerant grin. Then, abruptly, "Is this Haggerty fellow married?"

Eithne colored, fumbled for her handkerchief, and looked so guilty that Michael was almost sorry he had asked.

"No . . . but I could never leave Cornanagh, Michael, especially not now, when Catriona needs me so badly."

"D'you mean to tell me that you've had an offer from Haggerty?" he asked, his eyes narrowing.

She twisted her handkerchief nervously, evading his glance and reddening to her ear tips. He gave her shoulder a little shake to make her look up.

"Has he, Eithne?"

Her eyes held by his, she nodded slowly, once again looking close to tears.

"And you said no?" She nodded again, biting her lip. "Because you don't want to marry him?" After a moment she gave her head a quick shake. "Eithne Carradyne, I have had one martyr in this household, and I absolutely refuse to have another. If you want to remarry, do so. It's time you started thinking of your own happiness."

"But . . . but . . . Catriona? I can't desert her."

"As long as there is a horse or a pony in Cornanagh's stables, Catriona will not feel deserted," Michael said firmly. "You marry the man, d'you hear me? I'll give you away myself! And be glad for you. And we'll do just grand with Bridie in the kitchen and a housekeeper to see to the rest!"

They both heard the click of the door. Grinning at Eithne as he strode across the floor, Michael wrenched open the door to see Bridie scurrying down the hall.

"Bridie Doolin!"

Thus it was not difficult after all to sort Bridie out. But she was not pleased at the idea of sharing her domain with a housekeeper.

"Ye hired me as yer cook, and you can't complain that I don't set a good table for ye, come what may," she maintained stoutly. "But I'm having no jumped-up parlor maid telling me how to run my kitchen, so I won't. And you'd better make that plain as a pikestaff, Captain, or I'll leave ye to fend for yerselves, so I will."

"I promise you, Bridie, we'll find somebody quite suitable," Eithne replied.

"Mrs. Healey knows of several likely candidates," Michael added, praying he was right.

Bridie was instantly mollified. "Ah, well. She'd know, she would." Then, smoothing her apron in a final gesture, she marched out of the lounge, head high.

"What d'ya wanna bet she put her ear to the door as soon as we left?" Patricia asked Catriona as the cousins made their way to the yard after finishing the washing up.

Catriona giggled. "I've never seen her put things away so fast in my life. Bridie's been just poisonous to Auntie Eithne, and all for no reason at all."

"I wish I could hear what your dad says to her. He sure had a look in his eye that bodes no good for Bridie Doolin—the old bitch."

"Pat, you mustn't say such things. Bridie's . . . well, she's Bridie." They were getting down saddles and bridles now, and Catriona paused, looking worried. "Cornanagh wouldn't be the same without her somehow," she said softly.

"Yeah, well . . . sometimes you have to go on without things, like without—" She stopped. "C'mon, let's ride. It's too pretty a day to waste. And we promised to meet Mary."

They tacked the two ponies and were swinging out of the yard when Patricia exclaimed, "Cat, why can't I ride one of the horses? My feet are even with his knees."

Catriona looked down, surprised. "No, they're not. And you're much better on the Prince than Sean ever was. You don't let him scare you."

"I'd much rather ride Annie. She's sweet, and besides that, she's a horse."

"She's exactly the same height as the Prince."

"Yes, but she's made like a horse, not like a pony, and she acts like a horse, too."

Catriona gathered her reins. "Come on, we can trot to McBride's Lane."

Patricia's soft chuckle followed Catriona down the pleasant lane and into the shade by the stream.

After the three girls had hacked about Mary's place and practiced vaulting on the placid Champers, Mrs. Evans invited the visitors to stay for tea. She rang Cornanagh and spoke to Eithne, who gave permission.

"Aunt Eithne's become a consultant for a big Houston firm of interior decorators. It's a new career. Maybe she'll even open up her own business," Patricia informed the table at teatime.

"Really?" Maura Evans exchanged glances with her husband.

"Yes, she's been commissioned to buy things at auctions. She got a load delivered at noon, and there were these real neat writing chests that fold out into these super writing tops, with little pockets for writing papers and envelopes and stuff underneath."

"We've got one of those, don't we, Dad," Mary said proudly.

"In fact, we do," said Donal Evans. "I found it when we were valuing a house in Carnew. In very good nick it was, too."

"My aunt says she can sell all she can get." Patricia cocked her head expectantly.

"You are cheeky," Maura said with a laugh. "I think we'll keep this one. Have you girls signed up for Pony Club camp yet?"

"Camp?" Patricia asked skeptically.

"It's not like your kind of camp," Mary explained. "You get to pass your Pony Club tests, and there are neat instructors, and you only go during the day. Your pony can stay there overnight and stuff, but you have to take off their back shoes. So they can't kick other ponies."

"I think you'd enjoy it, Pat," Maura Evans said with a twinkle in her eyes. "It's a very Irish thing to do."

Patricia laughed. "Well, I'm here to get Irishized, and no

Irish camp would be as corny as American. Where do we sign up?"

After the girls had done the washing up, they played card games with Mary's parents and her brother. At ten o'clock the phone interrupted their rather hilarious game: it was Michael, inquiring if there were a pair of lost girls and ponies about the premises.

Maura Evans apologized. "I hadn't realized how late it was getting. I'll send them home directly. Did you want me to follow in the car?"

"No, I don't think so, Maura. There's plenty of light, and they're both cautious."

"You girls had best saddle up and scoot on home," she said when she had rung off. "I'd no idea it was so late."

"Wow! It's like ten o'clock, and the sun's still shining!"

Donal and Maura came out with Mary to assist them and walked with them down the long drive to the road, before waving good-bye.

"Gee, Mary's got the grooviest mother," Patricia said wistfully when they were on their way.

"Yes, she does," Catriona agreed, and sighed deeply.

"And her dad's almost as nice as mine . . . and yours."

The two girls trotted home, envious in their separate ways of Mary Evans.

25

"A housekeeper?" Selina said, blinking in surprise at Eithne's unusual greeting. The woman had evidently been waiting for her, for she had run out the door and popped the question as soon as the red Lancia had pulled into its usual parking space in Cornanagh's yard. "Well," she said with a laugh as she swung her legs out of the car, "I'm sure we can find one. For Cornanagh?"

Eithne colored prettily, managing to look both confused and pleased.

"Do come in and have a cup of coffee with me, Selina," she said. "Michael's out in the hay fields, so he won't be riding quite yet. I did hope that you'd be here a trifle early this morning." She guided Selina into the house and paused, listening for a moment. Then she nodded her head and ushered Selina into the drawing room. "This is a bit more private," she said, gesturing to the table on which a coffee tray had been placed. "You see, keeping a house as large and busy as this is quite time-consuming. And lately . . . well, the fact of the matter is, I've been helping to buy antiques for an interior decorator in Texas. It's become something more than a hobby for me, and yesterday, while I was explaining everything to Michael, things sort of came to a head—with Bridie, I mean. She will"—Eithne dropped her voice, her eyes going instinctively to the door— "listen!" She paused for emphasis. "And she takes things up entirely wrong. A year ago she overheard a conversation I had with Davis—the man who shops in Ireland for the firm—and totally misunderstood. And ever since then she's been . . . well, nasty. With no reason at all. Then yesterday, when the furniture came and I was explaining all about it to Michael, Bridie was listening at the door."

"I trust you were saying something scathing about her little habit."

Eithne giggled. "No, but Michael caught her, and when she started being awkward, he said that you'd help us find someone suitable."

Selina burst out laughing. "He did?"

"And Bridie calmed down right away." Eithne grinned back at Selina.

"Well! I certainly can't let the old waggon down, now, can I?" Selina replied. "Have you the morning *Times*?" Eithne lifted the paper from the couch end table and handed it to Selina. "Thank you. Now, let's see . . . 'Housekeeper's position wanted by respectable widow, accustomed to large houses and country living.' And it's a Wicklow number. Here's another: 'Housekeeper available for adult family only. Excellent references.' It's a Dublin number."

She passed the paper to Eithne, pointing to the entries.

"Now why is that phone number familiar?" Eithne said when she had scanned the first entry.

"Well, let's ring it and find out. Where's the phone here?"

"There's one in Michael's office."

"Discreet!" Selina grinned, and the two women, coffee cups in hand, retired down the hall to the office.

It was rather a dark hole, Selina noticed, but very workmanlike, with bound copies of the Irish *Field* and various well-used veterinary volumes on the shelves, an aged wooden filing cabinet, and a massive mahogany desk strewn with work papers. The phone was on the right-hand side, near a note pad that had several sharpened pencils beside it.

"I don't think Michael will mind," Eithne said. She sat down

on the edge of the swivel chair and dialed the number. It took
her several attempts to get through to the Wicklow exchange.
As the call was finally answered and she recognized the voice
at the other end, a series of expressions crossed Eithne's face,
mirroring her surprise, dismay . . . and delight.

"Mrs. Comyn?" She smiled enthusiastically at Selina, nodding her head in approval as she pursued the conversation.
"Mrs. Comyn, you might not remember me—Eithne Carradyne? My American associate, Mr. Haggerty, and I visited you
earlier this spring."

"If you are looking for more furniture, Mrs. Carradyne, it's
too late," was the droll reply.

"Actually, Mrs. Comyn"—Eithne's voice was very gentle and
kind—"I'm phoning in response to your advert in the *Times.*"

"Oh!" The pause that followed made Eithne wonder whether
or not the connection had been disrupted. "I see."

She plunged on. "I can't imagine that you are aware my
sister-in-law, Isabel Carradyne, passed away recently."

"In fact, I did know, Mrs. Carradyne. Shocking tragedy. You
have my sympathy."

"That's why I'm calling, Mrs. Comyn. This house is quite
large, and busy, and my brother-in-law needs someone to manage it for him. Would you, could you possibly consider coming
to Cornanagh? There is a cook, an old family retainer, and
someone to do the heavy cleaning. Captain Carradyne needs
someone to take entire charge. The household consists of the
Captain, of course, his son Philip, who's twenty-three and working, and his daughter, Catriona, who's thirteen. There's a lovely
corner bedroom with a back burner, so you'd be quite warm
and toasty in the winter, and—oh, dear, I haven't a notion what
sort of salary Michael has in mind. But you're exactly the sort
of person I'd hoped we'd find, because you do know big old
houses and horses . . . . "

"My dear Mrs. Carradyne, if I may interrupt, I'd be more than happy to be considered for the post."

"Oh, Mrs. Comyn! How marvelous!"

Mrs. Comyn then insisted on setting up an interview. After all, Captain Carradyne had never met her, and while she was extremely grateful for Eithne's unqualified recommendation, she felt it wiser not to take anything for granted. And she did not have to vacate Rathderry House until the fifteenth of July.

"Vacate?" Eithne was appalled.

"Yes, the new owners are taking possession then. I've had a month to arrange matters."

The details were fixed, and Eithne rang off, her expression slightly dazed. She gave a long sigh, her mind churning with pity for Mrs. Comyn's destitution. And all because Desmond Comyn had lived it up like a lord, in a mortgaged house on mortgaged acres, not caring that his wasteful ways would leave his widow without a penny to bless herself.

Watching her, Selina smiled and patted her arm. "So that's your good deed for the day, Eithne Carradyne. And well done it was, too. Now I'd better see what Captain Carradyne is doing with the horses this morning."

"You've been so marvelous, Selina, with Conker and Catriona: she's very attached to you, you know," Eithne said earnestly, her eyes searching Selina's face.

"You don't know how much Catriona means to me. If I ever have a daughter, I'd want her to be exactly like Trina. But we don't always get our wants, do we?"

Eithne blushed and looked shyly away, her eyes troubled.

"Besides," Selina went on in her social drawl, noticing her friend's distress, "with David away in the North, there isn't that much to occupy me. Most of our friends are on their holidays." She reached out to squeeze Eithne's hand, smiling. "And I really enjoy working with Michael's horses. It's a challenge and rewarding."

301

Eithne's expression cleared, and she smiled back at Selina, relieved.

"Thanks for the coffee," Selina said. As she came out into the hall, Bridie peered out of the kitchen. "Good morning, Bridie. Marvelous weather, isn't it?"

Michael was just coming in from the Ride as she left the house, and his face immediately brightened at the sight of her. Sensitive now to his mood and expression, Selina knew that passing the Tulip's paddock on his way from the fields had reminded him of his loss. She wanted to comfort him but waved instead, smiling at him and waiting until he reached her. To her surprise, he slipped an arm about her as he turned her toward the yard. His fingers cupped her left shoulder with a loving pressure, and his intensely blue eyes crinkled at the corners with pleasure at her presence.

"Where're the girls?" she asked.

"They'll be around again." He looked over his right shoulder and cocked his head to listen. "Here they come."

"Why, Michael, you've put Trina up on Charlie—and is Pat up on Annie?"

"At her request." He smiled tolerantly. "Americans never keep you in doubt as to their preferences. Patricia prefers Annie to the Prince."

Selina grinned. "Well, she certainly is riding very kindly."

"So I notice."

They both waved as the girls came out of the shadows of the double beeches and trotted past the house. Michael watched, his eyes narrowed critically, until they were lost in the shadows of the copse. "I don't want to rush Annie," he said, "but perhaps by the end of the summer she'll have enough condition to be shown. She's got a nice little pop, and God knows she's a trier. Give you her heart, she would. . . . So, did you and Eithne solve the housekeeper problem?"

Selina nodded. "A Mrs. Comyn—Eithne knows her—is coming for an interview Sunday at five."

Michael grinned at her. "Did she tell you about this Haggerty fellow?"

"Reluctantly, and with blushes."

"She confessed to me that he had proposed, but she'd refused because, of all things, she felt she couldn't leave Cornanagh, and Catriona." Michael gave a contemptuous snort.

"That does Eithne credit," Selina said, "but it's you that Catriona needs, Michael. You do know that, don't you?"

He nodded. "And horses. Speaking of which, missus, I've a lot of horses to exercise today."

"So, what's the drill?"

"The girls have one more round to do on that lot, then they can hack the ponies out with us, if you wouldn't mind riding Emmett while I cope with Temper."

"Michael, I shan't be able to come to the Galloping Green show," Selina said, blurting it out abruptly. "David and I have been invited to spend the weekend at Erinwood."

"I see. . . ." To ease the awkwardness of the moment, Michael threw open the tack room door and continued casually, "I'll have to use a big saddle on Emmett, he'd be pinched by that saddle tree of yours. And you'll need the breastplate or the saddle slips." He handed her the various pieces of tack, grinning. "Mick will be scandalized, my making you tack up your mount."

"That is, if I can remember how, of course!" She grinned back at him, her equanimity restored.

Temper lived up to his name on that ride, indulging in many airs above ground and elegant displays of fear at such unlikely obstacles as the white lines in the center of the road, a protruding branch, and a sudden burst of birdsong. Perversely, he ignored the air brakes of a lorry and the two tractors they had to pass. It took a good half an hour of the hack before he settled.

Selina was more amused than concerned and more than once envied Michael his deep seat and strong hands. Patricia was not as lucky. The Prince had decided that if Temper could misbehave, he could, too. As a result she was bounced all over; but she always managed somehow to regain her balance and stay in the pad.

"That was not the best ride I've ever had," she remarked, dismounting in the yard with a sigh of relief.

"What's the next lot?" Selina asked Michael.

"I've the three to school."

"In the menage?" she asked. Michael nodded. "Well, then, there are three of us, and you could get it all over with in one go."

"Oh, Unk, that'd be super. I love riding horses!" Patricia cried.

"Could I please ride the gray gelding, Daddy?" Catriona asked urgently, unexpectedly bold with her choice.

"C'mon, Michael," Selina said, grinning. "It'd be all over with then."

The girls danced about, squealing their delight at such a plan. Michael didn't hesitate very long because Temper's antics had strained his leg, and he had not looked forward to more hours in the saddle.

"I'll take that hunter cob, and Pat would be fine on the bay," Selina said, cheerfully taking matters out of his hand once he had given his consent.

The multiple ride worked out quite well, and the young horses seemed to enjoy it almost as much as the riders. Just as Michael dismissed the class, the haymakers arrived in from the field, and Sybil drove into the courtyard, her two children in the car with her.

"Hello, Dad," she called cheerfully out the window. "I've

come to steal a sister and a cousin. It's such a beautiful day, I thought we should all go to Brittas!"

"Brittas! Oh, Daddy, could we?" Catriona cried, jumping off the gray and hauling him behind her to give her sister a grateful kiss. "We haven't been to the beach in just ages! And it is hot today!"

"Yeah, we've done all the work. Now can we have some fun?" demanded Patricia, cocking her head impudently. "You could do with some, too," she added after a moment's thought. "Or maybe you can't swim?"

"He can so," Catriona said so stoutly that Michael gave her a hug. "Please. The hay's all turned, and we'd all help to do a second turn this evening, wouldn't we?"

Patricia nodded enthusiastically.

"Will you come, too, Selina?" Michael asked. "Or do you have another engagement?"

"Not one that would be as much fun," Selina said. "Let's put the horses up."

"No, put them out," Michael suggested. "Less work for later, and they deserve a break."

So, while the three walked their mounts down to the paddock, Michael helped Sybil with her children until their doting great-aunt came bustling out. The noon meal was a chaotic jumble of conversations. Sybil heard just enough about the housekeeper and Eithne's antiques to whet her curiosity, and Eithne offered Selina a swimsuit, saying that she was expecting a phone call from Davis and had better wait in. Michael was gratified to notice that she had perked up considerably from Sunday's gloom.

The two girls traveled in Sybil's car to help with Perry and Ann, and Selina went in Michael's Austin, with Artie and his brother, Billy—who had been invited along—silent as mice in the backseat.

The drive, at least, was quiet, but once they arrived at Brittas

Bay, Perry raced off, screaming with delight, pursued by Patricia and Catriona. Sybil gave conflicting directions on where to place the rug and picnic things. And when Michael told Artie and Billy to go swimming, it turned out that neither boy knew how, so he escorted them down to the placid sea and oversaw their entry into the water.

"I don't think those lads ever eat anywhere but at Cornanagh," Sybil said to Selina as they watched. Both boys were bone thin, their torsos reddened from two days' haying in sunny weather.

They both heard Patricia giggling.

"Gawd, ninety-pound weaklings," she said as she and Catriona gave a practiced swing to Perry to land him right by his mother on the blanket, sand and all.

"Well, they work just as hard in the fields as Barry and Mick do," Catriona said in their defense.

"I didn't say they didn't. I wasn't poor-mouthing Artie or his brother, Cat, but they are sort of all angles. Aren't they, Selina?"

"Well, they could both afford to put some condition on," she said matter-of-factly.

"Good heavens, Selina, you're as bad as my father," Sybil said with a laugh. "Completely horse-oriented."

"And if you watch him, you'll discover that he's unsound on the near hind!"

"Selina!" But Sybil was laughing too hard to have been offended. "Now, will someone enlighten me about Auntie Eithne and this housekeeper business?"

"Auntie Eithne's doing a fab line of antiques," Patricia began eagerly. "You should see the stuff that came in Sunday."

"How long has this been going on?" Sybil wanted to know. "And who's this Davis Haggerty fellow?"

"Apparently he works as a buyer for an interior decorating firm in Texas," Selina replied, "and has engaged Eithne as a kind of antique 'scout.'" She hesitated. "And if Eithne's blushes are any indication of her state of mind, I'd say she's gone on him."

"Well, I think it'd be great for Auntie Eithne to marry again," Sybil said. "It wasn't that she didn't have suitors before, but I know that Mother discouraged their calling on Eithne whenever she could—" She broke off to rescue the baby powder from her son, who thought it made a nice icing on the sand. "I'd hate to think of Eithne cloistering herself forever in Cornanagh out of a misplaced loyalty to the Carradynes!"

"How could Auntie Eithne leave Cornanagh? A housekeeper just won't be the same. And what would Owen do?" Catriona asked, beginning to feel uneasy.

"Owen's old enough to fend for himself, Trina," her sister said. "And even if Auntie Eithne married this fellow, it doesn't mean she'll disappear forever. If antiques are his business, they'd both have to come back often. I think it'd be great." Then she realized how pensive Catriona had become. "Oh, come on, now, pet, everyone grows up and leaves their home. You will one day."

Catriona shook her head slowly. "I won't ever leave Cornanagh. It's my life!"

While Sybil and Patricia regarded her with tolerant scepticism, Selina took her statement at face value. It was apparent to her that Catriona loved Cornanagh as intensely as her father did.

Suddenly they were all sprinkled with cold water. Complaining at the outrage, they looked around to see a grinning Michael flinging droplets from his fingers on them, two blue-looking Costello brothers shivering beside him.

Sybil immediately organized towels to rub down the boys, poured hot tea from a Thermos, and chided her father for a total lack of sense.

When they returned to Cornanagh, Selina and Sybil insisted on examining and exclaiming over Eithne's purchases, then everyone sat down to tea. On the whole, it was a very pleasant afternoon.

By Wednesday the hay was ready to bale. It was a fine crop with almost 120 bales per acre, which pleased Michael and made Barry strut with pride. When Philip and Owen arrived home from work that evening, they helped stack the bales to dry in the fields. Then Michael took son and nephew down to the Willow Grove to wet their whistles after such dry work. There he managed to sell a thousand bales to Jack Garden, enough to pay his own baling costs. On Friday most of it was stored, for the wind had been constant and the bales sufficiently cooled to take in.

Bridie, on her best behavior since Monday, cooked a superb dinner for the weary haymakers. Replete and well satisfied with the week's labors, Michael reminded the girls that they'd best check their tack for the show the next day.

"Show?" Patricia exclaimed, and sat upright, groaning at muscles misused during her enthusiastic attempt to outwork her cousin in the field. "I don't think I could sit on the wretched little pony, really I don't. Why doesn't Cat ride him? She's much better at it than me."

"Catriona is not the right age for that class, Pat," Michael replied firmly.

"So who'd know?"

"I would. That sort of subterfuge may be practiced in the States, but it's not the way I conduct affairs at Cornanagh."

Eithne noticed that Catriona was unable to finish her gateau, although the girl had eaten a very hearty tea. As Catriona was quiet by nature, and Patricia talkative, not even Mick noticed that she was silent as they readied horses, ponies, and tack for the two-day Galloping Green show.

They pulled out of the yard at nine-thirty in the morning, since the Galloping Green venue was a scant fifteen miles away, just beyond White's Cross on the main Dublin road. Once again the lorry as well as the two-horse box were needed, for the two ponies had their jumping competitions, and mares and foals would be judged this first day of the show.

When they arrived, the mares and foals had to be unloaded first: Lady Madeline had a bucking fit and narrowly missed her foal, who was white-eyed with apprehension and trembling nervously. It took the combined efforts of Mick and Artie to calm the little filly down while Michael lunged the fidgets out of the mare. Then they had to rub the sweat marks dry and get her settled.

Catriona was pleased to see that Tulip's Son walked placidly down the ramp, although he stared about him with pricked ears and an occasional high snort. "Like a crown prince surveying his realm," Patricia said in approval. Placid as always, Frolic paced beside him.

"Pat, Trina," Michael called, and the two girls trotted over to him. "I want you girls to go over to the entries caravan, get your numbers, and have a look at the course. At least this show is starting on time, and the 12.2s are already jumping. And Pat, I expect you to behave yourself. The ground here is rock hard. No bounding about, no charging fences, spare the ponies. Understood?"

"Yes, sir!"

"Don't forget," Catriona muttered as her father went off.

"Oh, Gawd!" Patricia turned on her cousin with a scowl. "I'll take it from him, but not from you, cousin dear—Miss Perfect, who always does exactly what she's told!"

With that scathing retort, Patricia turned on her heel and strode off toward the entry caravan. Catriona stared after her, then walked slowly back into the horsebox and threw her arms around Conker's neck. The Prince extended his neck toward her, rubbing his nose against her arm to offer consolation.

Conker stood without moving, lending her the support she craved.

Patricia couldn't know just how deeply her snide accusation had cut, coming right after another disturbing revelation. For Catriona had a worry chasing around and around in her head since last night. What would happen if her father ever found out that she had ridden the Prince's speed round? Her mind revolved unceasingly around this agonizing question and emerged each time with two wounding truths: she had done something her father would deem unforgiveable; and she was not the meek and obedient girl Patricia thought her.

The horsebox was hot and stuffy, but its odors gave Catriona an odd sense of safety. The noise of a show swirled outside from every direction, horses whinnied and kicked, dogs yapped, grooms cursed, lorry engines rumbled . . . and suddenly her name, anxiously called in Patricia's clear loud voice, cut through the nearer sounds. Then she heard Mick's voice raised in query.

"It's where she's likely to be," she heard him say, as he grew closer. Giving herself a good shake and Conker a final pat, she opened the door.

Mick had his hand raised to the door handle, and Patricia, two pasteboard numbers trailing their ties in her hand, looked surprised.

"How long have you been there?" Mick demanded.

"Not long," Catriona said. "I heard some kicking and thought it might be the Prince. You know how he can be sometimes."

Patricia gave her a long hard stare. "I thought you'd at least stand in line with me at the entries' caravan. I couldn't imagine where you'd got to."

Mick gave a snort. "Where else but with the ponies!" He turned and beckoned to Artie, who trotted over. "Now, no time to waste. Artie, get in with Cat and take the Prince. I'm to lunge him to see if that won't settle him. Pat, make yourself useful and get me the lunge line from the lorry. Artie can help Cat tack Conker."

Once the Prince and Conker had been led down the horse-box ramp, Catriona really didn't have time to fret herself. She got Conker saddled while Artie did up the plait that had come loose and oiled his hooves. Pat went off with Mick to lunge the Prince, who kept up an urgent whinnying at being parted from his stablemate. Conker's ear twitched, but he didn't reply.

"You're too well mannered, so you are," Catriona whispered to him.

When she was in the saddle, Conker between her legs, it was easier to forget everything but the job at hand. If she did exceedingly well on Conker, maybe her father would be able to forgive what she had done on the Prince. If only . . .

Then she saw her father leading Frolic and Tulip's Son back, the large red first rosettes fluttering from their headstalls. The colt, his near-black coat gleaming in the sun, continued to behave like a visiting princeling, contriving to look as if he were walking an inch above the rough meadow grass. Michael Carradyne was grinning.

"Hop off Conker, Trina, and help me load these two! You should have seen this little fellow! He's the consummate ham. Just like his sire!" He gave the colt a congratulatory slap.

Catriona obediently secured Conker to the lorry with a spare lead rope and then held mare and foal while her father opened their partitioned space in the lorry. Frolic, tail swishing, ambled placidly up the ramp and into the stall. Tulip's Son, however, was not eager to be penned up again and hauled back on the lead rope, nearly pulling Catriona off her feet.

"Don't let him go, Trina!" her father said in a low but urgent voice.

"There now, who's a silly boy?" Catriona said soothingly, going hand over hand up the taut lead rope. The colt regarded her down his aristocratic nose with white-rimmed eyes and flaring nostrils. "You'll be thirsty, and wanting a bit of lunch now, won't you? And you with such a pretty ribbon." She had reached his head now and gently touched his velvety nose. She blew into his nostrils, and all of a sudden he relaxed his opposition.

"Take the ribbon off, Trina. That may be spooking him, blowing across his face."

She removed it, talking all the time and stroking his neck and shoulder. She looped the lead rope properly, with a double twist of the end around her left hand, and took a firm hold on the cheekpiece of the leather head collar.

"Now, up we go. C'mon, fella. Mother wants you."

She felt the resistance and gave the barest of tugs, while he snorted, his left eye rolling white to see her.

"You're some tulip, you are! Walk on."

As if he'd been waiting for exactly that command, Tulip's Son set his dainty hooves on the ramp and scampered up beside her. With the smoothness of long practice, she unclipped the lead and slid out of the stall while her father closed it securely, sighing with relief.

"You handle him with a great deal more expertise than Owen did. I think I'll have you show him with me from now on," he said. "Better get going. The 12.2 class was just about over. I'm waiting for Phil and Owen, but I'll see you later."

The 13.2 course wasn't difficult, not even tricky, since this was not a qualifier: not one of the twelve fences could cause either Conker or the Prince a bit of bother. But the ground was rock hard, ruts baked into the surface. A hoof placed wrong, and a pony could stumble on landing. Catriona fervently hoped that Pat would obey her father. The concussion would be brutal, and it just wouldn't do to have the Prince laid up with bruised soles or sore legs.

There weren't as many Northern entries to this show, but there were hordes of girls and boys her age and herds of ponies of all shapes and abilities entered in the 13.2 jumping competition. She and Conker, the twenty-fifth pair in the event, were only the third to go clear. Then, as Patricia put it, things began to pick up, and more clear rounds were achieved. All in all, it took two hours before every first-round contestant had had a chance.

There were a mere eighteen entries in the second round and only six fences, each four inches higher now but spaced to make awkward turns in the final speed round. Catriona and Conker were once again the third double clear.

"Well, someone else has to go first, so you'll know what speed you have to beat," Patricia said with some satisfaction.

Catriona kept her eyes on the other competitors, trying to decide which pony looked speedy and agile enough to cut seconds around impossible corners. She had decided where she and Conker could make up a few seconds.

Then she was in the ring again, making her bow to the judges and cantering Conker in a circle until the bell sounded. She felt Conker's impulsion build as she turned him for the start. She dug her heels into him as soon as they were past the electric eye of the timer, and he responded with such a surge that he took off a long way from the first fence of rails; but he lost no time in the air, answering her pull on the reins to land already turning on his off fore. He made the next turn on his haunches, forefeet suspended briefly before he plunged forward. She could feel the jolt of the ground under them as he took the first element of the double, two strides and then out again. Instantly she angled him toward the wall, and they flew out across it. Once again Conker came down hard enough to rattle her teeth, but she kicked him on—the faster they went now, the sooner it was over.

She had only to angle him slightly to the left to put him in line with the rustic; over that, and then the barrels. Once again Conker seemed to suspend himself a moment over the jump, and then he was scampering for the finish. She heard Patricia's cowboy yell and felt like answering it. She almost did when the announcer gave her time as 23.4 seconds, a full two seconds under the best so far.

And this time, she won. If only Selina were there with her father, she thought how pleased she'd be, watching Conker's sedate lap of victory. Then, as she reined him back to a trot, she caught her breath, acutely aware of the unevenness in his stride. She pulled him up as soon as she could and dismounted. Holding her breath, she picked up the foot he had favored, the off-fore pierced by glass on the day she had not opened her door to her mother. She choked back tears of remorse as she felt her father's presence.

"I'd say it might just be the hard ground, Trina," he said, tapping the hoof with his pocketknife. The pony did not react to the test. "Walk him out."

She did, and he walked sound, but when she trotted him back she felt the same hint of unevenness.

"What's wrong?" Pat demanded.

"Probably nothing. But remember it when you're riding the Prince," Michael advised. "Are you on the board yet?"

"Yeah, I'm nineteenth to go, and we got here early, too."

"Let's load Conker in the lorry, Trina. Then, when the yearling class is over, Mick will drive him back and stand him in the stream a while."

As it happened, both Cornanagh vehicles pulled out of the show grounds at the same time. Patricia misinterpreted her uncle's directions and forced the Prince to go slow. Struggling all the while to get his head, the pony racked up a total of fifteen faults before Patricia realized her error and allowed him to finish the course without interference.

"These things happen," Michael commented philosophically when she drew up beside him, red-faced and anxious. "The perils of competing. You'll do better next week, Pat. Off you go now, and load him up. Then we'll be off."

As Michael watched Patricia walk the sweating pony up the hill to the horsebox, it struck him that her unflagging exuberance might be having a bad effect on Catriona. The girl certainly hadn't been herself today, despite her faultless performance on Conker.

Eyes narrowed thoughtfully, he walked away to join Philip and Owen, who were showing the yearlings for him since he'd had to be on hand for Patricia's class.

26

The next day Conker exhibited no further unevenness, but to be on the safe side, he was kept in. Catriona gave him a thorough grooming, an attention he always enjoyed.

Michael called the girls over when he was ready to leave with the horses to be shown that day. "Now, Patricia, I'll want you to take Annie. . . .

"Can we hack out?" Patricia asked eagerly.

"On the ride only. That little horse must be worked very, very carefully, d'you understand me?"

"Yes*sir!*"

Michael cleared his throat. "And Trina, I want you to school the Prince for me."

"Oh, Gawd!" Patricia looked down. "I really goofed yesterday, didn't I?"

"As well you realize it." He gave her shoulder a squeeze to take the sting out of the reprimand. "Two laps at the working trot, Trina, and then I want you to take him up the jump alley, calm, controlled. I'll be back before Mrs. Comyn arrives at five."

"Good luck, Daddy, Pip," Catriona called as her father hauled himself beside Philip in the lorry cab.

"C'mon, Cat," Patricia urged when they'd gone. "It's going to be hot today. And those flies are unbelievable! Let's ride now before they all wake up."

To Catriona's intense relief, Pat was fairly quiet when they were riding. Of course, she really enjoyed riding Annie, which was obvious by the kindness in her hands and voice. Annie's

ears flicked back and forth, and she seemed to respond as
quickly to voice commands as to seat and legs. Someone had
schooled her well. The Prince, however, needed restraint today
as much as Annie needed encouragement, and Catriona had
her hands full throughout the hack.

Bridie had announced at breakfast that she wasn't cooking
any big dinner just for three women—there was plenty to pick
from in the fridge. However, she was still in the kitchen when
Catriona and Patricia got back from their ride. Scrumptious
odors wafted out the open window. They could also hear the
old cook muttering under her breath, so they quietly went to
change their clothes and attend late Sunday Mass.

Bridie was gone when they returned, but they found a plate
of sandwiches and a warning that they weren't to go rooting
about the kitchen in her absence.

"She's baked up a storm for Mrs. Comyn," Patricia said, sniffing appreciatively.

Catriona nodded, hopefully interpreting Bridie's preparations as a good sign as far as Mrs. Comyn's visit was concerned.

Patricia decided to write a letter to her parents in the lounge,
so Catriona had her room to herself. She took out her sketch
of the Tulip and her father. She wanted to have it finished, and
framed, as her birthday present for him. If it turned out well.

Taking out her drawing pencils and eraser, she began to
make a few judicious corrections. She was rather pleased with
the Tulip's graciously inclined head, the pricked ears—the
Tulip had had lovely ears, just like his son did—the arch of
the proud full neck. But she hadn't quite the same skill with
human bodies. Her father's shoulder looked . . . well, misshapen somehow. With a frown of concentration, Catriona
went to work.

Twenty minutes before five, the lorry turned into the yard,
triumphantly sporting three red and two blue ribbons above
the windscreen. Sybil pulled into the courtyard not three min-

utes later while her father was rattling off quick orders to Mick, Philip, and Owen before he dashed up for a quick shower and change.

He was just coming down the stairs when he heard Tory's frantic barking and saw a brown vintage Morris Minor pull into the courtyard. Sybil came out quickly to control Tory, and Michael also noticed the flick of the kitchen curtain that meant Bridie had had a look, too. Then Eithne joined Sybil to usher the woman into the house, and he met her in the hall, guiding her to the drawing room.

Mrs. Comyn seemed far more at ease than he felt. She took in the room, and the view out the front windows, with one shrewd, appraising glance, then accepted the Victorian chair Michael held for her. There was nothing obsequious in her manner, despite what Eithne had told him of her reduced circumstances. She wore a neat gray dress, white cotton gloves, beige stockings with gray leather pumps, and a straw hat trimmed with a gray ribbon. She'd been a handsome woman when she was younger: she had smooth skin, a direct gaze in her gray eyes, and a generous mouth. Her hair was more white than gray, cut short but not exactly what he'd call styled. He couldn't judge her age.

"You do realize, Captain Carradyne," she began, "that I have no references to offer you, never having been employed in any capacity before." Her tone was matter-of-fact, and she spoke with an educated accent.

"Mrs. Comyn was, however, often the chairman of several administrative committees within the ICA, Michael," Eithne said with a nervous smile. "And Rathderry House is larger than Cornanagh and so beautifully appointed."

Mrs. Comyn inclined her head graciously at the compliment. "What duties would be required, Captain?" she asked.

"Actually, Mrs. Comyn, what we need is someone to take over complete management of the house," Sybil said, giving her father a reassuring grin. "My aunt has her own home to care for, and while she's been marvelous at turning to, it's not really fair to impose on her good nature. If you're accustomed to running a big house, it'd just be more of the same. Dad may be a tyrant in the yard and the menage, but as long as he's got hot meals, a clean bed, and an orderly house, I've never heard him complain."

"We have someone to do the heavy cleaning and laundry," Eithne added, "and, of course, Bridie—Mrs. Doolin, that is— does the cooking."

"Does Mrs. Doolin do the marketing?" Mrs. Comyn asked.

"Not anymore," Sybil replied. "She was never safe behind the wheel of a car, and anyway, Mother preferred to do the shopping. Would you mind?"

"I venture to suggest that it would be wiser to follow established routines, and I would naturally discuss menus with Mrs. Doolin or . . ." She turned politely to Michael.

"Oh, Dad'll eat anything, Mrs. Comyn, that won't eat him."

"Sybil!" Eithne cried, dismayed.

"Actually, the family's a good deal smaller now," Sybil went on, unperturbed, "really just my brother Philip and my sister, Catriona—oh, and my American cousin, Patricia, for the summer. Auntie Eithne and her son, Owen, usually take tea over here. Sundays, though, the entire clan might gather." Sybil rolled her eyes. "I can promise you one thing, Mrs. Comyn, Cornanagh is never dull," she said brightly. "That is, if you don't mind nonstop talk about horses and endless tracks of dirt in the house."

"Sybil!" Michael called warningly.

Eithne cleared her throat. "Perhaps Sybil and I should show you about the house now, Mrs. Comyn?"

Michael shot his sister-in-law a grateful look and stood as the three women went off on their tour.

"She's come, has she?" Bridie poked her head around the hall door as soon as the women had left.

"As you saw, Bridie Doolin, peeking out the kitchen window." Michael waggled a finger at the old cook but tempered his warning with a smile. "You give her half a chance, Bridie. She doesn't seem to be the sort who would interfere unnecessarily."

Bridie came round the door, her face screwed up indignantly. "Now, Captain, sor, and me as fair a person as ever lived. A' course, it's not up to me who comes into this house over someone who's labored hard for more years than I care to name."

"Bridie, Cornanagh wouldn't be the same place without you in the kitchen, and you know it. Eamonn and Paddy both said so when they were here."

The old woman lowered her eyes coyly and began to twist her apron. "Oh, Captain!"

Just then, they both heard the women descending the stairs. Bridie closed the hall door quietly behind her, retreating unobserved to meet them in the kitchen.

Michael found that he had his ears pricked for the sound of voices, but he could hear nothing. He fidgeted nervously, hoping Bridie and Mrs. Comyn would take each other's measure without prejudice. He hoped the matter would be settled today, if Mrs. Comyn was willing to give the place a try, for he most certainly did not want to repeat this sort of nonsense.

Sybil was chatting away in a very relaxed manner to Mrs. Comyn as they reentered the lounge, but Eithne's eyes met his anxiously. "Well now, Michael, Mrs. Comyn has seen the house and met Bridie. A cup of tea, perhaps, Mrs. Comyn?"

Mrs. Comyn inclined her head graciously in acceptance. Eithne left her in his charge so gratefully that Michael began to wonder if something had gone wrong. "Well, Mrs.

Comyn, I trust the size of the house has not put you off?" he ventured.

"This is a lovely old home, Captain Carradyne, and has been well maintained." Her eyes met his in a level gaze. "What had you in mind for salary and perquisites?"

Michael cleared his throat. "You would, of course, be considered a member of the family," he began, and sensed that this found favor with her. "I can offer a salary of one hundred pounds a month, with a yearly review, as well as a full day off each week and half days as required. I'm sure that you were shown the room you would occupy, and we can certainly make it more comfortable to suit your needs." He smiled encouragingly and was rewarded by another of her almost royal nods. "If you have no objection, then, I thought perhaps a month's trial to see if we suit . . . ?"

"That would be most satisfactory, Captain."

"When would you be able to take up the position, Mrs. Comyn? On the fifteenth?"

"Shall we say next Sunday, Captain, the twelfth? I'd prefer to vacate the premises before I'm required to."

Rather than be forced out of her own home, Michael thought, and experienced a stab of sympathy and respect for the woman's pride. "That suits me perfectly, Mrs. Comyn. Now, would you require any assistance in removing?"

"Thank you, no. I have that in hand."

Almost on cue, the door opened to admit Patricia, who gave Mrs. Comyn a long sharp look, Eithne carrying the tea tray, and Catriona, bringing up the rear with the cake stand. Michael kept his expression neutral, as if the tea parade were an everyday occurrence. Such a spread meant Bridie was prepared to surrender to the inevitable.

As if Patricia had officiated frequently at formal teas, she moved the table into position for Eithne to set down the tray, held her aunt's chair, and then stood quietly while Catriona set the cake stand by Mrs. Comyn with a shy smile.

"May I present my daughter, Catriona, Mrs. Comyn?" Michael said formally, and Catriona curtsied. "And my niece, Patricia Carradyne, from Connecticut, who is spending the summer with us." To his utter amazement, Patricia, as demure as a convent resident, also dropped a graceful curtsy.

Eithne served tea with the willing and deft assistance of her two nieces, while Sybil rattled on about her children and the various other members of the Carradyne family. Bridie had outdone herself in the dainty sandwiches, iced lady cakes, and freshly baked tarts. There was a momentary lull after everyone had been served. Then:

"Do you like horses at all?" The question seemed to burst from Patricia as if she had been actively suppressing it.

Mrs. Comyn smiled: in Michael's eyes the first spontaneous reaction from her.

"Yes, Patricia, I do. Do you have a pony?"

"We both have," Patricia said, now taking charge of the conversation. "I've got Ballymore Prince for the summer, and we've qualified for the 14.2s at the August show. So has Catriona, on Conker, only she's in the 13.2s. She got a first yesterday at Galloping Green. I got fifteen faults." Her candor won another smile from Mrs. Comyn. "You'll come and see us jump at the RDS, won't you?"

"I should be delighted to watch. The Horse Show, if weather permits, is always a splendid event." She turned to Michael. "You mentioned that you often have foreign buyers, Captain Carradyne?"

"Yes, in fact, we sold four show jumpers last year to the Italians. If the proposed Horse Board Bill is passed, I think more Europeans will look to the Irish horse market once they can be sure of an animal's breeding and performance."

On the breeding and showing of horses, Mrs. Comyn was

able to comment intelligently, and Michael's anxiety over her reserved manner began to dissipate. She quietly displayed considerable background and information about horses in Ireland and agreed with him about the main problems facing the industry. By the time tea was finished, and a good many of the little cakes and tartlets had been consumed by Patricia and Catriona, the atmosphere in the lounge had eased considerably.

"I must be on my way now, Captain. There seem to be so many people on the roads these summer Sundays." Mrs. Comyn got to her feet in a graceful movement. "It has been a pleasure to meet you, Mrs. Roche, Catriona, Patricia." Each came forward and gave her hand a formal shake. "Thank you for the lovely tea, Mrs. Carradyne, and my compliments to Mrs. Doolin. I shall look forward to Sunday, Captain Carradyne, with pleasure."

She turned toward the door, which Michael opened hastily. They all escorted her to her ancient Morris, and Michael again opened the door for her, closing it politely when she was settled in the driver's seat. With a gracious nod of her head, she started the car and drove sedately from the courtyard.

"I think she'll do very well indeed, Dad," Sybil commented when the car was out of sight. "Grandmother can't complain about her respectability."

"My word, she has changed," Eithne said at Michael's elbow. "She's so . . . so reserved. But she did seem to thaw a bit when the girls came in."

"What did you think, Trina?" Michael asked.

"I think she seems awfully sad and . . . well, kind of brave," Catriona replied. "D'you think she'll really like it here?"

Michael and Eithne exchanged glances. They had mentioned nothing of Mrs. Comyn's circumstances.

"But did you like her?" Sybil persisted.

Her head tilted to one side, Catriona regarded her sister for a minute. "Yes, when she does smile, it's a nice one. And she understands horses." Michael ruffled her hair, and she grinned.

"I wonder what Mrs. Doolin thinks," Patricia said mischievously. "But that sure was the most elegant tea I've ever et!"

All through the long, tedious weekend, Selina kept wondering what was happening at Cornanagh. She had even toyed with the idea of phoning Michael on Saturday evening to see how the girls, and Tulip's Son, had done but decided it would be unwise to do so.

She couldn't understand why wives were needed on what was patently a working weekend. The men would have been far better served in their offices, with their secretaries or personal assistants at hand, than cluttering up Elizabeth Murray's gracious lounge or locking themselves in Declan's billiard room.

Their hostess had done her best to entertain the three wives, two of whom had no conversation at all and were quite content to sunbathe around the luxurious swimming pool or bat a few tennis balls on the grass courts. Selina and Elizabeth ran out of social chitchat by late Saturday afternoon.

An elaborate but well-presented dinner on Saturday evening was graciously attended by the men, who carried on oblique and cryptic conversations and drank far too much. To Selina's chagrin, they joined the women after their port and cigars, apparently determined to turn the evening into a drunken free-for-all. Their convivial host called in the butler, who was kept busy for the rest of the night serving the guests whatever drinks they fancied.

Inevitably the jokes became coarser, and anecdotes about absent friends grew malicious, if not downright slanderous. At one point, the banker, George, began a drinking competition with Francis, and their wives joined in the spirit of the occasion, cheering them on.

Fortunately David had the good sense to remain on the sidelines and get quietly plastered on his Scotch and sodas. Unfortunately, he failed to notice when Declan plumped himself down beside her, pinning her against the arm of the low couch. As she tried to rise, he put his arm around her, his fingers lightly feeling the bare skin of her shoulder. When he drunkenly insisted that she try a sip of the rather bilious concoction in his glass, she took the tumbler, let it slip through her fingers, and spilled it over both of them. That brought Declan to his feet with a slurred expletive and caught the attention of her hostess, which had been Selina's aim.

"Elizabeth, have you something to use on stains?" she asked. "I'm terribly fond of this gown, and I feel so stupidly clumsy."

Elizabeth had a spot remover to recommend, and Selina was thus able to leave the room in her company. When she reached the dubious safety of her bedroom, she locked the door. Around dawn, she had to get up to let David in. He was exceedingly drunk, and she could barely get him to the bed. He would be very sorry tomorrow morning, and she was glad.

She and Elizabeth were the only ones up for breakfast, and the meal was served out on the sun-drenched flagstones beyond the sitting room. Elizabeth looked haggard and tried her best to sound cheerful. Selina fretted over wasting such a beautiful day and resented not being able to join Michael and watch the girls jump.

With a little effort and a rare go at the crossword puzzles, she managed to let the Sunday papers occupy her the entire morning. Around noon, the men finally emerged: George and Frank looking badly dyspeptic, Declan sullen, and David obviously suffering from hangover as well as indigestion. After drinking several cups of coffee, they decided that what they needed was a good round of golf. The women were not invited.

Selina spent a tedious afternoon with the women at poolside, and when the men got back, looking considerably more alert, she tried to sound sincere in her thanks to Elizabeth as they all said their good-byes. She also managed a deft evasion of Declan, who had been using farewells as an excuse to claim slobbery kisses from his women guests.

Needless to say, David took her to task on the way home.

"I do not like parties," she told him firmly, "which end with half the guests drunk and disorderly. I don't care how important they are in the world of business and finance, David. Nothing excuses such excess. And if Declan Murray ever attempts to maul me again, I'll slap him. It's beyond me why I had to come on a weekend clearly devoted to business discussions!"

"Declan particularly asked me to bring you this weekend. He thought you and Elizabeth would get on well together."

"So we did, watching her husband pay attention to everyone but her."

"I don't know what's come over you lately, Selina."

"Not lately, David, if you're referring to Declan. I've told you before that he's a lecherous man, and I will not be fondled like a whore. And don't tell me again how valuable he is as a financial wizard. That doesn't excuse his personal behavior."

"You obviously had too much sun, Selina," David declared as if this were the only plausible explanation for her behavior.

Selina closed her eyes and shook her head wearily. "If you say so, David." She rested her head against the seat back and let the motion of the smooth Jaguar and the sound of its throaty engine lull her into a doze.

David turned the radio on for the news at some point, rousing her just when she was on the point of falling asleep. But they were already in Dalkey.

"Will you be at home at all next week, David?" she asked as he tooled the Jag through their gates.

"No. This month could be critical; I'm afraid I'll have to be off early in the morning for Belfast."

"In spite of Declan Murray, it was lovely today in West Meath." She forced a note of conciliation into her voice. After all, she'd have one whole week without him; she could afford to be pleasant.

"We aren't often blessed with such lovely weather, are we?"

His response was equally amiable, and they parted civilly to go to their separate rooms.

At eight o'clock the next morning, Selina turned the Lancia into the yard with an incredible sense of reprieve. Catriona and Patricia were lying in wait for her and surged forward to be the first to open her door, babbling so about the Galloping Green show that she had to silence them both for an intelligible recital of Cornanagh's successes.

"Did you have a nice time, Selina?" Catriona asked, remembering her manners.

Selina smiled. "I would much rather have been with you two. How did you get on with the housekeeper?"

"She'll be okay," said Pat.

Catriona frowned. "She looked so sad and lonely."

"Bridie gave us a super tea, and Mrs. Comyn comes next Sunday," Patricia added. "C'mon, Cat, we've got to finish tacking up. Uncle Mihall's down checking the field horses."

Michael was at the top of the far field, looking larger than life and so handsome that Selina's heart began to race. Seeing him again, after such a long, lonely weekend, filled her with longing and an almost physical pain. Perhaps she would have to stop coming to Cornanagh. . . . Ah, no, she couldn't do that. She'd simply have to watch herself. After all, it wasn't as if there were any sort of understanding between them.

Michael answered her wave with a vigorous gesture of his own. His smile when she reached him was tender and caressing, and he put out a hand to catch her by the shoulder. She felt a surge of tremendous affection and relief: despite the many demands upon his time and attention, he had missed her, as she had missed him.

At that moment a shout alarmed them both. Artie was pelting down the ride, waving both hands and yelling. Michael and Selina ran to meet him.

"What is it, Artie?"

The boy came to such an abrupt halt that he had to balance himself with one hand on Michael's arm. He swallowed, his eyes wide with apprehension.

"There's a man in the yard, sir," he said, gasping, "with a shotgun, and he's threatening to kill Owen."

"Owen?" Michael shot Selina a startled look and then began to run, half limping, toward the yard.

For a man with a damaged leg, Michael managed a pace that left Selina, as well as Artie, well behind. He only slowed down to get round the strap-iron gate that Artie had left open in his haste.

They halted at the sight of the tableau in the courtyard. Mick, pitchfork in hand, was standing at the entrance to the yard, with Barry and a frightened Billy ranged beside him, one with a shovel and the other with a yard broom. A battered green Wolsley, the driver's door hanging open, occupied the center of the court, its wheels cut to the left as if the car had braked suddenly. Selina could see a girl crouched in the passenger seat. But her attention turned immediately to the menacing figure of the man, his stocky frame hunched as he trained the heavy-gauge shotgun on Owen.

Owen stood a trifle apart from the others, who had evidently followed him out into the court: Patricia and Catriona were very close together, Pat's arm about her cousin's shoulders. Eithne was standing by Philip, hands to her mouth, her face stark with fear and confusion; Philip looked on in surprise and apprehension, while Bridie peered around the door frame, her mouth open in a round of horror.

"I've got ya, ya gobshite, ya evil fornicating bastard. You'll not sport with another gel, for I'll blow 'em off ya."

To give Owen his due, he stood straight and calm, his eyes steady on the man without so much as blinking to acknowledge his uncle's arrival.

"I don't think so," Michael said calmly, and with unexpected swiftness he moved forward. The surprise was sufficient to cause the assailant to swivel toward a new danger. Seizing his advantage, Michael pushed the barrel of the shotgun up, wrenching it away, then brought the butt up and slammed it into the man's chest with such force that he was pushed back against the car. "Now," he said, pointing the shotgun at its owner, "who are you, and what is your complaint?"

"He knows who I am," the man said, brandishing an agitated fist at Owen. "He knows. Look at the guilt writ all over him."

Michael turned to his nephew. "Owen, can you enlighten me?"

"It's Jim Fitzroy from Kilcoole," Mick answered, coming to stand by Michael Carradyne. "Owns a dairy farm halfway down the Newcastle road."

"Mr. Fitzroy, we can adjourn—"

"Don't try that fancy talk on me!" Fitzroy rubbed his chest with one thick, reddened hand. "We'll go nowhere till this is sorted out, and it's best that all know what sort of a fucking bastard lives with 'em."

"That's enough of that kind of language, Fitzroy."

"It's enough of fucking about, is what it is, Carradyne." Fists clenched, the farmer took two steps toward Owen before Michael stepped in his way, the barrel of the shotgun now aimed straight at Fitzroy's chest. "That bastard has got my Cathleen with child!"

Selina saw the incredulous expression in Owen's eyes, and then his face cleared. His whole body relaxed, and he shot Philip a malicious grin.

"Cathleen?" he said with a snort of amusement. "You'll be looking at half the county in that case, Fitzroy."

With an inarticulate cry of rage, Fitzroy flung himself toward Owen and was intercepted just short of his goal by the concerted actions of Philip, Michael, and Mick. It was Mick's pitchfork, pressed remorselessly into the man's waistcoat, that finally constrained him. He was mouthing obscenities, eyes narrowed to slits in his weather-worn face as he tried to avoid the prongs of the fork and reach Owen.

Once assured that Fitzroy was restrained, Michael opened the door of the Wolsley and pulled the weeping, protesting girl out of the car.

"Now, miss, to his face, accuse my nephew of violating you!"

The girl turned as far from her father and Owen as Michael's grasp would let her. In doing so, the thickening of her waist became apparent.

"How far along are you?" Michael asked, in a firm but kind voice.

"Bastard, for shaming a girl so," Fitzroy shouted. "How would an innocent girl like my Cathleen know such a thing?"

"If Owen is to blame, surely you remember when, Cathleen," Michael said, ignoring the farmer. His tone was conciliatory, even kind, but with an undertone that made Selina shiver. Catriona's eyes were huge in a face gone deadly pale, her expression one of horrified recognition. She had seen Cathleen Fitzroy before. Patricia, on the other hand, was absolutely fascinated by the scene. "Speak, girl, when was it?"

But Cathleen could only blubber. Whatever prettiness might have been hers in happier times was now blurred by puffy eyes and a swollen, bruised cheek bearing the imprint of an open-handed slap.

"Answer, girl!" roared her father, and she gave a shriek of terror, crowding now against Michael for protection.

"February. February fourteenth, it was. After the disco."

There was a fleeting but satisfied grin on Owen's face, and Philip looked immensely relieved. Michael dropped Cathleen's wrist, his expression more disgusted than scornful. "Then I know you're mistaken about Owen, Cathleen," he said, "because on that weekend Owen and I returned two mares to the Allargard Stud in Waterford. I can have Mr. Alford verify that if you like."

Michael broke the shotgun, removed the shells, and handed it butt first to Fitzroy, then gestured pointedly to the Wolsley.

"You've shamed us all, Carradyne," Fitzroy said, his eyes pig stubborn, his jaw set. He grabbed his daughter by the arm and propelled her toward the car with a vicious shove. "I'll get ya for it. I'll get y'all for it, and God is my witness!"

Cathleen slid into the rear of the Wolsley, as far from her father as possible. He gunned the engine and the car bounded out of the court.

"Owen, a word with you before you leave for work," Michael said, striding to the house. "The rest of you go on about your business." He gestured peremptorily to the yard personnel.

Eithne caught Owen by the arm as he followed his uncle. "Did you molest that girl, Owen Carradyne?" she demanded.

"No more than anyone else in North Wicklow, Mother."

"She's got a name for it, Auntie Eithne," Philip said, nodding. He put a gentle arm about his aunt and guided her away from Michael and her son, in the direction of the kitchen. "Come along, now, I think we could all do with a cuppa." Selina, Catriona, and Patricia agreed and followed on his heels.

"Oh, Pip, I never thought it would come to this," Eithne said, her hands twitching restlessly. "How could he?"

"He's done no real harm, believe me," Philip replied soothingly. "Cathleen's been twitching her skirts at everything wearing pants. God knows who the father is. I doubt if she does. So stop worrying." He held out a chair for his aunt at the kitchen table.

"Well, are you satisfied now, missus, to ruin the reputation of Cornanagh all over the county?" demanded a fierce Bridie, pouncing on Eithne.

"Bridie, for God's sake!" Philip cried. "Put the kettle on, and if I hear any more from you, today or any day, I'll boot you out of Cornanagh myself!"

Everyone stared in utter amazement at Philip's fury and forcefulness. He made quick gestures to his sister and his cousin to get cups and nodded at Selina to sit beside his aunt and comfort her.

"Did I make myself plain, Bridie Doolin?"

She was still staring at him, her eyes bulging out of their sockets. Of a sudden, she collected herself, gave her apron a swipe, and flounced about to plug the kettle in. "The colonel to the spit of him," she muttered.

"Pip!" Catriona murmured wonderingly.

"Well, she's not the conscience of this house," he said, his eyes flashing with righteous anger. "There now, Auntie Eithne. Owen's only been acting the boyo." He patted his aunt's shoulder encouragingly. "And it's not the first time someone's tried to plant an indiscretion at Cornanagh."

He caught his aunt's attention with that. "Whatever do you mean?"

He pointed surreptitiously at Bridie, who was listening to every word. "You remember, don't you, Bridie," he said cheerfully, "when old Mr. Kirwan tried to blame my sainted brother Jack?"

Bridie whirled, her face white. "You nivver heard that!"

"I did indeed," Philip said brightly. "Look, I've got to rush or I'll be late. And thus ends yet another melodramatic scene at Cornanagh. See you, Selina." With an impish grin, he waved to everyone, gave his still distraught aunt another pat on the shoulder, and left.

"You know," Patricia said matter-of-factly, "she didn't look six months gone to me."

"Patricia!" cried Selina.

"Well, she didn't."

"There will be no further discussion of this episode," Michael said, entering the kitchen. In the hush that fell, every eye was on him, and he held every gaze just long enough to impress the order on them all. "Is the tea made, Bridie?"

She hurried to the table with the pot and without another word poured tea for everyone.

27

*M*ichael said no more about the episode in the courtyard. He gave the fretting Eithne a reassuring nod and a pat on the shoulder, much as his son had done, and spooned sugar into the tea Bridie had poured.

But the Cornanagh melodrama, as Philip had called it, was not over for the day. As if taking a cue from the still tense atmosphere in the yard, all the horses turned unexpectedly nappy. Temper was almost impossible to control. Michael hung grimly on to his patience, and Selina admired him the more for it. But the gelding shed Artie three times in a row, the last almost as soon as he felt the boy's weight in the saddle. It was obvious to Michael and Mick that Artie, while game, had been too badly shaken by the last toss to be useful.

"He plain doesn't like men," Mick told his employer.

"He plain has to learn," was the Captain's response. "Give me a leg up!"

"Aw, now, Captain dear, I seen you limping."

"Mick!"

Shrugging, Mick complied. Temper sagged briefly against the unexpected weight on his back. It gave Michael time to find the irons, set himself in the saddle, bridge the reins and grab a judicious hunk of mane, before Temper took off. The gelding plunged up and straight forward, fighting to get his head. When he couldn't budge Michael's iron grip, he reared and took such a clout from Michael's fist between his ears that he staggered, his knees momentarily buckling. He backed and found spurs in his ribs, requiring him to go forward. He spurted ahead then, evading the pain, still trying to dislodge his rider. But there wasn't enough room in the cramped confines of the menage to run, and the bit in his mouth and the implacable hand on the rein forced him to circle to his right, and circle and circle until his nose was almost touching his own flank. Trembling with rage and impotence, Temper balked completely, refusing to move.

Michael eased the bit slightly in his mouth, allowing him to straighten. Temper stood there, shaking, the sweat pouring off his neck and shoulders. The spurs pricked. He shifted his feet. A second prompting and he reared again. And again a terrific clout on his poll rewarded this attempt. So he continued to stand, shaking and blowing.

"Just one step forward, boy. Just one."

The voice was calm but commanding. Temper shifted his feet in place, trying to get more slack on the reins and ease the metal that pressed hard against the bars of his mouth. But Michael held him too firmly, with too much understanding of what the horse might do next. Temper continued to stand, though the spurs became urgent on his sides.

"Just one step forward, boy, and we'll end the day's lesson." Michael's voice was inexorable. "The lunge whip, Mick. Try flicking first. He's got to go forward."

Temper felt the switch on his flank and quivered. The spurs reinforced the message, the weight on his back seemed to urge him to take that forward step. He shifted his hind legs away from the lash, but perversely kept his front feet firmly planted in the sand of the menage.

"Give him a good one, Mick. He's got the devil's own will. And I haven't got all day to spend on one tantrum."

The lash curled harshly about Temper's rump and he squealed, scattering on all four feet. The spurs dug into his tender flank, prodding the sore points. He danced in place, fighting to get his head, fighting to get away from the lash and the spur, fighting to win.

"Again, Mick."

Spur and lash struck again and, frantic, Temper leaped high and with a massive effort, twisted to the left. Without success. Defeated and exhausted, the gelding trotted forward, refusing to halt on Michael's signal and breaking into a disunited half trot, half canter of rebellion.

"Now that you've got him going forward, Captain dear, will he ever stop?" Mick said, loud enough to be heard over the erratic hoofbeats.

"He'll drop before I do," Michael Carradyne vowed. The next instant, Temper dug both front feet in and slithered to a stop by the barred exit where Selina Healey was standing. The momentum of that stop combined with Michael's sudden loss of balance in the saddle was sufficient to make him dismount. On his feet, to be sure, but not what he had intended.

"I am impressed," she said, her smile mocking him gently. "So gallant. Poor Temper," she said, patting the gelding who was heaving with his exertions.

Michael was blowing almost as badly as the gelding and his leg ached abominably from the strains put on it. "Spare some sympathy for Artie," he suggested, pointing to the corner where Artie slouched, arms lapping his ribs. "Are you all right, there, Artie?"

Mustering a grin, Artie pushed himself upright. "I'll be grand in a tic, Captain. That was a great ride, sir. A great ride." But as Artie approached and made to take the reins from the Captain, Temper reacted in a flash, lashing out at the boy, the hind hoof almost catching him in the belly. Selina, standing at Temper's head, hauled him painfully down by the bit and clouted him across the neck: instant retaliation for his bad manners.

As they headed back to the yard, Michael decided he felt depressed, as he had not been in some time. He longed to take Selina in his arms. Over the weekend he had missed her far more than he had any right to. So many times he had wanted to point out something that he knew would interest or amuse her. He needed to talk to her just for the pleasure of her company, the sparkle in her eyes as she listened, and her often droll responses.

"Look, Michael, it's been a brute of a day on top of an awful weekend for me," Selina said in a rush. "David's away North again. I'd love a few drinks this evening to unwind. Say, the Castle again, eightish?"

Michael tried not to let his relief show as he agreed.

Suddenly the day was not quite so bleak.

As Michael turned down the sea coast road to the Castle that evening, he was slightly bemused by his present circumstances. The incident with Owen that morning had unearthed a host of memories . . . old Paddy Kirwan charging up to Jack at Cornanagh, shotgun in one hand, weeping daughter in the other . . . Isabel at his side, keening, unable to believe her precious son—a boy destined for the priesthood—had been capable of "doing that." Isabel . . . He remembered, too, a conversation he'd had with his father, shortly after he had announced his intention of marrying Isabel Marshall. Tyler Carradyne had tried to impart some wisdom about Isabel, but Michael had failed to recognize the meat of the caution. It had been wartime, and every one of his comrades had been caught up in the hysteria, the never voiced, always understood possibility that one might not return. At nineteen, he was certain that he could endure every hardship and challenge, surmount any obstacle, if only he had Love to come home to.

Isabel had been so pretty, had danced like a feather in his arms, had languished with adoring looks and sighs at him in his Guards uniform; she had seemed the perfect wife for a young lieutenant. And, miracle of miracles, she had accepted his proposal. They had been married in the imposing nuptial ceremony Mairead Marshall had insisted upon, and he had had two weeks with Isabel before the Army required him to join his unit.

If his blushing bride had been ignorant, and turned white with fear and revulsion of him, that was no more than any husband should expect of a gently reared, convent-bred girl. It would all come right, he'd assured himself, when they could spend a little more time together. Michael had never had reason to doubt his charm or virility; many girls had already succumbed to it.

It had taken him seven years to understand what his father had tried to explain—that for all her prettiness and charm, Isabel was neither demonstrative nor giving. Old Tyler was a knowing one where women were concerned; he had recognized her innate frigidity, but Michael had been helpless—it was impossible to discuss sexual matters with a woman of Isabel's breeding.

And now Selina—just by being at Cornanagh, riding his horses, spending time with him, and sharing her *self* in those brief magnificent intimate moments—had showed Michael all that his original choice had lacked. Until she had come into his life, Michael had simply not been aware of the sterility of his existence: how he had permitted his love of horses to substitute for the simple human pleasures of an intimate relationship.

As he turned the Austin into the carpark, he saw the red Lancia topping the rise from the opposite direction. Their timing made him smile, and he was still smiling when she brought the car to a halt beside him.

"This time I'm paying," he told her firmly as they entered the lounge.

She gave him a quick gamine grin and settled herself in the booth as the barman came to take their orders. "I had a mar-

velous idea on Sunday, Michael," she began in the determinedly bright way that told him she was uneasy. "I was thinking that if only horses were like drugs, or illegal weapons, you
could make a fortune—you know, bootlegging Irish horses."

Surprise wrung laughter out of him, which echoed in the
nearly empty room and caused the barman to look their way.

She grinned. "It's about time we Irish *exported* bootlegged
goods."

"Illegal horses!" Michael was still chuckling when the barman returned with their ale. "I must remember to tell that one
to Philip; he'll embroider it suitably. Would that we could
invent a market in illegal horses! They're one of the few things
that are reasonably legitimate, even in Ireland."

They raised their glasses in a mutual toast, then sipped at
their drinks, loath to interrupt the sense of companionship
that settled between then.

"Selina—"

"Michael—"

They smiled at each other.

"All right, we must talk," Michael said, covering her hand
with his and curling his fingers about it. Her lovely eyes met
his, their expression ineffably sad. "Your presence at Cornanagh has become very important to me," he continued, "personally, quite apart from your kindness and understanding of
Catriona and your help in showing Charlie."

"This weekend I thought I would die of boredom." Her eyes
widened and flashed with exasperation. "I wanted so much to
be at the show with you, and the girls. The irritating thing was
that there was absolutely no reason for me to be at Erinwood.
It wasn't as if David needed a partner or a hostess." Her lips
tightened. "They talked business the entire time, and the wives
were left to themselves. Then this morning, when I met you
on the hill, I thought that perhaps I ought to stay away from
Cornanagh for a while. . . ."

His hand tightened on hers, and he shook his head. "Have I the right to ask how matters stand between you and your husband?"

"Badly, as you must certainly have noticed, when I am so willing to throw myself in your arms."

He smiled wryly. "The vaunted Carradyne charm must be slipping if it was pique with your husband that brought you into my arms."

She shot him a quick look, a faint smile curving her lips. "The Carradyne charm is very potent stuff, Michael. Anyone's bed might do if it were only pique. But I'm terribly afraid it's more than that for me with you, and I don't know what to do about it now."

She leaned back against the banquette, her body relaxed against his, her fingers limp, willing, in his. A surge of triumph and anxiety swept through him.

"I am old enough to be your father, Selina," he began.

"My feelings for you are not the least bit filial, Michael Carradyne. Though it's true that I've always been partial to older men." She gave a bitter snort. "Which is why I married David Healey. My father tried to warn me, but I knew what I wanted." She looked at Michael ruefully. "It's awful to be so cocksure at twenty-one. It oughtn't to be allowed."

He smiled gently at her, fondling her hand in both of his, feeling the firmness of the flesh beneath the soft skin. After a moment she continued.

"If it was just a tumble in the hay I wanted of you, it'd be very simple. I could lure you into my bed often enough to bore you. Or me." She gave him an impish grin. "But it isn't just you. It's Cornanagh and the horses and Catriona. And Patricia, Eithne, Philip, Mick—and I can't leave Charlie right now, and I don't want to board my mare anywhere else but Cornanagh because that's where life seems to be these days." Her gaze met his, wistful, yearning. Then she straightened herself up in a purposeful way, as if to dismiss her sweet fantasies. "Michael, what is the matter with Trina lately? She's so quiet all the time, so . . . sad. Or is it just that Pat talks nonstop and Trina has given up trying to get a word in edgewise?"

Michael shook his head thoughtfully. "I thought at first she might feel that she should have had the ride on the Prince, but Sybil feels it's because she hasn't quite absorbed Isabel's death."

Selina remembered all too clearly her conversation with the girl. "No, I think she's as relieved her mother's dead as you are. Only it's not the sort of thing she can admit, is it?"

"No, it isn't," Michael said slowly. "I don't think she could be upset over the way Conker's going, either, and I don't think it's Pat. I'll see what Sybil can find out."

"Or what I can. Because whatever it is is recent. And I do hate to see her so blued."

"Yes, maybe she'll talk to you where she won't to her old father."

Selina gave him a jab in the ribs. "The dear old dad who's been attracting swarms of eager unattached women at the local horse shows, all setting their caps for the handsome widower of Cornanagh!"

"It is not amusing," Michael said sourly, then paused as a new thought struck him. "I wonder . . ."

"You mean, Trina might be worried about you remarrying?" Selina asked insightfully. "If the intended likes horses, I don't think you'd have trouble with Trina. A point to remember when you consider the second Mrs. Carradyne." She grinned slyly at him.

"Selina, I have no intention of remarrying." He caught her eye in a stern gaze, and the levity disappeared from her expression. "Unless you're free."

"We Anglicans do not regard divorce with the same aversion as Catholics," she said, trying to control the surge of joy at his declaration, "but I don't even have grounds for a separation, much less a divorce. You can't really present boredom as grounds. After this weekend, I know we're not even compatible. If there'd been children . . ." She shook her head. "But I did marry David in full possession of my senses."

"And Anglican or Catholic, there's no divorce in Ireland."

"No state divorce, that is."

"I am much older than you, Selina," he said, "too old to be romantic—"

"You are too romantic! And marvelous in bed." She grinned unrepentently up at him, thinking how very handsome he was.

"Selina!" Michael protested, torn between embarrassment and amusement. But the more he thought about it, the stronger he felt about their relationship. Selina had confirmed that her attraction for him was more than physical, that there was already a deep and lasting bond between them. She wanted to continue their liaison despite everything. And he . . . well, he intended to cultivate that bond as deftly as he could, whatever the future might bring.

"All right, pet," he said at last. "We will be discreet and sensible. But if I find a handsome widow with a fine dowry . . ."

She laughed softly, aware that Michael was feeling the intensity of their situation as keenly as she, and so had to conceal his vulnerability with flippancy.

"Now, do tell me about Mrs. Comyn," she asked conversationally, to give them both time to recover.

Michael gestured to the barman for a second round, laughing as he recalled his sense of inadequacy during that interview. He proceeded to render an amusing account of the afternoon, suffering Selina's sly teasing good-naturedly.

When the story had been told and the second round polished off, Michael turned decisively to Selina.

"To prove I'm unromantic, my dear, I will now tell you that

I am knackered. I intend to go home and get a good night's sleep."

She grinned. "Sounds like a good idea. I'm knackered, too."

They parted, after a lingeringly gentle kiss, with considerable ease of mind—two people who had just decided to continue an affair.

Selina turned the Lancia up the narrow streets of Dalkey toward home, tremendously relieved to know that she would not have to give up either Michael or Cornanagh. Thank goodness David was so immersed in his business! And how fortunate that she had established the routine of visiting Cornanagh frequently and at length. But she must be very careful. David might one day look up from his earnest contemplation of strike, trouble, and crisis and notice her preoccupation. Insensitive he might be, but he was not stupid.

She was annoyed rather than alarmed when she climbed the shallow steps to her front door and found it slightly ajar. Surely she'd closed it behind her when she'd left earlier that evening. Had David returned unexpectedly?

She pushed open the door, listening hard. David, as was his custom, should have not left briefcase, hat, and raincoat on the hall table. But she heard sounds, and though she did not later remember the action, she grabbed her crop from the table and strode across to the lounge. That door was also ajar, and she could see signs of disturbance inside.

"Who's in there?" she shouted, moving forward, crop raised.

Muffled oaths greeted her call, and she ran toward the sound, through the lounge, into the dining room, and down the hall toward David's office. She was halfway down the hall when the office door flew open and several figures darted out toward the kitchen. Instantly she gave chase, flailing with the crop. She caught one lad across the back, but he turned on her, striking out with what he held in his hand. She cried out, for the heavy metal box caught the side of her face and shoulder.

The blow stunned her, but a surge of anger cleared her head quickly enough, and she charged after the burglars. They made it out the back door and were halfway across the garden to the high wall, two of them with sacks banging their sides, the third with the cash box clutched in one hand. All three were dressed scruffily with heavy boots on their feet. They had the leanness of youth, and none of them was very tall. They were too far ahead for her to give chase now. And even as she watched, they had flung themselves over the rear wall. She tried to memorize details that might help her identify them: the boots, the scruffy jerseys, their size, and the color of their hair.

Then, cradling her battered cheek, she returned to the house and dialed the emergency number on the kitchen extension. It took far too long, she thought savagely, for the call to be answered. Later she was pleased at how calmly she reported the burglary. Yes, she would remain in the house for the detectives. No, she couldn't tell what had been taken, apart from a cash box that was kept in her husband's desk. No, she didn't know how much it might have contained.

The moment the call was disconnected, she phoned Cornanagh. Though she knew that Michael could not yet have reached home, she desperately needed reassurance. Philip answered.

"Dad's not here, Selina. What's up?" She gave him a quick rundown. "My God! All right, now, don't panic. Just be calm. Get yourself a stiff drink. I'll leave a message for Dad and be right over."

She gave a little laugh as she stared at a phone gone suddenly dead. Then, abruptly, she began to tremble. With both hands she put the phone back in its cradle and dropped, rather than sat, onto the chair, shaking violently. Her face began to sting and throb. Annoyed, she took several deep breaths to steady the tremors and touched her cheek. Her fingers came away bloody, and she stared at the stain objectively. She reached for the box of tissues on the telephone table and extracted a wad, which she then pressed carefully against her cheek.

Her legs were rubbery, but, supporting herself with one hand on the wall, she made it to the mirror in the front hall. The whole side of her face was beginning to swell, and when she took away the tissues, she saw a long shallow gash from the corner of her eye to just above her mouth.

It was then she realized that she also had to tell David about the burglary. She started to close the front door and then laughed. The Gardái would arrive shortly.

It took two double scotches before the shaking in her midriff settled. She was unsuccessful in trying to reach David and left messages at the various numbers he had given her. She had just replaced the phone when the two Gardái arrived. Michael, Philip, and Eithne pulled up behind the police Renault before the Gardái had emerged from it.

Eithne took one look at Selina's face and disappeared to the back of the house. Michael poured her another drink while the detective, who introduced himself as Brian Clooney, tried to take control of the situation. Halfway through Selina's account, Eithne reappeared with a towel full of crushed ice, which she placed gently along Selina's injured cheek.

"They got in the side window, Sergeant," said the second gardá, having returned from a tour of the premises. "There's nothing disturbed upstairs. You must have surprised them before they'd done much, missus."

"You took a terrible risk, Mrs. Healey," the detective said. "What if they'd been armed?"

"They were in my house, Sergeant, stealing my possessions. Of course I went after them. And it gave me a great deal of satisfaction to know that one of them will have a painful weal on his back from my crop. I just wish I'd had a lunge whip."

Michael and Philip chuckled, but Eithne clucked her tongue in dismay. "I'd like to get you settled in bed, Selina," she said firmly, and gave the detective a pointed look.

He shook his head. "First we'll need to know what's missing from Mr. Healey's study."

"I'm not sure if I could tell you or not," Selina said, grimacing. "It is his private office." It annoyed her that Clooney reacted as if her attitude were only proper. "He's in the North on business, and I haven't been able to reach him yet."

"If you don't mind, I'd like to see the study, please." The detective gestured politely but firmly for her to lead the way.

Selina rose as gracefully as possible despite uncooperative legs, but she was relieved when Michael's hand appeared suddenly under her arm, supporting her.

The young burglars had had a time of it in David's study. Every drawer of the fine old Sheraton desk had been jimmied open, their contents strewn about the floor. David's neat shelves were empty and his priceless first editions scattered about. Some looked torn, and certainly the thieves' roughness had done the fragile bindings no good.

"The desk set and clock and the calculator are gone," she said. "And I don't see some of the ornaments. There should be a green jade statue of a Chinese mandarin, eight inches high, quite old and valuable. And easily broken. And an enameled Fabergé egg, an alabaster box with gold filigree edging, and a carved ivory Chinese street scene." She described three more pieces of small but valuable statuary that had been David's particular treasures. "Mr. Healey is going to be furious about this."

"I've rarely met someone pleased by a burglary, Mrs. Healey," Clooney said wearily. "But some of this"—he tapped the list—"is unusual enough so that we should hear if it goes through a known fence."

"Otherwise?"

The detective shrugged. "You might be lucky enough to find 'em in a ditch."

The phone rang, breaking the silence. Clooney raised his hand when Selina made a move toward the kitchen and signaled his partner to take the call.

"Yes, Mr. Healey," they heard him say, "this is Constable Varney. I regret to inform you that there has been a burglary in your residence. Mrs. Healey is giving the detective particulars. . . . No, sir. . . . Yes, sir. . . . We'll certainly do our best, sir, you may be sure of that. . . . Yes, sir, I'll put her on directly, sir."

Selina lifted her chin as she walked to the kitchen. She smiled at the gardá and caught his sympathetic glance as he handed her the receiver.

"Yes, David."

"Where the hell were you when the house was broken into, and what was taken? Did they get into the safe?"

"I went out after tea on an errand. I was home at nine-thirty and surprised them at their work. No, they did not get into the safe, but they got whatever you had in the cash box in your study."

His explosion at the other end of the line made her take the phone from her ear. "That is quite enough of that, David," she interrupted when it began to look as if he had no intention of winding down. "Just tell me how much was in the cash box, and then the detective will go away and I can go to the hospital and get my face treated."

He paused. "Your face treated?"

"I told you I interrupted them. I also nearly caught one of the little buggers, only he stunned me with the cash box. My face is cut."

"Well! Well, I'm sorry to hear that."

"Thank you. Are you coming down?"

"There is no possible chance of that, Selina. I'm in the middle of some extremely delicate negotiations. Have one of your friends stay with you until you get over your fears."

"Thank you, David. You are all consideration." She dropped the phone rather forcefully back into its cradle. Her face was throbbing, the ache in her shoulder was more insistent, and she had discovered that she actively hated her husband.

"Selina?" Michael was standing there, his face drawn with concern. She bit her lip to control the desire to seek comfort in his arms. Instead, she took a deep breath and walked past him into the study.

"My husband said he had only about a hundred pounds in the cash box."

The sergeant nodded. "You've been lucky, then, Mrs. Healey. Too many people are keeping a lot of cash in their homes, what with the bank strike and all. It just encourages young gurriers to chance their arm. It's no consolation, I know, but you're not the only house to be hit hereabouts." He folded up his pad and replaced it in his coat pocket. "If you think of anything else, please let me know. I'll circulate the list of valuables. Don't count on getting the cash box back, though. And," he added as an afterthought, "if you keep anything valuable upstairs, put it in a safe place?"

"D'you mean there might be a repeat of this break-in?" Michael demanded.

"I hope not," the sergeant replied, but his tone of voice was not reassuring.

Philip saw the man to the door as Selina sagged wearily onto the sofa.

"Look, Selina," Michael said, sitting down beside her, "would you like one of us to stay with you tonight?"

She dared not look at him. "I'm not worried, no matter what the sergeant said."

"Well, I am, and I'm staying," Eithne said firmly. "I've no intention of leaving you alone here. And I think that a doctor should see to that cut."

Gently Michael moved the ice pack away from Selina's cheek and peered at the cut. "It's not very deep," he said, "more a scratch than a cut. But you're already coming up in vivid bruises." His eyes flicked to hers and held them for a moment before the corners crinkled in amusement. "D'you have any honey in the house?"

"Michael!" Eithne was disgusted. "As if Selina were a horse!"

Selina laughed. "I do have honey, and if it works for horses, it'll be just fine for me. So long as I can get to bed. Between the fuss and all that scotch, my head's spinning."

"Look, Dad, I'll stay, too," Philip suggested. "It's convenient enough because I can just walk down for the bus tomorrow morning. That is, if Selina would like a man in the house tonight."

"I'd be very grateful, Philip, very."

"Then we'd better let Eithne settle you in bed. And I want you to stay at home tomorrow," Michael said.

"Nonsense. Cornanagh's exactly what I'll need, to clear my head of all this!" She moved to the fireplace and pushed aside the seascape to the left of the mantel, revealing a wall safe. "But I'll sleep a lot more securely if you could store some things at Cornanagh for me."

When she had worked the combination and opened the safe, she was rather surprised to find large packets of banknotes as well as David's securities folder and her jewel cases.

"Oh, dear, there's rather more than I thought."

"I'll get a sack from the kitchen," Philip offered, and disappeared.

"The safe at Cornanagh is a little better disguised," Michael remarked as he took possession of the sack. There was a distinct twinkle in his eyes. "Your valuables will be secure there."

She smiled back at him. "And that will be a tremendous relief."

"All right, now, off with you. Eithne, get her up to bed. Philip will fend for himself."

That night Selina slept sweetly and deeply, without a single nightmare.

When Michael got back to Cornanagh, he found all the yard lights on. Mick, Barry, and the two girls were rushing around, and Tory was barking up a storm.

"Tory got us up," Patricia told him, rushing to the Austin as Michael drove into the yard. Her eyes were sparkling with excitement, but Catriona looked terrified. "I ran for Mick and Barry, and then we all went to investigate."

"Can't find anything wrong, Captain," Mick said, coming up to the car. "All the horses is fine." He looked accusingly at Tory as if the dog might have been misleading them.

"Tory doesn't sound false alarms."

"No, he doesn't," Mick agreed, patting the collie apologetically. "He don't bark like that unless it's someone he doesn't know. Like Fitzroy!"

"That's a possibility, isn't it?" Michael said wearily.

"Give me the shotgun, Captain, and I'll just sleep in the hay barn tonight with Tory. Just in case."

"I'd appreciate it, Mick."

The old groom nodded, then stepped back so Michael could park the Austin. Wearily, Michael made his way upstairs to bed, too tired even to reflect upon all that had happened since morning. He fell asleep instantly but woke several times during the night, unaccountably disturbed.

28

"There isn't a horse in the field with a tail, Captain, sor," Barry announced the next morning, cap crushed between nervous hands. "There's tail hair all over the paddocks, sor. Great wads of it."

Everyone raced out of the kitchen and down to the fields. Only the foals had been spared. Swearing profusely under his breath, Michael ordered Mick and Artie to check the brood mares and the young horses for injury. Everyone pitched in to help, while Catriona, stunned by the vandalism, began to gather up the shorn horse tails. Most had been cut off in hanks.

To Michael's great relief, the horses had suffered no real damage, though some of the younger stock were skittish about being approached. There was something to be said against constantly handling young stock, Michael thought bitterly. He'd hear about this from Jack Garden, who tended to let his run wild in the fields.

"Fitzroy!" Owen stated furiously. "He's got five sons, enough to make it a quick night's work."

"Jesus, I'll get the fucker," Mick said.

Michael knew he should say something, but he was so consumed with anger at such wanton disfigurement that he couldn't trust himself to speak. Then he saw the forlorn, anguished expression on Catriona's face as she clutched her armful of horse tail hair.

"Trina . . ." he began, trying to find some way to comfort his daughter.

"Yeah, Cat! Boy, that's using your head," Patricia said, rushing up to her cousin and fingering the wads of horse hair. "Gee, at least they cut it long. It'll work in easy."

"What are you babbling about, Patricia?" Michael demanded.

"Making false tails, Unk. We just braid 'em on. They even left enough hair on the docks to sew on to."

"Braid it on? Sew it?"

"Well, you sure as hell couldn't show Frolic without a tail, could you? She'd look ridiculous with just that scut left." Patricia giggled. "But with hair this long, we just braid it on the dock and sew it tight to what's left. No big deal. There isn't a Standard Bred that isn't shown with a false tail. Wait, you'll see. You won't be able to tell she'd been shorn. That'll show Fitzroy!"

Michael's face began to brighten as he recognized the possibilities in Patricia's suggestion. To everyone's astonishment, he even began to chuckle. At first Catriona was confused, but as she saw the others begin to look less grim, she, too, felt better.

"Good old American know-how," Michael said. Pulling Patricia to his side, he gave her a fond embrace and ruffled her hair. "All right, then, Artie, you help Pat gather up tail hair and bring it back to the yard. C'mon, Trina. The day is saved!" He gathered Catriona to his other side and gave her a reassuring squeeze. "A nuisance, no more or less, and exactly what one could expect from Fitzroy. It'll take more than that to stop Cornanagh." He gave her a bright smile. "Good thing the show horses are all stabled. None of them were shorn, were they, Mick?"

His question startled Mick, who had been stamping along behind, a furious grimace on his weatherbeaten face. "No, not a one of them was touched. Iffen he had . . ." Mick's right hand closed into an aggressive fist. "Goddam culchie!"

Eventually, Michael marched everyone back into the kitchen,

insisting they return to their breakfasts. At table, Bridie was both sour and smug, darting fierce looks at everyone. Her attitude sent Catriona into a deeper depression.

"What's the matter with you?" Pat asked when Bridie had left.

"I don't see why the horses have to be hurt if God is punishing Owen."

Michael put down knife and fork and stared in total amazement at his daughter. "God in heaven, Catriona, where on earth did you get that idea?"

"Bridie said it was retribution," Catriona said, her chin quivering.

Michael reached across the table and gave Catriona's forearm a little shake to make her look at him. "Catriona, thinking that God punishes you, me, Owen, anyone, is just superstition. And Bridie is full of it."

"She's full of something else, too," Patricia muttered. Michael shot the girl a stern look.

"I will not have my daughter thinking so about such things. The horses' tails were cropped because Fitzroy is a vindictive man and chooses to believe that Owen is responsible for Cathleen's pregnancy. He did it out of spite. Surely you can't believe he's an instrument of God, can you?" He tried to coax a smile from her and gave her arm another squeeze when she avoided his glance. "Catriona Mary Virginia, God is not spiteful. Nor did He send this act of vandalism on Cornanagh as discipline for what we have or have not done. To think so is to pull God down to Fitzroy's level. Don't you agree?"

Catriona glanced anxiously up at him, her blue eyes revealing her inner anguish.

"Kitten, ignore Bridie's superstitious prating and . . ." He hesitated. "And your mother's obsession with prayer and divine retribution. It is not God who is responsible for what happens to us, but ourselves, since He gave us the free will to make our own choices. If you make a bad choice, things go wrong. But *you're* responsible for that choice, not God. Let's be big enough to admit that we're responsible for the bad as well as the good things that happen to us." He could see the muscles in her jaw relaxing. "And there is little question in my mind that Fitzroy and his sons are responsible for cutting the tails. But you, Catriona Mary Virginia Carradyne, are not guilty in any way, shape, or form for *their* sins. Right?"

Catriona gave him a wan smile and a tremulous sigh before she pushed back her chair and took her plate to the sink. Michael regarded her soberly, hoping she'd take his brief sermon to heart. He hated to see the child accepting the grim doctrine her mother had embraced. He had never felt comfortable with the guilt and repentance aspects of Church dogma. "God's will" had always struck him as an easy way out of taking responsibility for one's own actions. "God's will" had been Isabel's excuse for avoiding a candid look at the results of her choices, good or bad. And one way or another he would make certain Catriona did not grow up to do the same.

Just as he was returning to the yard, the phone rang. It was Philip calling from Crawford's to say that there hadn't been so much as a mouse squeak all night. Michael thanked him for a job well done and rang off without mentioning the shorn tails; there'd be time for that later.

When he reached the garage Patricia and Catriona were already at work, sorting hanks to make a tail for Frolic. Catriona seemed absorbed in the task.

"It's no fun being burgled, Cat," Patricia was saying. "It's scary at first, and then you get mad that someone had the unmitigated gall to rob *you* of your things. Getting mad's the first step to a cure."

"Good God, Pat, was your house robbed?" Michael asked.

"Yeah," she said sourly, "the house got stripped two years ago while we were on vacation." She shrugged. "But Dad's insurance covered everything. Everything except my Beatles' collection. They didn't consider *that* valuable!" Pat was plainly disgusted by such prejudice. "Here's a better piece, Cat. Use this."

"Can we get something of a tail on her today, Pat?" Catriona wanted to know. "The flies are wicked mean, and she's nothing to switch with."

"We'll give it a good ol' Yankee try," Pat assured her, and winked at her uncle. "Now, what we need is some of that thread you sew plaits with, and a big needle, and—"

"In the tack room," Catriona said, and ran off.

When Michael got into the yard, he realized that Mick and Artie were taking the vandalism even more to heart. They were mucking out as if every fork of manure were a Fitzroy. He considered warning Mick about retaliation. Perhaps he should present the matter to Sergeant Quinn at the Newtownmount-kennedy Gardái Station; he wanted no more incidents. What he really needed to do, he thought darkly, was find out who was to blame for Cathleen's condition.

"It's bloody good, Cat," Patricia said, "and that's the Tulip to a T!" The girls had worked in special harmony all morning and after the noon meal Catriona had pulled out the sketch to show her cousin. "I think you've even got Unk right," Pat continued, "though there is something a bit funny with his shoulder here."

"It's just the angle he's standing at," Catriona replied defensively.

"Doesn't matter. I don't think anyone's going to notice *him*. It's the Tulip you've got right. Gee, he was a great horse! Your dad must miss him horribly."

"He does," Catriona said softly. "Sybil's collecting it today to get it framed for me for Dad's birthday."

"When's that?"

"Just before the horse show, July twenty-sixth."

"Patricia . . ." Eithne's clear call reached them in their bedroom. "Telephone for you. From the States, I think."

"Wow!" Patricia flew out of the room and clattered down the stairs. "Dad?" Catriona heard her exultant cry as she took the receiver. Then there was a long silence, the sort that propelled Catriona out of her room to lean over the banister.

She couldn't see Pat from that angle, but she could see the concern on her aunt's face and made her way quickly down the stairs. When she reached her cousin, Patricia's eyes were dark with sadness and conflict.

"Mother," she began, and now that Catriona was close, she could hear the strident tones issuing from the instrument but could only distinguish an occasional word. "Mother, I don't want to."

There was a stunned pause at the other end. Then: "What?" That came through loud and clear.

"I want to stay with my father."

"So he got to you, did he, with his trips to your horsey cousins and backwater Ireland. Well, I'll contest it. He's not going to get my daughter. I'll see to that. And you'll see, young woman. You won't get around—"

"Mother, I'm fourteen. I've the right to choose!"

"I've rights, too, goddamn it. You'll see. You'll see!" Abruptly the connection was broken.

Patricia looked at the receiver blankly for a moment, gave a little shrug, and replaced it.

"Drunk, and she expected me to jump at the chance to live with *her,*" Patricia said, glancing from Eithne to Catriona. "Well, I told her."

"Patricia! She's your mother!" Eithne said.

"And I'm supposed to want to live with my lush of a mother? And nurse her hangovers and clear up her vomit?"

"Patricia!" Eithne was aghast.

"Thank you, no. I've had enough of it. Dad gave her every chance to dry out, but all she has to do is smell liquor and she's high. She doesn't need a daughter: she needs a nurse. She's made Daddy's life miserable, and she's embarrassed me and my brothers once too often. I'm glad Daddy's divorcing her. I'm glad!"

With that, Pat whirled and rushed up the stairs, sobs tearing from her throat. Eithne stared helplessly, but Catriona touched her arm gently.

"I'll go up, Auntie Eithne. I know how she's feeling."

Catriona climbed the stairs to her room and found that Pat had flung herself on the lower bunk, her face buried in the pillows, her clenched fists flailing.

Carefully Catriona put away the Tulip's portrait and then sat down on the floor beside her cousin. She remembered, all too vividly, how she had felt and said nothing until Patricia's sobs began to ease. Then Pat pushed her head around on the pillow, reddened, watery eyes accusing.

"Your mother's dead. Everyone feels sorry for you when your mother's dead. But when she's a disgusting, sniveling alcoholic, no one wants to know," she said in a low, bitter voice.

Catriona said nothing, merely pulled a wad of tissues from the box and passed them to Patricia, who almost wrenched them out of her hand.

"She didn't believe Daddy when he said that he'd filed for a divorce. She called because her lawyer just told her that he has a better chance for custody of us than she did with her record of drinking. She was so sure that I'd want to stay with her. . . ." Pat's voice caught on another sob. "I hate her, Cat, I just hate her."

"You can't hate your own mother. . . ."

"Oh, yes, I can," Pat replied fervently, glaring balefully at Catriona. "I can, and I do. You've no idea what it's like living

357

with a drunk; afraid that if your friends come home with you she'll be raving, stinking stoned out of her tiny mind. Daddy tried and tried and tried. He was so good. But Shirley"—Patricia accented her mother's name with a sneer—"didn't care so long as she could get tanked up. It was bad enough when she set out to seduce someone else's husband, right in front of everybody, but she couldn't see how disgusting she was, all blurry in the face and the voice. Revolting. Oh, yes, I hate her. She handed me the right on a bar tray." Pat broke into sobs again and buried her head in the pillow.

Catriona sat there, unable to find any words of comfort. You couldn't hate your parents: you had to love and respect and obey them. The Church said so. Yet she really could see how Pat had come to hate her mother. It was all very confusing. She felt so sorry for her cousin; she'd never thought anything could upset Pat so badly. She was so strong and so sure of everything. Catriona drew her knees up and hugged her legs, rocking a bit, then jumped when there was a gentle rapping at the door.

"Pat?" Eithne called.

Pat lifted her head slightly from the pillow. "Yeah?"

"Perhaps if you phoned your father . . . ?"

Patricia's face lit up as she scrambled off the bed and opened the door. "Gee, could I, Auntie Eithne? I know his office number, but I hate to run up Uncle Mihall's phone bill." Hastily she wiped her wet cheeks with the backs of her hands.

Eithne smiled at her niece. "I don't think he'd object. And it occurred to me that perhaps your father should know that your mother phoned you. Mind now, don't talk for hours," she called as Pat raced down the stairs.

After the evening meal, Michael phoned Selina to see if she would prefer to have Philip spend the night there again.

"I know whom I would prefer to spend the night here," she

said, her voice rippling with laughter, "but I've stout new locks, and some interim burglarproof catches on all the ground-floor windows. Besides, a young handsome man like Philip spending two nights in the house is going to cause comment. Now, a distinguished older gentleman . . ."

"I thought we agreed to be discreet," Michael said, chuckling.

"Oh, but we would be. That poor Mrs. Healey . . . that's what all the neighbors think, as well as half the people who've been here today. And *everyone* was here, it seems. The glazier to fix the front window. A man from David's insurance brokers. A Securicor specialist for the locks. I'm supposed to've been frightened out of my wits by the occurrence. Actually, I'm seething that those louts had their hands on my things. Not to mention David's."

"Is your face all right? Maybe we ought to have taken you to hospital last night."

"No, no, Eithne insisted that I go see the doctor and he said the ice had been the very best therapy. Who rode my bonnie Charlie today?" she asked, changing the subject deliberately.

They went on to discuss the various horses in training, and when she rang off, Michael realized that he had not mentioned the vandalism. Just as well, he decided. Selina needed a good night's rest with nothing to worry her.

The next morning Selina arrived early and was greeted by Catriona and Patricia, who were shocked when they saw the livid bruising of her cheek.

"You're making far too much of a silly scratch," Selina said, comforting a distressed Catriona.

"But it's on your face," cried Catriona. "Daddy never said you'd been wounded."

"Even the bruising will be gone by the weekend," Selina said, "thanks to your aunt's ice pack." Then she caught sight of the open garage door and the hanks of horse hair festooning the place. "What on earth . . . ?"

"It was that bastard Fitzroy," Patricia began.

"Pa-*trisha*-a!" Michael held up a finger in warning.

"Do you mean to tell me," Selina said, running her hands down a huge swatch of black horse tail hairs, "that he cut off all the tails?"

"The field horses," Michael said, "but not the stabled ones, so Charlie and your mare are intact."

"But Frolic was in the field, and Tulip's Son . . ."

"They're okay, Selina," Pat assured her. "I know how to make false tails, so Cat and me made some yesterday. Mick said Frolic's stayed on all night long, too. We're going to work on the others today. The flies are fierce, and all the field horses need tails to switch with."

"I'll lend a hand later this afternoon," Selina offered.

She and Michael were schooling Charlie when Eithne approached them anxiously, a letter in her outstretched hand.

"Michael, it's from Jack!"

"All right, Selina, take a break," Michael called, and took the letter from his sister-in-law.

Tearing open the flimsy air-mail envelope, he extracted the equally thin sheets of tightly written script. In the first sentence he realized that Jack had not received word of his mother's death until a month after the occurrence. Neither had he received Michael's subsequent letter, for he begged details of her sudden demise, demanding that the hospital be sued for incompetence. For the remainder of the letter he alternated between describing his proposed schedule of prayers to speed her soul into the keeping of the Heavenly Father and offering anecdotes that testified to her piety and goodness. Seven pages of such effusions were more than Michael could bear. He skipped to the last paragraph, which contained the only deviation from piety and remorse: advice to his father to have a care for the welfare of his now motherless sister.

"Jack is clearly upset," Michael told Eithne, who was still waiting anxiously beside him, "but there's nothing I can do for him that his religion can't do better. He hasn't received my letter, and our telegrams didn't reach him until June."

"Oh, Michael!"

He heard the quaver in Eithne's voice and looked down at her.

"Now, Eithne, you're too kind-hearted. Jack's a big boy. His decision to join the priesthood made his mother proud and happy."

"Not bad news, Michael?" Selina asked as she joined him, noticing that Eithne was weeping as she read the letter.

He shook his head. "My son Jack. The mail from Latin America is rather slow."

Selina's expression also mirrored her compassion, and Michael was inexplicably annoyed with Jack for producing this effect in a woman he had never met. The letter's arrival depressed him, not as it did Eithne, but because it reminded him, through Jack's words and the personality behind them, of Isabel.

"Forgive me, Selina, but I think we'll call it quits now." He smiled at her, then turned back to his sister-in-law. "C'mon, Eithne pet, you need a cuppa. And Bridie will doubtless be wanting to hear Jack's letter, too." He put a comforting arm about Eithne's shoulders and led her back to the house.

When he returned from the kitchen, he heard Selina's laugh issuing from the garage and found her busy helping Catriona and Patricia stitch tail hanks to lengths of old tail bandages.

"Y'see, Unk, some of the young stock don't have enough to sew onto," Patricia explained. "We did a tail count to see who's okay."

"Ingenious!" Selina said, grinning broadly as she held up a nearly completed tail swatch.

"We've got five more done, Daddy," Catriona said, "and they're so relieved to be able to switch off flies!"

"Well, you must be sure not to tie the bandages too tightly or circulation will be cut off," Michael cautioned them.

"Gotcha, Unk," Patricia replied, holding aloft her finished work. "Paleface counts coup!"

Selina was making her adieux when they all heard the throaty and familiar growl of Bob Doherty's Mercedes coming up the drive. He pulled into the courtyard, smiled briefly in greeting, and beckoned to Michael.

"How's Sean coming along?" Michael asked, bending down to the car window.

"Oh, he's well enough," Bob replied, his gaze shifting beyond Michael to the girls. "That the niece who's been showing the Prince for us?"

"Yes, and she qualified him for the RDS at Mount Armstrong. I phoned Aisling and told her."

"Hmmm." Bob frowned a bit. "Then what happened at the Galloping Green show? A friend of mine said the pony went very badly. Fifteen faults, and he said it was rider error."

"It certainly was," Michael agreed amiably. "The ground was rock hard, and I'd told Patricia to make it an easy round. She kept the pony on such a tight rein he lost his rhythm and stride. But she realized what she was doing and flew the last six fences."

"But the Prince is still qualified for the RDS?"

"Yes indeed."

"Well. I guess that's all right, then."

"If you've another rider you'd prefer on the Prince, you've only to say so," Michael remarked.

"Oh, no, no. Wouldn't think of it."

Michael merely smiled. "Good to see you, Bob. My regards to Aisling and Sean." He tapped the roof of the Mercedes and stepped back, allowing Bob to reverse and make his way out of the courtyard.

As soon as the Mercedes was out of sight, Catriona and Patricia came running up to him.

"What's the matter, Unk? Have I lost my ride?" Patricia demanded.

Catriona looked so anxious that Michael quickly told them exactly what Bob Doherty had said. He wondered about Catriona's almost comical relief. She sagged against him, hooking her fingers in his belt as she used to do. He put a reassuring arm about her.

"How'd he hear all that so soon?" Patricia asked.

"Ireland's a small country. It's hard to keep secrets."

"Well, let's hope he doesn't hear about the tails! C'mon, Cat, we gotta get back to work." She hauled her cousin away from Michael and back to the garage.

"Michael?" Selina asked, standing in the open door of the Lancia.

"No trouble," he said. "I merely said that if he had another rider in mind . . ."

"And spiked his guns neatly."

Michael grinned, wanting very much to give her a hug, too.

"Michael, after what happened I don't like the idea of leaving the house unoccupied in the evening while David's away," Selina admitted. "Kathleen heard that people three houses away were done last night. But if you felt like coffee and a liqueur, it wouldn't surprise anyone if Captain Carradyne came to reassure Mrs. Healey." She looked at him with eyes that sparkled with mischief. When he nodded, she murmured, "Eightish?" and then, quickly disengaging her hand, slid into the driver's seat.

🌿 *29* 🌿

*I*t took the rest of the afternoon for Catriona to relax from the terror at seeing Bob Doherty pull into Cornanagh's driveway; she'd been sure he'd come to expose her as a cheat and a deceiver in front of her father. Then, just as she'd recovered from her anxiety, she was rocked by another, totally unexpected piece of news.

The girls were in the loo washing up before tea when the phone rang. Patricia went all tense, her lathered hands dripping into the hand basin, her head cocked, listening. Although she had been her usual self after she'd had a chat with her father, Catriona noticed that she was wary whenever the phone rang.

"Yes, Paddy, I'll just go fetch him," they could hear Eithne saying. "He's doing evening stables. There's nothing wrong, is there?" A pause. "Well, that's good to hear. I'll just get Michael."

Catriona made to leave the loo in order to run the message for her aunt, but Patricia restrained her.

"Let's stay here. That way we'll know what's going on," she whispered. Catriona stared at her. "Oh, don't worry. If we're washing our hands, it isn't the same as eavesdropping on purpose!"

Catriona was not all that reassured. She didn't need to get into any more trouble. Then the girls heard the crisp tread of Michael's boots on the parquet floor.

"Paddy! How are you? . . . Yes, all well here, and yes, it's been a good showing season. Old Tulip's foals are doing us proud, and so is Pat. She's shown tremendous improvement in her riding." Patricia grinned at her uncle's praise. "Yes, yes, though I've not mentioned it to him. . . . You have? Oh, that is splendid, Paddy, really splendid. Junior account executive— whatever that means. When can he leave? . . . Well, as to that, he'd have to hand in his notice and work out his time. But I'm sure he'll jump at the chance. . . . Don't be daft, man. Of course I'd miss him, but I won't stand in his way. I really appreciate this, Paddy. . . . Well, it's five here now. He'll be home in the next hour. Shall I have him ring you then? . . . Yes, I've your office number. . . . Grand. Thanks again, and my regards to Marita."

Patricia opened the loo door a crack and saw her uncle's back, head slightly bent, his left hand rubbing the back of his neck. Then he wheeled abruptly and walked out of the house and back to the yard.

"Does he mean Owen?" Catriona asked in a careful whisper.

"No," Patricia said decisively. "Philip."

"But it's Owen who needs to leave Cornanagh!"

"Well, Uncle Paddy was more impressed with Philip. At least that's what Daddy said when he got home."

"Philip?" Catriona sank to the toilet seat.

"You heard the same thing I did. Frankly, I think Philip would do just great in advertising. He could charm the spots off a tiger. And they'll love his accent."

"Pip doesn't have an accent."

"Of course he does. Nothing broad, just a lovely lilting way of putting words together, and, believe me, it won't hurt him on Madison Avenue."

The two girls left the loo and went to lay the table for tea. Catriona decided that advice not to eavesdrop made sense after all. It was awful to know something you couldn't talk about. Especially when it meant yet another change at Cornanagh. When would it all stop?

When Philip arrived home, Catriona and Patricia contrived to be in full view when Michael Carradyne casually told his son that he was to phone his uncle Patrick at his office.

"I don't believe it, Dad," Philip said when he had spoken to his uncle and discussed the job offer. "It's just what I wanted, but I really don't believe it!" Then incredulity warred with concern. "But what'll you do about showing?"

"Pip, you're going," Michael said, clasping his son's shoulders firmly in both hands. "It's too good a chance for you to pass up. Not the way things are going here in Ireland."

Philip caught sight of his sister's sorrowful expression and swooped her up in his arms, hugging her affectionately. "Now, don't pull a long face on me, Trina. America's not the end of the world, and I'll get home for Christmas, sure I will! With the pots of money I'll make as an advertising executive."

Catriona buried her head in his shoulder, not wanting to dampen his excitement but overwhelmed by the prospect of Cornanagh without her adored brother. Philip gave her a squeeze and released her to accept the drink his father handed him. He sat down, cuddling his sister at his side.

Owen received the news with equanimity when he arrived; to Catriona he seemed almost indifferent. He sat down on the couch beyond her, and when Michael was busy settling Eithne with her sherry, he leaned across her to speak in low tones to Philip.

"It's arranged. Artie's older brother is going to nose around at the Barking Pig to see what he can learn, and Mick's going down to McDyer's."

Having delivered this cryptic message, he assumed his usual sprawl on his end of the couch until Bridie announced that tea was ready.

It was a lively meal because Philip made it so, and Catriona could not remain somber when her brother was such a gas character. Patricia was rolling on her chair, and even Eithne enjoyed herself.

Afterward, while Catriona and Patricia were carrying out the dishes, the men discussed security arrangements. Everyone had "important" meetings—"Yeah, at the pub," Patricia muttered—that would take them from Cornanagh until eleven. Even Mick would be out. So it was decided to leave Tory loose in the yard and alert Barry should his assistance be needed.

"Not that there'll be any reason to rouse him," Michael assured Eithne.

"Can we have the shotgun, Unk?" Patricia asked, her eyes dancing.

"You may not!" Michael said, and left.

"I was only joking," Patricia murmured to his retreating back.

Later, Captain Michael Carradyne called on Mrs. Selina Healey to see how she was faring after the unfortunate burglary.

"You'll miss him," Selina stated after he had recounted the evening's events.

"Yes," Michael said with a sigh, "I will. Whatever hope I might have had that he'd refuse this opportunity disappeared when I saw his face. He was thrilled. Mind you"—Michael accepted more coffee with a smile—"I'll give the boy his due: he worried about who would show for me."

"And did you not remind him you had a candidate?" Selina pretended to be coy.

"Selina . . ." Michael's tone was both chiding and wistful. "You do enough for Cornanagh. And I worry about what Healey will say when he comes back and finds out just how much time you spend at Cornanagh . . . riding for me."

"The more horses I show for you—and you must admit that that is a perfectly respectable pastime for David Healey's wife if he wishes to get on with Charlie Haughey—the more credence we give the situation."

"I will not put your reputation at risk."

"You're a pet, Michael"—she smiled warmly at him—"but my reputation is scarcely at risk if I'm busy winning show classes for you on your very well bred beasts. Besides that, didn't you notice Catriona this morning?"

"What should I have noticed about her?"

"Well, I must admit that I only realized it this morning myself—she's put on inches! She's nearly as tall as I am, and certainly the same height as Pat!"

Michael shrugged. "What has that to do . . . Ah, I see. You're conniving with Mick."

"Not that I know of," Selina said, puzzled.

"Mick has spent all winter trying to convince me that Trina's soon going to have enough leg to ride horses."

"And she has. She already rides Charlie a treat."

"She's thirteen!"

"And tall. Under a hard hat and in a showing class—oh, certainly the provincial shows to start with—no one will know, and there's no rule against it. Next year, maybe the sidesaddle class or ladies' hack."

Michael allowed himself to be persuaded to accept the idea. Trina was, he admitted privately, a superb young rider, with a great deal of sympathy and feel for her mount. Lacking a bit still in strength, but skilled beyond the standard of most adults. And she loved horses and Cornanagh as much as he did. But a girl?

"Don't rule out the possibility that Catriona would make an admirable heir to Cornanagh, my dear," Selina said gently, watching him. "There are changes in the wind, Michael, changes in the wind."

Michael put his coffee cup down with great care. "Were you reading my mind?"

"No." She lifted one hand to stroke his mustache and trace the shape of his mouth. "Merely an educated guess. Sometimes you are remarkably transparent when you think. Probably due to lack of practice."

"I'm putting that niece of mine in quarantine. Her manners are contagious." He pulled her into his arms, knowing the surest way to stop a conversation in which he found himself at a severe disadvantage.

Reluctantly he left Selina's at ten o'clock, late enough for a social call but not too late to have a quick pint at the Willow Grove. Relaxed and feeling very well within himself, he failed to mark the presence of a familiar Mini. It wasn't until he stepped into the lower lounge of the pub and had been hailed by Jack Garden and Robert Kelly that he noticed Fiona Bernon in her usual corner with the Mulvaneys. Too late, he thought. Nodding pleasantly in her direction, he proceeded to the bar to be greeted effusively by his friends.

"Christ, Carradyne, where have you been lately?" said Jack Garden. "Out politicking every farmer in the east?" He nudged Robert Kelly in the ribs, adding, "If that damn fool bill passes, we can blame this man entirely."

"When I'm only trying to put you in the way of making a few bob?" Michael pretended hurt surprise. In his estimation, Jack Garden was exactly the sort of casual horse-breeder the Board was geared to help.

"It won't work, Carradyne," Jack Garden said emphatically.

"Why not?"

Jack regarded him in disgust. "Registering mares and foals, and keeping track of half and three-quarter-bred stallions? Why?"

"The European and American markets will pay good money for animals whose pedigree they know. And the foals of stallions who repeatedly produce good half-bred jumpers, like Chou Chin Chow and King of Diamonds. The passport scheme . . ."

Jack guffawed. "No deal is going to surrender that passport

to the new owner. The breeder's name and address'll be on it. So your man will go straight to the breeder next time and—" he flung up his hands—"bang goes the dealer's commission."

"Not all horses are bought through dealers. And foreign buyers want to know the sire and dam of animals we want them to pay top money for. It also proves a horse has been vetted, inoculated . . ."

"That's another expense," Jack broke in, jabbing his forefinger in Michael's chest. "I tell you it's the vets and dealers who're going to get rich from this fancy scheme, not me. Maybe you," and Jack's lopsided grin was tinged with malice, "because you've obviously figured out how this whole shagging scheme is going to profit Cornanagh."

"And being a generous sort," Michael replied with a grin, "I'm only trying to show you the way."

Robert Kelly guffawed, and received a black scowl from Garden. "Michael," Fiona Bernon said, smiling as she approached him, "we haven't seen much of you lately." She settled herself on the stool beside him.

"The show-jumping season keeps me pretty busy, Fiona," Michael replied pleasantly. He turned back to Jack, who was watching them closely, a sly gleam in his eye.

"No trouble down your way?" Jack asked to break a rather uncomfortable silence.

"Trouble? No, why?" Michael asked.

"Then you didn't hear what happened to Fitzroy?" asked Fiona.

"No, what?"

"Vandals!" Fiona said, her eyes alive with the gossip she had to tell. "They not only emptied all the petrol tanks, but they took the diesel out of the tractor, and the air out of every tire on the place, including the pushbike."

Michael cleared his throat and tried to speak casually. "Sounds more like a prank to me. No real harm was done."

"You wouldn't say that if you'd heard Fitzroy," Jack said. "He was turning the air blue in the Barking Pig. He's not on the phone and had to walk all the way in."

Michael grinned at that despite himself. "Well, we've had no trouble. But I'll keep my eyes open."

"I heard . . ." Fiona leaned against him, making him conscious of the softness of her full breasts. He shifted slightly, hoping she'd withdraw, but she merely draped an arm across his shoulder and leaned in even closer. "I heard that his daughter has been terribly indiscreet, and he wants to find the culprit."

"That's too bad," Michael murmured, and shifted away again.

"Are you showing in Kilmacanogue tomorrow?" Robert Kelly asked, coming to his rescue.

"Yes, I am."

"You're in the mare and foal and yearling classes?" Jack asked.

"Old Tulip's last crop."

"Christ, I might as well stay away!"

"Not a bit of it, Jack. I don't have anything to compete with that Irish draught mare of yours, and you know it."

"That's only the one class," Jack said disgustedly, waggling his forefinger for a fresh round.

"Not for me, thanks, Jack," Michael said, and downed the last of his pint. "The girls are on their own tonight, and if there've been vandals about, I think I'll just do a check before I turn in. And thanks for the warning!"

He included Fiona in his farewell smile and, with a salute to all, made good his escape. Once in the parking lot, he let out a long sigh of relief.

Friday was a good day for horses . . . and other concerns. For Mick and Artie's older brother, Peter, it had been a very good night to gather information about Cathleen Fitzroy. Her pregnancy was now common knowledge in Newcastle, and her sorry state was much discussed. Peter confirmed that she had been at the Valentine disco on the evening in question, and that Owen had not. On that night—and indeed on other nights when she consumed rather more than she ought—she had been quite free with her favors.

Michael gave him a pat on the shoulder. "It'd be helpful to narrow down the prospects, though, Peter. Does she 'favor' anyone in particular?"

"Well, there was this fella Nolan, Jere Nolan. He seemed upset about the talk. He didn't say much, but he got pretty pissed off and left in a huff."

"Jere Nolan?" Mick grinned cynically. "He's only a step above a tinker. Works as a casual. And he's worked at Fitzroy's. But Fitzroy would have sent him packing if he got near Cathleen."

Michael thanked Peter for a job well done and watched as the boy swung onto his pushbike and pedaled out of the yard.

"Good lad, that," Mick said, nodding approvingly. "And it could bloody well be Jere Nolan. Up at Kilpedder, everyone knew about Fitzroy's 'trouble.'" He chuckled slyly. "Sure it's all over the county and chalked up to vandals. But there isn't much sympathy for the man. He's a sorry bastard, mean to his wife and kids, never stands his round at the pub if he can avoid it. There's a fair rumor that he's sold on tubercular cattle the odd time or two. No, I wouldn't call him popular."

"It was the talk in the Willow Grove, too," Michael remarked. "Ah, Selina's come. We'll give Charlie, Conker, the Prince, and Emmett a light hack, then I'll want to school Temper, Wicket, and Racketeer. Has Barry gone off to check the fences?"

"He has that," Mick said as he started to the tack room.

The day's work went well. Even Temper was compliant, beginning to relax his jaw against the bit, with a good rhythm to his trot. Michael made much of him since there had been so few opportunities lately to appreciate the gelding.

Selina stayed as long as she could, helping the girls adjust the false tails on the field horses. But she left before tea, again explaining that Kathleen was leaving on the dot of five and she didn't like to leave the house unoccupied.

Cornanagh was up and breakfasted by seven, and by nine-thirty the horses were ready for the Kilmacanogue show, mares plaited and groomed and foals shining. Owen had helped, although he was staying behind with Barry, "just in case." Michael was making a note in his ledger of the entry fees when the phone rang. He picked it up in his office.

"Oh, Eithne," Selina said, her tone coolly polite. She seemed to have something in her mouth that muffled her words. "Would you please tell the Captain that I shan't ride this morning? You might suggest that he have Catriona ride in my place. She's well able. I'll call at the beginning of the week."

"Selina, is anything wrong?" Michael broke in.

"Of course," she replied. "And you'd do well to see the antiques at Beach House tomorrow at three. Would be worth your while. Tata." The phone went dead.

Michael cradled the receiver, reviewing Selina's tone and cryptic phrases. If he took the meaning of her words, something was very wrong and she could probably make it to Greystones strand tomorrow at three.

It took an effort to leave the office, and considerable will power not to go charging up to Dalkey and find out for himself what had really happened. He knew that was the worst thing he could do if Healey was there. Quite likely he was making too much of the incident, he told himself.

He managed to check that all was properly loaded in the Austin and the horse lorry, then ordered their cavalcade to proceed.

"But Selina's not here," Catriona said anxiously. "Is she meeting us at Duffcarrig? She said we could ride with her."

"Yeah, that Lancia's a real treat," Patricia added.

Michael glanced at the two girls, standing side by side, and realized that they were almost of a height, looking smart in their white shirts and Pony Club ties, clean jods, and polished boots. The Carradyne resemblance made them look like sisters.

"She just phoned," he replied. "Something's come up, and she can't join us today."

"Oh, hell!" Patricia dug a resentful toe into the cobbles, scuffing the leather.

"Stop that," Michael said more forcefully than he intended, and Patricia backed off, surprised. "Sorry, didn't mean to roar at you." He turned to his daughter. "Catriona, is your hacking jacket in the Austin?" She nodded, still uncertain, and he smiled at her. "Well, Selina says you're to ride Charlie."

"Wow!" Patricia hugged her cousin and danced about. "Boy, are you lucky!"

"Into the car with you both now," Michael said. "We're running late."

For all that Kilmacanogue was a local show, it was very well attended. They passed several groups of ponies hacking on the quiet back roads, and when they arrived there was a trundling line of horseboxes maneuvering the steep entrance. Michael led the Cornanagh contingent to the far side of the parking field. Mares and foals would be judged first, so Mick, Artie, Billy, and Philip gave the entrants final brushes and one more coat of hoof oil. Michael sent Patricia to the entries caravan to get numbers and register herself and Catriona. Michael decided that Catriona would lead the Tulip's Son with him; Philip and Patricia would team up for Lady Madeline, which left Mick, Artie, and Billy available to bring up the yearlings.

There was a stallion parade early in the morning that Michael particularly wanted to watch. He was still looking at stallions to cross with his mares—not that he expected to find one to equal the Tulip, but the mares would need to be serviced come March and April. Joe Delahunt's American stallion Lone Star was a fine-looking animal and might just do for Frolic, but he preferred to see all available animals.

Patricia's round on the Prince was better than last time—right up until the final wall. Then she let him speed up, and the Prince took off too close to the structure, hitting the top row of bricks with his knees and bringing most of it down. Patricia was going to have to learn that a quick check on the reins would prevent such demolition acts, Michael thought.

Catriona won on Conker, but she was disappointed by Selina's absence, and he was unable to cheer her. However, she brightened a bit when Frolic and Tulip's Son were awarded first. The colt behaved with impeccable manners in the ring, a nice change from some of the foals who had been hauled in from the field with their dams, all muddy and shaggy haired, for the show. Tulip's Son was so clearly a quality animal that the others didn't stand a chance.

Lady Madeline and her filly foal were first in their class, and the three yearlings managed first, third, and fourth. This triumph for the Tulip comforted Michael. As long as Tulip's get was creditably shown, the old horse wasn't gone.

The highlight of the show was Charlie's performance. Catriona had felt the weight of this class on her shoulders from the moment her father had told her she had the ride. It had nothing to do with Charlie: it was Selina not riding the horse she had schooled so patiently and the fact that Catriona had never shown a horse publicly and was terrified something might go wrong.

She had to go twice to the loo tent; the second time she had to wait her turn, and the need became critical before she got into the smelly, stuffy convenience. By the time she got back to the lorry, she felt nauseated. Her father tied the number at her back and gave her a leg up, instructing her all the while.

"You've seen the drill often enough at the ringside, Trina. And you know Charlie. Circle round if the other horses bunch up or take the inside track, but keep some space around you. When you're called on to canter, try to strike off when the judges are watching, and let him gallop on when requested. Charlie has a neat turn of speed, and they need to see it. Good luck."

There was so much confidence and pride in her father's smile that Catriona straightened her shoulders determinedly, then squeezed Charlie with her legs and moved off to the ring.

There were ever so many competitors, some of them on beloved nags that had no claim to breeding and probably little to performance; but that was to be expected at a local show, and no bad thing. There were, however, several very well bred animals getting experience for the August Horse Show, and Catriona immediately noticed two in particular: a dapple gray and a brown mare. She eased Charlie into a working trot, delighted at his quick response and his agility when the gray spooked suddenly at a brace of golden retrievers in the corner.

The horses seemed to be trotting a long time before the steward bawled out, "Canter, please." Catriona was elated to find herself right in the judges' line of vision as she lifted Charlie into his beautiful rocking canter. He was so responsive! Not all the others were. One lady was bumping about in the saddle for nearly a complete round before her horse finally broke into the requested canter. Two others were equally disobedient, and another showed a tendency to kick whatever came close to his heels.

"Gallop on!"

It felt as if Charlie lowered himself before he sped away. She'd never ridden him so fast, and the elation she felt was breathtaking. He was also lapping half the other horses; only the gray was ahead of him. One of the ungainlies came off, and there was a pile-up of horses in one corner, but she, the gray, and the brown mare avoided it neatly.

At last the steward ordered a halt, and the judges, bowler

rims touching, conferred as the horses circled around. The steward made notes on his clipboard and then began to motion the horses in. The brown mare was called in first, but Charlie was second, and she was bursting with pride in him, patting his neck surreptitiously as he stood so calmly in the line-up. Eight horses remained, and the others were excused. Thank God she and Charlie hadn't had to endure that sort of ignominy, she thought. She was called abruptly to her senses as the steward beckoned her to dismount. The judges were now ready to ride each of the eight horses.

One started with the brown mare and the other at the eighth horse. As she stood by Charlie's head while he rolled his bit in a sort of reflective way, she kept murmuring to him that he must behave and do his very best, or Selina'd be disappointed in him.

The brown mare gave her rider a nice round, Catriona had to admit that. The other judge was having a bit of difficulty getting his mount to canter, but eventually he succeeded. Then Catriona had to hand Charlie over. The judge merely nodded at her as the steward gave him a leg up. And Catriona held her breath.

He was a portly man, she noticed, and Charlie hadn't been ridden by that many men, nor one so heavy. Would he be upset? No, he moved out as smoothly as ever, nicely down on the bit to give his neck its elegant curve. Catriona was so entranced with seeing Charlie show himself off that she didn't realize at first how many circuits the judge was making on him at trot and canter, both reins, even a figure eight.

"Very nice manners, young lady," the judge murmured as he halted Charlie back in the line again.

It seemed forever before the second judge had worked his way up to her. He was a light, wiry old man, with a lean and humorous face. When he vaulted to Charlie's back, Catriona caught her breath at the surprise in Charlie's eyes, but he gave the man an equally faultless ride.

Then came the boring part, when the horses were stripped of their saddles and examined for conformation, stride, and general fitness while the judges, brims together, conferred. Mick and other grooms had come out, with stable rubbers and body brushes, to smooth down any sweat marks, though Charlie had only the saddle patch to be groomed.

"He gave 'em nice rides, Cat," Mick said, "and you looked champion. The Captain thinks so, too. You rode him a treat, you did. Be proud of yerself."

Finally the competitors were asked to mount again and trot for the final judgments. Catriona was certain that Charlie had given a better ride than the brown mare, certainly better than the gray. She managed to keep her eye on the steward, who was jotting down the judges' comments, and at last he glanced around, patiently looking for the winner. She held her breath—and nearly burst into tears when the brown mare was pulled in first. She steadied a bit when she and Charlie were beckoned to second place, and she managed to smile at the brown mare's rider, astonished to recognize the woman as a near neighbor in Willow Grove.

"You've a fine gelding there, Miss Carradyne," said the wiry judge as he fixed the blue second-place ribbon to Charlie's headstall. "Did you school him yourself?"

"I helped," Catriona managed to say, and remembered to smile and thank him. Suddenly Selina's words flew into her mind: "You can't always win, it's how you tried that matters."

Blinking back her tears, Catriona leaned over to pat Charlie's neck. They had tried hard. They really had.

Then it was time for the traditional lap of honor. Charlie deftly evaded the gray's attempt to charge into his heels, and then they were out.

Catriona was surprised to see her father and Philip with mile-wide grins on their faces. Pat was jumping up and down in a victory circle with Artie and Billy. Everyone acted as pleased as punch.

"But we were only second," she said when they crowded around her with their congratulations.

Her father threw up his hands. "Second? The first time in a showing class for the pair of you? You expect a lot of yourself."

"Don't you, Daddy?"

Michael looked at her in astonishment. "By God, girl, you're all Carradyne!"

Suddenly all sense of failure dissipated. Dismounting, Catriona hooked Charlie's reins over her arms and threw herself into her father's arms. As she felt him return her embrace, she remembered the spring show and the Prince.

How could she tell him now?

≈ 30 ≈

*M*ichael was impatient all day Sunday for his three o'clock rendezvous with Selina. He arrived at the Greystones strand promptly at three and scanned the parking lot. There was only a battered VW by the railroad embankment, and concern flared briefly. Had he somehow mistaken Selina's cryptic message? Then the driver of the VW honked the horn, and an impatient hand beckoned him from the open window.

When he got nearer, he saw it was Selina, wearing a head scarf and dark glasses in what he thought was a parody of discretion. She wrestled with the inner handle of the passenger door, which swung open with a metallic squeal.

"What on earth are you doing in this wreck, Selina?" He started to sit beside her, then paused, realizing her face and neck were covered with bruises that neither glasses nor head scarf could hide. "My God, what happened?" He reached out to embrace her, and she flinched instinctively. "Healey?"

She swallowed and nodded. Then all resistance melted, and she leaned over to cling to him, shuddering.

He held off all questions until she had herself under control again. Ever so gently, he rocked her, condemning the awkward design of the VW's front seat. Gradually the shudders ceased, and she lifted her head from his shoulder.

"It was so ridiculous," she began in a low, controlled voice, "and so totally incomprehensible for someone like David to . . . to lose his rag so completely over something that I'm sure you'd have thought amusing. I still don't believe it happened." She gestured helplessly with her hands, managing a weak smile. "I got home on Friday well before Kathleen left. I listened to the news at six, and then Brian Clooney rang from the Gardá station to tell me that the Dun Laoghaire police thought some of the stolen items had been recovered, and could I come down and identify them.

"That's what I was doing when the duty sergeant came in to tell me that the burglar alarm in my own house had just been tripped. Brian Clooney accompanied me, and when we got to Dalkey, there was a patrol car in the drive . . . and David's Jaguar.

"Now, I had phoned the number he'd given me, to tell him that the locks had been changed and the security system installed. I don't know who David has working for him, but . . . well, I did ring and leave a message, only I guess he didn't get it." Michael noticed with a sickening jolt that behind the dark glasses she had a black eye. But it was the marks on her neck that truly enraged him.

"Anyway," she went on with a weary shrug, "David's key, of course, no longer opened his own front door. So he had broken a kitchen window, setting off the burglar alarm. He was in quite a state, arguing with the Gardái over his right to be in the house. I knew he was furious, and I couldn't blame him. He prefers dignified homecomings. He doesn't have much of a sense of humor, certainly not enough to cover something like this." She paused, looking down at her hands in her lap.

"So he beat up on you!"

She nodded. "It's the irony that gets to me. I wasn't away indulging myself, diverting myself with friends. I hadn't deliberately left the house unattended, or for that matter schemed to have him 'humiliated,' as he put it, flying into an even greater rage once the Gardái had left." She paused to swallow, and Michael realized abruptly that her throat was sore—"I had only left the house to retrieve *his* possessions. And I hadn't been gone fifteen minutes when he reached the house. I know he's been worried, that he's been having a difficult time in the North, and that he has to blow off steam—"

"Not by wife bashing!"

"Oh, Michael," Her precarious calm dissolved at his fierce tone. "He—was savage, Michael. Savage. I never, never, never want to see him again. But what can I do? He's my husband!"

What Michael wished to do to that husband shocked him, for he did not consider himself a physically violent person. He was reminded of the many times he had fought with the desire to throttle Isabel for her archaic attitudes and insensitivities. But he had never so much as raised his hand to her. For Healey to seize on such a flimsy excuse to vent his outrage on Selina was inexcusable.

"He took the keys to the Lancia when he went out today," she continued, leaning against him. "I borrowed this banger from the college lad next door to get milk. That's why the disguise." Carefully she lifted the glasses from her face. "Monday morning I can tell Kathleen that I got tossed on Saturday. She'd be more likely to believe that anyway. She's convinced horses are dangerous." Selina's voice lifted with an unmistakable ripple of amusement. "Oh, do tell me how Catriona did with Charlie."

"Second, and she was bitterly disappointed. Where's Healey now?"

"Michael!" She pushed away from him, her eyes gray with pain and worry. "You're not to do anything stupid. I've underestimated David"—she gave a sadly cynical sigh—"but you're not to make the same mistake—much less give him any cause to think some of his accusations are true. Oh, Mr. David Healey thinks he's so very smart, but basically he's an insensitive, narrow-minded, power-hungry humorless piece of work, and I won't let him get the better of me again." The rigidity of her shoulders, the fervor of her tone, was reassuring to Michael.

"Not long ago I told you that I hadn't any reason to divorce David. I most certainly do now, and I shall phone the solicitor in the morning."

With that resolution to support her, she sat upright in the driver's seat again. "I must get back now, Michael. But I desperately needed to see you"—she put her hand on his thigh and gave him a faint smile—"to preserve my sanity. I don't know where David went this afternoon, but he was on the phone to Murray, so I suspect he's at Erinwood. I don't know if he'll be going North again or not. I devoutly hope so! He looks so . . . so pleased with himself!"

Michael felt a wave of concern for her safety, but she caught the look in his eye and patted his leg.

"I'll be all right. Please, don't worry."

"Oh, my darling!" Michael was overcome by her dignity and took her hand in both of his, bringing it to his lips. "Healey's up against Cornanagh, too. Don't be afraid to phone me!"

He eased out of the VW, taking care not to crack his head. The door squeaked on opening and closing.

"Quite a comedown, isn't it?" Selina said, wryly. The car started willingly, and with one last smile and a wave, she headed off.

Just seeing Michael had done wonders for her, as she had hoped it would. She had wanted him to see what David had done to her; she'd needed the support of someone else's outrage to fuel her own: to give tacit support to her determination never to endure such treatment again.

Another, deeper reason why she had so desperately needed to see him was to reassure herself that David's rape had not altered her response to Michael. In fact her feelings toward Michael had altered: now she felt an even greater need for his support and comfort.

Considering her not too clear conscience on the matter of adultery, Selina might have endured David's brutality as a well-deserved penance. But the manner in which he had conducted his domination over her, the excuse he'd given when finished, had put an entirely different complexion on the matter. He'd had to "show her who's boss," he'd said.

David's treatment of her had also revealed the extent and horror of sexual practices she had only heard whispered of, and his familiarity with such perversities suggested that he had often found "partners" outside his marriage. Indeed, that was exactly how he had treated her—as a prostitute, a public convenience. Selina laughed mirthlessly. To think she had once assumed he was too restrained, too inhibited, to enjoy variations in the sexual act.

She shuddered as she remembered what he had done to her. The memory infuriated her, filled her with a coldness and fury that would protect her from a repetition of such indignities.

She didn't know much about such injuries, but she fervently hoped she'd be able to straddle a horse in a few days. She needed Cornanagh now more than ever before.

As Michael drove back to Cornanagh, he was seething. There was no excuse for what Healey had inflicted on Selina. More than anything else, he resented being powerless to protect his lover from her legal spouse. Sybil had been on about marital rights and family problems lately, going to meetings with those friends of hers. Now he could appreciate the irony of what she'd said: the Republic maintained that the family was the basis of its society and must be preserved. With the back of the husband's hand, it would appear. Thank heaven Selina was Anglican—divorce was not the anathema to her that it was to Catholics. She could spend the necessary time in England to file and receive a divorce, and when she was free, he would ask her to marry him—if she'd have him.

He smiled as he made the turn up to Pretty Bush. That was

what he deeply desired, a marriage with Selina. God, he hoped she'd agree.

Just as he came up the dip to the Kilquade road, an astonishing cavalcade crossed the T junction: Mrs. Comyn's venerable Morris Minor leading a positively ancient van. It had the high, straight sides, thin-spoked tires, and small windows of prewar design—and, unless his eyes mistook him, running boards, too! It proceeded at a dignified pace, a speedy twenty-five miles an hour, and he caught up with it just as it turned into the courtyard.

Michael was so intrigued by the van that he took his time joining the Carradyne women welcoming Mrs. Comyn. He grinned as he saw that Philip, Owen, and Mick were equally enchanted by the van, circling it surreptitiously. It glowed with wax, and its paintwork was flawless.

"You are indeed welcome, Mrs. Comyn," he said when the babble of greetings had subsided. He shook her hand warmly, feeling it cool and dry in his. "You made a safe journey?"

"But of course, Captain Carradyne. Seamus is an extremely cautious driver."

The gentleman in question now descended from the cab of the van, and Michael decided he could not have envisioned a more suitable driver to match it. Seamus was several inches shorter than Mick, partly from bowed legs and partly from stooped shoulders. He looked like two parts of a man put together: burly in the chest and upper torso and spindly from the waist down. He wore an ancient cap—had he purchased it the same year as the van?—and a brown suit so shiny that Michael wondered the threads were still intact.

"Naw then, sor, I'll be needing a hand with the es-kit-tor. Would your lads there oblige?"

Michael gave permission even as Philip and Owen started forward to assist.

"A cup of tea, Mrs. Comyn," Eithne began graciously, "while

they unload, and then we'll see that they have everything placed to your satisfaction in your room."

"You are most kind, Mrs. Carradyne," said Mrs. Comyn. She glanced back once just as she entered the house, and a flicker of anxiety crossed her face as she heard Seamus's voice raised in orders to "be careful, now, lads. You'll be skinned for so much as a scratch."

With all the females officiating in the lounge, Michael made an early retreat, far too restless to endure the social amenities. He went to his office and stared at the phone. He wanted so to ring Selina, if only to reassure himself by the sound of her voice. But if Healey answered the phone, it might worsen her situation. He began to pace, then decided it would be better to see how Seamus was progressing. He ran into Philip and Owen in the hall as they were lugging cartons up the stairs.

"She brought enough books to start her own lending library," Philip said, pausing to lean his box on the banister. "Maybe we should bring up Grandfather's shelves." Michael laughed and continued on outside.

Seamus was inside his van, folding the tarpaulins that had covered his load. As Michael watched, he took down a small brush and swept the floor, nodding to the Captain in apology as a brief flurry of dust and gravel landed in the courtyard.

"This is a fine van you have, Seamus," Michael said, tapping the door appreciatively. "In first-rate condition."

"Thank'ee, sor. Good equipment should be well kept. Deserves it."

"What year would it be?"

"Why, sor, 1939."

"And you're the original owner."

"Sort of, sor. I was working for Mr. Comyn, God rest his soul, when he bought it, and when he decided to replace it, sure an' I bought it from him meself. Been with me ever since. And we do the odd bit of carting now and again."

"Mick, I think this gentleman could do with a cup of tea." Michael caught the merest flicker of dismay on Seamus's craggy face. "Or perhaps a pint might go down better. It's past four."

"Thank'ee, Captain, sor, the pint'd be more to my liking." Then he stepped close to Michael, a concerned expression on his face. "Mrs. Comyn is a foine woman, Captain sor, and there are some of us in the village as felt she'd been hard done by. But I can tell 'em now"—a hesitant grin began to brighten the man's stern features—"that she'll be grand here. Just grand!"

Michael thought that Elizabeth Comyn had been accorded the finest reference she could possess. Philip and Owen came back with questions about the van and were permitted a glimpse of its immaculate engine before all the men adjourned to the Kilpedder Inn for the promised pint.

Monday morning started out properly, with Mick's whistle rousing Michael as the old groom made his way up the Ride to the yard to feed the stabled horses and check the field horses. Later, when Michael was having a second cup of coffee and toast with the two girls and Eithne, a strange car pulled into the courtyard and set Tory to barking fiercely. Its occupant did not immediately emerge, and then the horn was honked in a sequence that roused Eithne to her feet with a cry of surprise. She tore out of the house and into the courtyard.

"By God, it's her Texan," Michael said, rising from his seat to peer out the kitchen window.

"It is?" Patricia left her place, Catriona right behind her.

"Girls!" Michael cried, grabbing hold of Patricia before she could charge out to greet the visitor. "Let's give them at least a moment or two alone!"

Before Patricia's impatience got the better of her, a radiant Eithne escorted Davis Haggerty into the house and introduced him.

Michael decided that he liked "the Texan," liked his firm

handshake, the direct way he returned Michael's appraising glance, the pleasantries he made on being introduced to the two girls, and his ease of manner in what could only be a trying situation. He especially approved of the man's tenderness in his treatment of Eithne.

They all adjourned to the lounge, and minutes later Mrs. Comyn came in quietly with a coffee tray and a basket of freshly buttered toast. Michael began to feel better about having a housekeeper, if this was a sample of the service, tact, and consideration he might expect.

They had only just started the coffee when there was an urgent rap on the door and Mick came stomping in.

"Captain, the tack's been nicked."

Eithne immediately began to cry. "Oh, Michael, I'm so terribly sorry. It's all our fault," she sobbed while Patricia swore under her breath and Catriona looked stricken.

"Don't be stupid, Eithne," Michael said angrily, and caught Davis's look of concern. "Sorry, Haggerty, but it has nothing to do with Eithne. We seem to be in a tit-for-tat situation with a vindictive neighbor. How did they manage to break in, Mick?"

"They pulled the bars right out of the stones, sor, and got in the small window. Allus said that should be blocked up. There's not so much as a stirrup leather left."

"Did they get the show saddles in the tack box?"

Mick shook his head. "Only because they couldn't get it through the window," he said with sour satisfaction, "and there's no way of breaking that lock short of shooting it."

"Thank God for that. You'll have to excuse me, Haggerty. Likely you'll want to have a long chat with Eithne."

But Davis was only moments behind Michael and Mick as they hurried to the yard. Artie was standing there helplessly, as if he couldn't grasp the loss.

The heavy Chubb lock had not been tampered with, but inside, the ragged outline of the small window, set high in the outside wall, confirmed the point of entry. The bridle and saddle racks, the rail where girths were stored, the hooks for head collars and lead ropes, the bags that held odd pieces of leather tack, the box of stirrup irons—everything was empty. The place had been cleared.

Michael stood, fists against his belt, for a long moment.

"Lemme go up to Fitzroy's, Captain," Mick pleaded. "I'll find 'em, or I'll beat it out of 'em."

Michael held up his hand. "We don't settle this that way, Mick." He frowned, trying to think as Fitzroy would. "Fitzroy will either try to sell the tack on or dump it in a ditch. I'd be amazed if he's stupid enough to hide it in a shed on his own property. First, I'll inform the Gardái."

Back in the house, he phoned the Gardá station in Newtownmountkennedy and reported the break-in and theft.

"We think they used either a tractor or a Land Cruiser to spring the iron grill on the window," he told the sergeant. "Someone might just have noticed such early morning traffic. It's light about four these mornings."

The sergeant assured him that he'd be down directly and rang off. Then Michael dialed all the evening newspapers and inserted an advertisement, giving crisp details of the more expensive saddles, including the fact that all were marked for easy identification. That would make it much harder for someone to sell the tack on for a quick profit. Still, he rather doubted that Fitzroy intended to sell; the theft was another vengeful act, this time in retaliation for the pranks of the other night. Like the tail cutting, it was meant only to harass. But this time, in stealing items of such value, Fitzroy had committed a crime.

"If Fitzroy took it—and I can't think who else would—we would have to find the tack on his property before we could have him charged," Michael said, trying to defuse Mick's fury before the old man did something dire. "And he'll know that his farm is the first place we'd have searched."

"Effing bloody jumped-up tinker," Mick muttered.

"Which is exactly where we'll go!" Michael cried suddenly. "Come on, Mick. We've a message to run."

Johnny Cash and some hundred other families of the traveling folk occupied the vast field between the railway and the Shankill road near Ballybrack. During the day the men stood around the bonfires maintained even in summer, while the horses, greyhounds, and children ran wild about the place.

When Michael reached their camp he asked a group of boys for Johnny Cash. One of the lads pointed sullenly to a caravan set off closer to the embankment, where three donkeys stood, hip shot in the sun.

Johnny Cash was sitting on an upturned box beyond his caravan, talking with several other men. A blond woman peered out the open door and said something to him, pointing toward Michael's approaching car. Johnny rose immediately, and the other men formed a curious ring just out of earshot as he came up to speak to Michael.

"Captain, sor, how be ya? How's the filly?"

"She's coming on a treat, Johnny. My niece is riding her out."

"You're a grand man, so you are, Captain. Knew you'd bring her right if anyone could." Johnny touched his cap respectfully again, grinning at the good news. "Now, I've a grand gelding, five-year-old, good blood, that I'd give you fer a keen price, seeing as how it's yourself."

"Johnny, I'm not buying. I need your help. . . ."

"Someone's nicked your horses again?" A look of indignation flashed across his face.

"No, not this time. My tack. Every strap, stirrup, and bit. I was wondering if you could keep your ears open for someone trying to pass the lot on. All our tack's branded with a C slash c, so it'll be easy to recognize."

"I remember, sor, indeed I do, and very clever of you it was, too. Well, I'll pass the word, so I will, an' come an' tell you anything I might hear. That's desp'rite bad, sor. You wouldn't be needin' the loan of a few saddles, now would you?"

Michael grinned, but not broadly enough to give offense. "I can manage, thanks." Then he beckoned for Johnny to lean closer. "I've an idea who might have nicked the stuff, Johnny. Now it's only a notion, but it would be something you'd have the better way of checking. So, if you just happened to be up the Newcastle road near a place known as Killaois, you might possibly run across something interesting. Or somewhere nearby, in a ditch or a gorse field, or maybe one of those ruined cottages."

Johnny straightened, closing one eye and nodding his head. "Sure, now, Captain, sor, I'll be keeping eyes and ears open, so I will, and bring you the breath of whatever you need to know."

When they got home, they had a welcome surprise. Artie came charging into the courtyard at the sound of their approach, brandishing a bridle overhead.

"Captain, young Robert Evans found it. In the ditch beyond Woodstock. I told him what happened. I hope that was all right."

Michael clapped him reassuringly on the shoulder. "That's grand, Artie. And I'm relieved that it's the Prince's bridle. Young Robert'll tell his dad, and Bobbie Evans is a great man for hearing what you need to know from time to time."

"The bridle was found beyond Woodstock, ya said?" Mick asked, his eyes narrowing. "There we are, Captain, proof!"

"In a sense," Michael replied cautiously. "Artie, get in the car. Let's do a reconnaissance and see if anything else dropped off the back of the lorry. Mick, the sergeant'll be here any minute, and I want you to talk to him."

Although Michael held the Austin to a bare five miles an

hour, they found only a cheek strap and considerably more odds and sods of junk than one would think roadside vegetation would conceal. However, the strap was found on the Newcastle road, a bend away from Killaois Farm.

Sergeant Pat Quinn from Newtownmountkennedy was still inspecting the premises when they returned. He made notes of the recovered items and Michael's belief that James Fitzroy might be able to help the sergeant with his "inquiries," then closed his notebook and promised to get on with the matter straightaway.

When he'd left, Michael told the girls to use the show tack and work the ponies. He left Mick to see if there were enough spare bits in the tack box to put a horse bridle together and went in to make a few phone calls.

His first call was to Bobbie Evans, who assured Michael he had more than one saddle he'd be glad to lend. He invited his friend to come up and take what he needed and promised to keep his ears open as well.

Gratified to receive such cooperation from his neighbor, Michael rang off and phoned Selina. Kathleen answered and bluntly told him that Mrs. Healey was not at home, and no, she didn't know when her mistress could be expected. Michael asked the woman to have Mrs. Healey phone Cornanagh, as they'd had a break-in and her tack had been taken. She said she'd leave the message and hung up on him.

Disgruntled and curiously uneasy, Michael went on to call those of his hunting clients whose tack had disappeared with his own.

Selina did not receive Michael's message until late afternoon, for she'd been to see the solicitor who had handled her father's Irish affairs. She doubted that Mr. O'Hara would sully his firm's name by drafting separation papers but felt sure he'd refer her to someone who would.

She had to shock the old gentleman considerably more than she intended after he tried to soothe her with platitudes and advised her not to make any rash decisions. In the end he had acquiesced and given her the name of another solicitor. On the phone, Ian Coghlan sounded younger and certainly more incisive, but he too had tried to wheedle and placate her. At last she cut through his rhetoric and demanded an appointment for the following morning, which he gave her.

She spent the afternoon shopping aimlessly, pausing for a meal or a drink whenever the aching in her body made it necessary for her to rest. She dawdled as long as she could and then returned home in time for a long bath before David could be expected home for dinner.

"He phoned to say he wouldn't be in, missus," Kathleen informed her when she returned at last. "He's gone to Belfast."

Selina felt faint with relief. "Thank you, Kathleen. Any other messages?"

"Yes, Captain Carradyne phoned and said your saddle got nicked."

"Oh, my God, what in the world . . . ?"

She went immediately to the phone and dialed Cornanagh, but the number was engaged. She slammed the phone down impatiently and stood there, thinking furiously. At last she turned to Kathleen. "Well, if my husband is away, I shan't need to keep you, Kathleen. So have a pleasant evening."

As soon as the woman had left, Selina tried Cornanagh again, swearing impotently when the line was still busy. Eventually she went up and drew her bath. Soaking relieved her aches, but she was beginning to wonder if she'd ever feel really clean again.

Dressed in a loose cotton robe, Selina managed to eat a little of the tasty meal Kathleen had prepared when the front-door bell chimed. Willing it to be Michael, she rushed to open the door, completely forgetting that she wore no makeup.

It was Sybil.

After one shocked gasp, she stepped inside and shut the door, setting down the parcel she was carrying. "I know bloody well you didn't get those bruises from being tossed!" she said, her eyes blazing. "What happened?"

Sybil's rage was like a match to tinder. Before she could stop to think, Selina had revealed everything. It simply poured out of her, all the sordid details festering in her spirit. And when she had finished, she felt lighter, easier in her mind.

"And now," said Sybil, "I'm going to phone a doctor friend of mine"—she raised her voice above Selina's protest—"a woman doctor, Maurie Woods, who's been helping us with cases like yours. If you ever want to file for a separation . . ."

"I'm seeing a solicitor tomorrow."

"Which one? Coghlan? Well, he's not the best but he's not the worst," Sybil said grudgingly, "Most of 'em don't want to know, even when we can provide hospital proof of brutal beatings. You may not know it, but a husband can beat his wife black, blue, and purple, and unless he does so in front of three witnesses who will testify in court—and that's the real rub, given a good old Irish reluctance to be seen in court for any reason—she can't even get a barring order."

Selina stared at Sybil, trying to absorb what she'd just heard. "You can't mean that!"

"I can and do. Most women can't even pay for counsel unless they have a private income. You'd be amazed at the number of women I talk with who have trouble even getting house-keeping money. But we're working on it." Sybil patted Selina's hand. "Now let me call Maurie Woods. Honestly, that's the first step."

When Sybil left the lounge to make her call, Selina found herself wilting against the sofa cushions. It was a relief to have unburdened herself, but it was also unnerving somehow. Talking about it had transformed the whole nightmare into an inescapable reality. Selina opened her eyes as a smiling Sybil returned.

"Maurie said she'd come right over. The sooner the better, as it were, so she can make a record of the internal damage. Oooh, you look puny. Like a drink? Tea, coffee, scotch?" Sybil spoke jauntily, but her eyes were so kind Selina felt the sting of tears. "There now, Selina, the worst is over. 'Once a victim has been able to verbalize the attack, she has a much better chance of rationalizing it.'"

Selina gave her benefactress a weak smile. "Oh, I'll be able to rationalize it all right. I just can't understand it. . . . By the way, what brought you here to me tonight?"

"Ah!" Sybil cried, leaping up from the sofa. "I couldn't resist showing it to you, and I have to smuggle it back in to Cornanagh." As she spoke, she went to the entrance hall and retrieved the parcel, unwrapping it as she returned. Then, with a flourish, she turned the front of the framed picture to Selina.

"Oh, my God," Selina said, sitting up and reaching for the portrait of the Tulip and Michael. "Oh, my God. It's . . . it's perfect."

"Well, there are a few flaws . . . but Janey Mack, when you consider that Trina's only thirteen and has no formal training, it's pretty bloody good, isn't it? She had me frame it for his birthday."

"His birthday?"

"I admit Dad seems ageless, but he gets one birthday a year like the rest of us. July twenty-sixth." Sybil winked. "He hates parties, but we always have a big family dinner. Would you like to join us this year? We'd love to have you."

Selina hesitated, finding considerable amusement in her circumstances. Would Sybil be as helpful and hospitable if she knew?

"Well, I don't want to push you right now, but you'd be very welcome."

"How could I miss the opportunity to see Michael's expression when he unwraps this? Catriona is so gifted."

"For a lot more than horses," Sybil said tartly, "but if that's what she wants, she has the right to fulfill herself. And I'll fight for that for her." Selina was a bit surprised at Sybil's vehemence, and Sybil caught her expression. "Oh, don't mind me. I've been at sword's point with my grandmother again. She's positively medieval in her attitudes, but then, that's the way she was brought up. It's just that things are changing in Ireland, and— Sorry, I shouldn't bore you with my pet hobbyhorse— the only kind I'll ride!"

Sybil's exuberance and enthusiasm were contagious, and as they waited for Dr. Woods, Selina decided that Michael and Catriona were not the only admirable Carradynes.

"Janey Mack, listen to me, forgetting the other marvelous news! Auntie Eithne's Texan arrived this morning, proposed to her, and then fell asleep. He'd been traveling since early Texas time yesterday, and he was so worried about Eithne, or her refusing him, that he never closed his eyes on the plane last night. Isn't that marvelous?— Oh, and has Dad rung you about the robbery? Would you believe it . . ." She chattered on, giving Selina all the details. "Can you imagine? Yanking out the grille with the tractor! Daddy and Mick admit to having had a few pints with Mrs. Comyn's carter, so they slept through everything. Just like men! Never around when you need them." Sybil's smile was full of loving tolerance.

"Never mind the robbery," Selina said when Sybil paused to catch her breath. "My tack is insured. I want to hear more about Eithne and Davis."

"Well, they're going to get married right away," Sybil told her. "Register office, probably, as you have to post banns for a church wedding. You see, Davis has got a job for Owen, but there's more chance of him getting a proper visa if he's got a relative in the States."

"Surely Eithne isn't marrying Davis to get her son out of Ireland?"

"No!" Sybil replied, laughing. "And you'd know that for sure if you could see the look on Eithne's face when Davis is in the room." She rolled her eyes. "Turtledoves. It has Pat in kinks. She and Trina're to be bridesmaids, if you have them at register office weddings."

"And Trina? How does she feel about all this?"

Sybil sobered. "She's been awfully quiet, but I think it's more the robbery than Eithne marrying. I mean—"

Sybil's observation about Trina was cut off by the doorbell. Selina rose nervously, suddenly dreading the examination even if it were to be conducted by a female doctor. Fortunately Maurie Woods's matter-of-fact but sympathetic attitude put her apprehensions to rest, and the examination was so deft that it was over before she could resist.

"There's no irreparable damage, my dear," Maurie said reassuringly when she was through, "but you will be sore for a while longer. Keep up with the soaks. The physical damage is far less serious than the mental. We do have a counselor, a woman, if you want to talk about it," she added kindly.

Selina smiled. "Sybil's already done a lot for me."

"Could you bear seeing your general practitioner? Two medical opinions are better."

"And there's the usual male suspicion of collusion?"

Maurie shot her a droll look. "Two would be better than one, but I won't push it."

She refused refreshment, saying she had a full surgery, then reminded Selina that she would be available at any time.

"I've got to rush, too," Sybil said apologetically as she rewrapped Catriona's framed portrait. "You'll be all right by yourself?"

"Yes, of course," Selina replied, smiling.

"Good. But I don't think you ought to ride for Dad for a while."

"I'm not. David's left for the north again, thank God, but I've told your father that I wouldn't be able to ride for a few days."

"Make it a week, at least," Sybil urged. "To give Trina another chance on Charlie."

Selina grinned. "You do know, don't you, that Michael bought Charlie for her, not me?"

Sybil returned her grin. "I know. You know. Daddy knows, but Trina hasn't twigged it yet. Take care of yourself, pet." And she was out the door, down the steps, and carefully placing the portrait on the backseat of her car.

That was when Selina noticed the dark gray sedan parked down the street. The driver was still in it—and he'd been there when she had come home several hours earlier. Selina waved good-bye to Sybil, watched as she drove away, then closed the front door, frowning. Well, it could be just a coincidence. Nevertheless, she fastened the door chain and made sure the burglar alarm was turned on. She also checked the kitchen door before she went upstairs to her room.

ꙮ 31 ꙮ

*B*y Monday afternoon, Catriona could stand it no longer. She sneaked into Philip's room, a place no one would think to look for her; she had to be by herself and try to sort things out. Philip's room was quiet and overlooked the Ride. This morning it still carried the faint scent of his after-shave. The walls were decorated with photos of him on various prize Cornanagh horses, the broken polo mallet he'd nicked from Phoenix Park the summer he was going with a polo player's daughter, and a nice collection of red firsts and blue seconds.

It was also uncharacteristically neat; Mrs. Comyn must have tidied it. All his clothes were either hung up or put away, the bed was smooth, pillow plumped under the tightly stretched spread. There wasn't even a spare shoe kicked into a corner or a half-open drawer in the press. But the room felt safe to her, and she went to the window, staring out at the sun-drenched Ride.

She would have preferred to commune with Conker, but the yard had been whiddershins this morning, with Mick as ferocious as a thundercloud and Artie with a face as long as a wet week—and all over the burglary. Catriona sighed. If it hadn't been for Owen . . . She didn't want Auntie Eithne to leave Cornanagh, but at least it meant Owen would be leaving, too. And once Mr. Fitzroy heard that Owen was gone, he'd leave Cornanagh alone. The robbery was Owen's fault, not Cornanagh's, and it wasn't fair, not the least bit, that the horses were the ones to be treated so unjustly. Especially when nothing bad would be happening to Owen, who had caused all the trouble. Being sent to America wasn't a punishment at all, not to Owen. It just wasn't fair.

The distressed knot in Catriona's heart tightened again at the knowledge that Pip, too, would soon be leaving. She felt wretched because he was over the moon at the thought of tackling Madison Avenue. But he deserved a chance, she had to admit. He was wasted as a car salesman.

In the deepest, most critical part of her mind, Catriona knew that Philip was not as committed to Cornanagh and its horses as she was. But he was such marvelous fun and the very best of her brothers, and she loved him so terribly, terribly much.

She moved from the window and did a tour of the room, blowing dust off the ribbons, straightening one of the framed photos, rubbing her finger against the after-shave bottle, and inhaling the scent. Soon all this would be gone, and the room would be just a room.

Desolate, Catriona sprawled facedown on the neatly made bed, pounding it with her fists. Pip, Auntie Eithne, Cornanagh . . . *Everything* had gone wrong since Blister died, and it was just too much! Bad things should happen one at a time so you could get over them more easily. Not like this— not all at once.

Out of the corner of her eye, Catriona saw the door swing open. She was both dismayed and relieved to see Mrs. Comyn enter the room: she couldn't have borne it if it had been Pat.

"Oh, èxcuse me, Catriona, I didn't realize you were here." Mrs. Comyn started to leave, then stopped. "Are you all right, dear?"

Her voice was soft and kind, not distant or cool, the way she sounded at other times.

Tears came unbidden to Catriona's eyes. "Everyone I love is going away. And I'll never see them again." Catriona buried her face in the pillow and sobbed.

"Now, now, child . . ." She was lifted against Mrs. Comyn's lavender-scented shirt and comforted with gentling hands and soothing words. "It must all be quite unsettling for you, losing your mother so suddenly."

"Blister died first," Catriona said, her voice muffled. "Then Mother, and nothing's been the same since. Now Pip's leaving as well as Auntie Eithne."

"Now, then, my dear . . ." Mrs. Comyn lifted Catriona's chin and smiled into her eyes. "Surely you don't begrudge your brother and aunt their good fortune. You haven't struck me as a selfish child." Catriona shook her head, somewhat surprised: she certainly did not want to be considered selfish. "Though I quite see how the events of the last few days would be unsettling, especially when it all seems aimed at your horses."

"They've never harmed anyone. Why do they have to be victims?"

"Sometimes, my dear, it's hard to understand the reason for events . . ." Mrs. Comyn hesitated for a moment. "But generally, if we look at what happened before, we can figure out, quite logically, how it could occur. And it is much more sensible to be logical, because emotion gets in the way of constructive thought.

"I haven't been here very long"—she gave Catriona a wry smile—"but I did hear that Mr. Fitzroy blames your cousin for his daughter's pregnancy and has sworn revenge. But to break in and steal all the tack was a stupid thing to do." Her voice grew steely, cold as ice. "And it will all come right very shortly, believe me. . . . Now, child, a spot of the weeps is quite understandable, but your aunt is already worried enough about you. You don't want her to feel as if she's to blame for this, too, do you?"

Shyly Catriona shook her head. "Mrs. Comyn, do you like Mr. Haggerty?" she asked.

"I believe I do," the older woman replied as if mildly surprised at her answer. "He is certainly devoted to your aunt and has gone to great lengths to show it. I think we must all be happy for her sake. And your brother's. Of course you'll miss him; he's very fond of you. But you must concentrate on how much better off he'll be in America. And it's not as if they've dropped off the edge of the world—they'll all be coming home for Christmas, so you've something to look forward to, don't you?"

"Yes . . ." Catriona suppressed the unworthy thought that Philip was sure to bring her an extra nice gift from America. "Christmas at Cornanagh is the greatest crack!"

"I expect it will be," Mrs. Comyn said in her droll way, and got up, signaling Catriona to rise as well. The two of them smoothed the rumpled covers. "There now."

"Thank you, Mrs. Comyn."

"You're quite welcome, Catriona, and you are welcome to come to me anytime you've got a problem. It always helps to talk matters over."

Mrs. Comyn smiled, and Catriona thought there wasn't quite so much sadness in her eyes today.

"Will you be happy here at Cornanagh?"

Mrs. Comyn gave a little start of surprise and turned to look at Catriona. "What do you mean by that?"

"I don't know. I just thought you looked sad, but I suppose that's logical, having to leave your home and all. That's much harder than watching people leave you. I know I couldn't ever leave Cornanagh."

Mrs. Comyn gave her a very odd look, one eyebrow quirked. "We'll hope you don't have to. You know, your cousin's been searching for you."

Catriona grimaced. "I love Pat, but sometimes she's a bit much. Do you like her?"

"To be sure, she's very much a product of her culture, but she's got a good disposition and a quick mind."

As they opened the door of Philip's room, they could hear the phone ringing.

"I'd better answer that," Mrs. Comyn said, hurrying down the stairs.

Catriona felt much better after her talk with Mrs. Comyn, and at teatime she made every effort to join in discussions about the wedding and travel arrangements. Then Sybil arrived, winking and grinning at Catriona and pointing surreptitiously to the car. In all the excitement, Catriona was able to get the parceled portrait up to her room unnoticed.

Once there, she unwrapped it carefully but with trembling fingers. What if it hadn't turned out right? But no, she could trust Sybil.

The narrow black frame and off-white matte gave a new, almost professional dimension to the portrait, and Catriona sighed in relief and delight. Yes, it was the Tulip. Even if she hadn't quite gotten her father's shoulder right, the eye traveled first to the Tulip's elegant, classic head and then to the fact that this dignified animal was accepting her father's outstretched hand as homage. Yes, the pose was what she had seen in her mind when she started it. As Catriona lovingly replaced the wrappings, she could barely contain her anticipation. This was the most original birthday present she had ever given her father. She hid it by the side of her wardrobe, concealing it with her school coat.

When she reached the steps, she heard her sister and her aunt talking softly in the hall below. Sybil sounded angry, Auntie Eithne distressed.

"But how could he?" Auntie Eithne exclaimed. "She's a lady."

"That never makes a difference, believe me," Sybil said acidly. "But would you object to her taking over the mews after you and Davis leave? She may not need to, but sometimes knowing you have a safe place to go can make a difference. I wanted to ask you first."

"Of course, Sybil, of course. Though it's really up to your father, you know. But I'm sure she would always be welcome here."

"Good! I knew I could count on you, Auntie Eithne. Damn," Sybil added as the phone rang yet again. "Cornanagh!" she said briskly, answering the call. "Yes, I'll get him."

Somehow, though no names had been mentioned, Catriona knew that they had been talking about Selina. Would she be coming to live in Auntie Eithne's little house? Selina at Cornanagh all the time, every day, would, Catriona felt, make up for a lot of the uncertainty and unhappiness of the last few weeks. With a considerably lighter heart, Catriona came down the stairs just as her father picked up the receiver. He winked at her.

"Yes, Angus, good of you to ring. . . . Well, actually, if you happened to have a big ringed snaffle—those German eggbutts are a bit heavy for a gelding I'm schooling. . . . Grand! I'll be down later. Thanks, Angus."

In the lounge, all sorts of plans were being made and almost as quickly revised. Davis had originally thought that he and Eithne could be married by the American ambassador or consul, but that wasn't permitted under Irish law. And a register office marriage—the most expeditious kind of ceremony—required that a notice of intent be placed in newspapers twice within a week. Davis decided to publish the first notice the very next day, and the wedding was set tentatively for the following week. Eithne was flushed and fluttered a good bit, but Davis, and Owen, were eager to arrange matters as quickly as possible.

Suddenly Tory's raucous barking cut through the cheerful maze of suggestions and plans. A moment later Mrs. Comyn entered the lounge.

"There's a traveling person to see you, Captain," she said.

With an eager grin, Michael shot to his feet and strode to the door, Catriona a step behind him. Outside, Mick was just closing the outraged Tory in the garage.

"Good evenin', Captain, sor," Johnny said, getting out of the van and touching his cap brim. He beckoned Michael to come round with him to the back and threw open the door with a flourish. There on the load bed with a gaggle of children around it was the old hunting saddle that had been Tyler's.

Michael all but grabbed it, stroking it before checking that the saddle tree hadn't been damaged. He brushed off the mud and ran a finger down the worst of the scratches, rubbing vigorously.

"How'd it come your way, Johnny?"

"Well, now, sor, not a half hour after you'd gone when two of those Moorhouses came to us with a tale of finding some saddles in a ditch."

Michael gave a snort of disbelief.

"Now, sor, I do believe him." Johnny held up a forefinger. "This once. He and the dummy with him had a fierce thirst on them, for we settled on a tenner." Michael immediately began fumbling in his pocket for bank notes. "Mind you, he was asking twice that, but I pointed out how old the saddle was, sor, and the flaps thin, meaning no disrespect, Captain, sor."

"You did well, Johnny. D'you think he'll be back to deal again?"

Johnny's face twisted into a grimace of doubt. "Sure now, sor, he's that feckless he won't stir himself till he's drunk the tenner up. 'Course, there're the two of 'em, so it'd go faster," Johnny added encouragingly. "Then, too, Captain, those Moorhouses are canny. They might not come back to me next time."

Michael sighed. "Johnny, I can't spend all summer waiting to get my tack back piece by piece."

Johnny held up a hand. "Ah, now, sor, I knows that. I knows that well. Don't you be worrying. I came with this one to give ya heart." He winked broadly. "Not to worry, Captain, sor, not to worry. You'll see."

He got back into his van and, with a final nod of his head and a finger to his cap brim, turned round and out of the courtyard.

"I'll take that from ye, Captain," Mick said, his fingers caressing leather still supple from years of care. He smoothed the scratch. "Only on the surface. Come to that, Tom Berney would put new flaps on."

Mrs. Comyn appeared in the doorway. "Captain? A Mr. Doherty on the phone for you."

Michael cursed under his breath. But at least the show tack had been spared, and the Prince's bridle had already been retrieved. He had good news for Bob Doherty.

Unfortunately Bob Doherty did not have the same for him. "What's this I hear about another four faults, and in the second round at Kilmac?" he demanded as soon as Michael had set his mind at rest about the show tack. "I thought you said the girl would improve."

"And so she did," Michael replied, keeping his voice level. "The pony flattened."

"Well, I'm not sure that's going to be good enough, Carradyne. The Horse Show's nearly here, and I want that pony showing well.

"He is. Saturday is Castletown show. Why don't you come to that? See for yourself how she handles him. You know as well as I that people tell you what they think you want to hear. Or don't want to hear."

"Should I put in an insurance claim for the other saddle?"

"Not yet. There's a good chance that advert will do the trick."

"What I want to know is, how'd the theft occur? Leave the door unlocked?"

Michael steeled himself against the obvious dig. "No. The thieves pulled the iron grating off that small window on the roadside. That's why your show tack wasn't stolen. Couldn't get the tack trunk through the window."

"Oh! Must be a nuisance."

"It is." Michael ended the call with obligatory regards to Aisling and cradled the receiver. He had taken one step when its shrill summons turned him back. "Cornanagh!"

"Michael?" Selina's voice sounded apologetic, and he realized he had allowed his irritation with Doherty to carry over. "Kathleen told me my saddle had been stolen? . . ." And since Sybil's visit to her had been more or less confidential, Selina listened dutifully as Michael told her the whole story—again.

"They actually pulled the grating off? How did they manage that?"

"With either the tractor or the Land Rover."

"And the Gardái?"

"Are investigating."

"No one's helping them with their inquiries?" Her voice rippled with amusement.

"I did point them in Fitzroy's direction. He has both tractor and Land Rover."

"And motive. Well, thank you, Captain Carradyne for informing me," she added in an abrupt change of tone. "Do keep me posted."

The dial tone sounded in his ear. Michael looked at the receiver for a moment, then replaced it slowly and walked away.

The next morning, when Selina set out for her appointment with the solicitor, she couldn't help but notice the dark gray sedan, still parked in the street, though not in the same spot as the previous day. She was not particularly reassured when the driver started the car as she was pulling out of her courtyard. When it stayed discreetly behind her, often letting another car come between them on the busy main road into Dublin, she made a mental note of the number and jotted it down when she reached Ian Coghlan's offices. As she waited to see the solicitor, she noted that there were several other professionals in the same house, including a gynecologist. She made a second note, smiling to herself.

It was the last time that morning she had occasion to smile, for Sybil had not exaggerated the difficulties faced by an Irish woman wishing to separate herself from her legal spouse. Selina was appalled at how little protection she received under the law. In essence she was no more than a man's chattel. Not even the house—which had been a wedding present from her father—was hers, for she had blithely allowed it to be registered in David's name. He could even sell it without her consent.

David could not, however, touch the income from Funds that had been her mother's legacy to her. Sybil had also been correct in saying that with money of her own, she was in a far better position than many who shared her dilemma. Coghlan also rallied when he realized she had some resources. A legal separation was possible under Irish law, he explained but neither party was permitted to remarry. Furthermore, it was difficult to obtain, a lengthy and expensive process. However, when Selina mentioned that she carried dual citizenship, Coghlan brightened noticeably. An English divorce was a possibility, although Healey could contest it; but she would have to establish a legal residence in England for at least two years.

Selina thought of two years away from Cornanagh and Catriona, away from Michael, and cringed. Coghlan misinterpreted her expression and again recommended that she think long and hard. He would, of course, be glad to assist her as much as he could.

408

"Are there such things as private detectives in Ireland?" she asked Coghlan at the end of the interview.

"Why, yes, of course there are. Why? Are you thinking of finding evidence against your husband?"

"On the contrary, I think it's he who wishes to find against me," she replied, and told him about the faithful gray sedan.

"You have the registration number?" he asked, reaching for the phone. Sure enough, Selina's hunch proved to be correct: the gray sedan was registered to a private investigator. "An expensive one," Coghlan declared, "but the firm is reputable."

"But if there is no divorce in Ireland, what good does that do him?" Selina asked, barely able to contain her fury.

Smiling cynically, Coghlan gestured to her. "With no offense intended, you're an attractive woman, Mrs. Healey. And Mr. Healey's evidently a very suspicious man."

"Oh!"

"I'd be careful, Mrs. Healey. I'd be very careful about everything. Including your visit to me."

Coghlan shook her hand courteously as she rose to leave, assuring her of his help should she decide to proceed.

"Oh, I'll proceed all right, Mr. Coghlan. I'll be careful, and I'll give this matter a great deal of thought, but never doubt for a moment that I will proceed."

In the vestibule, she replaced her eyeglasses and veil before she swept through the door Coghlan held open. He was careful not to be seen from the street.

The gray sedan followed her all the way back to Dalkey.

"Captain Carradyne phoned you again, missus," Kathleen told her when she set her things down in the hall.

"Maybe my tack has been returned; I'll phone later. Has Mr. Healey called?"

Kathleen shook her head and went back to her vacuuming. Selina wondered briefly if David was paying the woman to keep track of her whereabouts. She preferred to think that

Kathleen's first loyalty was to her. Then, with a sigh, she went upstairs to take a long, hot bath.

As she soaked, she grew more and more incensed by her situation, by all the indignities heaped upon a woman in her circumstances. She thought of ringing her father—he always had a soothing effect on her—but she didn't quite like to admit that she was unable to handle this problem herself. No, she decided, she'd gotten herself into this mess; she'd just have to work it out on her own.

She was patting herself dry when the phone rang. Kathleen knocked on the door to say it was Eithne Carradyne calling.

"Oh, marvelous," Selina said, and picked up the bedroom extension. She waited and a minute later heard the distinct click as the downstairs receiver was replaced.

"Eithne, I hear I must wish you happy, and I'm delighted."

"I wish it weren't such a rush and all, Selina. I phoned to tell you that the wedding's set for next Tuesday, and could you possibly attend a small reception after at Cornanagh? There isn't even time to send invitations or anything."

How like Eithne, Selina thought, to worry about protocol at such a time. "I think it's all very romantic."

"You do?"

"Very romantic, and you deserve every bit of happiness. Now, what can I do to help?"

"Help? Oh, that won't be necessary. I mean, Mrs. Comyn is just marvelous about it all. But I've been so concerned . . ."

"Don't worry about Catriona, Eithne," Selina said, anticipating her. "I love that child as I would my own. And I'm at Cornanagh often enough to keep an eye on her."

"Actually, Selina, I'm worried about you. Are you free to speak right now?"

Selina hesitated, hearing the concern in Eithne's voice. "Sybil told you, didn't she."

"Yes . . ."

"Well, she's been a positive brick, Eithne, and I'm all right, really I am. In fact, I'll be over tomorrow, if you'd tell Michael for me. And Catriona."

"Oh, she will be happy. She's missed you terribly, you know, although this morning she's much more herself. Michael's off right now with the Gardái about the robbery."

"Has the tack been recovered?"

"Not exactly, but Sergeant Quinn found a cheekpiece in Mr. Fitzroy's Land Rover, and Michael's gone to the station to identify it." Eithne sounded more upset than pleased.

"Eithne Carradyne, are you blaming yourself for Fitzroy's antics?"

"Davis says I'm enjoying a needless guilt trip."

Selina burst out laughing at the blend of meekness and satisfaction in Eithne's reply. "And so you are! You should be enjoying every moment right now, looking ahead, not backward."

Reiterating her promise to be at Cornanagh early the next morning, Selina rang off. As she began to dress, she found herself smiling—in anticipation of a trip to Cornanagh tomorrow . . . and a visit with Michael.

When Sergeant Quinn displayed the cheekpiece, pointing to the C/c brand on the inside, Michael readily admitted ownership. It also happened to be the same cheekpiece he'd already found once, but he kept quiet on that point.

"Do you want to press charges, Captain?" asked the sergeant.

"I shall have to, with such evidence, Pat."

Sergeant Quinn shook his head. "Fitzroy denies it."

"I'd be exceedingly surprised if he admitted it, wouldn't you?"

"He's also wanting to lay charges against you for letting his cattle into the barley."

"What?" Michael cried, genuinely surprised. "I'd nothing to do with that! When did it happen?"

"Yesterday afternoon." Pat Quinn eyed him carefully.

"Then I know no one at Cornanagh was at fault. Owen and Philip were at work and came home on time. Mick and Artie were in the yard all day, helping with the horses, and so were the girls. No, he'll have to look to someone else for that piece of mischief. And I want to know from him where he dumped my tack!"

Pat Quinn gave the cheekpiece a bit of a brandish. "Fitzroy can't deny this was found in his vehicle. And he was furious." He grinned. "But don't worry—we'll have your tack back, too."

"I sincerely hope so, Pat. I sincerely hope so."

Michael shook hands with Pat Quinn and left the station. On the drive home, he began to think about how much his world had changed in just a few days. There was Philip, of course. He was going to miss that boy, badly. Philip was nearest to him in personality and temperament.

Then he began to chuckle. Sybil was a chip off the old block, too. After she'd had a little word with him about Selina's "trouble," he'd begun to take a less patronizing view of her association with Nualla Fennell and women's rights. Sybil had practically demanded that he offer Selina Eithne's mews! How he had managed to keep a straight face, he did not know. Surprise and shock, probably, that his daughter was insisting that he allow the woman he loved to move into Cornanagh! Selina, he was sure, would appreciate the irony as much as he. But however it was achieved, he wanted Selina away from Healey. More specifically, he wanted her near him—now, and always. . . .

When Michael returned to the yard, he sought Mick immediately. "You'll have heard that Fitzroy's cattle got into his barley?"

Mick's surprise was as genuine as his delight. "Did they,

now? Well, turning the cattle into the barley would be one way to get everyone out of Fitzroy's yard, wouldn't it, Captain?" And Mick, with the beginning of a slow and malicious smile, laid a forefinger along his nose and winked broadly.

Michael pushed his hat back, smoothed his mustache, and indulged himself in a chuckle. So Johnny Cash had planted that cheekpiece, which Mick—no question of it—had slipped to him. Michael gave the old groom full marks.

"If we get the tack back, I won't press charges, but he'll be bound over to keep the peace," Michael said. "Now, I'll school Temper first and get it over with. Where're the girls?"

"They're out on the Ride, for they're to go shopping with their auntie this afternoon." Mick let out a gusty sigh. "Sure, with all the goings and no comings, there's been fierce changes here."

"Most of them to the good, Mick!" Michael gave the old man a friendly clap on the back.

💥 32 💥

O nce again, Selina felt an incredible sense of relief as she turned the Lancia into the courtyard of Cornanagh on Wednesday morning. She parked the car and emerged, inhaling deeply of the fresh, clean air. Safe at last.

"Selina!" With cries of joy, Catriona and Patricia flung themselves out of the house and stampeded across the courtyard.

"Hello, my darlings!" Selina exclaimed, hugging first Catriona and then Patricia. "How are you? I've missed you!" Arms about their waists, she allowed herself to be drawn toward the house.

"We got new dresses to be Eithne's bridesmaids, and Pip's going to Madison Avenue and Owen to Texas," Patricia said.

"And Johnny Cash got your saddle back, and Mr. Hardcastle's and Temper's snaffle bridle and a whole lot of stuff. Oh, there's so much to tell you!" cried Catriona.

Michael stood in the doorway, smiling warmly. "In the dining room, Selina," he said when she turned right to head for the kitchen. He grinned. "Mrs. Comyn doesn't approve of the master eating in his own kitchen!"

"Well, I think she's right," Patricia said stoutly. "And there's not enough room now with all of us. And you haven't met Davis Haggerty, Aunt Eithne's fiancé."

"I was aware of his interest in your aunt long before you were, young miss," Selina teased.

In the dining room Selina embraced Eithne and admired her truly stunning diamond solitaire ring. A proud and happy

Davis stepped forward to be introduced, and Philip and Owen looked up from their breakfast to say hello. When Mrs. Comyn appeared from the kitchen with a fresh pot of coffee and the cream pitcher, Eithne did the honors.

"How do you do, Mrs. Healey?" the housekeeper replied politely as she set the coffeepot down by Eithne. "Would you be wishing breakfast?"

"No, no, thanks. Coffee would be grand."

Eithne served Selina coffee, and fresh hot toast was offered. Selina was aware that Michael was watching her as she quietly buttered a slice, letting the conversation flow about her.

"We're going to have the grooviest reception, even if it is at short notice," Patricia told her. "Mrs. Comyn's a wonder."

"Oh, she is, Selina," Eithne agreed fervently. "She's just taken over as if she'd always been here. Said that there's nothing she likes better than preparing for parties, and I think she means it. She's got Bridie eating out of her hand." Eithne frowned. "I only hope it can last."

"Why should you worry, Mother?" Owen said. "You'll be in Texas."

"Oh, but I would worry. You don't live in a place for twenty-five years and forget it in a snap," Eithne replied gently.

"It'll last," Selina said reassuringly.

The phone rang, and a moment later Mrs. Comyn came in, nodding to Michael.

"Who is it, Mrs. Comyn?" he asked.

"I'd say by the accent it's your man again," she replied cryptically.

Michael pressed Selina's shoulder in passing, with a grin that promised an explanation when he returned.

"You wouldn't credit it, Selina," Philip began when his father had left the room, "but these culchies got Dad on the phone last night with a deal for his lost tack. We've already got half of it back, but they're scared of the Gardái, and Dad's having the worst trouble arranging a meet."

"What's this?" Selina asked. "I thought the tack was all stolen by Fitzroy."

Philip grinned. "It was, but he dumped it. In three places, as near as we can discover, and those guys on the phone right now found some."

"I think it's crazy, the victims having to arrange with the thieves to return the loot," grumbld Pat.

"So long as we get it back," Catriona said fervently.

"Amen," Philip replied, and grimaced at Selina. "Mr. Evans loaned Dad an eighteen-inch saddle, but it doesn't fit me like my own does. And I've galls to prove it." He rubbed his knees.

"Well, it fits Emmett," Catriona said, and was surprised when her brother laughed and tugged her hair.

"We're making progress," Michael said, rubbing his hands together as he came back into the room. "They've agreed to deliver the tack to Johnny Cash. I'm to leave the 'finder's fee' with him, but if they so much as see a Gardá car or bike, the deal's off. You know where Johnny's camped, don't you, Pip? I'll give you the cash to take in, with a backhander to Johnny for all his trouble. Now"—he clapped his hands together—"let's get to work, troop!" He winked at Selina. "Trina, Pat, you'll hack to the leg pond hill and to the top at a working trot. Off you go, now." He gave Eithne an unexpected hug and kissed her cheek. "And you are not to worry, Eithne!"

"Oh, Michael!"

"You heard him, Eithne," Davis said, and embraced his surprised fiancée before she could say anything more.

"Michael," Selina began as the room cleared, "David neglected to leave me any housekeeping money this time, so I'll need some of those notes you're holding for me."

"There was rather a lot in those bundles, Selina. I ought to give you a receipt."

"Really, Michael!"

He grinned and led her to the hallway, where he paused, listening. Then, with a sharp nod of his head, he went to the stairs and pressed two portions of the decorative molding. A panel slid back, and he gestured for Selina to enter with him, then closed the hidden entrance. Light filtered into the space from several openings high in the outside wall. Michael flicked a switch on the wall, and a dim bulb illuminated the huge antique safe that stood in the slope of the rising staircase.

As Selina took in her surroundings, Michael set the combination and opened the heavy door, which gave with a well-oiled snick. He offered her one of the sealed bundles, and she quickly removed two hundred pounds, then handed it back. From his own supply he removed what he needed and closed the heavy door.

"This couldn't have been a priest's hole," she said softly, glancing about her.

"No, it sheltered rebellious Irishmen, and women, or so the family history suggests."

"But I thought the Carradynes were Royalists."

"Not all." He winked at her, then opened the panel, listening a moment. Abruptly, he gestured at her to leave and shut the panel behind them. He grinned at their timing, for a moment later Philip came out of his room, and Owen, Eithne, and Davis entered from the courtyard.

As soon as they were alone again, Selina turned to Michael.

"David has hired a private detective to follow me. Someone in a gray Ford sedan. He's been trailing me for days—in fact, he's probably out there, now, waiting."

"What?" Michael's expression was a combination of outrage, fury, and incredulity.

"I spotted him the other day, and when I gave the solicitor the registration number, he had it checked."

Michael took hold of her shoulders. "Selina, listen . . . I want you to come here—to Cornanagh—to live. Once Eithne leaves, the mews will be empty, and it's yours—if you want it."

She smiled and patted his hand. "That's a good thought, Michael, but it might add more problems than it solves. I'm applying for a separation."

"Good!" Michael cried, relieved.

"That's not to say I'll get it," she added, unable to suppress a note of bitterness. "You men really have it all your own way here in Ireland, a fact I never previously appreciated."

"Nor I," Michael replied with dry sympathy. "But Sybil has been a mine of information." He spotted Mick standing in the yard entrance. "Come on, let's saddle up. We can talk as we ride."

"Out there?" She gestured to the road.

"No, we'll keep to the Ride for privacy. Though I don't like the idea of your being kept under surveillance."

"At first I was scared," Selina admitted. "Then I thought of the funny side—the idea that this poor man has to follow me all over town and sit in that car waiting on my next move. And I decided to make it as difficult for him as possible. The Lancia's a lot faster and handier than the Ford he's driving."

"You are marvelous, Selina, absolutely marvelous," Michael said, laughing.

"Morning, Mick," Selina said as they crossed the yard.

"Morning, missus. Get Charlie for Miz Healey, Artie," the old groom ordered, then turned back to Selina with a warm smile. "Your saddle took no harm a good soaping couldn't fix, Miz Healey," he went on, touching his cap brim. "Wish I could say the same for all the tack."

"Oh, Michael, was much damaged?"

"Hardcastle's saddle was in the puddle at the bottom of the ditch, and two of our hunting Berneys," Michael admitted. "Fortunately the numnah on yours absorbed much of the dampness, and the saddle dried out in the sun yesterday. The bridles'll come right, too, but we're still missing five saddles, the show bridles, all the bits, the spare stirrup leathers, girths, that sort of accessory."

"Is that what you're hoping will be delivered to Johnny Cash today?"

Mick was growling under his breath as he brought the excited Temper to where Michael could swing up on him. Charlie, ears pricked, walked quietly beside Artie.

"Hoping is right. It's amazing how much accumulates over the years. We've only one head collar in the place, and that's been borrowed from Bobbie Evans." He swung up on Temper, who backed against the weight. "Watch the off side, Mick!" Michael cried. Temper reared, and Michael brought his fist down on the gelding's poll. Temper landed hard on the cobbles, shaking his head in surprise. "That's enough of that! Let's go, Selina."

Mick gave her a leg up, and suddenly Selina was acutely aware of the pressure a saddle exerted between her legs. She tried to make herself relax and pressed Charlie's sides to follow the dancing Temper out of the yard. How was she ever going to explain to Michael why she couldn't ride all morning?

Once they turned down the Ride, Michael set Temper into a working trot to take the edge off his freshness. Rising to the trot made it easier for Selina, as Charlie had such a smooth gait. Then, with the inspiration born of necessity, she rose in her stirrups to the hunting position, which eased the pain in her crotch. Michael had his hands too full of Temper to notice.

Just when Selina wondered if she could last a full round of the Ride at their current pace, Michael pulled up. She reined Charlie in beside him, wincing as she settled back into the saddle.

"Now, then, missus," Michael said, "he caused more than the visible bruises, didn't he?" His expression—suddenly so severe and uncompromising, his eyes almost gray in their bleakness—startled Selina. "Dismount!"

Surprised, she swung down and was pulled into his arms. She had to fight an initial involuntary panic at the sudden contact. This is Michael! she told herself. This is Michael. His grasp was strong but tender, the difference palpable in the careful way he placed his fingers to avoid the bruises he could see and the way he moved his body to adjust to hers. She had to force herself to relax, but it was suddenly easier to do so as his mustache brushed against her forehead. Then he tucked her cheek against his and just held her, stroking her hair. They stood like that for several moments, quietly and tenderly. And as Selina experienced the essence of the man who embraced her, all her fears, all her tension, melted away.

"I love you, Selina," he said, tilting her head up to search her eyes. "I have no right to, but I will protect you any way I can. D'you want me to see if I can get that private detective arrested for loitering? What with the burglary and all, I know Pat Quinn would send him packing if I asked him to."

Selina shook her head. "I've decided to use it to advantage, Michael," she said, and gave him a kiss on the cheek. "Besides, I think it would be the height of folly to interfere with David's little plans. I also can't stay long today, Captain, sor." She felt his body tense, and she tightened her arms about him, stroking the firm muscles in his shoulders. "As soon as I get home, I'm phoning Coghlan to tell him to proceed with the separation plans. He wanted me to take time to consider the problem from all angles. Well, I've considered—all night!"

"From what Sybil said about separations, it won't be easy, dear heart," he said, his eyes clouding with concern.

"Then I'll just pack up and come to Cornanagh!"

"Good! I'd feel much easier having you near me."

"So would I," she agreed stoutly, "and it's nice to know I've a bolt hole. But the Dalkey house is mine, and I won't evacuate without a fight."

He gave her a little squeeze, pleased with her resolution. Suddenly Charlie gave an impatient tug of the reins, pulling Selina out of Michael's embrace.

"Let him go; he'll graze," Michael said, helping her disentangle the reins. Then he held her close and kissed her gently, and she responded willingly, pressing her body against his because he was Michael.

"I love you, Selina," he said when their lips parted, "and I want to marry you, if that's ever possible. You should know this, even if you don't feel the same."

"No fear on that score, Michael," she murmured, reaching up to touch his lips. "I do. . . . I'm only alive here at Cornanagh."

A wry smile touched his lips. "I'm only alive when you're here."

Just then Temper pulled him off balance, to reach out for fresher greener grass. When Michael made to release the reins, she laughed.

"I'd've said you were only alive whenever you're on horseback. I never thought I'd see the day when Michael Carradyne ignored his horses."

He grimaced. "And I can't ignore Temper, damn it. He can't be allowed to get away with anything. But I haven't had any time with you at all!" Temper pulled again, and Selina laughed. "Damn! Look, I'll just jump him down the alley, Selina. Charlie doesn't need work, so relax for a while." He pointed to the bank.

She watched as Michael schooled Temper down the jump alley, and she was able to see how much the gelding was improving. As Michael jumped him back down toward her, Temper's ears were pricked, and he seemed to flow over the fences, front feet well tucked up.

"He's come on enormously, Michael," she said, reaching up to pat the gelding's neck. "He really enjoyed that jumping."

She had gathered Charlie's reins to remount, but Michael was beside her in an instant, ready to give her a leg up. Then he rested his hand lightly on her left thigh, his eyes anxious.

"Really, Michael, I'll be all right."

When he had remounted Temper, he guided the gelding to her side and, stretching out his hand, held hers until they turned off the Ride into the yard.

"I've got to get back, Michael," she said as Mick and Artie led away the two horses. "I've errands I must get done today. But I'll be back tomorrow, early. Eithne's wedding gives me a valid excuse to be here, to help. So I'll stay longer tomorrow. And ride."

"You will be careful, Selina," Michael said urgently, leaning in the Lancia's window and gripping her shoulder.

"Of course," she said blithely, starting the car.

For one fleeting moment, she thought she had lost her shadow. Where he had been parked she never found out, but by the time she was driving past the cemetery, she caught a glimpse of him in the rearview mirror. The confidence she'd gained from her time with Michael supported her firmly. She would not yield to David's little ploys and indignities. She would also not let him contaminate Cornanagh.

Now that she had cash again, she did some shopping and returned, banners flying, to the house. Kathleen reported no phone messages at all, so Selina went up to her room to make a phone call she had too long deferred.

"I am filing for a separation from David, Father," she announced calmly after they had chatted for a few minutes. "He's gotten far too involved with his affairs in the North. He's there more than he's here in Dublin, and it's no way to conduct a marriage."

"Well, no one can predict the course of a marriage, Sellie."

The old boy sounds pleased, she thought. Well, he'd predicted this, and he does so enjoy to be right.

"D'you need money?" he asked brightly.

Selina chuckled as she thought of the several thousand pounds in notes lodged at Cornanagh. "No, actually, David was unexpectedly generous. I fear he'll take the house, though."

"Hmmm? Will you remove to London?"

She smiled, thinking of her father's cozy little male sanctuary. He had bought a flat in Chelsea, which was run by his aged butler and an equally elderly valet, and on her infrequent trips to London she had invariably felt herself to be an intruder. "No, I shall stay here in Ireland, Father. D'you remember my mentioning the Cornanagh stud, the place where I've been boarding my hunter? Well, I may go into horses after all."

"Left it a bit late, m'dear, haven't you?"

"We'll see."

"If Healey gives you any sort of trouble, you will let me know, won't you?" Generations of aristocracy rang through the amiable query.

"Of course," she agreed.

Her father's support, coupled with Sybil's comfort and Michael's concern, cheered Selina considerably, and she rang off a few minutes later, promising her father she'd keep in touch.

Eithne had informed her friends and the rest of her family—her Carradyne nieces and nephews and her sister-in-law, Margaret Coyne—of her impending nuptials, and on Wednesday all the women arrived for tea. Eithne was in a fine fluster making sure everything was prepared.

"Not that I need to worry with Mrs. Comyn in charge," she told Catriona and Patricia, "but you will change, won't you, girls?"

Both girls agreed to behave for the entire afternoon. Patricia, teasing that no one was going to notice *them* no matter how they looked, put on a pretty summer frock in a teal blue that accented her eyes and coloring. It was rather more mature than anything Catriona possessed, but Pat always looked more grown up than she did in any sort of clothes.

Catriona washed and plaited her hair, and put on her best dress, but she felt very gauche suddenly, especially when she realized the hem was much too short. She looked longingly at her bridesmaid's dress, hanging in the wardrobe. *That* made her look ever so much more grown up.

It was not a boring afternoon for Catriona, because everyone was really delighted about Eithne's getting married, but it served to emphasize the changes in Cornanagh. Catriona didn't want anyone to think she wasn't happy for Auntie Eithne, or glad to see Owen go, or sorry that Philip was leaving, too, so she smiled a great deal and remembered to ask her sister-in-law Susan about her nieces and nephews and Auntie Margaret about her cousins.

But when she heard Tory creating a stink in the courtyard, she had to look out the window. And because it was Johnny Cash's van, she forgot everything else and dashed out to see if he really had gotten the rest of the tack.

He had, and nearly everything was either dried mud or soggy with slime. Her father told her to change out of her good clothes and ask Bridie for something from the kitchen to feed Johnny and his kids.

Catriona told Patricia, and together they changed into work clothes and raided the kitchen without asking Bridie. They spirited the food out to the yard, where Johnny and his kids, Mick, Artie, and her father were carefully checking over the returned tack. All the saddles were there, even Pat's, and only one was damaged beyond repair. Then, when Johnny and his lot had been duly fed and thanked, the girls got buckets of warm water, and everyone pitched in to clean and soap the abused leather.

One hour later, Margaret, Susan, and Sybil found everyone muddy, soapy, and too involved with tack cleaning to remember their social graces. The younger women had the sense to realize how important the return was, but Michael's sister was less understanding.

"Michael, Eithne will be leaving, and you spend your time mucking about with dirty leather?" Margaret scolded. "Really, you may be my brother, but you are a . . . a . . . "

"Male chauvinist pig?" Patricia suggested, wringing out a sponge.

"Patricia!" cried her aunt, appalled.

"Once Eithne sees all our tack back in place, Meg, she'll feel a lot less guilty, so it'll have been worth the social lapse." Michael dried his hands off enough to give his sister a quick embrace. "Have a safe ride home, and give my regards to Tom."

Margaret's exit served to speed the other women, which allowed Cornanagh's diligent workers to get back to the important work at hand. By teatime everything had been cleaned and hung back in its usual place, and the tack room looked proper again.

"Well, we'll check against the inventory tomorrow," Michael said as he walked with Mick to the ride gate. "I think we've got almost everything back."

"No small mercy that, Captain. I'll nivver say a word against Johnny Cash, no matter what sort of crock he brings us," Mick promised fervently, and said good night.

Thursday and Friday found Cornanagh back to a more normal working routine. Selina arrived early, joining them at the breakfast table and hearing all the news. Although Michael let her school Charlie for half an hour and had her sit briefly on Wicket, he was relieved when she went off with Eithne and the girls in the afternoon to shop.

Friday was more of the same, but Selina joined them for tea.

"Trina is showing Tulip's Son with you tomorrow at Castle-town, isn't she?" she asked him before she left.

"Yes, she manages him better than anyone else."

"Much like your father and the Tulip?"

He was rather surprised at the analogy and had to think a moment before he agreed that yes, they were. The smile she gave him was so warm, so filled with understanding and humor, that he felt relieved of some of the anxiety her situation had been causing him. He ventured to ask about her progress with the solicitor, and she could only say that the matter had been set in progress.

"I haven't heard from David at all. He may be trying to give me enough rope to hang myself," she concluded as she settled herself in the Lancia. "But it may just hang him."

Michael slept badly that night, hearing in every night sound the ring of the phone or a strange noise in the yard. Dawn found him wide awake, so he got up, showered, and shaved. Mrs. Comyn was already in the kitchen, neatly dressed and brewing the coffee, when he walked in.

"Now this isn't necessary, Mrs. Comyn," he protested.

"These long summer days are too beautiful to waste, Captain," she replied, and actually gave him a smile. "And there's rather a lot to organize for next Tuesday."

"We've thrown you in at the deep end, haven't we."

"I like to keep busy. In a happy house, it's no chore." She left him to enjoy his first cup and reflect on their brief exchange.

Then he heard Mick's morning whistle and went out to help with the morning feeds, keeping himself busy until he saw Selina's Lancia pull into the courtyard. Contented, he watched Catriona and Patricia haul her into the dining room for a second breakfast.

Everything proceeded according to plan that morning, loading all the horses and the clean, recovered tack, and setting off for the Castletown show in their miniature convoy. In his rearview mirror, he saw the gray Ford sedan pull in behind the lorry and cursed. Then grinned.

"What's funny, Dad?" Philip asked.

"Nothing, Pip, nothing at all."

Castletown was a popular show, with many spectators enjoying the summer weather. The Cornanagh contingent managed to park well back in the field reserved for lorries and horseboxes. Michael, keeping watch, saw that the gray Ford was shunted into another field.

Selina went off with the girls to collect numbers and get programs. When she returned it was to find out that they would have to scurry to make all the various classes.

The mare and foal class was first, and when he and Trina came away with red ribbons, Michael began to feel better about the day. Philip had some stiff competition, but Cornanagh's quality and presentation won out in the end as both Emmett and Minister came away with firsts in their respective classes.

In the 13.2 jump-off, Catriona and Conker, next to last in the third round, carved three seconds off the best score to win. Selina gave her a big hug and kiss while Patricia did a war dance.

"Oh, Lord, here's trouble," Selina said, breaking off her congratulations as she watched an odd trio coming down the field toward the pony ring.

"Oh, Gawd!" echoed Patricia. "Just what my nerves need!"

Catriona looked around and recognized the Doherty contingent, Sean still in plaster, with his father on one side and an unknown man on the other.

The unknown was introduced as Barry Sweeney. In a slight northern accent, he congratulated Catriona politely on the red first prize ribbon in her hand and glanced out at the ring where the course was being walked for the 14.2 class.

"C'mon, Pat, Trina says that the turn from the double to the stile could cause the Prince trouble. Trina, give him a few pops while we're walking the course, will you?" said Michael.

Catriona tried to suppress her anxiety as she and Selina walked Conker back to the box. Mick was tacking up the Prince, who was, as usual, affected by the excitement of a show and crowds.

"Now, Trina, you're not upset at seeing the Dohertys, are you?" Selina asked, peering at her.

"Pat's been riding him ever so much better. She's a far better rider than Sean ever was—the Prince doesn't get away with half as much with her up." Catriona knew she sounded scared, but she had no way of expressing her true anxiety.

"Up you get, now, Cat," Mick said, "and don't you worry about a thing. Miz Healey's right: your cousin's turning into a good little rider, though she's not up to your standard, not by a long chalk."

Selina walked beside the Prince on the way to the practice fence, smiling up at Catriona so encouragingly that it made everything much worse. If Selina ever knew . . .

Then, the magic of being in the saddle of a nervy horse claimed her, and she began to work the Prince in, curbing his excitement firmly and easily until he began to settle. She put him over the jump three times and then saw her father waving her over, Patricia at his side.

"Now that he's warmed up for me," Pat said in an outrageously posh voice, "I'll take over, dear." She gave Catriona a sly dig in the ribs and a wicked grin.

Catriona could see the Dohertys and Mr. Sweeney watching as the change was made. The Prince fussed a bit as her father took the stirrups down for the longer-legged Patricia, but when she let him move out, he went smoothly. Twice Pat popped him neatly over the practice jump, and then it was time for him to enter the ring for the first round.

Catriona was aware that she held her breath the entire time.

She had spots in front of her eyes when the Prince and Patricia cantered out with a clear round. Then she saw that Mr. Doherty did not appear pleased and was talking to Mr. Sweeney. Sean looked unhappy and uncomfortable and wouldn't meet her eyes.

In the second round Patricia provided a couple of nervous moments. The Prince had done a scrabbling turn to the stile and taken it at an angle, almost overshooting the next fence. But Patricia checked and corrected him, and he took the next four fences flawlessly until he was headed for the pocket and out. Then he picked up speed and began to flatten, coming up to the wall. Patricia was seen to lift him up and over, and the brick he displaced remained on the wall until they were past the finish marker.

"Well ridden," Michael said, coming up to put a hand on the sidling pony.

"Yeah, I did that right, didn't I? I asked the question, and he gave me the right answer." Pat was excited, her face bright with exertion and triumph. She slapped the Prince's sweating neck as the Dohertys came up.

"Carradyne, a word with you!" Bob Doherty looked odd; his eyes were narrowed, and his jaw sort of jutted out as he beckoned to the Captain. Catriona felt a stab of pure terror. She stared at Sean, who was avoiding her—had, she realized, avoided her all morning. Guiltily!

She saw her father listening intently to what Mr. Doherty was saying; then he leaned back and half-smiled, glanced over at Catriona, and shook his head. Mr. Doherty did not look pleased at that, but her father merely bowed slightly to both Doherty and Sweeney and left them. Next he had a word with Mick, who shrugged off what her father said with a grin and a quick phrase. Only then did Michael come back to her.

He knew about the spring show! Sean *had* told his father. Catriona wanted to die. Why hadn't she confessed when she had a chance? Why had she let him find out, here, in the most public spot?

"What was that all about, Michael?" Selina asked when he reached them. "Doherty can't be displeased with Pat's ride. She lifted him over that wall like Iris Kellett."

"He wants me to put Trina up for the final round," her father said, a funny grin on his face as he glanced down at Catriona, "just as we did in the Spring Show."

"What?" Selina stared at Catriona, stunned. Catriona bit her lip and closed her eyes. "Well, I'm glad that mystery's been solved. I couldn't imagine how on earth Sean did it. Why, Catriona, how clever of you to save the day!"

Startled, Catriona opened her eyes to stare first at Selina and then at her father. She couldn't believe it, but he didn't seem angry, only sad.

"Is that what's been tormenting you, Trina?" he asked, slipping an arm about her shoulders.

Wanting to sob out her relief that he didn't hate her, she clung to his belt loop and hid her face against him. Then she felt Selina's hand on her head, stroking her hair.

"Trina, it's all right," her father said, and tilted her head up. "It's not something I ever want you to do again, mind, but Mick said it had been all his idea, with the boy sicking up his guts in the pocket. But I think this is Pat's last round on the Prince."

"Why?" Catriona could barely get the question out.

"Well, Bob Doherty didn't take kindly to my refusal, although I pointed out that such a substitution was not only inadvisable but illegal. He was stuck with Pat as the rider today. So, since he wants the pony to win no matter what rules are bent or fractured, I told him that I'd drop the Prince off at his stable on the way back tonight."

"But Pat's qualified him for the horse show!" Catriona was appalled.

"True enough, and the qualification holds. But for another rider."

Selina put an arm around her waist, and her father gave her a little squeeze before he released her. Pat's cheerful voice warned them of her approach.

"We'll say nothing right now before the speed round," her father said, and walked over to give his niece a final word of advice.

"Pat's going to hate me," Catriona murmured.

"I doubt it," Selina said with a laugh. "She much prefers Annie, you know. And I must say, I'll be glad to see the last of the Dohertys."

"But what if—"

"Catriona Carradyne," Selina said, giving her a little shake, "do you enjoy being miserable?"

"No, of course not."

"Then stop it. There's so much to be happy about today. Don't spoil it. And if there's anything bothering you, tell us. Don't fret yourself."

Selina tipped Catriona's head up, and she could see the sadness and anxiety in the lovely blue eyes, so candid in their gaze, so trusting, and so very, very young.

"But I know Daddy's disappointed in me . . ."

"Not a bit of it, Catriona. Oh, c'mon, Pat's started!"

Selina took Catriona's hand and raced with her to the sidelines, where Michael, Philip, and Mick watched Pat going flat out with the Prince's full cooperation. If only they could go clear, she prayed. That'd show Bob Doherty! She caught her breath as Pat hauled the Prince around a standard; it set him to a jump at an angle but gave her a good line for the next obstacle. She checked the pony and for an instant seemed to hang above the saddle, losing both stirrups. Catriona gave a little moan, but by some miracle of balance, horse and rider remained together. Pat retrieved one iron, banging both heels against the pony's sides as she approached the triple. One stride between, over, then two more strides and out over the parallel. The pony executed a turn on his off fore and somehow lost neither balance nor impulsion heading for the final wall. The Prince took off a long way from the hurdle, but he soared over it neatly and sped past the electric eye. Pat dropped the reins to link both arms about the galloping pony's neck in her enthusiasm. She hadn't needed the announcer's confirmation of their winning time. Spectators gave way, applauding her as she collected her reins to pull the blowing Prince to a walk. Her face was flushed with triumph, and she was beaming with satisfaction as she came to a halt by the Cornanagh contingent.

"Well, that was a spectacular round, Patricia," Michael said heartily, giving the Prince an approving slap on the rump.

Selina and Mick rushed up to add their congratulations, and even Catriona put aside her worries to offer her cousin the praise she deserved.

33

*E*xcept for Bob Doherty, the first day of the Castletown show was an unqualified success. Lady Madeline and her filly foal, whom Pat had nicknamed the Bridesmaid, were again second in their class, and the yearlings had been first and third. Charlie got the blue second in the three-year-old in-hand, but as Selina told the disappointed Catriona, he'd been in excellent company.

Pat, of course, had to be told that the Prince was being returned to the Dohertys at Foxrock.

"What'd I do wrong? I won, didn't I? Whadda they want out of a free rider?" she demanded, more surprised than insulted.

"Owners are capricious, Pat," her uncle told her. "Frankly, I'll be glad to see the last of Ballymore Prince."

"Me, too," Mick said, scowling. "Little sod!"

Michael put the Prince and his tack in the horsebox with Charlie and detoured from the homeward-bound Cornanagh convoy to drop the pony off at the Foxrock residence. There was no one there, so he put the pony in the first clean stable, gave him hay and water. Then he and Philip put the tack box in an empty stable and left.

By Monday, Selina was finally comfortable enough in saddle to go on a long hack with Michael and the girls. When they returned to Cornanagh, the atmosphere was close to frantic with preparations for Eithne's wedding and reception, and the riders escaped gratefully to school the second lot of horses, leaving Susan, Sybil, Margaret, and Mrs. Comyn to cope with Eithne and all the arrangements.

When the riders returned, Mrs. Comyn told the captain that an Italian named D'Albretti had rung, asking if he and some friends, the Bartolomeo brothers, could come and see the Cornanagh horses.

"I conferred with Mr. Lenahan, and he felt it wasn't wise to delay an answer, so a meeting was arranged for three o'clock this afternoon."

"My God, thank you, Mrs. Comyn. That's perfect." He turned to Selina and grabbed her by the shoulders. "God, the Bartolomeo brothers! They're exactly the market I've been aiming at. But where's Harry, dammit? I can't ask Pip to take time off from work right now."

"Why bother Harry? I'm grand now, Michael," Selina said. "With four Italians around, I assure you I'll feel a lot safer in a saddle. Unless you think I wouldn't show the horses off properly?" She glanced at him slyly.

"You wouldn't mind? Of course, they might just want to see the horses lunged over fences . . ."

"They can't pinch me in the saddle, Michael." She winked at Mrs. Comyn, who was standing in polite attendance. Selina was sure she saw the woman's lips twitch briefly. "How's your Italian, Mrs. Comyn?"

"Sufficient. For refreshments, I think they'd prefer aperitifs to tea, Captain. I'll have Bridie make some of those hot savories she does so well."

"Thank you, Mrs. Comyn, you're a marvel," Michael said. Grabbing Selina's hand, he pulled her back to the yard, calling for Mick and the girls.

By three o'clock, when the chauffeured Mercedes limousine purred through the gates of Cornanagh, there wasn't so much as a blade of grass out of place in the two yards. Mick had organized clean shirts and vests for himself and Artie, while

Catriona and Patricia were turned out in Pony Club fashion. Selina had sponged the saddle soap from her jods and commandeered a clean shirt and smart linen waistcoat from Eithne.

The effort was worthwhile, for when Ignacio D'Albretti introduced the Bartolomeos to her, they were properly flattering. Selina managed to respond with courteous Italian phrases and was rewarded with such a spate of Italian that she had to laugh and admit to her poor command of the language. She was pleased when Raimondo Bartolomeo was just as attentive to Patricia and Catriona. Although he was courteous enough to Patricia, he surprised them all by caressing Catriona's cheek and muttering appreciatively in Italian. Catriona flicked a glance at Selina, who smiled encouragingly, and then curtsied, shyly grinning up at the solemn Italian.

Thus the ritual began. First, the horses were shown in hand so that their conformation could be appreciated. Next, Emmett and Minister were lunged over uprights that Mick, Artie, and Barry had hastily constructed in the menage. Finally, saddles were brought, and the entire group hiked down to the jump alley, over which the Bartolomeos exclaimed with delight and many Italianesque gestures.

"Two is all you have?" Raimondo Bartolomeo demanded after Selina had jumped both horses down the alley.

"Two produced and ready to be schooled on," Michael said. Then, catching the disappointment in the Italians' faces, he admitted that he had several more in training.

Temper, Wicket, and Racketeer were consequently brought out and lunged over the jumps. Temper understandably caught their eyes, with his proud and upright carriage and audacious manner, though they also lingered over Racketeer. The brown gelding was the bigger animal, standing 16.3 hands high with the superb front end of his sire. But when the Bartolomeos asked to see Temper ridden over jumps, Michael hesitated. He didn't want to outface the animal, particularly with his volatile personality. But before he could decide one way or the other, he saw Mick saddling Temper and Selina ready to mount. She winked at him, and then Mick gave her a leg up.

Fortunately Temper responded well to Selina and took both uprights with an economy of movement, tucking all four legs neatly out of the way as if he were a seasoned jumper. The Bartolomeos nodded their heads and made admiring grimaces. When Selina offered the reins to Raimondo, he gestured at his dress slacks and grinned his refusal.

To Michael's deep gratification, the Italians then asked to see his young horses and were thus conducted to the fields. The conformation of the yearlings and two-year-olds was examined and exclaimed over, and the brood mares were inspected with their current foals.

The ritual completed, Michael offered refreshment. Catriona and Patricia served the hot canapés that Mrs. Comyn brought in, and as the Italians took their leave, Raimondo bowed over Catriona's hand and offered her a charming compliment, which flustered her completely. Patricia managed to flirt with the man, and he pinched her cheek.

"We see you at the show, Capitano?" the elder Bartolomeo asked politely as they were escorted to the limousine.

"Yes, indeed, Major Bartolomeo."

"We talk again, then. At the show."

Everyone managed to contain their jubilation until the Mercedes had left the yard. Then every moment of the afternoon was carefully reexamined to decide whether there was genuine interest in the Cornanagh horses.

"I think they're going for Temper," was Selina's opinion. "He just flew those fences. He gave me a great feeling."

"Yes, but the Bartolomeos need international-caliber horses."

"And the Tulip hasn't produced any? Come on, now, that

horse had great heart and scope," Selina said, and Mick nodded emphatically.

"I think they liked Racketeer more," Patricia said. "They had their heads together all the time Selina was showing him."

"Well, they'll be in every other yard in Wicklow, Kildare, and Meath, so let's not raise any false hopes," Michael reminded them.

"I think you were done a signal honor, Captain, sor, when they wanted to see everything you have here," Selina said, grinning.

"Everything except Charlie," Patricia said bluntly.

Michael saw the disappointment on Catriona's face as well. "That, my dear niece, was because I do not wish to be offered a price for Charlie that I can't refuse!"

"Oh, my God," Selina interrupted, glancing at her watch. "I've got to fly. Kathleen's terrified of setting the burglar alarm off if she leaves the house."

"We can't thank you enough, Selina," Michael said, walking her to the Lancia. "You were marvelous today."

"We won't be sure of that," she teased, "until we sees their wads of lira!"

She could see that he wanted very much to kiss her, but they had to be content with shaking hands. As she pulled out of the courtyard, she grinned ruefully; it had never occurred to her that a simple handshake could also convey sensuality.

Eithne's wedding day dawned bright and clear, and Selina was out of the house as soon as Kathleen arrived. Wedding notwithstanding, there were horses to be ridden and a great many last minute preparations for the luncheon reception. Selina had packed an overnight case with a change of underwear, cosmetics, and the dress she planned to wear at the reception. She had elected not to attend the ceremony, as the register office was going to be crowded with Carradynes, Coynes, and

Gavaghans: even Bridie's presence had been specifically requested.

Of course, there were enough minor crises that morning to keep everyone on the hop: Owen's brother Harry couldn't find his tie, Eithne had a fit of last minute qualms, and Catriona's hem came adrift and Mrs. Comyn had to sew it in. Owen and Michael, on the other hand, were ready ahead of time and passing remarks about people in dithers and hysterics on auspicious occasions. Selina was very glad to see them all depart in their various cars at last. Sometimes so many tall Carradynes could be overpowering, she thought.

"A cup of tea, Mrs. Healey?" Mrs. Comyn suggested, and Selina gratefully agreed.

"We've about an hour before any of the reception guests will arrive, Mrs. Healey," the housekeeper said as Selina sipped her tea. "Why don't you take a little rest before you change?"

"Only if you promise me that you'll put your feet up for a bit, too, Mrs. Comyn," Selina said, trying to sound stern.

The woman shrugged. "I'll do just that, Mrs. Healey."

Yes, Selina thought wryly as she left her checking the reception rooms. When pigs fly.

At Catriona's insistence, Selina had deposited her case in the girls' room. She sponged off quickly and changed her lingerie, then lay down. She didn't think she'd dozed off, at least for not more than a moment or two, when she heard a car drive into the court. Startled, she glanced at her watch, then rose and shrugged into her dress. They must have made very good time, she thought, and started for the door. She had her hand on the doorknob when she heard the voice bellowing her name. David's voice.

Astonished, she opened the door and saw him charging up the stairs, his face contorted with fury.

"I've caught you, you bitch! Where is he?"

"Where is who?" Selina backed into the room, startled and confused.

David pushed her roughly aside and began opening closet doors. "Your lover! I know you've got one, you—you cunt!"

"David, I was changing my dress for the reception," she cried, desperate to calm him down. "Look, this is a child's room, not a love nest." She gestured at the bunk beds, the schoolbooks on the shelves, the ribbons that adorned the walls.

"Where is he?"

"There's a wedding in this house today, David. I'm an invited guest. Didn't Kathleen tell you that? I left a message last night for you at the Belfast number. Where the hell do you get your staff in the North?" She tried to sound more annoyed than frightened.

David, having finished his tour of the room, whirled on her again. "You close your face, bitch. I use what means I can to rescue the business which permits you to play gracious lady and get invited to weddings!" He mimicked her with a sneer. "What else do you ride here, every day, all day?"

"Well, you should know, shouldn't you? The man you hired to follow me should have a full report of all my activities!"

David's eyes narrowed, and he began to clench and un-clench his fists.

"What's the matter? Did you think I was so stupid that I wouldn't notice your little shadow? Ah . . ." Suddenly Selina realized what had brought David down from the north. "He saw me leave this morning with an overnight case and came to the only logical conclusion for a man of his occupation—that I was off to meet a lover. Well, the only lovers in this house are the two who are getting married today. Sorry, David, it won't wear!"

"You sneaky bitch, Declan's right about you!" Moving far more quickly than she had expected, he crossed the distance between them and slapped her viciously across her cheek. The left one, of course—she even felt the skin break across the barely healed cut. "You're my wife!" He punctuated that with another slap, and she felt blood trickling from her nose.

I should at least have ducked, she thought, stunned by the successive blows.

"You tend to *my* house and *my* needs, not some jumped-up culchie horse trader!"

David grabbed her by the arm and hauled her out the door and around to the steps. She collided with him as he stopped, for on the top step was Mick, shotgun in hand, and behind him were Barry with an axe and Artie with a pitchfork. As if at a great distance, she heard Mrs. Comyn talking urgently to someone.

"That's far enough," Mick cried. "Miz Healey, you step back!"

"And what the fuck do you think you're doing?" David bellowed. He made no attempt to move on, however, so Selina wrenched her hand free and tried to step around him. He yanked her back.

Mick took one look at her face, and his eyes narrowed with fury. "I'm holding you here, you bastard, until the Gardái arrive."

"Don't bother. They can't interfere in a domestic matter," David sneered. "She's my wife."

"You're her husband?" The shotgun barrel wavered briefly, but then Mick recovered quickly and put his finger on the first trigger.

"You down there," David yelled. "If you're phoning the Gardái, call them off."

"You have broken into and entered a private house without permission, sir," Mrs. Comyn said calmly, coming to stand at the foot of the stairs.

"Why, you interfering old cow!"

Mick gave him a prod with the shotgun, and David stepped

back, his anger cooling slightly now. Selina wondered if she
could slip past him.

"Now, listen here, my good man," he began in a conciliatory
tone.

"Your good man I'm not. And you'll not batter Miz Healey
about—"

"I'll do with my own wife as I please, goddamit! Now stand
aside, I'm taking her home. Where she belongs. Call him off,
Selina!"

Suddenly they heard a car squeal into the court. Mick looked
around, grimacing in relieved wonder. "Jaysus, for the first
time in their lives the Gardái arrive in time."

David swore viciously, his face contorted in rage, as Sergeant
Quinn rushed to the staircase.

"Now, what seems to be the trouble here?"

David roared down but one explanation, and when taxed,
Pat Quinn had to admit that he had no jurisdiction in a domestic dispute, no matter where it was being conducted. To
his credit, Quinn took a long time writing down his notes—
hoping, Selina thought, that it would cool her husband down.
Unfortunately the delay only made everything worse.

As soon as the Gardái car had left the courtyard, David
grabbed her wrist and hauled her to the front door. "Out of
my way," he snarled when Mick did not move fast enough.

Once again Mick leveled the shotgun at him. "Not if Miz
Healey wants to remain here."

"Didn't you hear?" David cried, waving his arms about. "Even
the Gardái know that I've the right to deal with my wife as I
see fit."

"Only it's not fit, ye gobshite!" the old groom bellowed back,
and Mrs. Comyn ranged herself beside him, startling Selina
with eyes as fierce as Mick's. "You're not stirring from this
house with Miz Healey, not while I'm here. Beating a woman's
against the laws of God and nature, so it is!"

Before Mick could protect himself, David scooped up a nearby lunge whip and caught Mick across the eyes with a quick slash. The loyal old groom staggered against Mrs. Comyn, but she held on to the shotgun when David tried to grab it. He pushed her back against the kitchen door, knocking the breath out of her, then renewed his attack on Mick with the lunge whip, beating the man into the yard.

"Draw a gun on me, will you, you frigging bastard—take that! And that!"

Barry and Artie rushed forward and hauled the half-blind Mick out of range. David then wheeled around and rushed at Selina, who had been trying to peel Mrs. Comyn's fingers from the shotgun stock. The first lash caught her across the face, and she lurched away. Barely able to see, she reeled toward the steps, trying to shield herself by the banister, but the enraged David grabbed her ankle, pulling her back down and beating her with the handle when he could no longer wield the lash effectively.

Then, abruptly, all motion ceased. She heard an oath, the unmistakable crack of a fist on flesh, the thud of a heavy object hitting the floor, and a seemingly endless screeching. The next thing she knew she was being picked up from where she crouched on the stairs. Although she couldn't focus her eyes, she realized that it was Michael who held her, and she clung to him, too shocked to consider who might witness her reaction.

"There now, Selina, there now. I'm here, I'm here."

"He's gone mad . . . David's gone mad. Is Mick all right? He beat him, Michael. And Mrs. Comyn stood up to him, too, but they weren't enough. Oh, God, I can't ever go back to him. Nothing can make me go back to him. I never want to see him again. Never!"

As Michael shifted to bring her farther down the stairs, she saw David's sprawled body and knew that he was unconscious.

"Boys, get some ice— Oh, thank you, Mrs. Comyn. Pip, cope with Bridie. I will not have a banshee at Eithne's wedding."

The screeching, Selina soon discovered, was coming from Bridie. Then the coolness of an ice-cold cloth eased the stinging across her eyes. She reached up and found thin, trembling hands holding it in place. Mrs. Comyn!

"Oh, God, we can't spoil the wedding." Selina struggled to release herself from Michael's grasp. "That's not fair to Eithne. They're not here yet, are they?"

"No, thank God, not yet," Michael said. "The boys and I brought Bridie home once the vows were exchanged. Everyone's involved in getting their pictures taken right now, so we've got some time to spare. Mrs. Comyn, see if you can find a long-sleeved blouse or dress in Eithne's press. The weals mustn't show." Michael examined her gently. "This dress is torn, Selina, and dirty, but you're about the same size as Eithne, and she'll be too excited to notice."

"What'll we do about him?" Philip asked, nodding toward David. "I think he's coming to. Why didn't you hit him harder?"

"Wrong angle," Michael said ruefully. "Look, throw some water on him. I think we'd better handle this right now. Selina, stay here. We'll bring him into the other room."

She made a feeble grab at his sleeve as he rose. "Michael, he's gone berserk."

"Perhaps," Michael said, smiling crookedly. "But I think he's had enough rope today. You've told me often enough that Healey has political aspirations." She nodded, puzzled. "Well, I'm reasonably sure that your father would take a very dim view of what happened here today. And it only takes three witnesses, doesn't it, to swear to a public beating?" He patted her hand, then strode into the lounge to join the others.

Selina could hear snatches of the interview, but, feeling understandably weak and cowardly, she was glad to be absent. When Michael, Philip, Owen, and Harry re-joined her, their faces reflected a certain smug satisfaction. Philip even went so far as to clap his hands together as they all heard a car roaring out of the courtyard.

"I don't think he'll be bothering you anymore, Selina," Michael said, smiling slightly. "We were able to get him to see reason."

"Oh, Michael . . ." Selina felt drained with relief. "Is Mick all right? He and Mrs. Comyn were tremendous, you know."

"Mick's grand, Selina," Philip answered, grinning. "No permanent damage to anything but his pride. And a cuppa's helping that."

"Mrs. Comyn's gone over to Mother's, Selina, to see about a dress for you," Harry said, pressing her arm lightly.

As soon as the door closed behind them, Michael took Selina in his arms, embracing her as tenderly, she thought, as if she were Catriona. Then he tipped her face up to his and looked into her eyes.

"That's it, Selina. You are not even to see David without witnesses. Strong ones. That's a dangerous and vindictive man. But he also cannot afford the sort of publicity that I would make certain he received. Much less what your father would do in England. Healey's businesses right now require too much assistance from City bankers for him to risk it. . . . I told you once that Cornanagh would protect you, Selina."

He kissed her, then escorted her back up the stairs to Catriona's room, telling her to rest until she heard the wedding party returning.

"I've got to have a few stern words with our local banshee now," Michael said, grinning as he closed the door.

As she lay on Catriona's narrow bunk, Selina could hear the noise Bridie was making in the kitchen, a curious blend of weeping, shrieking, and moaning. She positioned the ice pack on the pillow and turned her left cheek to its cooling surface,

hoping that she could find enough strength to play a con-
vincingly debonair role at the reception.

It took considerable willpower, but except for acknowledg-
ing Eithne's startled recognition of the dress she wore, Selina
behaved at the reception as if nothing untoward had happened
to her. The weals were mainly on her body and upper arms,
covered now by long sleeves, and the ice had stanched the
blood on her cheek. With heavy concealer and foundation,
she'd even managed to hide the lash mark near her eyes. She
took the first opportunity to explain to Eithne that she had
clumsily spilled salad dressing down the front of her own frock
and apologized for taking one of Eithne's, explaining that she'd
had no time to go home for a change. Eithne was too elated
to care about such minor accidents, although she did give Selina's cheek a long, puzzled stare.

For hours the happy bridal pair were feasted, feted, toasted,
and teased. Davis was indeed a merry groom by the time he
and his bride drove off to spend a few honeymoon days at
Kelly's in Wexford.

Shortly after their departure, the party began to wind down,
and people made their farewells, while the Gavaghans settled
in for a quiet natter among themselves. Michael managed a
moment alone with Selina to tell her that reservations had been
made in her name at the Glenview Hotel and that her overnight
case had been put in her car, along with some things Mrs.
Comyn thought she might need. She was to rest and try to put
what had happened out of her mind.

So Selina was able to make gay farewells to the girls and
assure them that she'd see them in the morning as usual. On
her way down the drive, she stopped at Mick's house.

"I don't hold with beating man or horse or woman, to make
it go," Mick said stolidly. Looking at him, Selina knew the lash
marks on his face were as painful as hers. "No, I don't hold
with beatings, missus. And I'd not have let him take you out

of the yard iffen I'd had to shoot his—legs off." Mick smiled at her. "Captain told me that you're not going back." When she nodded he cried, "Good! No man's got the right to beat someone for the joy of it."

Rights, Selina recalled as she drove up the Kilquade road, had little to do with her present circumstances. At least that wretched little man in his Ford sedan was no longer shadowing her.

34

The next morning Patricia and Catriona rose early and escaped to the yard. Having so many relations around really wore on the nerves, Catriona thought, listening to Patricia's usual chatter.

"I tell you, Cat, something's going on around here." Pat tossed the body brush back into her kit. "Everyone—your dad, Philip, Mick, even Mrs. Comyn—everyone's been acting funny somehow. Smug, pleased as punch. I don't know what it is, but I tell you, we're missing something!"

Catriona didn't try to argue with Patricia. It was true: no one was acting as they ought, and it didn't have anything to do with all the relatives staying over. "Sybil'll know what's happening," she said to her cousin. "She was looking awfully satisfied with herself yesterday, and it wasn't about Auntie Eithne. She said she'd be back this morning."

"It's nearly time to eat," Pat complained, rubbing her stomach.

"No, it's not. We just ate awful early, that's all."

They both heard a car pull into the courtyard, and Pat went to see who it was.

"Hey, it's Syb," she called, beckoning urgently to her cousin before running to meet the arrival. "No," Pat was saying when Catriona joined them, "we haven't seen her this morning. Uncle Mihall said she had some errands."

"I'll just bet she does," Sybil said so drolly that Catriona knew Patricia had been right after all.

"Okay, Syb, what's happening? You can level with us."

Sybil laughed. "I would if I could, but I can't. It's not for me to tell. But I assure you, it's nothing bad. In fact"—she grinned and ruffled her sister's hair—"it's all to the good. You'll see. Now, I'd better get cracking. Tell Selina to phone me when you see her, will you, pets?"

She had driven away, one hand fluttering back at them from her window, when both girls heard Tory's distant but frantic barking. Turning toward the front fields, trying to place his location, Catriona saw the young stock galloping around the big field. And they weren't galloping for the fun of it. She caught Patricia's arm and pointed.

"Tory's out with Barry, isn't he?" Pat said, unconcerned.

"If he was with Barry, he wouldn't be barking. C'mon, let's go see."

Catriona ran back to the yard, loosing the knot that tied Conker to the wall ring.

"Mick, something's scaring the horses," she called as the old groom emerged, a puzzled frown on his face.

She vaulted to Conker's back, saw out of the corner of her eye that Pat had mounted Orphan Annie. Their clattering brought Artie from the stable he was whitewashing. She heard her father call out, saw him leading Temper from the menage. She pointed to the fields, yelling to him about Tory and Barry and the horses. Then she realized that the strap-iron gate to the Ride was closed. She dug her heels into Conker's ribs, and gallant pony that he was, he soared over it. She heard Patricia's bitter curse and was fleetingly grateful that Pat had not put the green Annie to such a formidable barrier.

Almost unconsciously, she guided Conker right, down the Ride, to see what the horses were running *from*. Conker had sensed her urgency and was going full pelt. Frolic and Tulip's Son were in the big field with the other young horses.

Catriona knew beyond a shadow of a doubt that mare and

colt were in danger. She urged Conker faster, heard shouts behind her and loud voices coming from beyond the hill in the big field. Without pausing or checking for an instant, Conker cleared the five-barred gate into the field, landing with a jar that threw Catriona against his neck. She hung on to his mane and squirmed erect. As they charged to the flat top of the hill, Catriona saw several men below, saw Frolic protecting her foal, driven into a corner against the hedgerow, rearing and striking out from side to side. She also saw Tory, barking hysterically, standing over the prone figure of Barry.

Catriona stampeded down the hill, yelling at the top of her lungs and waving her arms. It was when she saw that the men carried lunge whips and ropes, and one was poking a cattle prod at Frolic, that she realized she had absolutely nothing, not even a riding crop. And the lead rope, which she might have been able to swing defensively, was attached to Conker's head collar. So she hauled Conker around to charge the man nearest her—Mr. Fitzroy. Too well behaved a pony to knock into a human, Conker swerved at the last moment, just as the farmer jumped aside, and Catriona nearly lost her grip on his smooth sides. Feeling his rider slip, Conker swerved and slowed. One of the other men made a grab for her, but she kicked Conker on, clinging to his mane and breaking the man's hold on her shirt. Then she was through their blockade and galloping toward Frolic.

Frolic tried to elude her as well, but she permitted Conker near her, as if she considered him an ally. Catriona tried to grab Frolic's head collar, but the mare flicked up her head, evading capture.

Fitzroy was rallying his men, and it was then that she saw the flash of knives in the sun and knew what he had intended: not kidnapping the prize Cornanagh mare and her foal, but hamstringing them, damaging them so badly they'd have to be put down.

Enraged, Catriona wrenched Conker around and set him in front of the mare, making him bounce under her as she gave the confused pony conflicting aids. Grim and determined, the men began to close the circle.

Suddenly she heard a bloodcurdling yell and saw Patricia come flying up over the brow of the hill on Annie. Just behind her galloped her father on Temper, wielding a lunge whip, and Artie, armed with the sickle, bareback on Charlie.

The Fitzroys scattered, racing for the far corner of the field and the hedge that separated Cornanagh's land from the Kilquade estate next to them. Catriona did not join that charge but stared, openmouthed, at the sight of Temper, neck extended, teeth bared, an equine variation of his rider.

Tulip's Son nickered at the disappearing horses and would have gone to investigate, but Frolic rumbled a warning, and Catriona quickly blocked his way. She felt utterly drained, her mouth dry and her arms and legs trembling from exertion.

Frolic nuzzled her, nickering softly.

"It's all right, Frolic. You were marvelous, protecting your baby. And so were you, Conker! Good boy! Good fellow!" She leaned down on the sturdy neck and stroked it, pulling Conker's pricked ears.

Tory's bark, less urgent now but still excited, reminded Catriona of Barry. She turned Conker up the hill and squeezed with legs that were still quivering. Tulip's Son nickered in his high-pitched voice and cantered beside them. Assured that this emergency had passed, Frolic put her head down to graze.

Barry, holding his head, was struggling to rise, while Tory danced about him, barking approval.

"It's all right, Barry," Catriona called out as she and Conker trotted up. "Dad's gone after them. Are you all right?"

"Oh, Jesus, I'm not," Barry said, reeling on his feet. There was blood streaming down his neck, and he fumbled in his pocket for a handkerchief.

Instantly Catriona was off Conker. "Come on, Barry, get on Conker."

"That I couldn't," he said, but he clutched at the pony's neck and looped an arm about it. "Oh, by Jesus, I don't know what they hit me with. Sure I thought Tory'd seen a badger or that ferret that lives in the hill. I didn't so much as look around until wham! Did they hurt the foal?"

"No, they didn't, and we've Tory to thank for that again." Tory immediately trotted up to be caressed.

Catriona, anxiously watching Barry's stumbling progress, led him and Conker back to the house. They were just turning into the courtyard when Pat and Artie came trotting back.

"We got 'em! We got 'em!" Pat cried. "Caught 'em in the act! You should have seen your father! He and Mick have them cornered like the rats they are, waiting for the Gardái. . . . My God, Barry, are you all right?"

"Here, I'll help," Artie said, and ran to Barry's right side to support him.

"God, Cat, you were marvelous! You should've seen the look on your father's face when you and Conker took the iron fence like that. Then he realized there was trouble, told Mrs. Comyn to call the Gardái, and took off after you. And there you were, holding off an army of Fitzroys! Wow!"

Mrs. Comyn was waiting for them at the door and quickly helped Artie bring Barry into the kitchen. Both girls heard Bridie's banshee wail and decided that they'd best put the horses up.

"Lord, we've got to groom all over again," Pat said in exasperation, fists on her hips as she surveyed Annie's sweaty hide and muddy legs. "And my dad said I'd have a quiet summer in Ireland."

Fitzroy was not one to lay down a quarrel easily. Brannigan, the estate caretaker, roused out of the fields by all the commotion, had stopped the Fitzroy retreat by discharging one barrel of his heavy-gauge shotgun at their feet. Then Michael galloped up, halting with a shower of pebbles from the drive just as Mick pulled the Austin across the drive, and pointed another weapon out the window. The Fitzroys were cornered.

Even after the Gardái arrived, and Fitzroy was formally charged with assault, grievous bodily harm, trespass, and breaking the peace, he was snarling threats through the spittle on his lips.

"I'll get ya, ya bastard. I'll get ya yet, Carradyne!"

"Sure, it's Jere Nolan you should be getting, Fitzroy," Brannigan cried. "It's him's knocked your datter up!"

"What?" Fitzroy whirled on him.

"Sure the world and his cousin know it, man," Brannigan said. "He's bragging about it. Ask him yerself. When you're out of the 'Joy, that is!"

Fitzroy writhed against the handcuffs, and his sons shouted loud denials and threats.

"I must get home, Pat," Michael said, having trouble now controlling the overexcited Temper.

"I'll be seeing you soon, then, for the particulars," Pat Quinn replied affably. "I might as well rent space at Cornanagh this weather." He grinned and waved Michael on.

Thoroughly pleased with himself, Temper swung into an extended trot, high-blowing all the way back to the Cornanagh entrance. "Good lad, Temper, good lad," Michael said, soothing the gelding. Too bad, he thought as he slowed Temper to walk into the yard, that there's no more cavalry. Temper would have made a magnificent charger. He might just contact Billy Ringrose anyhow. The Army was concentrating on three-day event horses these days.

Catriona and Patricia were in the yard when he walked Temper in, and a look of apprehension immediately crossed Catriona's face.

"It's all right, pet, it's all right," Michael assured her. "Fitzroy won't bother us anymore, I promise you."

Artie came rushing up to hold Temper, his face eager for news. Patricia too was impatient, but Michael ignored her until he had taken Catriona in his arms and hugged her hard.

"Oh, Daddy, I couldn't let them hurt Tulip's Son and Frolic! They had knives!"

He could feel her slight frame tremble, and he held her, stroking her hair. "Catriona Mary Virginia, don't you ever, *ever* take a fence that way again." Then he kissed her solemnly on both cheeks and smiled.

"Well, I knew Conker could, Daddy!" she said, grinning proudly.

An hour later, when the mounts of the irregular Cornanagh cavalry had been duly groomed and given a handful of nuts as reward for their valor, a triumphant Mick drove back into the yard to confirm that the Fitzroys had been taken off in the extra Gardái cars that had arrived from Wicklow town.

Selina started her day with a bath, but the warm water did not prove as effective for whip weals as for bruises. Mrs. Comyn had included a small jar of comfrey ointment, which when applied had certainly soothed the weal across her face and those on her body that she had been able to reach.

She waited until 10:30 to call Kathleen, but there was no answer at home at all, so she tried Cornanagh next. Mrs. Comyn answered.

"Oh, I'm so glad to get you, Mrs. Comyn, because I never had the chance to thank you yesterday for coming to my rescue."

"I did very little, Mrs. Healey."

"You did more than you know. . . . Is Captain Carradyne available?"

"He's just come from the yard, Mrs. Healey. One moment, please."

In the ensuing silence, Selina wondered idly just how much Mrs. Comyn had divined about her relationship with Michael. A moment later he was on the phone, sounding both pleased and anxious to be hearing from her.

"Selina? Are you well? Were you able to sleep?"

She smiled. "Not as well as I'd like. You weren't there to comfort me."

"That would have been a lot more palatable than catering to Eithne's boring relations."

"Michael! You're terrible. Did you see the paper this morning? The Horse Board Bill was passed last night."

"I know." He didn't sound as triumphant as she'd expected.

"Michael! You won! It's gone through. And seemingly much as you hoped it would."

"On paper, yes. That was the easy part. Now, it's got to be sold to the farmers it's supposed to help. And then there's the problem of who'll sit on the board and who'll be elected chairman. No, I think the real work is just beginning." There was a slight pause, then: "Have you decided yet, Selina? I mean, about coming to stay at the mews?"

She hesitated. "Yes . . . I think I'll hold off on that for a bit, Michael. I'm going after a barring order today; I want to see to it that David can't get back in the house. I don't want to give it up, you see. I'll also have to find out if I can prevent him from selling it without my consent. Mind you"—she laughed—"the mews is a very tempting offer."

"I know." He chuckled with her.

"But if I did move into Eithne's place, we would be sorely, sorely tempted."

"I know! We'll be tempted anyhow. We'll just have to be sensible."

She gave a long, low laugh. "Yes, we will."

"Listen, Selina. The Gavaghans're down, and I must play host. When will I see you?"

"I've a lot to do this morning, but tell the girls that I'll be there this afternoon. And congratulations again! I just know Bord na gCapall will succeed—I feel it in my bones."

"Politics ruin many good ideas," Michael said.

After she rang off, Selina took a deep breath and tried her number again, but there was still no answer. Troubled now and distinctly uneasy, she rang for appointments with Maurie Woods and Dr. Treacy, then took great pleasure in telling Ian Coghlan to get a barring order against her husband: she had the requisite witnesses. After she'd made all her calls, she drove to Kathleen's council house in Dun Laoghaire.

"Oh, missus"—Kathleen's eyes went wide as she opened the door and got a clear look at Selina's face—"I was afraid for you when he came storming into the house yesterday noon. He was raging. Raging! I never would've thought a man like Mr. Healey could act so wild."

"What exactly did he say, Kathleen?"

Kathleen flushed and looked away. "More'n I cared to hear, missus, he was so about in the head. He throws money at me and tells me to get out, that I was sacked for good and all— and with no reference, what with all that's been going on in his house." Kathleen shot Selina a querying glance. "I did tell him then, missus, that there's been nothing going on, an' that's the truth! But he wasn't listening, just throws me coat in me face and tells me to get out." Kathleen managed to look both affronted and piteous.

"Don't worry about a reference, Kathleen," Selina said. "I'll give you one, and a good one, for you've been excellent."

Relief flooded the earnest face. "Ah, thank you, Mrs. Healey, you're a real brick."

"Not at all, you deserve it. I'm only sorry you had to get

caught in the middle of all this. I'll be in touch in a few days, when I'm settled again."

When she reached the house, Selina discovered that David had changed the locks. She stood on the steps of the front stoop, jiggling her now useless keys, and wondered what to do. The clothes didn't matter so much, but there were things she'd brought with her from her family's old home in Kildare that were precious to her. David didn't own them, too. Or did he?

So she kept her first appointment with Maurie Woods, which didn't take long, and then went on to Dr. Treacy. Treacy was appalled at the marks on her body and tut-tutted throughout the examination. But he seemed most grateful when Selina spared him a blow-by-blow account of David's brutality.

Having elected not to conceal her battle scars, she was gratified by Ian Coghlan's swift intake of breath at his first sight of her. She gave him the names of the Cornanagh witnesses, the fact that the Gardái had been called in, and her assumption that the private investigator, too diligent by half, had precipitated this latest attack.

"Healey has fired my housekeeper, terrifying her in the process, changed the locks on the doors to a house that was a wedding present from my father—"

"But is in your husband's name."

She held up her hand. "There are some items of furniture, a few paintings, and prints of mine"—she stressed the pronoun—"that have been in my family's possession for many years, and I certainly don't want those sold out of hand. Can you prevent it?"

"I can try," Coghlan replied. "I've already initiated proceedings for a barring order. But if you're not in the house . . . "

"Does a barring order prevent him from entering any place I occupy?"

"Yes, but where are you?"

"I'm at the Glenview Hotel in Glen o' the Downs for a few days, but then I shall be taking up residence at the mews cottage, Cornanagh Stud, Kilquade."

Coghlan promised to get a barring order as soon as possible, and Selina believed he was sincere. From his office, she dropped in to Brown Thomas and purchased enough clothes to go on with. She was told by an embarrassed floor manager that her husband had cancelled her account the previous afternoon. As she paid for her purchases with cash, she remembered, with a certain malicious satisfaction, that the bulk of David's cash was securely in Cornanagh's safe, along with her jewels. Feeling quite jaunty, she dumped her parcels in the back of the Lancia and returned to the hotel.

She found three telephone messages waiting for her, all from Sybil.

"What news, Sister Anne?" asked Sybil when Selina rang her back. "I've been trying to get you all morning."

"Let's see . . . David fired Kathleen and changed the locks on the house, so I couldn't get in. So I went to see Maurie Woods, old Dr. Treacy, and Ian Coghlan, who's getting a barring order."

"Janey Mack but you've been busy."

"Strike while the iron's hot."

"Speaking of which, what're you going to do now?"

"I'm going to change my clothes and apply to your father for a job. He'll be losing Philip after the Horse Show, and Trina's a shade too young to compete in the big events."

"Then you're going to take the mews cottage?" Sybil sounded so enthusiastic that Selina had to laugh.

"Certainly until I can find something else nearby," she said.

"Good! There isn't a chance of your being depressed or lonely about this wretched business at Cornanagh."

"No, there isn't."

When Selina arrived at Cornanagh after lunch, everyone

crowded around her, babbling in unison about the Fitzroys' latest attempt on Cornanagh.

"This is the last one, Selina," Michael promised her when he saw how shaken she was at the account.

"Cat was the heroine," Patricia said proudly.

"Only because it was Frolic and Tulip's Son," Catriona mumbled, examining her boots.

Selina gave her a quick hug, and Catriona looked up shyly, only to draw back in horror.

"Your face—Selina, what happened to your face?"

Selina glanced uncertainly at Michael, who gave a reluctant nod. So she sat down on the couch, pulling Catriona to her right and keeping her arm about the girl. Patricia slid into the space on the left, and Michael, folding his arms, slouched against a nearby table.

"My husband has been in the north a great deal," she began, "with all the troubles up there and the bank strike, and when he came home and found I was at Cornanagh, he came looking for me and . . ."

"He beat you up," Pat said bluntly, her expression bleak.

Selina nodded. "And tried to force me to return home with him."

"When was that?" Pat asked, amazed that she'd managed to miss such an event.

"While you were all at Eithne's wedding." Selina felt Catriona's hand creep over to cover hers protectively, felt the girl's slender body lean against her. "Mick and Mrs. Comyn kept him here until your father and brothers got home. They've persuaded David—my husband—to leave me alone, and I'm seeking a legal separation from him."

Catriona put both arms about Selina's neck and hugged her close. "You're not to go back to that man, Selina—not ever! Is she, Daddy?"

Selina, unable to look at Michael at that moment, returned

Catriona's embrace. She felt close to tears suddenly, aware that she was being offered exactly what she had once thought beyond attainment—Michael, Catriona, and Cornanagh.

"I think Selina knows that she's welcome at Cornanagh for any reason," Michael said, his voice rough.

"You know, Selina," Pat said gently, "you can get divorced in the States."

As Catriona's hold tightened convulsively, Selina shook her head.

"Since I'm welcome, I don't think I'll leave Cornanagh!"

❧ *Afterword* ❧

Cornanagh pulled out all the stops for Michael's birthday: the horses did well at the day's show, the newlyweds returned from Wexford looking well pleased with themselves, all the nonresident Carradynes, including Andrew and the grandchildren, showed up, and Bridie, Mrs. Comyn, Susan, Sybil, Selina, and Eithne worked together to produce an unparalleled feast. For despite his protests, everyone was determined that Michael was going to have a proper birthday celebration.

When the lavish meal had been consumed, the birthday cake, sixteen inches across and elaborately decorated, was carried in by James as the eldest son and greeted with cries of admiration and delight. Bridie followed it into the dining room, and even Mick and Barry joined the family for the ceremonial toast that followed.

Then it was time for the presents. Michael was effusive in his thanks as one item after another emerged from all the gaily wrapped boxes and brown-paper parcels. Mick's gift was a beautiful brass-mounted head collar with "Tulip's Son" affixed to the cheekpiece. Philip gave him a new folded leather girth and Andrew a fine set of spurs. Soon, the table in front of him looked like a tack shop counter, and Michael was more than a little touched by such generosity. At last Catriona, looking apprehensive, brought him her package.

"Tack this is not," Michael said, and everyone laughed.

He felt the breathless silence in the room and took his time about undoing the gaudy birthday paper, sensing this was the high point of his party. He ended up unwrapping it backward, and there was a ripple of surprise and admiration from those opposite him who could see the picture. Grinning in anticipation, he turned it around.

As he saw the sketch, saw old Tulip in a pose that had often gladdened his heart after a long and trying day, his grin faded. It was such a powerful image that he could almost feel the touch of those searching lips on his hand. Tears welled in his eyes and spilled down his cheeks, and he was not ashamed. He turned to Catriona, saw her anxious face, and carefully put the portrait on the floor before he embraced her, hugging her as tightly as he could. He felt her relax, her arms wrapping about his neck as she accepted his love and approval.

Rubbing his eyes and nose with a napkin, he rose and went to the wall. He took the center hunting print down, set the Tulip's portrait in its place, and stepped back with a slightly dramatic flourish. Then, retrieving his champagne glass, he gestured for all to join him. When everyone had stood up, he inclined his glass to the daughter of his heart, then raised it high.

"Ladies and gentlemen, a toast: To the Tulip, alive forever in Cornanagh!"